Water Folk

Book Three of the Folklore Cycle

JOHN HOOD

DEFIANCE PRESS
& PUBLISHING

Water Folk

First Edition: 2024

Printed in the United States of America

10 9 8 7 6 5 4 3 2 1

DEFIANCE PRESS
& PUBLISHING

ISBN-13: 978-1-963102-62-8 (Paperback)
ISBN-13: 978-1-963102-61-1 (ebook)
ISBN-13: 978-1-963102-75-8 (Hardcover)

Cover designed by Spomenka Bojanic
Interior designed by Debbi Stocco

Published by Defiance Press & Publishing, LLC

Bulk orders of this book may be obtained by contacting Defiance Press & Publishing, LLC. www.defiancepress.com.

Public Relations Dept. – Defiance Press & Publishing, LLC
281-581-9300
pr@defiancepress.com

Defiance Press & Publishing, LLC
281-581-9300
info@defiancepress.com

To Martha Sue, my sister true,
Wise leader of the Walnut Clan,
A Naiad bold, with hair of gold
And eyes that far horizons scan.
May ever she, o'er land and sea,
Range free — her tales an epic span.

Prologue — The Campfire Tales

October 1832

THE AUTHOR *HEARD* THE CHARACTER before he ever saw him.

That wasn't the usual way. Whether his characters crept onto the page from a folktale collected during his travels, emerged from a stack of manuscripts, or simply sprang from his imagination like Athena from the head of Zeus, the author usually saw them in his mind's eye long before he ever bade them speak.

He saw them as lean and lanky, or plump and plodding, or reserved and regal, or gristly and grasping. They grinned or glared or glanced away. They strode forward, stumbled backward, or stalked in the night. Always wordlessly at first. Silent.

This time felt different. *And isn't that why I've come all this way, to feel something different?* the author asked himself. This time, he let his ears, not his eyes, meet his subject for the first time.

He heard heavy boots clomping along the porch outside Colonel Matthew Arbuckle's house. He heard planks groan and spurs jangle. He heard raucous laughter from a deep voice that belonged as much in a fancy opera house in Paris as a rough-hewn fort in the Indian Territory. And he heard the loud whack of one brawny frontiersman slapping another on the back.

"I head into the wilds, sir, on a mission of great urgency," the deep voice bellowed. "But all will not be toil. To the west may lie endless adventure and boundless fortune."

"You sound like my pa," said a second, softer voice. "Kept headin' west, too. Found more than his share of adventure, but no fortune."

"I once saw your illustrious father from afar, though we never met," the first replied. "He was a great man."

After a pause, the softer voice spoke again. "Not great in stature, like you, but great in courage, yes, and in deed."

Of what great man did the disembodied voices speak? The author thought of those larger-than-life figures he'd chronicled with his own pen. Christopher Columbus. Ferdinand and Isabella. American heroes such as Oliver Hazard Perry and Zebulon Pike. Surely the strangers outside were speaking of no one so august, so consequential to the course of history.

Then he recalled his own words, written a dozen years ago. *History fades into fable; fact becomes clouded with doubt and controversy; the inscription molders from the tablet; the statue falls from the pedestal. Columns, arches, pyramids, what are they but heaps of sand—and their epitaphs but characters written in the dust?*

The author had, after all, traveled across the Atlantic, then halfway across his native country to find fresh subjects for his pen—living, breathing subjects, not ones forever separated from his immediate senses by distance and time.

Perhaps such a subject waited beyond the door. The author opened it. His host, Colonel Arbuckle, was close on his heels.

"Welcome, my friends," the colonel said to the two men on the porch. "Please allow me the honor of introducing a gentleman just arrived from the east. He is Washington Irving, a writer not long back in America after extended residence in Europe."

Washington nodded graciously at Fort Gibson's commander, then studied the strangers. One, dark-haired and slender, was slouching against a rail. The other man, whom Washington guessed was the deep-voiced seeker of "adventure and fortune," stood ramrod straight and well over six feet tall. He had chestnut-colored hair, a pronounced cleft in his square chin, and sharp blue eyes resembling those of some giant bird of prey. His dress was an odd assortment: shiny leather boots, buckskin leggings and hunting frock, a cloth shirt, a multicolored blanket of Indian weave draped over a shoulder, and a white, broad-brimmed beaver hat on his head.

"We are well met, sir!" boomed the sharp-eyed man. "Have you come to Indian country in search of a retreat where you might 'steal away from the world and its distractions, and dream quietly away the remnant of a troubled life'? You'd hardly be the first."

Washington Irving blinked in disbelief. He'd journeyed deep into the frontier, far removed—and purposely so—from the genteel life he'd once known. And yet here he was listening to some rustic blowhard toss his own written words back at him.

"You're familiar with 'The Legend of Sleepy Hollow,' I take it," Washington said, trying not to let his incredulity show.

He failed.

The smaller stranger smirked and tugged on one ear. "We *do* read books in these parts, Mister Irving. Sometimes even the sort of tales you spin. My late father would have liked 'em. His favorite book was *Gulliver's Travels*." Then he lurched forward and held out his hand. "Pleased to meet you. I'm Nathan Boone."

"*Captain* Boone now," Arbuckle explained, "just arrived at Fort Gibson to take command of a new regiment of dragoons."

"And you, sir," Washington began, peering up at the man in the beaver hat, "you have an officer's bearing and a military mode of expressing yourself. Do you serve in the army as well?"

The big man's wide mouth formed a genial smile, but Washington fancied he saw something else in those blue eyes. Uncertainty? Regret? Shame?

This man may, indeed, be a character of fascinating depth. Perhaps I should be taking notes for my next story. Washington's hand brushed against the coat pocket where he kept notepaper.

"I was once a soldier, yes, and still bear the scars," said the man in the beaver hat. "Now I lead little more than a trading post on the Neosho River—and even that command will soon slip my grasp."

Colonel Arbuckle cleared his throat awkwardly. "Mister Irving, a truly remarkable man stands before you. Congressman. Governor. Major general of the Tennessee militia. Hero of Horseshoe Bend. The Indians call him Kolana, the Raven. I call him friend. All else call him Sam Houston."

~ ~ ~

After living seventeen years abroad—collecting folktales in Holland and Germany, translating plays in France, researching books in Spain, performing diplomatic work in London—Washington Irving had returned to his native land to prove to his critics, and perhaps even to himself, that he remained a genuinely *American* author. On a whim, he had traveled west with a group of friends, hoping to find adventure and inspiration.

Perhaps I've found both here, bouncing around in the middle of nowhere. Washington glanced ruefully at the little pony tethered next to the creek, wishing he'd secured a sturdier mount.

Shortly after arriving at Fort Gibson, the army's first outpost in the Indian Territory, Washington and one of his traveling companions, Henry Ellsworth, had tried to catch up with a patrol exploring the territory. Matthew Arbuckle, Nathan Boone, and Sam Houston volunteered to accompany them, along with some soldiers from the fort.

Washington welcomed the company. They supplied him both an interesting subject, Houston, and people to question about him. Most helpful were the soldiers from Tennessee, where Houston had spent much of his youth and to which he'd returned after sustaining grievous wounds during the War of 1812.

Less helpful was Captain Boone, another War of 1812 veteran who reentered army service during the brief war against Chief Black Hawk and was now tasked with keeping the peace in the Indian Territory. Boone was a Missourian, not a Tennessean, and reluctant to share secondhand rumors about Houston. "Never cared much for gossip," he'd explained, adding that his famous father, Daniel, was often annoyed by loose talk. "General Houston can speak for himself, or not. None of my business."

Still, with what Washington had learned plus his own vague recollections about the Creek War, he'd assembled a rough portrait of the man. Sam Houston was born in Virginia's Shenandoah Valley, then moved with his family to Tennessee around 1807. The young Houston struggled at first, even running away to live in a Cherokee town for a while, then found his calling as an army lieutenant during the second war with Britain. At the pivotal Battle of Horseshoe Bend in 1814, Houston took an arrow in the groin and musket balls in his arm and shoulder.

Miraculously surviving, Houston then worked as an Indian agent among the Cherokee and studied law in Nashville. Elected as district attorney, then congressman, he reached the pinnacle of his political success by winning the governorship of Tennessee in 1827 and helping his friend and political patron Andrew Jackson win the presidency a year later.

After which, misfortune rained down on Sam Houston's head.

Just weeks after Jackson's election, Governor Houston married a lovely young lady named Eliza Allen. Eleven weeks later, Eliza fled the marriage. Houston resigned his office and fled Tennessee to seek refuge among old Cherokee friends now living west of the Mississippi.

What happened? Washington had collected a range of conjectures. Some soldiers said Houston, known to enjoy strong drink, abused his wife and prompted her to fear for her own safety. Others said Eliza discovered on her wedding night that Houston's wartime wounds never quite healed, and she couldn't stomach the sight of his bare flesh. The Tennesseans insisted, however, that the real victim of the affair was Houston himself—that Eliza married the governor purely for social gain, and when Houston discovered the truth, his honor permitted no other course but resignation and exile.

Colonel Arbuckle eagerly repeated this version of the tale of Sam and Eliza. "'Whatever may be said by the lady or her friends,'" Arbuckle quoted Houston as saying, "'it is no part of the conduct of a gallant and generous man to take up arms against a woman. If my character cannot stand the shock, let me lose it.'"

Despite Arbuckle's enthusiastic rendition, Washington doubted the colonel's account. It sounded too scripted, too theatrical. *I ought to know*, he mused, thinking of his fictional Ichabod Crane's doomed rivalry with Brom Bones for the hand of Katrina Van Tassel.

Not for the first time, Washington struggled to remember exactly what had led him to write "The Legend of Sleepy Hollow." The source material itself was no mystery. Years before writing the story, Irving had actually met a woman named Katrina Van Tassel, as well as an awkward young officer with the memorably odd name of Ichabod Crane. Later, during his time in Europe, he collected folktales about spectral horsemen on wild nighttime hunts.

Still, what had motivated him to seek out such tales in the first place was a hazy mental picture Washington had tried to shake for years—an image of one cloaked rider chasing another through a New York forest. Where the fragmentary image came from, he couldn't guess. He just knew it wouldn't leave him alone. It walked his daydreams. It prowled his nightmares. Only by expanding it into a published story did Irving manage to excise it.

Nor was it the only strange idea to inspire his pen. One evening in 1818, an after-dinner conversation with his brother-in-law reminded Washington of a childhood cruise up the Hudson River and his first glimpse of the

Catskills in all their magical shapes. Suddenly, a flood of images and ideas overwhelmed him. Stooped figures in jerkins and doublets and other quaint clothing. Bewitching voices. Shadowy places where time itself stood still. With the briefest of apologies to his sister and brother-in-law, Irving had retreated to his bedroom and scribbled furiously through the night to capture his reverie before it could flee his head. By morning, the first draft of "Rip Van Winkle" lay on his table.

Other inspirations had similarly struck Washington during his travels on the Continent. An elderly German spinster held him spellbound for hours with stories of the Evil One, which the author later adapted for his story "The Devil and Tom Walker." During his time in Spain, a series of loquacious strangers offered Washington colorful tales of hobgoblins they called the Duende, of enchanted talismans of bronze and monstrous horses beset by hellhounds, of magical curses that turned invading soldiers against each other, and of underground caves where wizards practiced their dark arts in timeless seclusion. All these, he'd included in his new book *The Alhambra*, published shortly before his voyage home to America.

I have built many fanciful castles in the air, Washington thought, looking up at the night sky. *Time to explore real places and real people here on the muddy ground.* As he trudged toward the campfire in front of Colonel Arbuckle's tent, he heard raucous laughter and smiled.

~ ~ ~

"It was an outrage with few equals in the annals of our young republic!"

Sam Houston took another drink and slammed the bottle on the ground, trying to look infuriated even as his twitching dimples said otherwise. A few months earlier, it seems, he'd been in the nation's capital when a congressman made a speech accusing Houston of corruption. After a newspaper reprinted the charges, Houston had demanded a retraction and, when none was forthcoming, promptly beat the man with his cane. In response, the House of Representatives fined Houston for retaliating against a member for remarks made on the floor, a violation of congressional privilege.

Houston tossed his cards face down and turned to Washington Irving seated to his right. "I ask you, as an esteemed chronicler of arts and manners, what can be dearer than a man's sacred privilege to defend his honor? This privilege the congressmen claim, this shield for any sort of rat or rascal, where is it?"

Washington glanced around at the other players. Colonel Arbuckle chuckled and raised his own bottle. Nathan Boone kept his eyes trained downward, either studying his cards or maintaining a studied neutrality. The only one who returned Washington's gaze was his new friend and traveling companion Henry Ellsworth, the Connecticut judge President Jackson had appointed commissioner to the Indians.

"The customs of our national government are no specialty of mine, General Houston," Washington replied. "Perhaps Henry can offer more insight."

"Hardly," said Ellsworth. "My career to date has taken me no further than the banks of the Connecticut and the halls of Hartford. Of the banks of the Potomac and the halls of Washington, I know no more than any of you, and likely much less."

"Then count yourself lucky," Houston snorted. "I have seen enough of the nation's capital to last a lifetime. It is a place where once-wise men go to become knaves and fools. Once elevated to high office, they too often leave common sense out of the question."

Washington saw his opportunity. "So, you have given up politics for good?"

Houston voiced no response. Instead, he picked up his hand and held the fanned cards before his face. "Shall I raise the bet, gentlemen?"

Ellsworth, Arbuckle, and Boone gave a collective sigh and recovered their own hands, none seeming to welcome the prospect. Washington was not so easily diverted, however. "I heard you tell Captain Boone the other day you were on a mission of great urgency," he began. "Did you acquire it while in the nation's capital, sir? Perhaps from the president himself?"

Houston's eyes narrowed, though his cards revealed little of the expression on his face. "You fence and parry, Mister Irving, as if the sword were just as mighty in your hand as the pen."

"I'm no warrior, although I did hold the notional rank of colonel during the War of 1812. Was it during the same war that you formed your friendship with General Jackson?"

Houston's hand fluttered as if fanning himself. Washington arched an eyebrow. *Am I getting somewhere, or just under his skin? Careful, now. I wish only for the truth, not lasting enmity.*

Then, suddenly, Houston's eyes flicked away. Darting his own eyes in the same direction, Washington thought he spotted movement in the trees, but he couldn't be sure. When he turned back, he noticed the former governor's hand no longer shook. Nor was he blocking his face with it.

Smiling broadly, Houston offered a sly wink. "My apologies, sir. You are, indeed, no soldier. You made no attack by asking your question, so I had no cause to counterattack."

Arbuckle giggled nervously. "We are all friends here, of course. Just enjoying this fine night together."

"All friends here," Houston agreed, "some of longer standing than others." Again, his eyes darted to the trees. This time, as Washington followed his gaze, he glimpsed the barest outline of a figure sitting on an oak branch. It was the size of a small child, though more graceful of build. One moment it was there, legs dangling down from the tree—then, as if the candle illuminating its shadowy form were snuffed out, the figure disappeared.

Washington started. Something about the brief apparition tugged at his memory. Pulling a handkerchief from his coat pocket, he dabbed his eyes and tried to recall. Was it an exotic monkey he'd seen in the new Zoological Gardens in London just before sailing for home? Or was it—

Sailing for home! That's it!

For the moment, at least, Washington Irving's memory of the event was unclouded. It was during his recent voyage from London that he'd encountered a pair of oddly matched sailors. One was impossibly tall and broad, like some great ox stuffed into seaman's clothes and standing upright on massive hind legs. The other companion was impossibly short and slender, like some trickster from a fairy story, though seemingly more at home on the deck of a ship than in a dark German forest or a dank Spanish cave.

Had the little fairy somehow made its way here, now, to the Indian Territory? If so, could the great ox-man be far behind? Washington felt prickles on the back of his neck. His breaths became shallow.

"Are you well, Mister Irving?" Houston asked. "Shall we continue our game?"

If this erstwhile governor of Tennessee can see what I saw, however briefly, on that ship, he holds cards that are truly precious to me.

"By all means," Washington said, forcing a conciliatory smile to his lips and reaching for his greatly diminished stack of coins.

~ ~ ~

After the men played a few more hands, all won by Houston—and not always by Washington's connivance—the author deemed it timely to try again. "General, you talked earlier of attack and counterattack. Though I am no soldier, I do not lack experience with confrontation and combat."

"Oh?" Houston seemed more interested in gambling than gabbing.

"Some of my years spent overseas were in the diplomatic service. I have witnessed many contests of will waged by bluster, feint, and chicanery."

"Valuable tools of war," Houston allowed, giving his new hand an appraising look.

"Though I must say," Washington went on, "few contests were ever as memorable as the one I witnessed on the deck of the ship that brought me home—and none of the contesting wills was human."

Arbuckle, Ellsworth, and Boone dropped their hands and stared at him, clearly confused by the conversation's turn. Houston was staring, too, but his expression signaled wariness, not confusion. "No *human* wills, you say?"

Washington nodded. "Have you ever heard of the Galápagos turtle? It's really a tortoise, I'm told, but the 'turtle' label is widely used. For generations, traders, whalers, and pirates of the Pacific have come to the Galápagos Islands and departed with tortoises to keep aboard as sources of food."

"I recall reading about that," Ellsworth chimed in. "The beasts can survive with little to eat or drink for as long as a year, I understand."

"True enough." Washington watched with satisfaction as Houston took another swig. *That will aid my scheme.*

"On the ship were two gigantic specimens, both males. Normally the sailors kept one fore and one aft, for male tortoises can be highly belligerent to each other, but one day they were allowed on deck at the same time. One crept ahead slowly. The other eyed him cautiously. Suddenly, the first lurched forward, prompting the second to snap viciously. Again and again the two circled, reconnoitering each other, breathing deep, their eyes scintillating fire. 'Foo-foo-foo,' the first clucked. 'Foo-foo-foo,' the second retorted."

Nathan Boone shook his head. "Scintillatin' fire? 'Foo-foo'? You writers are always dressin' up ordinary things in fancy words."

"You wouldn't say so if you'd seen these two creatures preparing to duel to the death," Washington said, "but the truly extraordinary part was yet to come."

Cards forgotten, the players regarded him with a mixture of disbelief and impatience. "Do get on with it, man," Ellsworth prompted. "Which animal prevailed?"

"Neither, I suppose, and yet both. Before the duel could commence, the tiniest man I ever saw leapt out from behind a barrel and dashed between the sharp claws and snapping beaks of the antagonists."

Colonel Arbuckle cocked his head and tittered nervously. "A little...man?"

"Or something shaped like a man, yes." Washington only had eyes for Sam Houston. "I'd say he stood three feet tall, if that, and wore quaint old Dutch clothing. Putting his hands up as if in supplication, he called out: 'Show your true colors, Bull!'"

Except for the distracted Houston, the others looked flabbergasted. "Was the little man addressing the turtles?" Ellsworth asked. "I believe whales and seals are often called bulls if they're male."

Washington shook his head. "That may be, but he wasn't speaking to them. He spoke to his companion, a giant of a sailor whom everyone called Bull for obvious reasons. He stood motionless as the little Dutchman kept repeating those five words—'Show your true colors, Bull!'"

"A *Dutchman*, was he? Ha!"

Surprising everyone, including Washington, Houston scrambled to his feet. Swaying unsteadily, his bouts of laughter punctuated periodically by hiccups, the former governor pointed an accusing finger. "You've shown your cards too early, Mister Irving. We out in the west aren't barbarians. Think we don't know how many of your fantastic stories feature odd Dutchmen? We only hear his latest fiction, gentlemen—a fitting campfire tale for our campfire game!"

Has the fish slipped my hook? Washington studied the man's face for a long while. *Is he acting the fool to throw me off, or merely drunk?*

Colonel Arbuckle broke the silence. "Well, at least finish the tale. Did this Bull fellow separate the beasts?"

"He did not." Washington decided to play his full hand. "The sailor called Bull did take a couple of steps forward, but only to beckon the little man back to his side. 'Know 'em better than you, Gez,' he muttered. 'Leave 'em be. One'll get the better of the other.'

"'And tear him limb from limb?' the little sailor called Gez wailed. 'I will not watch such a spectacle!'

"'Won't have to,' said the giant. And he was right. Presently, one of the tortoises walked his forelegs onto a barrel lid, raising his head somewhat higher than his rival's. However slight the advantage, it was enough. The rival beat as quick a retreat as he could."

Nathan Boone shrugged. "An interesting account of strange beasts, Mister Irving, but hardly extraordinary."

Washington glanced up at Houston, who was no longer laughing and whose vertigo had mysteriously vanished. "What I found truly extraordinary, gentlemen, were the two sailors. Now that I see the matter plainly, I am convinced neither was human."

~ ~ ~

The card game broke up shortly afterward, the players turning to their respective tents for the night. An hour later, as Washington was about to slip from groggy frustration to slumber, he heard two sets of footsteps approaching—one the ponderous stride of heavy boots, the other a light patter, as if a raccoon were stealing close to camp in search of scraps.

"Mister Irving," boomed the voice of Sam Houston. "Might we have a word?"

We? Washington sat up. "I shall slip on my boots, sir."

"You will not need them," said a higher voice.

Then the hazy figure glimpsed earlier on the tree branch appeared in sharp detail beneath the flap of his tent. It was not Gez, the little man in quaint Dutch clothes. It was no man at all.

The newcomer's dark wavy hair cascaded halfway down her slender back. She wore a deerskin shirt that left her brown arms bare except for finely wrought bands of copper and precious stones, and her deerskin skirt left her brown legs just as bare except for two large anklets fashioned from, of all things, tortoise shell.

Something unexpected dropped into Washington's mind. *I always pictured her hair as blue.*

All at once, the drop became a torrent. Memories flooded his mind, in images, words, experiences, feelings. Their force shattered whatever internal dams and dikes had once held them back. He felt towering waves crash into his chest. He felt the icy spray sting his face as if propelled by otherworldly winds. He felt powerful currents ensnare his legs, trying to yank him below the surface.

Senses reeling, Washington Irving pitched back to the ground. He couldn't think. He couldn't breathe.

"Irving, can you hear me?" Houston bellowed. "Help him, Tana!"

Washington felt a rough hand pull him up to a sitting position. He felt one delicate hand stroke his cheek and the other grasp his arm. Help came not by touch, however, but by sound. Help came by song. Spellsong. *Her* song.

Piece by piece, melody by melody, the jumble in his mind resolved into clarity. He remembered it all. His childhood encounter on a Hudson River schooner with a disguised Water Maiden named Dela. Meeting her again, in the company of the real Ichabod Crane, at Sackets Harbor. Overheard conversation and frenzied supposition. Pursuit along the eastern shore of Lake Ontario. Pursuit through a forest. And a headless horseman, of a sort.

His breaths came easier. "I am…better, thank you," Washington whispered to the little fairy woman. "You…you are—"

"Tana of the Nunnehi," she explained. "Chief of the Azalea Clan, called Tana Song Snake by my people and"—she paused to glance at Houston—"by certain other intimate friends."

Over the next few minutes, the two intimate friends surprised Washington by answering every question he posed about fairies, magic, monsters, and more. Tana explained that her people had long lived atop a mountain in Georgia but were preparing to relocate now that the westward trickle of Cherokees would soon become a flood. Coming west to scout sites for a new Nunnehi village, she'd planned to meet Houston at his home on the Neosho River and ask for assistance, only to happen upon their campsite. When it became evident Washington's perceptions were overwhelming the memory spells previously sung to him, Tana and Houston deemed it prudent to intervene.

"And you, sir," Washington asked Houston. "Is this your mission here? A commission from President Jackson to help her Folk make a new home?"

The Tennessean grinned and then hiccupped, suggesting his earlier insobriety hadn't been entirely feigned. "Not precisely, no. The president has sent me among the tribes to learn of and try to resolve certain disputes. Still, I won't stay long in this territory. I journey on to a new land."

"What do you mean?" Tana asked. "Where are you and Diana going?"

Houston shook his head. "My Cherokee wife may share only my Cherokee life. That has now ended. I will leave to my lovely Diana our wigwam on the Neosho. I will leave her behind."

"Like you left your first wife behind?" It was Washington who hurled the accusation, not Tana.

His words seemed to sting. "Do not bring her into this, sir," said Houston, now glowering at the author. "I will speak to no man of Eliza."

Tana touched Houston's arm. "Why not speak of her to me? I have never heard the tale from your own lips. And you know I would never repeat it."

Glancing at her and then back at Washington, Houston seemed about to protest. Then Tana shook her leg, making her tortoise-shell anklet rattle. A faint smile briefly creased the big man's leathery face.

"There was blame enough for us both," Houston admitted. "I loved Eliza dearly, with a passion that sometimes bordered on jealousy. I used foul, ill-chosen words, particularly after drinking. Still, I *did* love her—which is far more than she ever felt for me, as she confided later."

Tana looked aghast. "Then why did she—"

"It was to please her father that Eliza agreed to my proposal," Houston continued after a loud sniff. "Her heart belonged to another, but I was governor and confidante to the new president. The Allen family thought to elevate further their already exalted station. Eliza had hoped to grow to love me. It was on our wedding night she decided…that could never be."

Houston sniffed again, then drew a ragged sleeve over his now-moist eyes. Tana stroked his arm consolingly. Washington felt like a heel for indulging his curiosity at the expense of a man's composure. He cleared his throat.

"There is a sacredness in tears," he said, trying to sound both apologetic and sympathetic. "They are not a mark of weakness, but of power. They speak more eloquently than ten thousand tongues. They are the messengers of overwhelming grief, of deep contrition and of unspeakable love."

Tana and Houston transferred their attention back to Washington. "What's that, sir?" the Tennessean asked.

"Such ordeals as you have experienced may earn a rain of tears, and more," the author continued, "while in no way diminishing you. I submit that little minds are tamed and subdued by misfortunes, but great minds rise above them."

The visitors exchanged meaningful looks. "Kind words, Mister Irving, and well spoken," Houston said. "I have enjoyed making your acquaintance."

Puzzled, Washington pursed his lips. "Is our meeting over, then?"

Tana rose to her feet and bowed her head. "Not just yet."

Understanding dawned in the author's mind. His moment of clarity would be fleeting. His answers would turn back into questions, half remembered, if at all. Even the truth he'd just gleaned about Sam Houston's tragic past and uncertain future would wash away like words traced on a sandy beach.

Tana broke the silence. "Your mind has been subject to multiple memory spells by multiple Folk rangers over the years. Such an ordeal is more than any human should have to endure. I think it best to clean the slate and start anew."

And then, as the Song Snake began to shake her rattle, Washington Irving experienced one more earth-shattering, if fleeting, realization. He finally understood what had led him to write not only "The Legend of Sleepy Hollow," but also "Rip Van Winkle" and "The Devil and Tom Walker" and the fantastic tales of *The Alhambra*. He finally understood that his encounters with magical beings hadn't ended that day in 1814 on the banks of the Oswego when he'd first heard the memory song of Dela the Water Maiden.

The German spinster. The Spanish strangers. How many more disguised fairies had he met on his travels? How many more of his stories were actually elements in some unknown grand Folk design?

How many more of my stories were never truly, fully my own?

Chapter 1 — The Springs

July 1834

WHACK!

Manuel growled. It was the finest throw he'd ever seen from José. *Must he beat me at everything?*

Whack!

Pedro was next in line. As usual, the stocky boy's throw was off the mark, although this time he managed to hit the trunk a foot above the target rather than missing the tree altogether.

Then Manuel stepped forward, raising the stiff brim of his felt hat and eyeing the small circle drawn in yellow mud on the pine tree some forty feet away. He weighed his well-worn hunting knife appraisingly in his hand, wishing he'd sharpened the blade that morning while the others were off shooting their bows. He'd long ago given up trying to best José at archery or musketry, on the rare occasions they were allowed to fire the settlement's precious few muskets, and he'd never really considered Pedro a challenge at any contest of skill. When it came to knife-throwing, though, Manuel had always defeated the much taller and stronger José. Indeed, fifteen-year-old Manuel Antonio Chaves was widely acknowledged to be knife-throwing champion of Cebolleta.

"Fortune smiles on us, brother," said Pedro, who stood to Manuel's right on the sunbaked clearing that separated their small settlement from the trees lining the nearby creek. "You nearly stuck center, José! And at least I struck wood."

His concentration broken, Manuel glared at Pedro, whose answering bout of laughter shook his heavy jowls and ample belly.

To Manuel's left, José had been lounging against a rail and chatting amiably with the other young men of Cebolleta who so often followed him around like puppies. In response to Pedro's jest, however, José drew himself up to his impressive full height and crossed his muscular arms over his broad chest. "Fortune had nothing to do with it," José said disdainfully. "It was hard work. I have practiced for weeks to perfect my throw."

And to show up your scrawny little brother, Manuel wanted to snap, but he didn't. When dealing with José, it was best to hold your tongue. Manuel had learned that the hard way. He was a good wrestler. José was better. He was a fast runner. José was faster. So, Manuel had to rely on skill instead of strength, honed senses instead of brute force.

I hear all clearly, he assured himself, as he had so often before. *I see all clearly. I know what others do not. That is why I am a champion.*

Manuel gave only a guarded nod in response to José, the eldest of the Chaves brothers, then returned his attention to his blade. If it was too dull, he might strike the target dead center and still lose. Manuel ran his thumb lightly along its edge, glanced down at his uncreased skin, and frowned. *I should have spent my morning at the whetstone.*

"Want to use mine, Manuel?"

The knife in Pahe's hand was the Indian boy's most cherished possession. It had been a gift from his late master, Julián Chaves, who'd also been Manuel's father. Its long thin blade of steel and long curved handle of horn marked it as a *navaja*, a traditional dueling weapon from Old Spain that little resembled the sturdy utility knives more common among the hardy settlers of Mexico's far northern frontier.

It had come into Pahe's possession only because, just before he died of the pox, Julián Chaves decided to give away what he had deemed a useless heirloom. Broken and rusted, the blade no longer folded into the handle as designed. "Here you go, boy," Julián had muttered one afternoon, tossing it into the dirt before his little servant. "A navaja for my Navajo! Perhaps you can salvage some iron for the forge."

That day, as the imperious Julián left chuckling at his own wordplay, he missed the gleam in Pahe's eyes. He also underestimated his Navajo servant's dedication and skill. First, the boy spent weeks cleaning and sharpening the fifteen-inch blade. Then he spent months teaching himself how to repair the blade heel, lug, and backspring so the navaja would open and close with ease.

Manuel studied Pahe's folded knife. Although the navaja was sharp, Manuel was accustomed to the heft and balance of his own blade. *It makes no sense to use the navaja instead.*

His brother José seemed to read his mind. "Best stick to the tried-and-true, Manuel," he warned, brushing a spot of dirt from his otherwise pristine shirt. "I do not want my first victory in knife-throwing to come from a change of weapon."

I need no advice from you! Manuel wanted to shout back in defiance. *I see all clearly. I will remain the champion, no matter which knife I use.*

He snatched the navaja from Pahe's hand, inclining his head in curt appreciation. He wasn't particularly friendly with the boy, who kept to himself when not doing chores for Manuel's mother, María and her new husband, José Baca. It was with Pedro that Manuel spent most of his spare time. It was with Pedro that he had the most in common, including their shared resentment of their late father, distant and strict and impossible to please, as well as their popular brother, who seemed intent on carrying on the family tradition. It was in Pedro that Manuel had long confided, though less often now that Pedro had married and lived in his own small house.

Grasping the blade of the navaja between his right palm and fingers, Manuel pulled it away from the handle until he heard the distinctive clicking sound of the toothed heel locking into place.

Pedro raised a beefy hand in protest. "Are you sure it's wise to—"

But Manuel chose to act before his resolve could weaken. With a single fluid motion, he drew back his arm and flung the navaja at the pine tree.

Whack!

The razor-sharp tip struck true and plunged deep. The twisted end of the horn handle still quivered, as if in excitement, from the very center of the target.

Triumphant, Manuel whirled to face the spectators. Most looked surprised and impressed. José looked shocked. Pedro looked relieved. Pahe looked pleased, and perhaps even a little proud. At that, Manuel felt his neck flush. *It was* my *doing, boy, not yours. My skill, not your skinny blade. You are just a servant. I am a champion.*

Pahe had been smiling. When he saw Manuel's steel-gray eyes trained on him, however, the Navajo bowed obsequiously.

Servant. Manuel snorted dismissively. *That's just a word we use to hide the truth, but I see all clearly. You were my father's slave, and you are nothing at all to me.*

~ ~ ~

Which is precisely why he was outraged to learn the next morning that José planned to take Pahe but not Manuel on an expedition into the western desert. "You would have a slave boy ride with you instead of your own brother?" he demanded, stamping his foot.

"We journey deep into Navajo country," José explained, tying a bundle of cookpots across the back of his horse. "Our safety may require someone who speaks their tongue fluently. It may also require someone who doesn't come in last in every horse race."

"I am never last!" Manuel insisted. "That's Pedro."

José laughed. "And you don't see him among our number, either, do you?"

Manuel scowled at the assembling company. A dozen young men of the town stood on the dusty square, strapping trade goods, bows, muskets, and other supplies onto their own mounts and bidding goodbye to friends, family, and servants. All were clad in light-colored shirts, dark-colored trousers, leather chaps, and high boots, with flat-brimmed poblano hats of black or brown felt on their heads. It was hardly the first expedition to set out from Cebolleta to trade with the Pueblos to the south or the Navajos to the west, nor would it be the last. Founded a generation ago under the shadow of the San Mateo Mountains, some forty miles west of Albuquerque, Cebolleta lay on the fringe of settled New Mexico. It was the province's gateway to the Indian lands beyond. Whether war or peace passed through that gate, however, depended on the time of the year and the whims of one side or the other.

Manuel was sure he knew what kind of "trading" expedition José had in mind—and he wasn't about to be left out. "You will return with more than hides and blankets. Your friends Diego and Amado wish to marry. They want native girls as servants for their wives."

"This is no slave raid," José insisted. "I want no part of that."

"I do not believe you," Manuel said. *I see all clearly. I see through you.*

"You should trust my judgment. Besides, what would Mamá say if I let your ride into such danger? You are just a little boy."

"I am nearly sixteen, and Pahe is shorter by half a foot!"

"We won't be counting on Pahe if raiders or wild animals attack. I take only warriors and servants on this journey."

"I am no servant like *him*," muttered Manuel, nodding at the Navajo boy loading his own pony with provisions.

"Do you claim to be a warrior, then?" José snickered, reaching down to tousle his brother's shaggy mop of chestnut-colored hair.

Manuel jerked away. "I can fight as well as anyone, if ever I get a chance to prove it!"

An uncomfortable silence fell between the two brothers. Seething, Manuel could feel José's dark eyes fixed on the back of his head as if trying to bore into his mind.

"You may well get your chance."

It took Manuel a few moments to comprehend. Then he spun on one heel.

"But only if you are ready to leave in half an hour," José added as he turned and strode away to help a friend load a feed bag onto a reluctant mule.

~ ~ ~

For the first two days of the journey, the youths remained in sight of the mountains looming over Cebolleta. As the expedition continued westward, however, they passed the final landmark they recognized—the volcanic plug known as the Awl—and proceeded through unfamiliar desert toward a distant soaring range of hazy peaks.

"They are called *Níłtsą́ Dził*, the Rainy Mountains," said Pahe, pointing them out to Manuel as the two rode side by side. "My family lives in their shadow, just as yours does in the shadow of the San Mateo."

José organized the little party in double file. Seven pairs of riders were spaced apart by several horse lengths with the fifteenth member, José himself, riding solo at the head of the column. *He was the one who brought Pahe along*, Manuel brooded. *Why do* I *have to ride with the slave?*

"Your family is nothing like mine," he replied, turning his head to scan the vast sea of dirt and stones around them. It was dotted with islands of saltbush and rabbitbrush.

"I meant no offense," Pahe sputtered. "I meant only that my people—"

"Where *are* your people? José says we should have met Navajo scouts or herdsmen by now."

Duly chastened, Pahe shrugged his shoulders and looked down.

A moment later, the sound of galloping hooves made both youths glance up. "We'll stop here for a bit," José shouted. Manuel bridled his horse to a halt, trying not to let his annoyance show. The trip thus far had proved tedious and exhausting—not at all the exciting adventure he'd expected. Although José insisted frequent stops were necessary to rest and water their mounts, Manuel preferred to press ahead, get wherever they were going quickly, and then head back home.

His brother rode up to them. "Pahe, take a look at that," José said, pointing northward at a low mesa surrounded by reddish slopes and topped by low brush. "I thought I saw something move."

The Navajo boy studied the hill. So did Manuel. After a while, he heard Pahe suck in a startled breath. "*Náshdóítsoh,*" he whispered.

"What is that you said?" Manuel demanded. *What could he have seen that I did not?*

"Our word for what you call lion of the mountains," the Navajo replied. "It is the guardian of my mother's clan, the *Honághááhnii*. The 'One Walks Around You Clan.'"

José looked surprised. "I thought mountain lions rarely prowled in daylight and are hard to spot even at night."

"You are right," Pahe agreed. "I have seen Náshdóítsoh only twice before. First, when I was a small boy, and then again from the trail when your father carried me away to Cebolleta."

Manuel noticed Pahe's hand touch the horn handle of the navaja thrust through his sash. The sight made him snicker. "Do you mean to slay the beast with your little pig-sticker?"

Pahe paled. "*Slay* Náshdóítsoh? I would never use Áláshgaan to—"

Manuel interrupted him with a guffaw. "A-lash-what?"

The Indian boy started and bowed his head.

"I take it you have named your knife?" José said in a low voice.

Pahe nodded, keeping his eyes averted. "I call it Claw. Claw of Lion."

"A fit name," José said. Then he smiled at the boy, spurred his horse into a walk, and headed for the back of the line. Manuel watched him go, silently cursing his brother for his indulgent tone.

If José was mocking Pahe and expects him to get the joke, the boy is getting more credit than he deserves. And if José actually meant to be kind, the boy is getting the credit I *deserve.*

~ ~ ~

It was late afternoon of the eighth day when José and the others discovered why they'd met no Navajos on the trail or on the sheep-grazing lands they'd passed.

"We call it *Tséyi'*, the Place Deep in the Rock," said Pahe as he, José, Manuel, and José's friends Diego and Amado peered over the ridge into the crowded valley. "Some of your people call it Canyon de Chelly."

Although thick clouds filled the summer sky, blocking the rays of the setting sun, blazing campfires made the inhabitants of the canyon clearly visible. Flocks of sheep and a great herd of horses grazed on the grass and brush of the valley floor below. The Cebolletans saw several clusters of *hogans*, the distinctively round houses of the Navajo. Hundreds of men, women, and children were entering or exiting the stone-and-mud structures or milling around the fires outside them.

The canyon wasn't just filled with lights. It was also filled with sounds: sheep bleating, horses nickering, children laughing, women singing, men shouting. Underneath all the bedlam was the relentless beating of Navajo drums and drumsticks.

José turned to Pahe. "Why have they all come to this 'Place Deep in the Rock'?"

The Indian boy gulped. "A ceremony. To sing and dance."

"Will it last long?"

"It may last...many days."

"Many *days*?" Diego exploded. "I will not wait that long. Not worth it."

His friend Amato snorted. "Do you really want to go back without the servants we promised our women?"

José jerked to his feet and thumped the butt of his borrowed musket on the ground. "I *told* you this was no slave raid! You assured me you understood."

"We thought you just said that for show," Diego protested. "Why be so squeamish? Our fathers raided the Indians for boys and girls. Our grandfathers did the same."

"Just as generations of Navajos, Apaches, and Comanches raided *our* villages and carried away *our* boys and girls," Amato added. "It is the way of things."

"Must it always be so?" José's deep voice now sounded not enraged, but plaintive. "Raid after raid. Violence and more violence."

Manuel sat back on a flat rock, his mind reeling. He'd long prided himself on his ability to see through pretense, but José's outburst seemed genuine. *Have I misjudged my brother so greatly? I always thought him a cruel, arrogant bully. Can he truly be such a sentimental fool? Or is he like so many other bullies—a coward at heart?*

"Do what you like, José," Amato sneered. "I do not plan to give up so easily." Then he turned to Diego. "Perhaps if we keep to the hills and wait for the Navajos to get drunk, we can snatch a couple of stray children to make the trip worthwhile."

"Are you mad?" José exclaimed. "Look at all those campfires! With such overwhelming numbers, they will never agree to trade with us. And raiding them is madness. We are but thirteen good shots, plus Pahe and my little brother. We must leave—now."

My little brother! "I am just as good with bow and gun as anyone here," Manuel asserted. "If it's a fight they want, I will—"

"Shh." Pahe held his finger against his trembling lips.

Manuel made no reply. The slave boy's interruption gave him and the other Cebolletans the chance to hear what Pahe heard: the crunch of dirt and stone beneath moccasined feet.

"Go back!" José urged, already clambering down the steep path toward the arroyo, the narrow gulley near the base of the ridge, where the others waited with horses and mules.

Manuel didn't follow. He'd brought a weapon with him to the lip of the canyon, just as his brother had—but unlike José, he was neither a fool nor a coward. He saw all clearly. And he was a champion. He would *not* run from a fight.

Drawing a steel-tipped arrow from the quiver strapped across his back, Manuel drew his fingers across its gray-feather fletching, fitted the nock into the string of his stout bow, and edged forward, eager to find a target.

The arrow flew fast and struck hard. But it was tipped with bone, not steel. Its feathers black, not gray.

Manuel first saw the black fletching at his left shoulder, contrasting sharply with the white cloth of his shirt, before he saw the red stain spreading beneath it.

"Manuel!" José scrambled toward his brother.

Pahe scrambled faster. As the younger Chaves tumbled back from the edge of the canyon, he found the Indian boy ready to break his fall. Waving José back, Pahe wrapped one arm around Manuel and used the other for balance as the two youths stumbled their way down the mountain path.

Arrows whizzed past their ears and skipped along the rocky ground beneath their feet. There were arrows flying the other direction, too—steel-tipped ones, sometimes accompanied by musket balls—from José and his friends.

Miraculously, and solely because of Pahe's assistance, Manuel made it to the gulley. He saw the other Cebolletans fitting arrows to their bows or laboriously loading their antique guns. *I am a champion!* he reminded himself, slipping under Pahe's supportive arm.

Whether the servant boy tried to object, he never knew—Manuel only had eyes and ears for the enemy. He saw Navajo warriors step from behind boulders or sagebrush, loose their arrows, then return to cover to reload. He saw Navajo warriors leap forward, holding clubs and tomahawks over their heads. He saw other Navajo warriors stalk forward with short knives or long spears. He heard Navajo warriors call, threaten, grunt, and moan.

Pahe was no Navajo warrior, so Manuel neither saw nor heard him.

The first enemy Manuel killed was tall and thin. The man's small buckskin shield offered inadequate protection when Manuel first slashed his thigh with a hunting knife, then opened the Navajo's throat. The second enemy Manuel killed was short and squat, an easy target for the expertly thrown knife that took the Navajo full in the chest just as he drew back his bowstring.

Were the other Cebolletans faring as well? Had his arrogant oaf of a brother managed to fell even a single foe? Manuel wanted to find out but couldn't spare the moment. More enemies were filing into the gulley. More black-fletched arrows filled the air.

Manuel winced as something sliced his thigh. Something else punched his unwounded shoulder, knocking him to the earth. He felt sharp stings on his side, his left arm, his right shin. Then he felt only pain, and pride, and vindication.

I am a champion. I am a warrior. I am the Chaves brother all should fear—and obey.

~ ~ ~

The agony that dragged Manuel back to consciousness didn't come from the arrow wounds in his shoulders, arm, side, or legs, but rather from his parched mouth. He opened his eyes. The clouds had thinned, revealing a sky of twinkling stars. He drew a breath of cool night air and coughed.

"Man…Manuel?"

The reedy voice came from his left. Manuel tried to sit up, groaned, and gave up. It felt like branding irons were pressing against his skin.

A face blotted out the starry sky. "Here," it said. Something cold and wet touched Manuel's lips. He drank greedily.

After a while, he made another attempt to sit up. This time he succeeded, though his wounds burned no less fiercely. What Manuel saw, however, sent a chill down his spine. He was surrounded by bodies. Bodies pierced, hacked, bruised, and sliced. Unmoving bodies, drenched with blood.

All except one. It was drenched in blood, to be sure, the wound in its chest clearly visible and inexpertly plugged. This body, however, was moving. Manuel watched Pahe crawl awkwardly to his side and hold up a wooden canteen.

"No, no," Manuel muttered. "Save it for later."

Pahe nodded. Both examined Manuel's wounded body. Every enemy arrow had been yanked from his flesh, leaving bloody holes.

"Where is my brother?" Manuel asked.

The Navajo's dark eyes closed.

Shocked, Manuel scanned the ground. One motionless body stood out. He recognized José's brown breeches and yellow shirt, but his fine leather boots were gone. His bare feet were twisted unnaturally.

"He saved me," Pahe said. "I could not save him."

"What do you—"

"An arrow hit me," the boy explained. "Then a warrior ran at me with a club. José was wounded, too, but he stepped in front of me and blocked the blow with his gun."

Manuel tried to picture the scene in his head, but was too groggy for it to come into focus. "Is that when José—"

"Another swing of his gun felled the warrior," Pahe continued. "Two others surrounded your brother as I crawled away. I did not see what happened next."

"You *left* him even after he saved you!" Manuel was incensed but couldn't fathom why. He knew Pahe would have been useless in a fight.

Then the bootless body moved.

"José!" Manuel cried. He started crawling toward his brother, whose bare feet flexed briefly before dropping back to the ground. Pahe followed him.

There weren't any arrows protruding from José, either. Indeed, Manuel suddenly realized *all* the bodies had been stripped of spent arrows, weapons, boots, belts, and personal effects. The Navajos had stripped everything of value from their fallen foes and hurried back to the celebration in the valley below.

They didn't even stop to make sure we were all truly dead.

"What…where are…why can't I…"

What gurgled out of José were mere fragments of questions, separated by coughs that left a pinkish foam on trembling lips.

Though he'd never felt great affection for José, Manuel flinched at the sight of his once-mighty brother contorted in pain and bleeding from half a dozen wounds. "Don't try to speak," he managed. "Pahe, try to find some—"

"Is that you, Manuel?" his brother hissed. "My eyes see nothing."

"I am here."

"And…the others?"

"All dead," Manuel replied, watching Pahe tear pieces of cloth from a nearby corpse.

"Not all." The next cough sent a trickle of blood down José's chin. "Brought glory and…honor to the name Chaves."

Manuel's eyes narrowed. *Even* now, *you brag of your exploits!* "Lie still, José."

"Papá never believed," José hissed. "Weak…headstrong…I knew better…proved him wrong."

With fumbling fingers, Pahe pressed a makeshift bandage over the hole in José's belly and secured it with a strip of buckskin. Manuel watched in silence, feeling his stomach clench and knowing it wasn't caused by his own wounds.

"I challenged...pushed myself...a step ahead." José's words were fainter now. "How else...can a cub grow...to be a lion?"

The last word rose like a thin stream of smoke from a snuffed candle. That word, the last José Chaves would ever utter, wriggled through the cold night air and curled itself around Manuel's throat.

Lion.

~ ~ ~

The second night's journey spanned many more hours than the first. They were also walking across easier terrain, flat and sandy instead of steep and rocky. Still, it seemed to Manuel that he and Pahe had covered more ground during their first night, though it was shortened by the need to bury José and to search, however fruitlessly, for any provisions the Navajos had missed.

Besides Pahe's ragged moccasins—not worth stealing—the only other items they carried away from Canyon de Chelly were the two Pahe had managed to hide during the battle. One was the wooden canteen, now fully drained. The other was the Indian boy's precious navaja knife, now caked with dirt after being pressed into service as a burial tool.

"Going too far south," Manuel complained. Hunger, thirst, fatigue, and blood loss combined to slow his normally brisk pace to a lethargic shuffle.

Pahe looked no less exhausted but shook his head firmly. "Cannot make it back to Cebolleta without water. Ojo del Oso is close."

Eye of the Bear. Manuel had heard others talk about the natural springs just north of the Zuni Mountains, but he'd never been there. It offered the prospect of water, shade, and perhaps something to eat. But was finding Bear Springs worth adding so many miles to their journey home?

Click-click-click. Click-click-click.

Manuel was absentmindedly opening and closing the navaja. Puny though it was, the knife was presently their sole means of defense. He'd insisted Pahe hand it over for the duration of their journey. *How can a mere slave wield the Claw of a Lion?*

Manuel smiled grimly and thought of his brother's last words. That José couldn't stop boasting about his fighting prowess, even as he lay dying, should have been infuriating. It wasn't fury, however, that consumed Manuel as he stumbled along behind Pahe. It was pity. *I never knew José felt that way about Papá. I thought only Pedro and I had cause to resent our father.*

"Look, Manuel! Do you see?"

Pahe stood atop a small hill, pointing. Trudging up the slope, Manuel felt his pulse quicken when he glimpsed a blue-green smear in the distance. After a few more steps, the indistinct smear took on the distinct pattern of oak leaves.

What lay ahead was a shallow pool surrounded by grass, clumps of cactus, and a stand of Gambel oaks. To Manuel's tired eyes, however, Bear Springs appeared before him as a tantalizing Garden of Eden. His strength momentarily restored, he quickened his pace and spread his arms, eager to submerge himself.

"Wait!" Pahe sounded panicked. "Something is in there!"

Already at the edge of the pool, Manuel fell to his knees and dipped his sunburnt face into the water. He gulped greedily, coughed some of it back up, then sipped more cautiously. With shaking hands, he scrubbed his grimy forehead, cheeks, and neck.

"There it is, again!" cried Pahe, who'd stopped far short of the water's edge.

Manuel lifted his head. "I do not mind sharing with some flapping fish or leaping frog. Come on in!"

When the Navajo boy shook his head, Manuel felt a twinge of apprehension. He scanned the little pool more carefully. Other than the ripples caused by his own actions, he saw nothing. Then he lifted his eyes to the far shore and the trees beyond.

What was that?

Several branches shook back and forth. Manuel stood up, lifting a wet hand to shield his eyes from the early morning sun. The trees were now still. *Am I a frightened child, or a man who hears and sees all clearly?*

He chuckled. "We need not fear the wind, Pahe."

After drinking his fill, Manuel tried to coax him into the water. The

Indian boy still refused, though he gladly drank from the refilled canteen. Then Manuel stripped off his tattered clothes and reentered the pool, gingerly rubbing his wounds to remove crusts of dirt and blood. Rather than wash his own chest in the water, Pahe removed one of his moccasins and tore off a strip of the sole to cover his arrow wound, which was discolored and oozing pus.

The two lay on the soft grass for some time, passing the canteen and nibbling on acorns and a few prickly pears Manuel had cut from the cactus and peeled with the navaja knife. "What did you think you saw in the pool?" he asked.

The Indian boy seemed hesitant to answer. "Could be the wind, like you said."

"Then why not get in the water?"

"I…I cannot say."

Manuel pressed the flat of the navaja blade against an acorn and pressed until he heard a crack. "*Cannot* say, or *will not* say?"

Pahe rolled onto his back, shutting his eyes tightly. "Our people do not speak of it. Great danger."

"Speak of what?"

Eyes still closed, Pahe clinched his jaw. Whether the boy was trying not to cry out from pain or trying to keep a secret, Manuel couldn't tell. He asked his question again but got no response. Pahe appeared to have fallen asleep. Just as Manuel was starting to drift into a fitful slumber of his own, however, the boy mumbled something in the Navajo tongue.

Manuel rolled over. "What?"

"*Yee naaldlooshii,*" the boy repeated, still looking half asleep.

"Yes?"

Pahe sighed groggily. "Skinwalker."

~ ~ ~

Growls jolted Manuel awake. Or perhaps they were howls, hisses, grunts, or roars—the noises were strange and indistinct. He sat up, making the wounds in his side and shoulders burn, and glanced around. Pahe was no longer next to him.

Grabbing the navaja knife and struggling to his feet, Manuel gazed across the pool at the line of oaks. One branch suddenly bent low, nearly touching the ground. Then came an unearthly scream. It seemed to leap across the water at Manuel.

Disregarding the protests of his aching limbs, he dashed along the waterline and into the trees. "Show yourself! I hear all. I see all. You cannot hide from me!"

There was no second scream, no sounds of struggle. No sound at all. No movement. Manuel saw only moonlit trees and moonlit grass, and the moonlit form of Pahe lying near the water's edge. His arms and legs were twisted and pale. His chest was painted in splotches of pinkish red and greenish black. His mouth and eyes were wide open.

Manuel heard no sound from the former. And he saw no life in the latter.

~ ~ ~

It killed Pahe. It wants to kill me, too.

Manuel had never been more convinced of anything in his life. As he pushed ever eastward and northward, the imminent danger from Pahe's killer was a constant presence in his fevered mind.

The *identity* of the killer did not, however, stay constant. Was it a wild beast, perhaps even the mysterious creature Pahe had claimed to see at Bear Springs? As he made his laborious way through the desert, Manuel couldn't shake the feeling he was being followed. Sometimes, when he looked back, he saw a shadowy figure on the horizon. Other times, he saw nothing but sand and stone and occasional patches of brush.

Still, whatever phantom trailed him, it was either unable or unwilling to close the distance between them. In his more lucid moments, Manuel recognized it could be a figment of his imagination. After all, the phantom's size seemed to vacillate between two extremes—a hulking shape as large as an elephant and a furtive shape as low to the ground as a dog. Moreover, Manuel couldn't be sure *any* beast was responsible for Pahe's death. There had been no other wound on the boy's body aside from the festering hole in his chest. Several of Manuel's own wounds were now discolored and oozed pus as well.

Perhaps such poison is what killed Pahe, and what is about to kill me.

Manuel glanced up at the stars twinkling in the night sky. Were they twinkling, though, or laughing? He licked his parched lips and felt his stomach lurch. Perhaps it was the land itself that had killed the Indian boy—the sizzling heat of the midsummer day, the freezing air of the lonely night, the barren ground that yielded so little to eat or drink. So many times during the three days—or had it been it three years?—since he'd left Bear Springs, Manuel glimpsed possible succor. He'd seen the spines of a cactus, only to discover its fruit and other edible parts had already been consumed by some denizen of the desert. More than once he'd followed faint tracks to a watering place, only to discover it was either dry as a bone or filled with a fetid liquid that only worsened his thirst.

Manuel's legs wobbled and gave way. He fell to his knees, the navaja knife and empty canteen slipping from his grasp, and then keeled over backward. His wounds scalded him. He tried to swallow, which only caused his throat to burn, too. He looked up toward Heaven. *I can go no further. Be you beast, poison, or thirst, take me now. Whatever killer you are, pray get on with it. I am a champion. I am a warrior. I deserve a quick death.*

He looked up, yes, but saw no stars. He saw only dark-brown branches and blue-green leaves. *Oak trees?* Had Manuel wandered so aimlessly that he'd doubled back and returned to Bear Springs?

No, said a quiet voice. *You are not so far gone that you cannot tell east from west. And where one thing grows, others may grow.*

Turning over and crawling beneath the leafy boughs of Gambel oak, Manuel soon found what he was looking for. He tore a piece off of the tiny cactus and gnawed on it desperately. He tore off another. The precious moisture and pulp revived his flagging spirits, as did a short rest among the sheltering trees. When he set off again, it was by walking, not stumbling.

Two days and many miles later, his second wind gave out. Again he sank to his knees, then rolled onto his back. Again he looked up and mumbled an anguished prayer. Again something blocked his view of the twinkling, mocking stars, only this time it wasn't an oak tree. The head and shoulders of a man leaned over the emaciated form of Manuel Chaves.

It was the head and shoulders of a shepherd from Cebolleta.

~ ~ ~

"They are back!"

Manuel jerked up when he heard the shout. He instantly regretted it, sinking back onto his bed with a grimace.

While his other wounds pained him less, having been properly cleaned, stitched, and bandaged by his mother María, the hole in his side was the deepest and still burned fiercely. It had only been a few days since the shepherd brought him back to town on a litter. Only a few days of rest—not nearly enough time to heal his two most serious wounds.

The arrow wound in his side was one of them. The other was the hole his ordeal had poked in the youth's once impenetrable confidence. *I hear all clearly? Then how did the Navajo archer get the drop on me at Canyon de Chelly? I see all clearly? Then how did I so badly misjudge José and Pahe?*

Confined to his bed, he'd done little but dwell on his ordeal. Contrary to his accusation, his brother had never intended to capture slaves. José had been telling the truth all along. He'd also rushed to Manuel's defense when the younger Chaves was attacked. And were his final words truly those of a swaggering bully? Manuel was no longer sure they were, though their meaning still eluded him.

As for the slave boy, he could have left Manuel and José for dead in the arroyo and tried to save himself, perhaps finding his way back to his own family. Instead, Pahe had stayed behind to help the Chaves brothers. His reward was to die, pitiful and alone, at Bear Springs.

I heard and saw much, but knew far too little.

The door flew open. Pedro burst into the room, round cheeks flushed with excitement. "Did you hear, Manuel? Ramon Sena and José Castillo are alive! Just rode into town with a bunch of Navajos!"

"Are we under attack?" Alarmed, Manuel swung his feet over the side of the bed. The two blacksmiths, Sena and Castillo, had left Cebolleta shortly after the Chaves expedition, heading north to sell jewelry in a Navajo settlement. When Manuel returned to town with news of the massacre at the canyon, the Cebolletans feared the Indians had killed Sena and Castillo too.

Pedro held up a hand. "Not yet. These Navajos say they come in peace. They claim they had nothing to do with the battle at Canyon de Chelly, and that they escorted our men back to town to keep them safe."

Manuel frowned, recalling his recent misjudgments. "How many are there? They could be lying."

"I am *sure* the Navajos are lying," Pedro said. "There are eighteen, all warriors on good horses. No little boys or old men. Still, many believe their story—our own mother does. She has offered to let them stay the night here."

"What?"

"She's being foolish, Manuel, but it may serve our purpose."

"Our *purpose*?"

"I have talked to the others." Pedro sauntered to the window and gazed thoughtfully into the courtyard. "If the Indians believe they are safe, it will make our task easy. We can fall upon them in the middle of the night."

Manuel rolled his eyes. "You are no warrior, Pedro. Even if you catch them sleeping, eighteen armed Navajos will be hard to overpower."

"Who says they are armed?" Pedro gave Manuel a conspiratorial grin.

"They offered to leave their weapons outside the house?"

Pedro snorted. "They were not even armed when they rode into town. Said they left their weapons near the creek as a sign of good faith."

Manuel scratched his chin. *I heard and saw much, but knew little.* "How can we be sure they are lying, then?"

Pedro looked incredulous. "*Of course* they are lying! It is a trick. No doubt their friends wait outside town to swoop in. We must jump them before they jump us."

"What do Sena and Castillo say?"

"That the Navajos were *kind* to them," Pedro sneered. "What fools. Big talkers, like José, without an ounce of common sense." It was the kind of crack the two brothers had made countless times at José's expense.

Manuel's ordeal had changed things, however. Now, the insult made him cringe. "Don't speak of him that way!"

Pedro's face reddened. "Though I had no great love for our brother, I regret what happened to him. Still, it is *you* who made it back from Canyon de Chelly. *You* are the hero. *You* are the Chaves all of Cebolleta is talking about."

Before he left, that would have thrilled Manuel. Now, remembering how he'd fallen to the ground in agony and prayed for a quick death, Manuel didn't feel much like a hero.

"You should be the one leading our attack tonight," Pedro insisted. "Do you not want to get back at them?"

Manuel shook his head. "These are not the men who attacked me."

"They are Navajos! They are all the same. If we do not kill them, they will surely kill us!"

Pahe was Navajo. He could have abandoned José and me, the sons of the man who made him a slave, or he could have killed us while we lay unconscious in the arroyo. He did neither. He helped, but only I made it home.

"No." Manuel felt a great weight pressing down on him, as if the mountain lion they'd glimpsed on their journey had found its way into the room and pounced, pinning him to the bed. "Mamá has offered shelter to these men. It is not right to kill them in cold blood."

"We have *every* right," said Pedro, his fists clenched. "Thirteen men of Cebolleta are dead. Will you not avenge them? Will you not avenge your own brother?"

The pressure intensified. It felt like Manuel's ribs were about to crack. "José would not want us to do this."

Pedro sighed. "You are not well, brother. You are not yourself. Just rest now."

Manuel shook his head again. "You must not—"

"Lie back and rest. Leave the Navajos to us."

~ ~ ~

It was about half past three in the morning when Pedro and a dozen Cebolletans crept into the courtyard of the Chaves home, muskets in their hands and vengeance in their hearts. What awaited them there, however, was no party of unarmed sleeping men. The Navajos stood in a circle, holding muskets and bows.

"It *was* a trick all along!" Pedro wailed. "We must run and wake the town!"

"No," growled a low voice. "You must stay here."

The circle of Navajos parted. Out limped Manuel, pallid and hunched over, holding a long thin blade.

Pedro was aghast. "What have you done? Have you lost your senses?"

Manuel gritted his teeth. "It is you who have lost your senses, if you ever had any." *I hear all clearly. I see all clearly.*

"They hid their weapons under—"

"These warriors were armed by our mother's hand, and my own," Manuel said. "They were telling the truth, Pedro. They gave their word. We gave ours. I will see it carried out."

There was nothing left to say. Pedro glared at Manuel. He glared back. Finally, cooler heads prevailed, and some of the Cebolletans escorted the Navajos out of the village. Pedro returned to his home, furious and shamed. Manuel returned to his sickbed, furious and determined.

His fury wasn't directed at Pedro or the others. It was directed at himself. *I am just as big and swaggering a fool as José ever was. Now I must become someone else, someone better—a champion of something other than hurling knives and insults and accusations. I must hone my senses. I must hear what is silent. See what is invisible. Know what is hidden.*

Only then will I swing my Claw.

Chapter 2 – The Vow

April 1834

PROPELLED BY LONG POLES, THE barge left the main course of the river and entered a narrow canal. Standing on the deck next to his best friend, and invisible to everyone else on the small craft, the traveler glanced wearily at the enormous white mansion in the distance.

He'd never met its primary occupant, but he knew the two shared something in common. Both had lost the women they loved.

For the lonely man who resided in the mansion, the loss was irretrievable. Andrew Jackson's wife, Rachel, had died shortly after his election to the presidency in 1828. She'd never lived in the great house that lay beyond the north bank of the canal.

The traveler shut his eyes tightly. *My story will have a different ending. I will find her. I will have my Dela again.*

Goran Lonefeather felt a heavy hand on his shoulder. The Sylph opened his eyes and cast a grateful look at his companion, Har the Tower, then turned his attention back to the south portico of the White House. Whether the two fairy rangers would have occasion to visit the president's mansion during their time in Washington, Goran didn't know, although he and Har would certainly consult their contacts in the Jackson administration. By now, Sighted humans serving in the government had surely collected reports of Elves occupying abandoned Folk villages across the frontier. Mass resettlement of Elfkind had been Prince Veelund's plan all along—and despite the best efforts of Goran, Har, Dela, and their allies, the prince's devious plan succeeded.

Worst of all, Veelund had used magical devices of his own design to escape the seemingly victorious allies at Spirit Forest, carrying off the Water Maiden in the process. Goran clung to the desperate hope that his American friends might aid his search for her. Dela's own people, so far, had given him less help than blame.

~ ~ ~

"I wish you never came here!" Dela's mother, Tesni, fumed, her pale-blue finger trembling before the Sylph's distraught face. "I wish you never met her!"

It was many weeks ago, as humans reckoned time in the Blur, that Goran and Har had last visited the Gwragedd Annwn village in Tennessee. Laid out as a series of tunnels, caverns, and grottos beneath Long Island-on-the-Holston, the village was home to a traditionally insular Water Folk who'd gone to war twice in reluctant alliance with the Dwarf colony of Grünerberg. The first time, intervening against the pro-British Sylphs and Pixies at Yorktown, the Gwragedd Annwn had turned the tide of battle, albeit at the cost of many blue-skinned warriors. Their second intervention against the Elf fortress in Spirit Forest had produced more casualties, but little else.

It had been many weeks since Goran stood before the Gwragedd Annwn to plead for assistance. Still, as the Sylph stood on the deck of the slow-moving barge, what he felt was not the gentle breeze off the Potomac River but the continued sting of bitter words and accusing stares.

"Because of our Folk's past sacrifices in the service of starry-eyed schemers like you, we face grave dangers," said Councilmember Gwyla during his visit. "And now you would have us put more rangers at your disposal?"

"Veelund must be headed for one of the new Elf colonies," Goran had replied. "If the Gwragedd Annwn could but help me discover which one, I promise I will find a way to rescue her without endangering any more of your—"

"We have heard such promises before." Gwyla rose from her seat at the council table. "Pretty words in the cool of night that turn to mist and vanish in the light of day."

Tesni crossed her arms defiantly. "Our rangers *should* search for Dela, but not in the company of this Lonefeather who led her astray."

At that, Har the Tower snorted dismissively. "Your daughter is not 'led' by others. She leads."

"You think you know my daughter better than I do?"

"I know when I was Veelund's captive, she never stopped looking for me—and I am but a friend," the Dwarf said. "Who is better suited to leading Dela's rescue than the man she loves?"

It had been the wrong thing to say, though Har couldn't have known that. Only Goran and Dela were aware of her mother's strong objections to their relationship.

During the ensuing debate between Tesni and Gwyla, the two visiting rangers were unceremoniously ejected from the council chamber. As they sloshed their way across the watery floor of the grotto, the noise of their exit drowned out by the impassioned voices of the debaters still inside, Goran realized his presence among the Gwragedd Annwn was doing more to incite resentment than cooperation.

So, they'd departed Long Island-on-the-Holston, heading first to Grünerberg for a brief conference with King Alberich and then on to the American capital on the Potomac, where they hoped to meet up with an old friend.

No longer lost in thought, Goran noticed the barge had left the river entirely and was heading eastward along the canal. The Potomac wasn't much like the Holston, and the bustling human city of Washington didn't much resemble the modest human town of Kingsport that sprang up around Long Island-on-the-Holston.

When the barge reached a sharp right turn, Har pointed to a five-story building on the north bank. Goran could read the name *Jesse Brown* on its sign, though what truly made it distinctive was the image of a human woman painted next to the words.

"That is said to be the likeness of Pocahontas," the Dwarf explained, hopping more nimbly from the barge than his immense bulk might seem to allow. "So they call it the Indian Queen Hotel."

Har's dexterity was no surprise to Goran Lonefeather, of course—he'd seen Har put it to far more consequential use. The Sylph stepped to the edge of the barge and leapt into the air, his wings bearing him gracefully over the tiny gap. He hoped the two rangers would have more luck with Har's friend than they'd had with the Gwragedd Annwn—and that they'd be lucky enough to find him in the first place.

~ ~ ~

In that last hope, at least, Goran was not to be disappointed.

After only a short time hiding in the bushes next to the hotel, Har nudged Gar and pointed at two approaching figures. One stood about average height for a human—that is, a little over a foot taller than Har the Tower—and wore the suit, waistcoat, shirt, and cravat of a Washington gentleman, though his stride marked him as better suited to stalking bears in a forest than dance partners at a ball. His companion was tall and stocky, with oversized hands and feet and an Indian blanket draped over his broad shoulders. His leathery square-jawed face shot the laughing man a sheepish grin of his own.

It was the bigger man, Sam Houston, whom the two fairies hoped to find at the Indian Queen, his favorite Washington hotel. Sighing in relief, Goran watched Har poke his head out from the bush and nod meaningfully as the humans passed their hiding place and entered the hotel. When the Dwarf turned back with a frustrated expression, however, Goran sucked in a breath.

"Did he not see you?"

Har shrugged. "Neither one batted an eye."

"*Neither* one?" Goran was puzzled at the choice of words.

"The other man has the Sight, too. That was David Crockett, the Tennessee congressman I told you about."

Allowing impatience to overrule caution, Goran suggested the rangers fortify their concealment spells and follow the men. It proved to be no challenge to find their quarry. The congressman's boisterous laughter beckoned them to the hotel's dining hall, where they saw Houston and Crockett greet three other humans rising from a corner table. Two were men dressed much like Crockett, though the resemblance ended there. Both were shorter and slighter than he, their light complexions and practiced reserve contrasting sharply with Crockett's ruddy face and easy manner. The other guest at the table was a stunning young woman in a rose-colored gown, her dark hair shaped into an inviting mix of parted lines and dangling curls.

"Mighty glad to make your acquaintance, Miss Walton," Crockett boomed, "and happy to see you and your friend again, Mister Kennedy."

Goran could see the lady's mouth moving but couldn't hear her words. "Let us move closer," he whispered to Har, who readily accepted the suggestion and pointed to an alcove in the opposite wall. As the fairies crept silently through the dining room, Goran saw Sam Houston's eyes widen, but he couldn't tell whether the big man had recognized them or was simply responding to something the lady was saying.

"You've been holdin' out on me, Sam!" Crockett exclaimed. "Miss Walton—"

"Octavia," she insisted.

"—*Octavia*," the congressman continued, "why would a fine young filly like yourself bother with a broken-down old plow horse when there are stallions about?"

Houston harrumphed. "Don't you have a mare back home?"

Crockett smirked and pointed across the table. "I meant these young bucks here."

"I am happily married to my own Elizabeth, Mister Crockett, as you are to yours," said the man named Kennedy, prompting everyone to snicker at the congressman's expense.

Well, not *quite* everyone. For the first time, Goran noticed the other stranger was turned sideways and twisting his hands in his lap. Beads of perspiration formed on the man's high forehead as he alternated between staring down at his hands and casting furtive glances at Octavia Walton.

"Oh, now, I meant no offense, Mister Kennedy," said Crockett with a placating gesture.

"Call me John," said the other just as good-naturedly.

"*John*, then. How's that book of yours comin' along? The one about the Revolution and Kings Mountain and such?"

Goran and Har exchanged startled glances.

"Made real progress," John Kennedy replied after sipping his drink. "The stories you passed along proved most helpful."

"The ones about my pa, you mean? Is good ole John Crockett in your book?"

Kennedy dropped his eyes. "Well, not as such. My main character is a Virginian named Sergeant Galbraith Robinson. His nickname titles the book: *Horse-Shoe Robinson*."

"He is the life and soul of the drama," muttered the nervous man, once more stealing a look at Octavia Walton. "The bone and sinew of the book. Its very breath."

Kennedy patted his friend's shoulder. "That is high praise coming from you."

Crockett looked dubious. "Never heard of this Horse-Shoe feller. What about the leaders at Kings Mountain, like Isaac Shelby and John Sevier?"

"Each gets his due," Kennedy assured him. "I've tried to preserve historical accuracy."

"Oh?" Octavia arched an eyebrow. "I trust you haven't drained your book of color, John. I thought you wrote for the general reader, not some clerk in the War Department."

Many snickered at that, including the author, but not his nervous friend. "Not at all," said Kennedy. "There are many romantic and picturesque features."

"So you seek to entertain, not teach."

"I seek to amuse all lovers of adventure," Kennedy replied. "As an example, I relate—"

"Nothin' wrong with teachin' folks about real heroes," Crockett broke in, "especially those from Tennessee. Men like Sam here, and the great John Sevier."

When Houston offered no immediate response to the compliment, Goran glanced over at the former governor and instantly figured out why—Har had finally gotten Houston's attention. The two were carrying on a silent conversation of winks and nods.

It was John Kennedy who took the bait. "Wasn't Sevier the governor of Tennessee at one point, too?"

"Our very first governor, and one of our best," Crockett agreed. "If only our once happy nation had such leaders today."

Har tugged Goran's sleeve. "Sam wants us to go back outside. He will join us as soon as he can get away."

The Sylph kept his eyes on the humans. "In a moment. I want to hear more."

Kennedy seemed to share that desire. "I seem to recall Governor Sevier and President Jackson were once political rivals."

"Enemies, more like," Crockett said. "Came within a beaver's whisker of a shoot-out."

Octavia's eyes went wide. "Were you a political ally of Sevier?"

Crockett shook his head. "He died before I won my first election.

Would've been honored by the acquaintance."

"You didn't used to feel that way, David," said Houston. "You were a Jackson man through and through."

"I am no man's man," Crockett insisted. "I bark at no man's bid! I will never come and go and fetch and carry at the whistle of some man in the White House, no matter who he is."

Then the congressman turned his face to the ceiling and howled in passable imitation of a wolf. Houston gave an exasperated sigh as Octavia Walton and John Kennedy chuckled. Kennedy's nervous friend seemed to give Crockett his full attention for the first time. The remaining patrons in the dining room shot the party a mixture of curious stares and censorious scowls.

Houston cleared his throat impatiently and rose from his seat. "Just idle talk at the end of a tiring day, my dear Miss Walton. David and I best be—"

"Congressman, if I may," Kennedy insisted. "You've been outspoken in your disapproval of President Jackson's policies on Indians and other matters. I understand Henry Clay and Daniel Webster are organizing a faction to oppose Vice President Van Buren should he seek the presidency in 1836. Have they enlisted you in their cause?"

Instead of answering, Crockett lifted his glass and gulped. His companions watched expectantly—even Houston, who'd sat back down so hard, his chair groaned in protest.

Relishing the attention, Crockett gave Kennedy a long, searching look, then shot a sideways glance at Houston. "Little Van fancies himself a sly fox," he began, "though I'm no stranger to the woods myself."

"But if the vice president should gain the nomination for—"

"I have almost given up the ship of state as lost," Crockett continued. "If the folks back home don't reelect me to Congress next year, or if the folks of America elect Van Buren the year after, I'll leave the United States. Before I submit to his government, I'll go to the wilds of Texas!"

~ ~ ~

Sometime later, when the two Tennesseans at last left the Indian Queen, Goran was surprised to see them engaged in a spirited argument, with

Crockett's arms flailing and Houston punching the air with his fist. As Har edged out of the bushes to signal their location, Goran recalled Houston really was "a Jackson man through and through," as he'd put it.

So politics explains their quarrel, Goran surmised.

He was mistaken.

"How was I to know?" Houston demanded as the humans came within earshot.

"Might've asked," Crockett said. "Or did ya figure a feller like me for a fool?"

Houston snorted. "You know I don't."

"See here," Har broke in with mock seriousness. "Is bickering any way to greet an old friend?"

"Well, now, that's the trouble," said Crockett, the corners of his mouth twitching in barely disguised glee. "Sam and me, we only just figured out we had you in common."

In an instant, Goran understood. Neither Houston nor Crockett had previously known the other possessed the Sight! That's why neither had acknowledged Har when entering the hotel—they were keeping the same secret, from each other. Only when Houston and Crockett made their excuses at the same time and tried to exit in the same direction had the two figured it out.

It took the fairies far more than an instant to narrate the events that had led them to Washington: the assault on the Elf stronghold of Spirit Forest by the alliance of Dwarfs, Goblins, Nunnehi, and Yunwi Amayine Hi, followed by Prince Veelund's flight with Dela as his hostage, to points unknown.

"Well, you say the villain and his entourage headed northwest from the chimney rock," Houston mused. "That's something to go on, at least."

Goran grimaced. "Not really. Once the Elves got out of sight, they could have turned in any direction—perhaps even doubling back toward Cherokee or Creek country."

Crockett pursed his lips and whistled. "Hate to say it, friends, but findin' their hidin' place now would be like findin' a peacock in a pine forest—or an honest man in Washington."

"Present company excluded, I gather," muttered Houston, glaring disdainfully at the congressman. Then he turned to Goran. "Such a bleak prospect is no laughing matter. You have our deepest sympathies."

The Sylph sighed. "It does not appear so bleak to me, sir. As one of your human poets once wrote, 'Hope springs eternal in the human breast.' Hope is no less a constant companion for us Folk. It once guided Dela and me hundreds of miles to rescue Har from captivity in Spirit Forest. Now, it accompanies us on our search for Dela."

The Dwarf again placed a comforting hand on Goran's shoulder. *Thank you, my friend.*

"And we do, at least, have *something* to go on," he continued aloud. "Winged Folk remain a rarity in America. Any sightings of flyers, by either Folk or human, could well signal the presence of Elf rangers employing Veelund's artificial wings—and perhaps Elf settlements nearby."

"Well, that *is* something." Sam Houston's voice, usually deep, rose in pitch. "I've seen wings in the sky more than once, in circumstances I can only describe as extraordinary."

Goran exchanged quizzical looks with Har.

"You'll recall the first occasion, David," said Houston. "Back in April of 1829, the day I resigned the governorship and resolved to share the exile of my Cherokee friends in the west."

"The business with Eliza, you mean?"

Houston nodded. "I left Nashville and booked passage on a riverboat bound for Cairo, Illinois. Eliza's brothers rode overland to Clarksville and overtook the boat. They came aboard and tried to get me to go back and exonerate Eliza of wrongdoing. I declined, though I defended her character to all in earshot."

Crockett guffawed. "The way I heard it, you said somethin' like, 'If any wretch utters a word against the purity of Mrs. Houston,' you'd come back and 'write the libel in his heart's blood.'"

"Sounds about right." A rueful grin creased Houston's face. "Despite my blustery words, I felt pretty low that night. Went to the upper deck and considered throwing myself into the river. Then I heard a strange sound overhead. Something swooped at me and let out a strange cry. I ducked, then searched the sky, but its form was already lost in the rays of the setting sun. An eagle? Or something more unnatural? I wasn't sure, but I took it as an omen that some great duty awaited me in the west."

Goran studied the big man now staring into space, eyes wide as if he were still trying to catch a glimpse of what had rescued him from despair five years earlier. *Is this Sam Houston simply a pompous dreamer with a flair for the dramatic? Or there is something more substantial to the man?*

"I saw mysterious wings on the horizon a second time when we reached Cairo," Houston continued. "Months later, I saw flying forms again in the Indian Territory, and on the first occasion I visited Texas. Always figured it was just my feathered messenger drawing me further westward to a glorious destiny. Now that I think about it, though, what I saw didn't much resemble a bird. It was large and oddly misshapen."

Crockett snorted. Har looked equally skeptical. Goran felt compelled to grasp the proffered straw, however, no matter how slender.

"They *could* have been Elf rangers following you," he said. "Perhaps they knew you were Sighted and wanted to discover your ties to the Nunnehi or other Folk."

"Sounds like a big leap to me," said the Dwarf. "There are many other—"

"Or perhaps, recognizing your political stature and ties to the president, they hoped to learn more about the Jackson administration's policy on Indian relations and westward expansion," Goran cut in, feeling his pulse quicken. "Prince Veelund likes to manipulate human affairs to his own ends."

Houston's eyes flitted to Crockett's for a second. "Yours may be a wild conjecture, Goran Lonefeather, but wildness and I are old friends."

I must explore every possibility, the Sylph told himself. *I must find her.*

Har's next words sounded as though he'd heard Goran's unspoken words. "Although I have my doubts, I will follow any trail that may lead to Dela's rescue. I know she would do the same for me. She already has."

Goran nodded appreciatively, his mind racing. "We already know the Elves have likely resettled abandoned Folk villages along the great rivers and lakes of the northwest frontier. We must return to the Gwragedd Annwn with this new information. Searching such places should be a congenial prospect to Water Folk, at least."

"No, *you* should return to Long Island-on-the-Holston while I investigate Sam's other sightings." Har removed his hand from Goran's shoulder and pointed it at Houston. "Am I right in guessing that you are soon returning to the west?"

"To the Indian Territory, yes, and then back to Texas," the human replied. "You are welcome to come along, but I can't promise it will bring you any closer to finding your friend."

Har inclined his head. "I ask only one favor: Can the first leg of our journey take us through the Shenandoah Valley of Virginia? I would first confer with my fellow rangers at Grünerberg."

"Suits me just fine," Houston agreed. "My relations in Rockbridge County are long overdue for a visit."

Congressman Crockett chuckled. "Wish I could join y'all, but the duties of office keep me here, tied and stuffed like some turkey bound for a Sunday table."

Houston shrugged. "And who placed you on that table but yourself? I once held high office, then chose to walk a different path."

"I will, too, if need be," Crockett assured him. "That vow I just made in front of Miss Walton and her friends? I meant it. If the people of Tennessee choose dishonor, they may all go to Hell, and I will go to Texas!"

Now it was Houston's turn to chuckle. "You'd be most welcome there. But remember what that young friend of Octavia's said? 'To vilify a great man is the readiest way in which a little man can himself attain greatness.'"

Crockett waved a dismissive hand. "That nervous little chipmunk? Wasn't much interested in what he had to say."

"Oh?" Houston seemed surprised. "I found the fellow rather poetic, in a dark and brooding sort of way."

Goran, who'd started mapping out a search plan in his mind, hadn't been closely following the humans' conversation. For some reason, however, Houston's description grabbed his attention. "Do you refer to the writer, Mister Kennedy?"

"No, the other writer," Houston clarified. "Kennedy's friend. Said his name was Edgar Allen Poe."

Chapter 3 – The Mask

MAKER OF ALL THINGS, *I know you are here with me. I pray for the strength to endure whatever may come.*

Dela opened her eyes and stared at the ceiling. Its surface was curved and pierced by two shafts, one allowing light to enter and the other for smoke to leave.

Maker, I know you are also with the ones I love. I pray they are safe and well.

Turning on her feather pallet, the Water Maiden pulled the woolen blanket up over her dark-blue gown and pale-blue shoulders. She looked across her dimly lit chamber to the far wall, shrouded in shadow. Both the planking of the floor and the door beyond had been recently constructed. They still smelled of freshly cut pine, of wide-open spaces, of freedom.

For a cell, it was far from uncomfortable. Expecting harshness after her capture during the Battle of Spirit Forest, she'd been surprised at her generous treatment when they arrived at the new Elf colony, located deep within an ancient Indian mound. Perhaps Prince Veelund hoped to gain something from her—information, entertainment, or even sympathy.

His scheme will fail. A cell is still a cell. A prisoner is still a prisoner. I lie buried, far from home. Far from him. *I must escape.*

Dela closed her eyes. Now, the cell was no longer dimly lit—it was ablaze in torchlight. She saw herself thrusting the prongs of her trident into one of the smoke shafts, twisting and digging until the small aperture became a large hole. She saw herself performing a great leap, her slender fingers grasping the edges, strong arms lifting her lithe body through the hole. She saw herself vanquishing an entire company of Elves and passing through the mound's earthen and Shimmer walls to see the open sky.

It was a glorious, hopeless dream. Dela had no trident, nor any other means of digging or lifting herself out. All she had at her disposal was her pallet, her blanket, and her resolve.

Great Maker, I must escape!

~ ~ ~

It was during her next audience with Veelund that a more sensible plan presented itself.

Two Elf warriors led her to the prince's chambers. Their journey was long and, she assumed, purposefully confusing, passing through narrow twisting tunnels as well as several massive caverns within which the Elves had erected market squares, guildhalls, and other public buildings. The Water Maiden was, however, far from confused by their circuitous route. She'd visited many Folk villages on missions for the Gwragedd Annwn or their allies. To her experienced eyes, the long trek to Veelund's chambers served only to help her form a mental map of the Elves' new stronghold—just as her daytime arrival on the back of a flying horse many days earlier had given Dela a valuable view of the complex of terraced grass-covered mounds the Elves had chosen for their new colony, as well as the human city located a few miles to the west on the bank of a mighty river.

"Did you enjoy the baked sturgeon yesterday?"

The Prince of Elves lounged sideways in his oversized chair, one amber-stockinged leg dangling over an armrest, as he nibbled on blackberries. He wore his usual long robe of forest green and yellow-green surcoat bearing the sigil of the Craftsmen Guild in silver thread.

In reply, she allowed herself a faint smirk. "There is no profit in starving one's hostages."

Veelund held up his hands in protest. "Hostage? Why, you are a *guest* here—though not of your own choosing, I admit. Can you honestly say you have been mistreated?"

"Not as yet." Dela met his mocking gaze. "Still, I am not the first 'guest' you have locked away in a cell. If Goran and I had not rescued Har from Spirit Forest, he would have died."

"The Dwarf killed one of my guards, and almost killed me. His rough…

handling by my warriors was not by my command, though surely you would admit it was understandable."

Dela would admit no such thing but saw no point in debating the matter. "What is the ransom for my return?"

"As I said, you are a guest here. I had originally thought to hold you hostage, yes, but I have since thought better of the idea. We will ask no ransom."

"Then why am I still alive?"

Veelund bolted up straight in his chair. "A provocative question! Can you reason your way to the answer? I hear you are a talented ranger. Among my Folk, rangers are diplomats. They are schooled in the art of negotiation. Do the rangers of the Gwragedd Annwn receive different training?"

The Water Maiden blinked in surprise. "No, we do not. But if ransom is not your aim, what would be the goal of—"

"Peace."

It seemed to Dela as if the word slithered from his mouth, then resolved into a hiss. She felt more like crushing it under her heel than answering it.

"Peace is what I seek," Veelund repeated, rising to his feet. "I can see you do not believe me. You let your passions enslave your intellect. It is a common failing, especially among the young. Still, after all that has been accomplished, why should peace not follow?"

"All that has been...*accomplished*?" Dela clenched her hands as if grasping a weapon—or perhaps the Elf's throat. "Your schemes produce nothing but suffering for your victims and dishonor for your Folk."

Veelund smiled. "You remain submerged in sentiment, Water Maiden. What is straight, you see as bent. What is sharp, you see as blurry. It is all illusion. Come up for air. Break the surface. See things as they really are."

"Your words are poison," she spat.

"An interesting analogy," the Elf allowed. "Poison has too few defenders, I think. If there is killing to be done, it is a great improvement over brute force. It strikes only its target and no other. It spares bystanders and those who merely follow orders. In my experience, only blood-mad warriors and glory-mad princes prefer war to subtler tools."

Dela's horrified expression prompted Veelund to chuckle.

"Nevertheless, I reject your analogy," he continued. "I speak not poison, but truth. Yes, we Elves fashioned the Gifts of Power and gave them to Indian nations. With spellsong, we bade them attack the United States, knowing the

Americans would ultimately prevail. Thus, we secured a great and necessary migration to the west. In the Blur, forests and fields once occupied by small bands of Indians will become the farms and towns of American multitudes. And in places congenial to *our* kind, where monster game abounds and Shimmer walls stand strong, surging throngs of Elfkind will thrive where other Folk managed only a doomed and miserable existence. Best of all, we did it with craft and guile, without the ravages of all-out war."

"More poisoned words," the Water Maiden accused. "Without war? You admit you *fomented* war among the humans. And what about all the Folk, both yours and ours, who died at Spirit Forest?"

"They owe their deaths not to me, but to the mad Dwarf king and other Folk who joined him in his madness." Veelund sank back into his chair. "Alberich attacked a colony we were abandoning. His bloody assault accomplished nothing. My bloodless plan accomplished a great deal."

He sounds like he truly believes his own lies. "And the humans?"

"The fate of Tecumseh and the others who died was regrettable, but necessary—and their wars were relatively small in scale. The North American war begun in 1812 was little more than a collection of skirmishes when compared to the titanic struggle engulfing Europe at the same time. And yet, this little conflict of ours has secured the future of a great nation and all our human herds who dwell within it, while thinning those herds by only a few thousand."

"So, you think historians will judge you a righteous leader, not a villain?"

Veelund shrugged. "I have made all the calculations. Fate will do the rest."

Lives are more than just numbers on a page! Dela wanted to shout, but she stifled the urge. *If he thinks it possible to convert me from enemy to emissary, that serves my purpose.*

"This peace of yours—on what terms would it be established?" she asked. "Must Elf lords rule every Folk nation?"

He rolled his eyes. "You still do not believe me. Otherwise, you would not suggest such absurdities. Lasting peace is founded on true interests, not capitulation. Now that Elfkind has what we need—homes for our teeming masses—it is time all the Folk of America recognize our common interests and unite against our common foes."

"Against Dwarfkind, I presume? This Eternal Conflict you wage is of no concern to—"

"Silence!" Veelund was on his feet again, now looking over her shoulder to the closed door. "My time is too valuable to waste on a fool."

I have "overplayed my hand," as Ichabod Crane would put it. "Please excuse the outburst, Prince Veelund," said the Water Maiden, trying to sound conciliatory. "Sometimes I do lack patience, as you say."

The Elf regarded her coldly for a moment. "Impatience *is* a great obstacle to success. You are poorly served by your impatience, and that of your leaders. Most Folk are as poorly led as the humans we herd. And the real truths of history are hard to discover."

"Then help me see them," Dela urged.

"King Alberich and the squabbling Dwarf lords of Germany are *not* the foes I mean. The common enemies of all Folk are ignorance, indolence, and the poverty they produce. Faced with the waning potency of spellsong and the declining stock of monsters to fuel our magecraft, far too many Folk resort to raiding each other's meager stores or retreating into the wild to perish in solitude. It is wiser to look forward, not backward. To craft new tools, not just wear out old ones. To embrace new ideas—even those borrowed from the humans."

"Like your idea to breed monsters."

Veelund nodded. "And many more. Now, perhaps, you begin to grasp my purpose. We must make common cause, unite behind enlightened leadership, and dispel certain…misunderstandings."

I grasp more than you know. I feel the hard fist beneath the velvet glove, though it suits my *purpose to pretend otherwise.*

"If others feel as you do, there may yet be a role for diplomacy in resolving our differences," she said. "If I may be allowed to meet with other Elf leaders, to learn more of their aspirations for—"

"If you may be allowed to wander the colony freely, you mean." Veelund chuckled. "I suspect you merely feign interest in my proposal, not admire it. But I shall allow you more latitude, though you will always be accompanied by one of my guards."

Dela inclined her head to show her gratitude—which was, in this case, sincere. *One Elf will be easier to defeat than two.*

~ ~ ~

The next day, she met the Elf in question.

Standing in the doorway of her cell was a grim-faced woman clad in dark green from her trousers to her tunic and cloak. A long knife was thrust through her belt, and a stout bow of yew was strapped across her back. "I am Thekla," said the Elf. "Here to escort you to the Greenweavers Guild."

That first meeting, with the grandmaster, proved of little interest. So did a second meeting later in the day with the grandmaster of the Hunters Guild. Neither Elf was particularly talkative, and neither volunteered anything of consequence. *No wonder Veelund was so quick to approve my request,* Dela mused. *I will glean no useful information from his minions.*

Nevertheless, every time she was escorted through the colony, her mental picture of its layout sharpened. Her cell lay near its central complex, which housed an assortment of living quarters and public buildings. The Greenweavers' guildhall was within the complex as well, but the Hunters' was at the end of a long tunnel lit by torches.

Nearly all of the complex predated the Elves' arrival. She assumed its builders had relocated westward as a consequence of Veelund's conspiracy. More puzzling was the fact that so many of the tunnels leading into the colony began at the top of the mound rather than its base. Had the indigenous Folk who once lived here induced the local Indians to carry humanwares up the mound as ceremonial offerings? She'd read about such practices for harvesting humanwares by the Folk of ancient Egypt and Mesopotamia.

It was only during the journey to the Hunters Guild that a better explanation for the upward-sloping tunnels suggested itself. As Dela and Thekla approached the guildhall, they'd been bowled aside by three Elf rangers hurrying down the tunnel. All wore sets of Veelund's artificial wings.

This village once housed a flying Folk, Dela had realized. *A Folk like the Sylphs.* The thought made her wince.

The next time Thekla appeared at her door, the Water Maiden greeted her with a playful grin. "Will I meet another of your silver-tongued lords today?"

Thekla's eyes narrowed. "Today I bring you to my own guildhall to meet the greatest ranger in history."

"*You* are a ranger?" Dela was taken aback. "I thought I had a warrior as an escort."

"Among lesser Folk, war may be the exclusive domain of warriors,"

Thekla sneered, "but among Elfkind, a mastery of the art of combat is universal. You may test mine anytime you like."

Not yet. "Oh, I am sure you are most capable. I was just surprised."

Dela followed the ranger along a narrow tunnel that led to a chamber where Elves sorted baskets of grain, vegetables, cloth, and other goods into wooden bins. "Newly arrived humanwares?"

Thekla gave a brief nod. "From St. Louis."

As Dela followed her into another tunnel, broader and inclined upward, she thought about a map she'd once seen of the land purchased from the French emperor Napoleon by her friend Thomas Jefferson. The southernmost part, a boot-shaped area encompassing the Mississippi River Delta, had become the state of Louisiana. Immediately north of it was the Arkansas Territory, to which Cherokees, Creeks, and other Indians had relocated from their original homes in the Carolinas, Tennessee, Georgia, and Alabama. Further upriver was the new state of Missouri, admitted to the Union in 1821. Dela's friend Daniel Boone had spent the final years of his life there. Its largest settlement, founded at the confluence of the Illinois, Missouri, and Mississippi Rivers, was St. Louis.

A plan began to form in her mind. Once she reached the Blur, her safest course wouldn't be the predictable direction—swimming the mighty Mississippi directly south to Tennessee—but rather to head west into St. Louis, where she might hide from Elf fliers. Later, she'd swim northward, up the Illinois River, then follow a more roundabout way home through Indiana and Kentucky.

First dive, then swim, the Water Maiden reminded herself. *I must find a way out of here.*

The hall of the Rangers Guild was a modest structure placed so far up the tunnel that Dela guessed it must be close to one of the exits at the top of the mound. Lounging at the entrance were a dozen Elf rangers, some armed with bows like Thekla's and others with knives and shortswords.

"I bring the prisoner to see Runa." Thekla sounded even less enthused about it than Dela felt.

The Elves ushered her past a small anteroom and library into the great room. The grandmaster waiting there was Dela's second surprise of the day. When Thekla had described her as "the greatest ranger in history," Dela envisioned some grizzled veteran of a hundred campaigns in the Blur. The woman sitting behind the high cluttered desk, though, was young and bony, her hair short and mousy, her sharp nose buried in the pages of a crudely bound book. When Thekla and Dela reached the table, Grandmaster Runa glanced up briefly, held up a rail-thin finger, then looked back down.

Thekla cleared her throat nervously. "I have…I have brought the—"

"Just a moment." Runa's watery eyes remained fixed on the text.

Dela took the opportunity to scan the hall. It was spare and utilitarian, with few of the celebratory artworks and decorative flourishes of other guildhalls. In addition to shelves crammed full of books and scrolls, there were rows of jars, flasks, bowls, and baskets, most filled with liquids, leaves, or powders. Several strange objects of wood, bone, and metal stood on small tables or shelves of their own. The place looked much like Har's description of Veelund's chambers back at Spirit Forest—only Runa was a ranger, not a craftsman.

Presently, the grandmaster seemed to reach a stopping place and closed her book. "You may go," she told Thekla, who quickly complied. "Dela of the Gwragedd Annwn. Take a seat."

As she did so, Dela flicked her eyes to the book. Its title, *Songs of Two Rivers*, was inscribed into the leather cover in ornate script. "Is that a collection of old spellsongs? I have never seen its like."

Runa ran her finger along the outer edges of the pages. "A curious tome brought to America by a ranger of the Samodiva. It has only recently been added to our collection here at Cahokia."

This was the first time anyone had mentioned the name of the new Elf colony to Dela. "Cahokia. Was that some Elf village back in Europe?"

"It is a local word—the name of humans who once lived nearby, as I understand it. Now they live in the west."

"As do the Folk who once watched over them from this mound, I suppose, because of your Elfish plot."

Runa shook her head. "Your supposition is uninformed. The mound complex was abandoned by its inhabitants long ago—long before your Folk or mine ever set foot on this continent. We have only begun to explore its extent. Only yesterday, we discovered the entrance to another previously unknown tunnel."

"So, this new colony of yours was *not* the result of Veelund's scheme with the Gifts of Power." Dela arched an eyebrow. "He led me to believe otherwise."

"Veelund is clever, but hardly all-knowing," Runa said, rolling her eyes. "We in the Rangers Guild possess knowledge of Cahokia he does not."

A crack in the door! Can it be widened? "It is not your duty to share such knowledge with him?"

"Do not presume to lecture me on duty," the grandmaster said in precisely measured words, failing to disguise her annoyance. "I commanded my rangers to carry out Veelund's 'schemes,' as you called them, though I disagree with his methods."

Dela sensed an opportunity. "As do many other Folk. To manipulate the humans into war for the sake of—"

She stopped when Runa raised a bony finger to her puckered lips. "Silence. Your ignorance is disappointing and your motives transparent."

My attack was premature. Time to parry. "I do not understand, Grandmaster. My motive is simply to learn more about Elfkind."

Runa returned her hand to the old tome. "Your kind wallows in sentiment. On this point, Veelund is quite correct. You lesser Folk neither recognize the true threat nor possess the strength and determination to counter it. So, it falls to us to lead."

Dela thought it best to hold her tongue.

"My disagreement with Veelund lies elsewhere—as he well knows," Runa continued. "Faced with the twin scourges of waning magecraft and weakening spellsong, he places his trust in the future, in modern arts borrowed from humankind and adapted for our use. I prefer to place my trust in the past, in ancient arts we Folk once possessed but have long forgotten."

The Water Maiden's eyes flicked again to the book.

Runa noticed. "Yes, arts preserved by past generations in works like this. The book is itself a copy of a far older text, inscribed on clay tablets by rangers scarcely a generation removed from the Arrival to Earth. I had hoped to discuss its secrets with you, to see if the Gwragedd Annwn had also managed to preserve any critical knowledge from that heroic age when Folk mages could expend great quantities of elemental magic without regretting its depletion, and when a single Folk ranger might bind thousands of humans to her will. But if your people waste their time in pointless moral preening about the fate of humanity, I doubt there is anything useful to be learned from you."

"I am a field ranger, not a scholar," Dela said. "If I may be permitted to send a message to my guild, however, we might determine whether—"

The grandmaster's chuckle was dry and raspy, although the cause must have been something other than age, for the brown-haired woman was Dela's age, if not younger. "You will have to do better than that. Our audience is ended. Perhaps I will send for you again when your dreams of escape have faded enough to make conversation productive. Assuming, of course, Veelund permits you to live that long."

~ ~ ~

Could that meeting have gone any worse?

After Dela emerged from the guildhall, Thekla's fingers clinched her arm. "Back to the cell you go," said the Elf with a renewed enthusiasm.

As they started down the tunnel, it occurred to the Water Maiden that the squad of Elves who'd been loitering by the guildhall were no longer there. Other than herself and Thekla, no one was in sight. And because the guildhall was located so far up the mound, the tunnel's opening to the Blur was surely nearby.

Dela considered her options. *None of my attempts to gain intelligence or stoke dissension has borne any fruit, or is likely to. Will I ever get a better chance?*

She decided the answer was no. Making herself stumble suddenly on the rough floor of the tunnel, the Water Maiden careened into the Elf ranger, knocking her off-balance and simultaneously grabbing at the hilt of the woman's hunting knife.

Thekla huffed. "You cannot—"

Her shriek was interrupted by the punch Dela delivered to her jaw. Relief washed over the Water Maiden when she realized that not only had her punch knocked the other senseless against the wall, but she was also now holding Thekla's knife.

What next? She considered the prostrate form of the Elf and the naked blade in her hand. Silencing the ranger forever might give her the head start she needed, but Dela recoiled from the idea of attacking a defenseless foe.

The decision was made for her when she heard two mingled sounds. One was of feet shuffling. The other was a voice. It was humming. *An entry song! Rangers returning through the Shimmer!*

Dela cursed her bad luck. Her exit now blocked, she turned and raced down the tunnel, hoping to find a place to hide or from which she might launch an ambush if the odds weren't too strongly against her. After a few dozen steps, she saw a bulge in the tunnel she hadn't noticed on the way up. Between mounds of earth and stone was a narrow crevice. Hurriedly, Dela turned sideways and slipped her left leg into the fissure. She could launch no ambush from its tight confines, to be sure, but there might be enough space on the other side to shield her from the passing rangers.

With difficulty, Dela managed to squeeze through the crevice and crawl inside. She kept expecting to run out of room but encountered only empty space before her. It soon became clear that the crevice opened not into a small cave but into another tunnel—perhaps the very one Runa had spoken of discovering the day before.

If so, I have chosen a hiding place known to the grandmaster, though they may not have explored it yet. Hope and despair warred in Dela's mind as she scrambled further and further from the crevice, its faint illumination soon giving way to pitch blackness.

How far she traveled along the tunnel, Dela couldn't tell. First crawling along blindly, then walking when she discovered its ceiling extended above her head, she resolved to put as much distance as possible between herself and any pursuers. With every step, she hoped to find a junction, a crevice, some indication that escape from the Cahokia mound, or at least this tunnel, remained a possibility. With every step, however, all she found was more dark, empty space. With every step, hope dimmed.

Then came a flicker of light. Dela saw it first reflected on the surface of a shallow pool of mud on the tunnel floor. She froze in place, tightening her grip on the stolen knife and straining her eyes to study the splash of light that broke up the darkness ahead. Hearing no sound, she proceeded cautiously. The bright blotch soon sharpened into the oval shape of a passage. Whether it opened into another tunnel, a cavern, or the open air of Missouri was impossible to guess at such a distance.

Nor, in the end, did it matter. The light flickered, then disappeared and reappeared several more times. Dela heard voices and the muffled thump of turnshoes on the tunnel floor. Elf rangers were approaching. When she halted in midstride to ponder her options, she heard similar sounds in the direction from which she'd come.

"We know you are here," said a voice Dela immediately recognized as that of Grandmaster Runa. "Escape is impossible. Your flight has come to its inevitable end."

Runa was behind her. Dela's mind raced. *If I surrender now, will Veelund ever let me out of my cell again?* She counted two sets of footsteps approaching from the front. Rushing them, in an attempt to reach the lighted area beyond, would be a desperate gamble.

Great Maker, help me!

Dela sprinted forward, her feet splashing through mud puddles and slapping the stony surface of the tunnel floor. Her two targets broke into a run as well, one carrying a torch and shortsword while the other held the fletched nock of an arrow to his whiskered chin.

As soon as the light of the bouncing torch revealed the danger, Dela ducked into a somersault, hearing the loosed arrow whistle through the space her head had occupied an instant earlier. Then the Water Maiden sprang, her left hand grabbing the wrist of the swordsman while her right hand drove Thekla's knife into his chest.

The man grunted and dropped to the floor, wrenching the knife firmly stuck in his chest from Dela's grasp. Undaunted, she spun to face the archer now fitting another arrow to his bow.

"Finish her!" Runa's voice echoed down the tunnel, along with the sounds of running feet and exclamations of dismay and anger.

The archer wasn't quick enough. Dela brushed aside his drawn weapon and kicked him in the stomach, leaving him doubled over and gasping. The torch of her first victim had fallen against the tunnel wall and remained lit, painting the scene in streaks of orange and shadow. Dela picked up the dropped bow and looked frantically for the dropped arrow.

A sharp point took her in the shoulder, its sting making Dela cry out. It was the point of a different arrow, of course, as was the second point that erupted from her breast in a spray of blood.

"No," she murmured, falling to her knees.

"No," she repeated in a whisper, turning awkwardly to face her killer.

But the triumphant face of Thekla, standing next to Runa and three other Elves, was not the last sight Dela beheld.

The second to last thing she saw was the opposite wall of the passageway, brightly illuminated by the flickering torch of the now dead swordsman as well as the torches held by other rangers. Filling the wall from floor to ceiling was an enormous painting rendered in lines of black, white, red, and green. The human it depicted wore a loincloth and cloak, an elaborate headdress, and an oddly shaped mask with a long, upturned nose painted in a brilliant red-orange.

Her strength ebbing fast, Dela found she lacked the energy, and perhaps the will, to turn her face away from the masked image on the wall. Then Runa entered her field of vision. The grandmaster studied the painting with great intensity herself, running her wiry fingers along its surface and chattering excitedly.

"Precisely what I hoped to find," she told the other rangers. "Its preservation is remarkable." Then she looked down at Dela. "In your foolish bid for freedom, you have done us a great service. Let that be a comfort as you take your last breath."

Runa, the Elves, the tunnel, and the painting all faded from Dela's view. The next thing she saw, the final thing, was the wondrous face of Goran, *her* Goran, smiling as he bent down to press his lips against hers, much as he had that glorious day on Iris Isle when their two broken souls were forged into one.

Though Dela's now lifeless eyes had not truly beheld this last lovely sight, that did not make it any less real.

Chapter 4 – The Prize

October 1834

"AS YOUR PEOPLE MIGHT SAY, we took the Bull by the Horn!"

Exasperated, the ship's captain rolled his great sepia eyes and ground his great white teeth from side to side, causing the great black whiskers protruding from his cheeks and chin to bristle and ripple.

The sight made the ship's boy laugh so hard, he nearly fell from his perch on the mizzenmast. "It is too easy," he teased. "By now you should know to let my jests bounce off your thick hide."

By now you should know when not to hurl them, Bull thought as he seized the ship's wheel with two huge hands and spun it clockwise. The *Courser* lurched to port, its three masts of square-rigged sails propelling the prow of the ship—and the great carved figurehead of a horse jutting from it—away from the rocks the captain had spotted through the salty spray.

"Not yet cleared the Cape!" Bull bellowed. "Eyes ahead."

Still chuckling, the boy climbed to the yard of the topsail and took several steps along the spar, looking in all directions. "The worst of the squall is far astern, as well you know. What remains is a mere trifle to an experienced seaman."

Being careful is how you get to be *an experienced seaman*, Bull wanted to snap back. He didn't bother, however. His companion already knew that, having spent even more years on the high seas than his captain. And so the man who called himself Bull—and whose crew called him Alfred Bulltop Stormalong—chose, characteristically, to remain silent.

Eyes twinkling, mouth curving into a triumphant grin, the boy sat back down and stroked his long gray beard.

~ ~ ~

To the three dozen other crewmen of the *Courser*, Gez *did* look like a boy. When they saw him hauling food to the deck, scrambling up the rigging, or peering from the crow's nest, they saw a slender, redheaded youth standing just under five feet in height and dressed much like they were, in loose-fitting trousers and a ragged work shirt.

To Bull, however, Gez looked quite different: less than three feet tall, chubby, nearly hairless—except for a bushy beard—and wearing a belted tunic of light-gray wool, a short blue cape, queer wooden shoes, and a stocking cap of blue and gray.

It was the latter, his Kabouter form, that was his true form—or so Gez had insisted when the little man first revealed himself to Bull. It was seven years ago in the North Atlantic, during the first whaling voyage of the *Courser* with Bull as captain, when they'd happened upon Gez and three Dutch sailors adrift in an oarless whaleboat. Close to death from hunger and thirst, the three other survivors regaled Bull's crew with wild tales of a doomed encounter with a monster of the sea. Only to Bull had the calm demeanor of the fourth Dutchman, the cabin boy, been of greater interest than the delirious ravings of the others.

Inviting the boy to his cabin, Bull had hoped to satisfy his curiosity about the ill-fated Dutch ship and the giant whale that must have caused its destruction. Yet the ensuing conversation went in a different direction, with Gez asking increasingly personal questions of *him*—questions Bull found increasingly difficult to answer.

On some subjects, Bull had an excellent memory. He knew every rope, knot, and trick of navigation. He knew every square inch of every boat, barge, or ship he'd ever served on. Every contour of reef or shoreline, every depth of bay or inlet, every current of sea or stream—if Bull had rowed, poled, or sailed it, he recalled it. And the names, backgrounds, and abilities of everyone he'd ever rowed, poled, or sailed with were carved into his mind like scrimshaw on whalebone.

About his own background, however, Bull knew almost nothing. His first memory was of washing up on Cape Cod and being discovered by a retired sea captain and his wife. They'd taken him home to their little cottage in Provincetown and named him Alfred, after a beloved uncle lost at sea. Judging him five or six years old, his adoptive parents had been shocked to discover the boy couldn't talk and concluded he must be mentally defective, yet they soon came to love him as fiercely as if he were their own child. His mother gave him the nickname Bull, no doubt because of his huge size, and Bull's father resolved to teach him the trade he knew best: sailing.

The youth took to it like a duck to water. Although Bull struggled to remember many details of his life in Provincetown, he *did* recall hours spent working the docks, sailing the bay, and strolling the seashore while daydreaming about the seas he hoped to conquer and the faraway lands he hoped to visit.

By the time he was nine, Bull could no longer resist their allure. Already larger than most teenagers of Provincetown, he left for Boston. Again judged far older than he was, the tight-lipped boy quickly found work. He crewed fishing boats, poled barges, and sailed schooners, first in New England, then beyond. A few years later, he joined the first of many whaling voyages on the high seas. As Bull was as stingy with prize money as he was with words, he eventually saved enough to buy the *Courser* from its former captain.

That first day they met, Gez had continued to pester him for details about his background. Pacing the floor of the cabin, Bull insisted over and over he couldn't recall. Annoyance turned to exasperation, then to anger. "Don't know!" Bull finally roared, the long blue tail of his coat forming a horizontal line as he spun and glowered down at the little Dutch boy. "Don't care!"

In response, the boy shrank—not cringing in fear, but actually diminishing in height. His youthful face melted into an older face, bearded and wrinkled, his mouth forming a self-satisfied smile.

That was how Captain Alfred Bulltop Stormalong learned the Wee Folk of legend were no mere inventions of scolding mothers, village hucksters, or lonely sailors. That they were truly present in the world. And in the ensuing years, Bull learned the value of having one as a friend.

~ ~ ~

"Still don't get how you tell the difference."

Once they passed Cape Horn, Bull had relinquished the *Courser*'s wheel to the helmsman and returned to his cabin for a meal of turtle stew. As usual, Gez had accompanied him.

"It is more a feeling than a telling," said the Kabouter, flicking an apple into the air and catching it on the back of his hand. "How many times must you ask the same question?"

"You're one to talk." Bull wiped his mouth with his sleeve.

Gez took a bite of apple and swished it around his mouth. It was the last of the fruit they'd bought in Buenos Aires. "You *know* why I ask about your childhood. If I keep jabbing at that big, blubbery mind of yours, memories may tumble out."

Bull swept the bottom of the bowl with his spoon. "What good'll that do?"

"What good is knowledge?" The Kabouter's eyes widened. "Why, knowledge is a *tool*, my friend. No less a tool than the sextant you use to navigate, or the harpoons in your whaleboats."

"Can't hunt with memory," the captain grunted.

"I would not be so sure about that." Gez bit the apple again, then turned his head to stare at the oaken wall of the cabin.

He's lost in a memory. Bull felt a twinge of envy. Gez often reminisced about his many exciting adventures. He'd been part of a Kabouter hunting party magically concealed within the hold of the doomed Dutch ship. According to Gez, such parties consisted of a mage, a ranger, and several hunters. They stowed away on ships for the purpose of capturing aquatic monsters and bringing them back to Kabouter villages hidden along the shores and rivers of the Netherlands.

It was the job of rangers to mingle among the humans, magically disguised, and look out for monsters, including those that didn't *look* like monsters at first. To handle smaller prey such as Kelpies, Selkies, Hippocamps, and Capricorns, the Kabouter hunters themselves—shielded from the dangers of the Blur by the mage and from human eyes by the ranger—were more than capable. When faced with larger prey such as Hydras or Sea Serpents, however, it would fall to the ranger to enlist the aid of the ship's human crew with spellsong and to the mage to use elemental magic to shrink the captured monsters for storage in the hold.

Or so Gez had explained—Bull struggled to understand. Even when he recognized words such as "Selkie" or "Hippocamp," he knew them only from silly stories about shape-changing seals and horses with the tails of fish. As for terms like "elemental magic" and "the Blur," he simply had no frame of reference for the Kabouter's explanations.

Bull decided to press the issue. "You say you feel when a monster's hidin' its true form. Ever been fooled?"

The Kabouter's head snapped around. He eyed Bull with an odd expression. "Not yet, though I suppose there is a first time for everything."

Having lifted the bowl to slurp the last bit of stew, the captain was about to reply when a fist pounded the door.

"What is it?" Bull demanded.

"Sightin', cap'n!" cried the man outside, whom Bull recognized as the Welshman Morgan, his second mate. "Black whale!"

~ ~ ~

By the time Bull, Gez, and Morgan reached the deck, it was swarming with seamen. The first mate, Gunnar the Norwegian, was already climbing into the larboard boat and directing the harpooneer and four crewmen to their places at the oars. The other three boats were being craned down to the choppy waters off the Chilean coast.

Bellowing orders to the shipkeepers who'd stay behind with the *Courser*, Bull shoved his short-brimmed black hat down tighter on his massive head and stomped to his own whaleboat, its distinctive red prow still visible just above the waterline. As usual, Gez was close on the captain's heels. Morgan and the third mate, Orcus the Haitian, would command the other boats.

The lookout had spotted the spout some three miles northeast of the *Courser*. Once fully crewed, the four boats knifed through the water in that direction. Clutching the steering oar of his own craft, Bull strained his eyes to catch a glimpse of their quarry.

"Der she blows!" called Gunnar from the lead boat, pointing straight ahead.

Bull felt his pulse quicken. "'Nother!'" he snorted, having seen a second burst of mist and foam to port. It was a V-shaped blow, the telltale sign of a black whale exhaling through its two blowholes.

"Cow and calf?" Gez speculated.

Bull nodded. *Two prizes in a day. A hard fight, but my men are up for it.*

On previous ships, Bull hadn't always felt so confident about his fellow crewmen. Some had been physically unfit. Others had been unreliable for other reasons, mainly drunkenness. Even capable ones like Mike Fink, with whom he'd served briefly during the War of 1812, were too interested in glory or booty to do their jobs well.

The men of the *Courser* were a different breed. Bull had recruited them himself, drawing from a lifetime of connections and experience. Their endurance, prowess, and courage were unmatched—as was their devotion to their captain, Alfred Bulltop Stormalong, whose legend they'd concocted by telling fanciful tales and singing colorful chanties.

Bull watched with pride as his men raised sail and readied weapons. The harpooneer would draw first blood, trying to sink his barbed blade deep into the back of his prey. Later, once the whale was exhausted, a longer-bladed lance would finish the job.

As the whaleboats neared the location of the blows, their crews stopped rowing, relying on sails to close silently with their targets. Presently, two sets of dark fins came into view, separated by a sizable stretch of water. The four boats divided into two squadrons, their commanders hoping to harpoon both whales at the same time to maintain the element of surprise.

"There she blow!" yelled Bull's harpooneer, a fierce Filipino named Bayani.

The V-shaped blow told Bull he was almost in range—and its size told him he was chasing the larger whale, the cow. Bull glanced to starboard and saw the dorsal fin of the calf. It was only a few dozen feet from the prow of Gunnar's boat. Nodding to Gez to steer, Bull strode forward, propelling his massive bulk as quickly as he could across the length of the whaleboat. Bayani looked disappointed but not surprised. Without a word, he handed the weapon to Bull.

Today, first blood would belong to Captain Stormalong.

Bull ran his hand along the oaken pole of the harpoon, still covered in bark, and checked the knot securing the tow line to the barbed iron shaft in the pole's socket. He glanced back at Gunnar's craft. Its harpooneer was ready, too. Bull raised his weapon to get the Norwegian's attention.

"Give it to 'em!" he yelled.

Then, with a force no other whaler could hope to match, Bull thrust his own harpoon at a spot just below the whale's dorsal fin. The point sank deep. The heavy pole fell away, bending the iron as it dropped into the water.

The cow bolted. "Stern all!" the captain shouted, though his oarsmen had already begun backing the boat away as fast as they could, trying to avoid being struck by the bucking body of the gallied whale or the flukes of its flailing tail.

The boat pitched. Steadying himself against the thigh board, Bull closed his eyes and reveled in the sounds of the fray. The splash of displaced water falling back to the surface. The crash of waves. The shouts of excited men. The whine of rope against the loggerhead and the smell of the smoke it produced as the wounded whale swam away, rapidly uncoiling the tow line.

Bull's eyes sprang open when the boat lurched. The now taut rope yanked the vessel halfway out of the water, then dragged it over the choppy waves as the tethered whale continued a desperate bid for freedom. Bull tried to spot the other whaleboats. Had Gunnar's man fastened the calf, too? Harvesting two at once would be an enormous enterprise, exhausting the crew as they raced to finish the job before the floating carcasses attracted too many sharks.

That his men would ultimately succeed, Bull had no doubt. He smiled and glanced back at Gez, who'd surrendered the steering oar to Bayani. The Kabouter didn't return his smile, however. The mouth of the normally jovial little man was twisted into a perfect circle, as if from astonishment.

The Kabouter's expression startled and excited the captain, but it didn't alarm him. As best he could recall, Bull had never felt fear. What made his heart race and muscles flex was the prospect of action, not danger.

"What d'you see?" he demanded.

"Not certain!" Gez yelled back. "It is a feeling I have not—"

The stern of the whaleboat pitched suddenly upward, tossing Gez, Bayani, and two oarsmen into the air. Then the vessel lurched forward again, but not because the hooked whale accelerated. It was as if some enormous hand had shoved the whaleboat from behind. When the oarsmen landed, they struck the steering oar, smashing it. Gez and Bayani struck the water behind the boat.

No longer concerned about the fate of the whale, Bull whipped out his rigging knife, intent on cutting the tow line. That proved unnecessary—he saw neither the rope nor their prey. The tow line was already severed.

"Cast a line!" he ordered, also unnecessarily. A crewman had grabbed a harpoon tethered to the spare tow line and tossed it. Soon Gez and Bayani were back on the boat, wet but unharmed.

"Hit a reef, cap'n?" Bayani asked.

Gez caught Bull's eye and shook his head.

"Not sure," said the captain. Then he noticed the splintered remains of the oar. "Raise sail. We steer by tiller. Must find the others, and the *Courser*."

The crew sprang into action. Bull put his knife away and turned to Gez.

The little man's eyes were round as buttons. "Best keep your blade out. We will need every weapon we have to survive this."

Bull was about to ask why when he heard the eruption.

Seven years earlier, during the same voyage when he'd met Gez, Bull had anchored off the coast of Iceland to take on supplies. While ashore, he visited what the locals called the Great Gusher. The geyser's periodic eruptions, launching water hundreds of feet into the air, produced a deafening roar.

The comparable roar behind him was no erupting geyser, Bull knew. When he spun around, what he saw left him gaping. The beast was gargantuan, extending perhaps eighty feet from teeth to tail—by far the biggest whale he'd ever seen. Its enormous head was covered in glistening barnacles, signifying extreme old age. Its body, ventral grooves, fins, and flukes bristled with iron spikes, signifying countless battles with harpooneers—battles won by the whale, not the whalers. Its row of cone-shaped teeth, from which dangled their severed tow rope, and its single blowhole, from which a geyser still roared, signified its identity as a sperm whale.

Most startling of all, its skin wasn't gray or black. It was white as wool.

"The great pale devil!" breathed Bayani.

"Mocha Dick!" Gez agreed.

Mocha Dick! So named for nearby Mocha Island, this old bull was the stuff of legend. Nearly a hundred whaling ships had battled it, and most returned to port with nothing but wild stories. The remaining two dozen hadn't returned at all.

"Hard to port!" Bull yelled to Bayani.

"The wind is strong," said Gez, pointing to their full sail, "but can we truly outrun it?"

Bull spoke no answer. Instead, he picked up the blade of the harpoon they'd used to cast the lifeline to Gez and Bayani. In the other hand was a wooden pole. He jammed the iron into the socket.

The Kabouter lowered his head. "We cannot defeat it alone."

"Won't have to." Bull pointed to the raging sea behind Mocha Dick, where three more sails were visible in the distance. "Got it surrounded. Four boats of *Courser* men can take any whale!"

Bayani and the others cheered at that.

Gez only shook his head. "It is no whale."

It took a moment for his meaning to sink in. Bull stared at the Kabouter. "You sure it's a—"

"Monster?" Gez gave a mirthless chuckle. "I told you. I can *feel* it."

~ ~ ~

How long the four whaleboats kept the beast at a respectful distance, Bull couldn't say. As his irritation grew, his sense of time dwindled. Had it been a minute? An hour? A day? He no longer knew. He only knew Mocha Dick must be destroyed.

From somewhere in the back of his mind, a voice whispered caution. If the creature was indeed a monster, Bull couldn't be sure of its capabilities. His instinct was to have three of the boats approach Mocha Dick from the front, shouting and beating their weapons to draw its attention, while the fourth boat slipped up quietly from behind to harpoon the whale in the back.

Follow your instinct, the whispering voice urged. It was answered by another inner voice, however—a louder, angrier one. This voice insisted Bull's instinct, honed from years of hunting whales, couldn't be trusted in a battle with an unearthly monster.

You hate it! the second voice screamed in his head. *Kill it now!*

The beast turned its body parallel to Bull's whaleboat and fixed its stare on the captain. Bull felt as though its gigantic blood-red eye was searing him with flame. His own fury felt like a cauldron of scalding water about to burst.

"Attack!" he heard himself bellowing. "Kill it now!"

"Fiend of the deep!" yelled another man.

"Send it back to hell!" screamed a third.

"Fight it!" The lined, bearded face of Gez appeared in Bull's field of vision.

"Yes, fight it!" Bull agreed.

"No—fight your *fury*!" the Kabouter insisted. "It radiates from the monster. Do not let the magic control you!"

Bull was in no mood for the little man's word games. "Attack!" he repeated.

The men of the *Courser* complied eagerly, shouting curses as they rowed their boats toward the barnacle-covered object of their hate. Bull, maintaining his position as harpooneer, fantasized about heaving the weapon right at the demonic right eye of the white monster. He imagined it passing entirely through the monster's brain. He saw then himself holding not his short rigging knife, but one of the long, thin, razor-sharp boarding knives his crew used to harvest blubber. He saw himself carve gristly trophies from the flesh of his prize. And in his head, he heard sailors singing a new chanty about Captain Stormalong:

With righteous fury faced the foe,
To my way hay, storm along, John!
And slayed the devil with one blow,
To my aye, aye, aye, Mister Stormalong!

It would be a glorious new verse to his epic—a legendary adversary worthy of a legendary captain and his legendary crew.

But it was not to be.

When the converging boats came within fifty feet of their prey, Mocha Dick disappeared from sight, sinking as if suddenly transformed into solid stone. When seawater rushed to fill the void, the resulting suction pulled hard on the whaleboats, accelerating their already rapid speed.

"Avast! Avast!"

Bull heard someone cry out, a voice other than the ones still arguing in his head. It was issuing commands—no, he realized, the new voice was *singing* commands. Bull could hear the words and melody. He felt himself drawn to them. Yet still, in his mind's eye, all he could see was the white-skinned fiend he hated.

Only when Bull found himself sinking into the ocean as well did he awaken from his fury dream. All around him were tools, planks, and pieces of whaleboat. He saw thrashing bodies and dangling feet above him.

I must see to my men. Bull clawed desperately with his hands and kicked with his feet.

And continued to sink.

For all his great strength and prodigious skill, Bull felt like a helpless child. Was he still trapped in the suction effect of the monster's dive? That was his first guess. Then Bull felt the viselike grip on his left ankle. He glanced down. It wasn't an irresistible current of water drawing him into the heart of the sea—it was the clenched teeth of Mocha Dick.

On they sped through the water, the formidable giant of a man and the eighty-foot monstrosity with complete dominion over him. Their course switched from vertical to horizontal, then to vertical again. It gradually dawned on Bull, his attention mainly focused on his bursting lungs, that the beast was dragging him up rather than down.

What sort of death does it plan for me? What cruel tortures?

Even then, at the end, Bull felt no terror. Only regret for his errors and the loss of his friends, plus no small slice of morbid curiosity.

Then confining water became unconfined space. His arms and legs, no longer pinned to his sides, flailed wildly. He had time to take in only a single greedy gulp of air before his body struck the water. It skipped twice more along the surface and then came to rest against a solid wall of wood.

Bull looked up to see the horse-shaped figurehead of the *Courser* bobbing above him.

~ ~ ~

The collision of the whaleboats had, miraculously, produced little more than mild injuries and a couple of wrecked but reparable vessels. Of course, by the time the men were all reassembled on the deck of the ship, Mocha Dick and the two rescued whales were gone.

"Not over," Bull insisted as Gez bandaged his ankle wound. "I'll find the beast again. I'll chase it round the Horn and round the—"

"No, you will chase him no more."

The captain growled and glared at the little old man who was his ship's boy. "*Courser*'s mine, not yours."

"Yes, but it will not chase Mocha Dick, not so long as it flies your true colors."

Again he speaks this nonsense about my true colors! What does he mean?! "Figure you can—"

"He saved your life, Bull, when he could easily have taken it," said the Kabouter as he tied off the bandage. "He ignored the rest of us, when he could have smashed the remaining boats to bits and drawn us all to a watery death."

The captain ground his teeth, making his stiff whiskers roll and ripple. "Smart, they may be, but whales ain't people. Don't do good deeds."

"Mocha Dick is no whale," Gez reminded him. "That blind rage you and your fellow humans felt? That was his magic clouding your minds. It works much like my spellsong."

"Act of a villain. Shows monsters need huntin' even more than whales."

"*Was* he the villain, though? By tricking us into disaster, he saved not only whale lives but human lives. A battle of his brawn against our iron would surely have produced casualties."

It was only then Bull noticed the Kabouter's choice of words. "Callin' the beast 'he' rather than 'it' now?"

"In light of his actions today, it seems more fitting."

Bull pounded a meaty fist into the palm of the other. "Didn't you see all the spikes in its hide? Haven't you heard the tales? Many a good whaler's died fightin' Mocha Dick."

Gez, looking pensive, did not reply.

"Spent your life huntin' monsters, aye?" Bull pressed. "Why not this one?"

"Because over that lifetime I have learned a great deal, or so I like to think," the Kabouter said. "Because the creatures I was taught to see as mindless brutes sometimes act in ways that puzzle and trouble me."

Then Gez paused, looking intensely into the eyes of his captain.

"Because I have come to believe that not all monsters deserve captivity or death."

Chapter 5 – The Weaving

THE PASSAGEWAY TO THE COUNCIL chamber was cold, damp, and dimly lit. As Goran waited outside, he found it hard to concentrate. His mind wandered from cherished memories to idle speculations and back again. It wandered because of how long he'd been waiting. It wandered because the task he was waiting to perform was so hard. His mind wandered because it kept finding pain and fleeing it.

As his eyes meandered, they lingered on a rectangular picture hanging from a wooden peg. The artwork was woven, not drawn or painted, and made entirely of stems, leaves, and flowers. Goran spotted daffodils and bladderworts. His late mother, Wenna, a greenweaver, would have scolded him for failing to recognize the rest.

Studying the layered textures and subtle shades, Goran found himself thinking of afternoons spent on the Holston. Of river grasses swaying and beckoning in the breeze, of leaves sewn beautifully into the seams of a short blue gown and thrust jauntily into long blue hair.

He found Dela in the picture. He found pain.

So, Goran changed the mental subject. He thought about the many Folk villages he'd visited and their differing decorations. The walls of Grünerberg bore paintings of battles won and the mounted skulls of monsters hunted. In the guildhalls and royal chambers of Spirit Forest, visitors were more likely to see artistic depictions of natural landscapes, the night sky, and elaborate mechanical devices. Tana's Folk, the Nunnehi, displayed richly contoured pottery and finely crafted jewelry and beadwork. The Ceasg, a Merfolk who lived in North Carolina's Cape Fear River, preferred sculpted swirls of coral, stone, and bone. Goran's own Folk, the Sylphs, filled their new village in Iris Isle with depictions of the hills and mountains they'd once called home:

the Knob, Pennsylvania's Haycock Mountain, Cornwall's Brown Willy.

Sylphs. Home. As Goran stared at the woven artwork, he found within its twisted stems and leafy whorls the faces of his sister, Ailee, his father, Brae, and his brother, Kaden—all lost to him, perhaps forever. Again, he found pain.

Once more he redirected his mind, but where it might have wandered next, he would never know. Goran heard feet splashing along the puddled floor of the grotto before a pale-blue face appeared at the entrance. It was long and thin, with a high forehead and sharply pointed chin. The man's dark-blue hair was cut short and swept to one side, though a couple of unruly locks jutted down over an arched eyebrow.

"You may enter," said the man, a ranger named Dyl. "The elders will see you one final time."

One final time.

After returning to Long Island-on-the-Holston, Goran had tried repeatedly to convince the Gwragedd Annwn of the significance of what Sam Houston had told him. The human had seen flying Folk—almost certainly Elf rangers with artificial wings—on the Cumberland River and later at the confluence of the Ohio and the Mississippi. The sightings suggested the possibility of Elf settlements nearby. In one of them, Goran insisted, they might find Dela.

His requests for rangers to help investigate the sightings were repeatedly rebuffed. Goran knew he couldn't really blame them. Viewed dispassionately, his information wasn't much to go on. Although they cared about Dela's fate, the Gwragedd Annwn faced more pressing problems—the same ones other Folk faced. They needed food, humanwares, and magic-bearing monsters to provision their colony. Their comparatively few rangers needed to spend their time searching for resources, not for a single captive.

In desperation, Goran had even turned to Dela's mother, Tesni. Though she despised him, the Sylph hoped she might grab at the chance he offered and take his side. His hopes had been dashed when Tesni refused to listen and demanded he leave.

And so Goran tried one last gambit: He'd planted himself outside the council chamber and refused to budge until the elders granted another audience. The Gwragedd Annwn were a distracted and divided Folk, yes, but hardly an unfeeling one. Demonstrating his devotion to Dela might gain him sympathy, he reasoned—or at least motivate the elders to rid themselves of an annoying interloper by granting his request.

His gambit had worked, it seemed. *Now I need to make it matter*.

He was surprised to find more than just a small number of councilmembers conferring around their driftwood table. Half a dozen other Gwragedd Annwn were engaged in conversation in the corner, some standing in the shallow stream that trickled through the grotto and others standing on its bank. Other than Dyl, who'd hurried over to join their discussion, the others were strangers to Goran. Tesni was present as well, standing against the opposite wall and glaring at him. Like the unfamiliar rangers, she must have entered the grotto from the rear, no doubt so she wouldn't have to encounter him.

"Our visitor has come," announced Gwyla, grandmaster of the Greenweavers Guild and leader of the council. "Let us conclude our discussion of Diri's proposal."

I thought you brought me here to discuss my *proposal. Who is this Diri?*

Goran's unspoken question got an immediate answer. "It is not my proposal, Gwyla, nor just that of the Folk of River Conwy." One of the strangers, a stoutly built ranger with widely spaced eyes and elaborately braided hair, walked briskly from the stream. The others followed. "All the Gwragedd Annwn of Cymru speak with one voice on this matter."

"You cannot speak wisdom with just one voice," Gwyla replied tartly. "Do you think we have forgotten what made us cross the great ocean in the first place? Or the harsh words left in our wake?"

Diri shook her head, rattling the shiny shells bound into her braided blue hair. "Nothing is forgotten, Gwyla, though circumstances require us to forget old quarrels. The future of our Folk is as stake."

"You come late to a conclusion we drew *years* ago," said Gwyla, who was taller and thinner but otherwise resembled Diri in her facial features and thickly braided hair. "With great effort and tragic losses, we built a new home in America. Now you ask us to put it at risk."

"If I may, Grandmasters?" The youthful voice of Dyl might have been expected to waver in the presence of so many elders, but Goran heard only reproach in it. "You requested the Sylph be present, yet he cannot be expected to know why, or to understand your words."

At first, both Gwyla and Diri looked affronted. Then the latter inclined her head. "Well said, ranger of River Holston. We have journeyed long through the Blur, over sea and land, and are the worse for wear from it. You there, the one called Goran Lonefeather—I apologize for poor manners. I am Diri, grandmaster of the rangers of Conwy and emissary of the Great Council of the Gwragedd Annwn."

"The Great Council?" Goran was unfamiliar with the term.

"It represents a new path for us, one we swim with unfamiliar strokes. Yet swim it, we must."

Gwyla rolled her eyes. "Our visitor needs explanations, not metaphors."

"They are one and the same—or so we were both taught in our youth, you and I, by the same teacher." Diri's serious expression softened into a wry smile. "Goran, we have always been an independent, insular Folk. Rarely did we venture from the wilds of Cymru, the land the English-speakers call Wales, to engage the world beyond our deep lakes and flowing streams. We formed no sprawling confederations like those of Elfkind. We sought no common cause with our cousins, the Nixies of the Northlands and the Naiads of the Mediterranean. We held no grand assemblies to settle differences peaceably, as do the lords of Germany in their Dwarfmoots."

Having heard much about Dwarfmoots from Har, Goran knew the grandmaster described them too charitably.

"Our communities remained separate and inwardly focused," Diri continued. "The Folk of the River Conwy stayed apart from those of Tyno Helig, Llyn Cau, or the Pistyll Rhaeadr. When, on occasion, our villages clashed over game or humanwares or some matter of honor, we warred. One village would defeat the other, the victor claiming the spoils and the vanquished relocating to some more remote location. Or both would lose so many lives that the origin of the conflict became moot or forgotten. It was a disastrous waste of—"

"It was better than the alternative!" Gwyla interjected. "Better than subjecting ourselves to tyranny!"

"The creation of the Great Council was no tyranny," Diri said. "You vastly overstate your point. Each village sent representatives, and no action could be taken without at least three-fifths of—"

"I was there," Gwyla broke in again. "I know the words written in the charter. I also know the words written not in the charter, but in the hearts of those few who aspire to rule the rest."

Diri rested her hands on her hips. "You, of all people, should know that combining even opposite elements can produce something stronger and more durable. What else is the Shimmer but a mix of earth, air, fire, and water? Does your guild not weave together opposing forces—heat and cold, cultivator and inhibitor, the living and the dead—to serve your Folk?"

"Do not lecture me on greenweaving," Gwyla snapped. "Our arts are subtler than those of craftsman or mage. They require precise knowledge. From our studies, we know not all combinations are possible. Some are too dangerous even to attempt."

This time it was Goran who spoke, not Dyl interceding on his behalf. "With respect, I fail to see what the political arrangements of the Gwragedd Annwn have to do with finding Dela."

Gwyla snorted. "Those political arrangements have failed, just as we dissenters predicted before we departed for America. Its failure brought Diri here. It is what breathes new life into your frail hopes."

"The Great Council did *not* fail." Diri turned to Goran. "It brought unity to a Folk facing common threats. A dramatic and inexplicable decline in game. Encroachments from other Folk of the British Isles, themselves increasingly organized into larger, more dangerous federations. Alas, these threats proved beyond our collective power to overcome."

"And so you propose to bring all your problems, and your accursed Great Council, to the land we chose for *our* new home."

"We do not propose to settle in your territory, Gwyla—as you know," Diri said. "That is why, ranger of the Sylph, we requested your presence at this final meeting before we take our leave."

Surprised and puzzled, Goran stayed silent.

"We were prepared to banish you from our village," Gwyla said. She glanced at Tesni, still standing against the far wall. "When Diri learned of your reports of flying Folk on the western rivers, however, she made a request that served our own interests."

"More Gwragedd Annwn wish to leave the Old World and settle in the New," Diri explained. "It was our intention to find suitable locations for villages along the western rivers—the Cumberland, the Tennessee, the Ohio, perhaps even the great Mississippi. Such settlements would be close enough to maintain cordial relations with Long Island-on-the-Holston while not encroaching on its territory."

Gwyla blew out an exasperated breath. "So you *say*."

"So we *mean*," Diri insisted. "We ask you, Goran Lonefeather, to assist us. Show our rangers the places where your human saw the flyers. Warn us away from places where Elves or other hostile Folk may already reside. We have neither the strength nor the stomach for more war. We seek only the opportunity to create a new home."

Goran finally understood why he was there. His words hadn't been persuasive. His stubborn refusal to leave the passageway had neither inspired nor shamed the elders to give him another chance.

What had truly changed the situation was Diri's arrival, supplying the necessary thread for Gwyla to weave a brilliant plan. If he said yes to Diri's proposal, Goran would depart Long Island immediately in the company of her rangers, presumably never to return. If he subsequently found suitable sites for new Gwragedd Annwn colonies in the west, that would ensure they settled far enough away from Long Island to allay Gwyla's concerns. And if his information *did* lead to the discovery of Elf colonies, he and the other rangers discovering them might well be killed—or, however improbable it may seem, they might find and rescue Dela without risking any of Long Island's own rangers.

From the look of triumph on Tesni's face, Goran concluded that either outcome—his death or Dela's rescue—would bring her great joy.

Chapter 6 – The Refugees

June 1835

MANUEL ANTONIO CHAVES LOWERED THE brim of his hat to shield his eyes from the morning sun. The upper ridge of the mountain, mostly green but dusted with lingering snow, loomed hundreds of feet above him. He hadn't decided yet whether to push on to the summit. Climbing the extinct volcano—named *Tsoodził,* "Turquoise Mountain," by the Navajo—was no great feat. He'd done it many times. What Manuel hadn't yet done was find and slay the great lion of the mountains—and do so alone.

Well, not entirely. Manuel glanced at the pack mule grazing on a patch of grass. She'd dutifully carried his weapons and supplies up the trail, and she'd carry his trophy back down to Cebolleta if the hunt proved successful.

Then he touched the handle of the navaja knife thrust into his belt. Lionclaw was always with him, too—as were the spirits that he believed were forever bound to its shining blade. The spirits of two lost companions, his brother José and the Navajo boy Pahe.

Manuel smiled grimly. *I hear what is silent. I see what is invisible. And I am never truly alone.*

Then the long-dead volcano of Turquoise Mountain rumbled to life.

~ ~ ~

In the months since his late brother's ill-fated expedition into Navajo country, Manuel had thrown himself into hard work. He helped his stepfather and pregnant mother with the farm. He herded sheep and broke horses. He worked the forge and anvil of the blacksmith shop. After the birth of his half-brother, Román Baca, Manuel shouldered more duties around the house. When not at work, he spent his time hunting in the arid plains and hills surrounding Cebolleta, seeking to perfect his skills at stalking, shooting, and knife-throwing.

In his labors, he toiled alongside many other Chaves relatives—with one notable exception. His married brother, Pedro, constant companion of his childhood, seemed always to leave a room, stable, or corral as soon as Manuel entered. Pedro would claim to have pressing duties at home, but both knew the real reason Pedro avoided him. He resented Manuel's arming of the Navajo lodgers on the night Pedro and the Cebolletans had planned to murder them. Pedro clearly considered it a personal betrayal. To Manuel, it was Pedro who'd attempted to betray his mother's hospitality and his family's honor.

Lately, the brothers' relationship had become even more strained. Since Mexico secured its independence from Spain in 1821, the central government had largely left New Mexico alone and allowed prominent local citizens to lead the remote northern territory. Its first governor, Francisco Xavier Chaves, was the brother of Manuel's grandfather. More recently, Manuel's uncle Mariano served as acting governor. Then Colonel Pérez arrived in the territorial capital of Santa Fe, carrying a proclamation from President Antonio López de Santa Anna. It named Pérez, a stranger to New Mexico, as its new governor. That had irritated the local population, and once Pérez revealed himself to be a boorish bully, their irritation turned to anger. Still, the new governor had managed to attract a few sycophantic supporters. One was Pedro, much to the disgust of the Chaves family.

Manuel's newfound frustration with the Mexican government was another reason to spend all his time either working or hunting. He'd let childhood frustration with his father and eldest brother turn to resentment and anger. Neither served him well. They had made him blind and deaf to the truth. He resolved never to let that happen again.

~ ~ ~

That morning on Turquoise Mountain, however, Manuel's finely honed senses proved superfluous. Even Román, his infant half-brother, would have heard the series of booms from the dormant volcano. And the easily distracted Román would have also noticed the ground rippling and bucking violently.

The baby couldn't yet stand. The quake made Manuel feel just as weak. Twice, he staggered to his knees. He'd have fallen over entirely if not for the butt of his musket that he used to steady himself. His snorting mule proved more sure-footed as it took off down the hill.

There was, however, no scent of ash or sulfur in the air. Manuel looked up. No smoke billowed from the mountaintop. He'd never witnessed an eruption, though he'd read about them. What was happening bore little resemblance to the active volcanoes described in books.

Then came the laugh. Manuel didn't so much hear it as *feel* it. There was no merriment in the laugh, no playfulness, no joy. It dripped with contempt. Indeed, Manuel felt its contempt drip onto his skin, burn him, flow over him, smother him—much as he imagined lava from an erupting volcano might. For a moment, Manuel *became* a little child. He felt tiny, puny, an insignificant speck on the side of the tallest mountain on earth.

Then the man of Cebolleta shut his eyes and stood up straight, willing his arms and legs to stop shaking. *When the Navajos shot me full of arrows, I was not afraid. This is only a sound. I must show no fear.*

Manuel opened his eyes. What was framed against the blue sky would have caused even the bravest heart to skip a beat.

Well above the ridge line was a strange object shaped like a gourd, though of huge proportions. Its texture looked rough and its coloring mottled, mostly grays and browns with several black streaks running from rounded bottom to tapered top. Imbedded in the middle of the object was a smaller multicolored disc glistening in the morning sun. With its brown outer band, broad middle ring of light yellow, and center circle of deepest black, the disc resembled a giant eye. The image reminded Manuel of the bedtime stories his mother used to tell of a cunning Greek hero and a giant one-eyed monster.

Only the enormous gourd looming over the ridge wasn't the head of a Cyclops, and the ringed disc at its center was no eye. Manuel realized that when two slits below the disc opened and blinked.

That was what he *saw*. What Manuel Chaves *felt* was the earth trembling again, even as the face rose higher, revealing a broad neck and massive shoulders also mottled in grays, browns, and thin black stripes. And what he *heard*—unexpected words from an unexpected source—was a low, raspy voice from behind him. "Run, Manuel!" it growled. "Be brave, but run!"

Manuel spun around. Somehow, the realization that the head peering over the ridge was that of a gargantuan humanoid, and that its ponderous strides were causing the ground to shake, didn't keep him from being shocked by his next discovery: the voice warning him to flee belonged to no man.

The shaggy creature before him was unnaturally large for a bear. Standing on all fours, the span from its oversized claws to its light-brown shoulder hump was at least a dozen feet. And when the beast reared up in alarm, its glowing yellow eyes staring intensely into Manuel's astonished gray ones, its full standing height of twenty-five feet left him speechless.

The Monster Bear wasn't. "Run, Manuel!" it growled again. "I will try to slow the Yeitso!"

When Manuel glanced over his shoulder, he understood why the shaggy beast hadn't promised to do more. While towering mightily over any living creature Manuel had ever seen, the Monster Bear was scarcely a third the height of the colossus now plodding down the mountain. Along the latter's rocky hide were protrusions shaped like knives of flint. Unlike the bear's glowing yellow eyes, the Yeitso's black eyes seemed to crackle and swirl, like storm clouds about to emit bolts of lightning. From its jagged mouth came continuous contemptuous laughter that chilled Manuel to the bone.

None of it made any sense. Lightning-eyed giants with the power to make the earth tremble? Monstrous bears with the power of speech? Witnessing such preposterous things would have made any ordinary man question his sanity. That it had no such effect on Manuel Antonio Chaves proved, not least to his own satisfaction, that he was far from ordinary.

"I will not run." Smirking at the notion of conversing with an animal, Manuel cocked the hammer of his musket. "I came to the mountain to hunt."

"Your firestick will only enrage it," the bear warned. "Flee to the lake and hide!"

Manuel's only response was to lift the gun to his shoulder and aim at the approaching giant. The spot between its crackling eyes seemed as good a target as any. He squeezed the trigger.

Nothing happened. If the bullet struck the Yeitso at all, it didn't so much as slow the giant's advance.

"Run!" the bear roared one last time. Then it sprang, its claws extending into sharp knives of its own.

Now doubting his gun's utility against the rock-skinned giant, Manuel knew he should take his newfound protector's advice—yet he found it impossible to tear his eyes away. Snarling, the bear swiped at the Yeitso's left leg. To Manuel's surprise, its claws didn't bounce off the craggy armor. They sank into the Yeitso's flesh just below the knee, showering the ground with golden sparks.

One instant, the giant was howling in rage and pain. The next, it was the bear howling in rage as it soared through the air, then howling in pain as it struck the thick bole of a pine tree. *If a single kick of its leg could do that to the bear,* Manuel wondered, *what would it do to me?*

At last, he fled.

~ ~ ~

For much of the way down the mountain, Manuel heard the fight no less clearly than if he'd stayed to watch it. Tough claws battered and scraped against rocky hide. Massive stone fists and feet smashed against furry hide. The bear grunted, growled, and roared. The Yeitso grunted, growled, and laughed.

When the trail crossed a small brook, Manuel altered his course to follow it, guessing it might lead to the lake the bear had suggested as refuge. He soon found it, a large body of water contained in a deep natural bowl of rock.

Manuel looked around in confusion. *What sort of hiding place is this?*

Then the ground shook. Again he heard the dreaded cackling of the Yeitso. An intense feeling of vulnerability washed over him, but Manuel balled his fists and willed it away. *Whatever fate has in store, I will face it with courage.*

Not knowing what else to do, Manuel loaded his musket. Then, although the action felt foolish, Manuel heeded the bear's command and waded into the lake until the water nearly reached his waist. As he watched and listened, another feeling washed over him—a feeling that he wasn't alone in the lake. It prompted him to recall the day he and Pahe had stumbled on the oasis in the desert. Suffering from hunger, thirst, and multiple wounds, Manuel had rushed joyfully into the pool while his companion held back, claiming to sense a dangerous creature in the water.

Just as I sense one now.

His eyes darted around. They saw nothing but clear water and rocky lake bed.

He felt ridiculous. After all, what could be more dangerous than the giant clomping toward him?

Manuel looked up to see the face of the Yeitso. The glassy disc on its forehead shone with reflected sunlight. Its dark eyes seethed with energy. Its mouth gaped open, revealing rows of jagged teeth. Another enormous stride brought the rest of the giant's body into view. Manuel was amazed to see its flinty armor was torn away in several places, exposing soft flesh from which dripped a dark liquid.

The bear earned first blood. Did my protector also earn a quick death?

It took only two more steps for the Yeitso to reach the water's edge. Accepting the futility of the gesture, Manuel nevertheless raised his musket to fire. This time he would aim for the shining disc.

Then a wall of water knocked him off his feet—and the gun from his hands. Kicking and splashing, Manuel lost sight of the Yeitso for a moment. Then he heard it bellow with laughter.

Once he regained his footing and recovered his musket, Manuel looked for his foe. It was still there, in all its enormity, but the laughing face wasn't. Only the back of the Yeitso was visible, heading *away* from the lake. Manuel trudged his way through the water, intent on following the giant.

"Let it go, Manuel. Aki will lead it away."

The raspy voice came from his left. Turning his head, Manuel saw the shambling form of the bear, its brown fur dotted with patches of red. It sank to its knees in the shallow water, then keeled over. Once again, it seemed as though Manuel's keenly developed senses were fooling him. The pitiful moans of his protector became progressively less bestial. Its brown fur dissolved into brown flesh. Its enormous bulk shriveled until the body shivering in the shallows was as small as Manuel. And human. And female.

Many questions jockeyed for primacy in Manuel's mind. He finally settled on one. "How do you know my name?"

~ ~ ~

How long he knelt beside the woman, holding his neck rag against her most grievous wound, Manuel couldn't be sure. It *felt* like a short time, a feeling confirmed by the absence of long shadows from the surrounding trees. That suggested it was only midday, but that was hard to reconcile with the rapidly improving condition of his protector. Manuel initially thought her close to death. By the time he heard the patter of rapidly approaching feet, however, the woman had turned, smiled, and raised herself up to a sitting position. With a gentle hand, she removed his from her side.

"Thank you," she said, and for the first time Manuel noticed her Spanish was heavily accented. "I will soon be well enough to travel."

"How could you have healed so—"

His question was interrupted by the sound of rustling leaves. Glancing into the nearby shrubs, he glimpsed a dark shape wriggling behind some branches. Manuel shot to his feet, gun in hand.

"Do not be alarmed," said the woman, smiling broadly. "It is only Aki."

An instant later, a bare-chested man emerged. He was taller and thinner than Manuel, though lithe and sinewy. He wore deerskin leggings and moccasins, and in his hands were several other garments. When their significance dawned on Manuel, he blushed and wheeled around.

After a time, he felt the touch of a hand. He turned to see the woman smiling at him. She was dressed in Navajo fashion, a blanket dress of yellow cloth worn over knee-high leggings and sashed at the waist. "You must have many questions," she began. "I am called Shash. This is Aki, my husband."

Manuel inclined his head. "I would introduce myself, but you already know my name."

"We know much more than that," said Aki, slipping a light-blue shirt over his head. "We know you are brave, Manuel Antonio Chaves. Trustworthy. A man of honor."

Such unearned praise from a mysterious stranger made Manuel feel both mystified and giddy.

"You wonder how we know this," Shash guessed, correctly. "We know because we are witnesses. We were there last summer when you and your Indian friend arrived at Bear Springs. We saw how the boy's death pained you. We followed to ensure you made it home, witnessing your courage, hearing your prayers. Then, some days later, we met Navajo herdsmen on the trail and learned of your role in saving them from ambush by your own people."

Her words made no sense at all. "How could this be? I have never seen you before."

Shash arched an eyebrow. "Is that so? When we first encountered you at the springs, we thought you spotted us. So we hung back and followed you at greater distance, at least until you fainted that second time and Aki helped the shepherd from Cebolleta find you."

Manuel racked his brain. Although he knew he'd become delirious at the end, he didn't remember seeing any Navajos during his trek through the desert. Then it came to him—during his ordeal, he *had* felt he was being followed. Sometimes his pursuer looked massive, like an elephant. *The bear called Shash.* Other times, his pursuer looked low to the ground, like a dog. *Aki.*

"What...what are you?" Manuel asked the man.

"The Navajo call our kind *yee naaldlooshii,*" Aki replied. "It means 'with it he goes on all fours.' In your tongue, the word is skinwalker."

Skinwalker. The last word Pahe spoke before he died.

"No," Manuel clarified, "I mean what...*skin* do you wear?"

Aki and Shash exchanged bemused looks. "That is a harder question than you think," Aki said. "You have seen Shash transform before your eyes, so you wonder by what magic a woman can assume the shape of a bear. You see a man standing before you, so you wonder what sort of monster shape I can assume. Your eyes are sharp, yet they deceive you."

Manuel pursed his lips. *What manner of riddle is this?*

"You mistake the root for the flower, and the flower for the root," Aki continued. "The skins we wear are human."

Shash moved next to Aki and drew him close. "The bear you met on the mountain—*that* was my true form," she said. "As for Aki's true form, the Navajos who have seen it call him *Tieholtsodi*, the 'Water Monster.' And they call me *Sasnalkáhi*, the 'Bear That Chases.'"

Manuel stared. "Then...you are truly—"

"Monsters?" Aki smiled. "It was as 'monsters' that we met and fell in love, Shash and I, at the place the humans call Bear Springs. How long we lived there, safe and content, we do not know. Just as neither of us remembers much about our lives before."

Although he was struggling to understand, Manuel did experience a flash of insight. "Shash must have stayed at Bear Springs long enough, and been seen enough by others, to give the place its name."

"Perhaps," Aki allowed. "We *did* encounter Navajos on occasion, when we went hunting or when they brought herds to drink at the springs. Our memories of those encounters are cloudy. What we do recall clearly is why we were finally forced to abandon the springs, to seek refuge elsewhere."

Manuel glanced at the unmistakable indentation of a giant foot in the nearby ground. Shash noticed and shook her head.

"The Yeitso? No. It is dangerous, but as far as we know it is just a mindless brute, not a reasoning creature. Aki and I learned long ago how to evade it. You see, the Yeitso's eyes are large, but weak. It finds and tracks its prey by magical means. It can sense when another feels vulnerable, scared, and small. With its enchanted laughter, the Yeitso provokes such feelings."

"Except in you, my fearless love," Aki added. "I am, however, no stranger to fear—and I can run much faster. So it falls to me to trick the Yeitso and lead it away, as I did today."

Shash hung her head. "You exaggerate, husband. The Yeitso's magic does not work on me, that is true, but of the others I remain terrified."

"The...*others*?" Manuel's mind reeled. "Are there really monsters more dangerous than the Yeitso?"

"Not monsters, no." Aki turned and stared into the lake. "They came to Bear Springs one summer morning. Shash and I had just bathed and were nibbling on prickly pear when the first arrows flew."

"Two struck my leg," Shash said with a shudder, "while a third sank deep into Aki's back. He managed to crawl into the water and hide in its depths, while I turned and hurled myself at the archers."

Manuel had seen the Monster Bear attack in all her savage fury. She'd given a giant three times her size a serious fight. A few Navajo hunters would have stood no chance against Shash.

Which is why her next words were so puzzling. "They were amazingly fast and nimble, dodging every swipe of my claws, and I felt my strength draining away even before they shot two more arrows into my side. Without help, I was done for."

"While you kept them occupied, help arrived," Aki pointed out. "The two captives they brought with them woke up and attacked the hunters from behind. You also gave me enough time in the water to recover enough strength and enter the battle."

"Which you won," Manuel surmised.

Aki nodded. "We had two strokes of luck that day. One was fending off the hunters. The other was helping free the two captives, who taught us much about the hunters and how best to escape their notice. They taught us how to use powers we did not know we had."

By now, Manuel was used to the imaginative leaps required to follow their story. "The two captives were other monsters. From them, you learned to how to adopt human form—through some obscure sorcery, I suppose."

"How it works remains a mystery to us, too," Aki admitted. "It is an act of will, not at all like the ceremonies and incantations we have seen the medicine men of the Navajo perform. When we first saw you at Bear Springs, we had hoped to learn more about it from you. Only later did we discover our mistake."

Manuel blinked. *Well, I* thought *I was getting better at following their story.*

Shash read his face and laughed. It was no contemptuous laugh meant to demean or belittle. It was playful.

"We saw you with Pahe," she explained. "We witnessed his devotion to you, and you to him. We watched you mourn his death and bury his body. So, naturally, we thought you knew the truth about your friend."

The truth about my friend? The truth is that I was no friend to Pahe, though the boy repeatedly tried to be one to me.

Then Manuel grasped the truth she meant. "Pahe was a monster? A skinwalker?"

"It was Pahe and his mother whom the hunters captured that morning on their way to Bear Springs," Shash said. "He was only a small cub, of course, but she was one of the fiercest fighters I have ever seen. It was largely her doing that the hunters were forced to flee, since their poisoned arrows had left Aki and me so weakened. I am sure she would never have been captured in the first place had she not been hampered by the need to protect her cub."

"Her capture left her deeply ashamed," Aki added. "She blamed herself for leaving the safety of the Navajo village and taking Pahe into the desert. She felt he should spend some time in his true form, so he would never forget his heritage. After the battle at Bear Springs, she resolved never to let him shed his human skin again. Indeed, when the men of Cebolleta raided the Navajos and stole Pahe away, his mother chose not to rescue him. She considered him safer among your kind than among the Navajos."

In that judgment, she was proven wrong. "So you reasoned that Pahe and I were friends, close enough for me to know his secret?"

"Yes," Shash said. "It was why we developed our own bond of affection for you, though only from afar."

Manuel lowered his head, feeling unworthy of such a bond. "You spoke of Pahe as a cub. What sort of monster was he?"

"Feline," Aki explained. "Shaped and colored much like the animal the Navajo call *Náshdóítsoh*, though much larger and fleeter of foot."

Manuel winced. His hand brushed the handle of the knife in his belt. Pahe had named it *Áláshgaan*. Lionclaw. Had the boy known the truth about himself all along? If so, why had he not turned into a monstrous cat and defended himself during the battle with the Navajos, or later during their trek through the desert? Manuel had already witnessed Shash's miraculous power to heal, and Aki had spoken of a healing power he possessed while submerged in water. Such power could have healed Pahe's wounds, surely.

No, Manuel concluded—the boy must have forgotten his real form. Perhaps his years as a slave in Cebolleta had caused him to suppress the memory of his earlier life. *Or perhaps clouded memories are a trait of all enchanted monsters.*

There was still one thing about Shash and Aki's story, though, that Manuel didn't understand. "What manner of Indians attacked you that day at Bear Springs?"

The two monsters in disguise clasped hands. "They are not Indians, Manuel, or even humans," Shash said. "They wield enchanted weapons of wood, bone, and copper. A human tribe of the far north, the Omahas, call them *Gada'zhe*, the 'Wild Ones.' The Shoshones name them *Nimerigar*, the 'People Eaters.' The Osages, the Crows, the Cheyennes, the Comanches—all know and fear these creatures."

"Only the Navajos, Zunis, and other tribes of New Mexico tell no tales of them," Aki said. "That is why we and so many other skinwalkers have taken refuge here. The Nimerigar village must be so distant that they do not raid this far south very often."

Their words both excited and unnerved Manuel. *Today, I have taken my first steps into a larger world I never knew existed. I have truly heard what was silent, seen what was invisible, and found what was hidden. And this is only the beginning.*

"These Nimerigar, these People Eaters—are they also giant in stature?" he asked.

Shash shook her head. "As we said, Manuel, they are not monsters at all. They are far more dangerous creatures, though they stand only a little over two feet in height. And they do not call themselves People Eaters. We are told they use a simpler word. They call each other Folk."

Chapter 7 – The Fort

September 1835

THE REBELLION IS STARTING—AND I'M hundreds of miles away!

Crumpling the letter within a meaty fist, Sam Houston shook it in frustration at the orange orb looming large over Nacogdoches. Manifestly unperturbed at his defiance, the harvest moon continued to bathe the roofs, barns, and streets of the town in restful autumn hues.

Sam was walking home along the tree-lined San Antonio Road that formed one side of the town square. Now, the prospect of spending another night in his rented room left him cold. He leaned on a rail fence and launched a thick wad of spittle at the dusty ground. It struck his boot instead.

That figures.

Over the past three years, Sam had thrown himself wholeheartedly into his Texas enterprise. He'd crisscrossed the territory, which constituted the northern two-thirds of the Mexican state of Coahuila. Sam had settled in the town of Nacogdoches, opened a law practice, and gotten elected a delegate to the Texas Convention. He had met dozens of leaders, from the empresario Stephen Austin and the militia leader William Travis to San Antonio Mayor Juan Seguín and General Perfecto de Cos, the brother-in-law of Mexico's president.

When Sam first arrived in Texas in 1832, his official mission was to write reports to the Jackson administration about the Indian tribes in the borderlands. Unofficially, President Jackson asked him to investigate the possibilities of Texas declaring independence or being purchased from Mexico by United States. Sam bided his time, criticizing the increasingly tyrannical Santa Anna's dissolution of the Mexican Congress while also trying to restrain the hotheads who sought immediate independence. Separate statehood within Mexico was the right answer for now, he'd argued. "Mexico is acting in bad faith, and trifling with the rights of the people," he told fellow Convention delegates. "Plans formed without the assent of Texas are not binding upon Texas." He even devised a plan to resettle hundreds of friendly Cherokees and Creeks from the Indian Territory so they could help defend Texas against both Comanche raiders from the north and Mexican soldiers from the south.

Now, despite his careful planning, the political struggle between Texas and the central government had erupted into open revolt. Many years ago, the Mexican army had sent a bronze cannon to Gonzales to help defend the town against the Comanches. Now, the army was insisting the cannon be returned. The suspicious residents of Gonzales refused, even capturing the Mexican soldiers sent to retrieve it. The crumpled letter in Sam's hand was from Juan Seguín, reporting that a hundred Mexican dragoons had left San Antonio for Gonzales. Sam knew the Texians wouldn't give the cannon up without a fight, but he also knew they weren't ready for that fight. They lacked military organization. They lacked training, discipline, and supplies. Few of the settlers had ever tasted battle.

As I have.

Sam slowly rolled his right shoulder and winced in pain. Decades earlier, at the Battle of Horseshoe Bend, a musket ball smashed the shoulder. It had never fully healed, nor had the deep arrow wound in his groin. He found himself wishing he hadn't refused the invitation to share a bottle with some old friends visiting from Tennessee. Although Sam knew he needed a clear head to plan his next steps, liquor was the only sure say he'd found to make the pain go away, at least for a little while.

Maybe just a little drink wouldn't hurt.

Sam glanced back at the house he'd just passed, the largest in Nacogdoches. Back in 1790, the town's founder built the two-story house out of adobe bricks, walnut planks, and, most distinctively, slabs of iron ore. Known ever after as *La Casa Piedra*, "the Stone House," it played a central role in the history of the town. A trading center, land office, mayor's office, military base of operations—the Stone House had been all these things and more.

Now it was the property of Judge Córdova. That made it, in effect, the courthouse of Nacogdoches. Córdova was among those Tejanos who opposed Santa Anna and championed the cause of Texas—though only as a separate state within Mexico and with all the rights and powers that came with it, not as an independent republic or a new acquisition by the United States. A fresh conversation with Córdova could be useful, Sam reasoned.

Of greater interest at the moment, however, was that Judge Córdova stocked the finest wines in town. Sam retraced his steps and was soon leaning against the old oak in front of the Stone House. The flickering candles in the windows beckoned to him. He craved what they signified.

Then different images sprung to mind, powerful memories asserting their own claim on his will. Sam thought of the many other times he'd turned to the bottle for relief, escape, or courage. His youthful fling with the Cherokees of Tennessee. His later exile among the Cherokees of Arkansas—after the collapse of his marriage and resignation as governor—where even his friends had called him *Oo-tse-tse Ar-dee-tah-skee*, "Big Drunk." The many days he'd started off with a swig to get him through a challenging legal case or political debate. The many nights he'd downed a bottle to deaden the pain in his limbs—and his soul.

What Sam Houston yearned for was just a few feet away. Since his youth, he'd had no more constant companion. *But the pain always comes back.*

As he hesitated before the Stone House, Sam pondered his youthful exploits in Tennessee. He'd made several lifelong friends there, including the Cherokee chief the whites called John Jolly, the future president they called Old Hickory, and the Tennessee congressman they called Davy Crockett.

Former congressman, he corrected himself. Sam had received another letter reporting the news that Crockett had been defeated for reelection and would soon leave for Texas.

Good. I can use a man like him, if the hotheads of Gonzales don't lose the war in the meantime. Sam recalled a favorite line from the *Iliad* of Homer: "'*Tis man's to fight, but Heaven's to give success.*"

There's another lifelong friend I made in Tennessee. When Sam had first read Homer as a child, he much preferred the colorful adventures of the *Odyssey* to the grim epic that preceded it. Later, as a young man, he came to appreciate the grandeur of the *Iliad*—and even to memorize much of Alexander Pope's translation. Gazing up at the oak, Sam recalled another favorite passage, from the speech of Glaucus to Diomedes. Clearing his parched throat, Sam recited it in the most theatrical voice he could manage:

Like leaves on trees the race of man is found,
Now green in youth, now withering on the ground:
Another race the following spring supplies,
They fall successive, and successive rise.

"No truer words were ever spoken. Seasons pass swiftly in the Blur."

Sam stiffened. If by reciting the *Iliad* he hoped to bring his friend to the porch—and thus resolve his indecision in favor of going into the Stone House for a drink—he had failed. It wasn't Judge Córdova who responded to the recitation. The reply came from behind him, high and reedy, like a whisper on the wind.

He spun around. Four children were coming toward him.

As they approached, their shapes grew more distinct. Sam cracked a smile. One was wide and burly, the end of a stocking cap draped over one shoulder and a battleaxe slung over the other. *That will be Har*. The next was smaller and thinner, manifestly female, with long dark hair. *Tana Song Snake*. The third walker was also short and lithe, with light-colored hair and a spear in her hand. *Could that be Dela, the Water Maiden? They must have rescued her from the Elves.* As for the fourth fairy, he wasn't walking at all—he flew on feathered wings. *Goran Lonefeather, of course*.

"Welcome to Nacogdoches, my friends," Sam began. "To what do I owe the pleasure of your—"

"You presume too much, as Sighted humans tend to do."

Shocked into silent inaction, Sam merely watched the four newcomers surround him.

The stockiest of them did, indeed, resemble Har, though he wasn't nearly as tall and his cap was blue instead of red. Also positioning herself behind Sam was the woman he'd mistaken for Tana. Her features were dark and her skin coppery, to be sure, but her clothes were fashioned of interwoven roots, stems, leaves, and moss, not animal hide, and she clutched a long flute in her hand, not Tana's trusty blowgun. The other female, her sparkling yellow hair swept over two shapely shoulders and extending well past her narrow waist, wore a gray shift and carried a spear with a single barbed point of polished bronze. And when the archer landed in front of Sam, retracting his green-feathered wings and lifting a beechwood bow to nock an arrow, the expression on the fairy's angular face was anything but friendly.

Sam's mind raced. While immune to spellsong, Sam was outnumbered. If they meant him harm, his only chance would be to whip out the big knife his friend Jim Bowie had given him and strike first. On the other hand, over the years he'd met more than a few Folk, including some of Tana's fellow chiefs of the Nunnehi, who were gruff but not inherently hostile. If he struck first, that would start a fight he might otherwise avoid.

Come on, Sam. Time to do what you do best.

"Why, I intended no such presumption," he bellowed in an unnecessarily loud voice while bobbing his head around. "Just making new friends. First time in Nacogdoches?"

The winged archer rolled his eyes at the golden-haired woman, who replied with a stream of words Sam recognized as Folktongue. He also recognized her voice as the one who'd originally called to him. From behind came an exasperated grunt from the axe-wielding fairy and a melodious chuckle from the flute-wielding one.

"I do not bandy words with drunken fools," said the blonde fairy in English, presumably to make sure Sam understood the insult.

"Even a fool can have his uses, Aya," said the archer, "especially if his tongue be sufficiently loosened."

The male behind Sam grunted again. "Lum speaks truth. This pitiful 'village' clearly has no proper fortification. Perhaps the human can narrow our search."

The one called Aya, whom Sam took to be the leader, shrugged. "Perhaps he can, at that. What about it, human?"

"What about...what?" Sam had no need to feign confusion. He didn't understand what she wanted to know.

The fourth newcomer, the dark-featured one carrying the flute, stepped into his field of vision. While the others regarded Sam with disdain, she flashed a playful smile. "We will get to that. But first, introductions. I am Oina, ranger of the Duende. And you are?"

Ah, the diplomat of the bunch. "Sam Houston's my name, ma'am. Pleased to meet you."

"Likewise. My companions are Aya, Lum, and, behind you, Kitu."

Sam staggered onto one foot and made a show of craning his neck slowly backward. The stocky Kitu, his axe resting on one broad shoulder, offered him a curt nod.

"What sort of Folk are you, sir?"

"I am a ranger of the Duende," Kitu muttered.

Puzzled, Sam whipped his head back to the others. "And what about—"

Lum opened his mouth as if to reply, but Oina beat him to it. "We are *all* rangers of the Duende, human. Guardians of the Unity. Servants of the Throne."

Mystified at the unfamiliar words, and curious about the sullen expression on the archer's thin face, Sam chose to respond with a loud, theatrical hiccup.

"A waste of time," Aya snapped. "We should find another human."

"A moment more," Oina insisted. "Our new friend has yet to hear the question. Sam Houston, we have come to your village in search of something. Might there be a fort nearby?"

A fort? Here in Nacogdoches? Sam had seen a variety of fortifications in his life. Army camps and Creek strongholds during the War of 1812. Massive Fort Monroe at the mouth of Chesapeake Bay. Frontier outposts in the Indian Territory. There was nothing of the sort in town, or anywhere in Texas, for that matter.

Unless by "fort," they mean anything that may have once been used as...

"What about the house before us?" Kitu asked. "Plenty big. Walls of stone."

Sam licked his lips. Why were these Folk searching for a fort? Did they seek a new home? Their use of a Spanish word for "fairy," *Duende*, suggested another possibility: that they were magical allies of the central government in Mexico City. Had the Duende come to snuff out the flame of rebellion in Nacogdoches—or perhaps even to scout for an approaching army column?

We're not ready to contend with Mexican soldiers here.

"Uh, well, some soldiers *did* use the Stone House as a headquarters a few years back, but that hardly makes it a fort," Sam stammered, trying to sound dismissive. "Our little town's never been important enough to fortify."

Aya eyed the house. "Should not take long. Then we can move on to more promising territory."

The archer gave a brief nod, then turned to the others. "Standard approach?"

"You up, I down," Kitu agreed.

"And I play!" Oina added.

It quickly became clear what they meant. With a great sweep of his wings, Lum leapt into the air and headed for the second-story porch. Kitu stomped toward the front door. Oina took only a couple of steps in the same direction, then drew the long flute to her lips.

Her song began soft and slow. Sam felt his mind wandering back to his youth, to leisurely days spent reading by a placid lake or wading in a gently flowing stream. Gritting his teeth, he looked at Aya. Of the four Duende rangers, only she remained in the road with him.

"There's no call for this, ma'am," he said. "No one in there worth worrying about. No one you need to charm." *If Judge Córdova is home, I'd rather have him in his right mind tonight.*

Aya shot him a withering glance. "What we need is none of your concern."

"I tell you, there's no fort here. And if you're looking for rebels, you've come to—"

"We have the Texas matter well in hand," she snapped. "I did not come all this way to suppress some minor uprising among the humans."

"Well, then, what *does* bring you here?"

Aya's eyes narrowed. "You ask many questions for a human who was so drunk, he could hardly stand a moment ago."

Sam felt his cheeks flush. *Stick to your role, Houston. The play's not over yet.* "Just trying to be helpful. We in Nacogdoches are only—"

"If there are other humans here, Oina's spellsong will shield us from prying eyes. You pose a special problem, however."

The problem of how to silence a Sighted human. With the other three Duendes otherwise occupied, Sam would have no better chance to even the odds. Aya was probably skilled with her barbed spear, but Sam was no stranger to battle. Bending into a purposefully unsteady bow as a distraction, he let his hand drift down to his Bowie knife.

Then Sam heard a rattle. And smiled.

Aya heard it, too. She shouted in Folktongue, thumping the butt of her spear against in the ground in time with Oina's song. Still, the *other* song—the one accompanied by rattles and something akin to a guitar—quickly surpassed the Duende melody in volume and intensity. Sam couldn't see its players but could tell they were converging on the Stone House from multiple directions.

Lum and Kitu exited the residence, adding their voices to Aya's voice and Oina's flute. Sam had never witnessed anything like this, a battle of fairy magic waged entirely by song. As a Sighted human, he was largely immune to the effects, as were the combatants. Presumably the Duendes feared the approaching Folk were accompanied by charmed humans, while the other Folk suspected the Duende had comparable allies of their own.

"Are you in danger, Sam Houston?"

Although he'd been expecting the voice, its reassuring familiarity washed over him like a warm bath. "Not anymore, Song Snake."

Tana emerged from behind the oak tree, placing her steps in time with her friends' spellsong so the turtle-shell rattles at her ankles punctuated its rhythm. Clutching her blowgun close to her mouth, Tana flashed a grin at Sam. He returned it, and not only in appreciation of her prowess. He'd also seen another familiar figure lumbering behind her, a much larger one with hands strumming a long-stringed instrument.

"Har the Tower!" Sam exclaimed.

The Dwarf nodded but did not speak. He was still singing, as were the three other Nunnehi rangers who emerged from the shadows around Tana and Har. The Duendes were assembled in front of the Stone House, with Kitu holding his battleaxe, Aya her spear, Lum a nocked arrow to his chin, and Oina the flute to her lips.

All nine fairies seemed to realize at the same time that Sam was the only human in the vicinity. Their competing spellsongs came to abrupt ends.

"You are far from home, Nunnehi," Aya said icily.

"Not so far as you," Tana replied. "Do the Xanas not live in the Pink Lagoon of the Yucatan? That lies a great distance away, over the Gulf of Mexico."

"You know much but understand little," Aya said. "The Duende herd all the humans in our domains. You are the strangers in Mexico. We will tolerate no intrusion."

"But you yourself are a Xana," Tana insisted. "I recognize each of your Folk. The Enano with the axe. The Trenti with the flute. The winged Ventolin. My friend Har here has told me much of the Folk of Iberia."

Aya gave the Dwarf a sour look. "Our Folk came here from Spain, yes, but we are all now Duende of Mexico. Guardians of the Unity. Servants of the Throne."

"We are indeed of the Nunnehi," said Tana, smiling and inclining her head. "I am Tana, chief of the Azalea Clan."

"Aya," said the other.

"May we find a more secluded place to continue our meeting?" Tana asked. "I would learn more of this Unity you guard and this Throne you serve."

"I am sure you would, but diplomacy is not our task."

"The Duendes came here looking for a fort," Sam ventured. "No such thing, I told them."

Aya exchanged brief looks with the other Duendes. "Then our duty calls us elsewhere. As should your own."

Tana raised her hand. "May I suggest we exchange—"

"You may not." At a jerk of Aya's head, the other Duendes turned to go. "Heed my warning, Nunnehi: Mexico is our domain. Its herds are ours. Its humanwares are ours. Respect our claim or face the consequences."

"We seek no conflict with you. Indeed, we came here to investigate rumors of another Folk entering your domains, a rogue Folk whose scouts possess mechanisms for flight."

"Elves, you mean. We are aware of the threat they pose. It is none of your concern."

"On that, you are mistaken," Har rumbled. "We have tangled with Prince Veelund's Elfish hordes before. They are devious and deadly. And they hold hostage one of our friends."

So Dela remains a captive, Sam concluded. Now the presence of Tana and Har in Nacogdoches made sense. They'd come looking for signs of Elf habitation, perhaps even drawn here by rumors of flying creatures.

Lum was, at the moment, rising into the air on green-feathered wings. Oina and Kitu had already slipped into the shadows, Aya not far behind them. "Your quarrel with the Elves is your own affair," the latter called over her shoulder. "Whatever the fate of your friend, you will not discover it here."

Sam watched the yellow-haired figure until she was out of sight. *A Xana, Tana called her. Something like a Water Maiden, I'll bet.* He turned to face his friends. "Sorry to hear Dela's still missing."

"Just as I am sorry to learn that tales of winged fairies in Texas may be nothing more than another false trail," said Har the Tower, his bearded face twisted into a dejected expression.

"They sought a fort?" Tana cocked her head to one side. "To what end?"

Sam related the story of his encounter with the Duendes. He then described the complicated situation in Texas and his determination to offer his services to the people of Texas. "I don't rightly know why the Duendes are looking for a fort, but it's likely bad news for the Texian cause," he said. "We sure could use some magical help of our own."

Tana shook her head. "I agree with the Xana ranger in one respect: the fate of Texas is not for my Folk to determine. The Nunnehi have other responsibilities, Sam, as you and I have often discussed."

"Helping the Cherokees settle their new home in the Indian Territory." Sam knew she was right, but that didn't make the reality any harder to accept.

The Dwarf frowned. "We cannot yet be sure the trail to Dela is a false one. Perhaps Elf fliers *do* range nearby. We should investigate further."

"That, *you* should, Har," agreed the Song Snake, "but my scouts and I must journey east for a time. You will have to go on alone."

"No he won't." Sam clapped the Tower on the back. "I'll do what I can to help find Dela, though I now have my own mystery to investigate as well."

A faint smile came to Har's lips. "You speak of the Duendes and this fort of theirs. Perhaps we can help each other, at least for a time."

And perhaps, Sam mused, the two mysteries were not as unrelated as they seemed. Another favorite passage from the *Iliad* sprang to mind: "*For I must speak what wisdom would conceal, and truths, invidious to the great, reveal.*"

Chapter 8 — The Roar

October 1835

IT WAS ANOTHER DRY HOLE—FOR Goran.

The ancient mound they had discovered near Lewistown, Illinois, was close enough to the river for a Gwragedd Annwn settlement. Indeed, the thick tangle of thaumaturgical vines around it and rich veins of thaumaturgical stone beneath suggested habitation by some ancient Folk.

"I regret we have yet to detect Dela's abductors," said Diri, giving Goran's arm a squeeze. "Perhaps we will have more luck downriver."

"The confluence of the Illinois and the Mississippi is near," Dyl offered. "The humans we questioned at Lewistown passed along intriguing rumors about it."

Vague rumors. Chance sightings. These are the only threads of hope left to me, and yet I grasp and tug as if they were skeins of rope.

Goran stepped from the riverbank into the shallows of the Illinois, wetting his hands and drawing them across his sweat-streaked face. Though sunny, the autumn day wasn't particularly hot, but to permit conversation, he and the others had spent the last hour traveling by foot rather than their preferred modes of flying and swimming, respectively. Perhaps it was the resulting exertion that brought the flush to his cheeks and forehead. Perhaps it was only frustration.

"Do you need a rest, Lonefeather?"

Dyl stood next to him, spinning his trident and eagerly scanning the water for fish. Many hours had passed since their modest breakfast of dried meat and fruit. The young ranger's gesture made Goran think of Har the Tower, who was searching for Dela in Texas. The Water Folk were no substitute for his favorite fisherman, but Dyl and Diri proved to be excellent traveling companions.

The Sylph turned to find the woman regarding him with inquiring eyes. Other than their shared ancestry and easy manner, the two blue-skinned rangers couldn't have been more different. Diri was cautious and deliberative, Dyl brash and impulsive. After decades spent in the Blur, Diri was grandmaster of her guild and emissary of the Great Council, while Dyl had only just become a journeyman ranger for the Gwragedd Annwn of the Holston. Diri was short and stout, like Goran's Goblin friend Betua, while Dyl was taller than the Sylph and slighter of build. During their game hunts on the trail, young Dyl demonstrated impressive skill with his Folk's traditional weapons—bronze-shod trident and beaded net—while Diri was as adept an archer as Goran himself.

"River junctions are prime locations for settlement, Folk or human," she said, tucking a stray lock of hair under the braids that framed her periwinkle-colored forehead. "And as I understood the humans' words, we are not far from the confluence with the mighty Missouri, where the humans built a bustling city."

Dyl nodded. "Named after a famous monarch of the French, I think. A great warrior."

Goran smiled. "Great, perhaps, but as a warrior, he met only defeat. The humans venerate him for his faith, not his military prowess. They call him Saint Louis."

"You know your humanlore." Diri looked pensive. "We Folk are quick to dismiss humans as violent and puerile, yet I believe there is much value in studying them."

"I have always thought so," Goran agreed, "though some lessons are more valuable than others."

"Which lessons do you mean, ranger of the Sylph? Do you share Gwyla's opposition to the creation of our Great Council? I admit the government of the Britons was an inspiration, but necessity impelled us to act. Only by uniting into a single Folk can the Gwragedd Annwn hope to survive the present crisis."

Goran *did*, in fact, have concerns about putting too much power in the hands of an elite few, given the decisions of Grandmaster Bren and King Briafael during the American War of Independence. *Now is not the time to discuss them.* "One questionable lesson we learn from humans is how to make our weapons more destructive."

Dyl snorted. "I fired one of the muskets our craftsmen forge of brass and bronze. It makes a fearsome noise, I grant you, but I credit neither its accuracy nor its rate of fire. One skilled with bow, net, or trident can easily outmatch one armed with a gun."

"One to one, perhaps," Goran said, "but fire many muskets in volleys, or many cannons as batteries, and the results can be devastating."

"Your words ring true," said Diri, "yet this would hardly be the first time Folk have employed arts first developed in the Blur. For generations, we have worn the products of human looms, eaten the produce of human hoes, and replicated the patterns of human forges and sewing needles. For generations, we have harvested the fruits of their ingenuity while weeding out their worst ideas and protecting them from their worst impulses."

Or so we have told ourselves. Goran had seen too much suffering and death at the hands of Folk, or of humans guided by Folk rangers, to accept this oft-told tale at face value. Still, he had no desire to argue the point with the grandmaster. *She is doing what she thinks is right for her Folk. And she and Dyl have been nothing but helpful in my search for Dela.*

He decided to come at the issue from a different direction. "Why do Gwyla and the Folk of the Holston mistrust your intentions so fervently?"

Diri opened her mouth as if to reply, then shut it when a rumbling sound came from downriver. *A thunderstorm?* Puzzled, Goran glanced up at the cloudless sky.

The woman did the same, then shrugged. "About the motives of other elders, I can only guess. As for Gwyla, it has been our way since childhood. I speak and she contradicts me, as if by reflex—though I suppose I contradict her at least as often."

"You grew up in the same village, then?"

The grandmaster chuckled. "The same village? Why, my dear Sylph, I thought you knew—we grew up in the same *room*. Was it not the same in your family?"

Gwyla and Diri are sisters. Goran chided himself for not realizing it before. The resemblance of their faces. The multiple references to their common teacher. And the sibling rivalry that, in retrospect, lay at the core of their contentious debate. *Yes, it was indeed the same in my family—though my rivalry was with my big brother, never my little sister.*

He assumed that Ailee still lived with their aged father in the Sylph village at Niagara Falls. Where his Blur-struck brother Kaden lived, or *whether* he still lived, remained another unresolved mystery. "So, when you and other leaders of the Water Folk of Wales decided to unify your villages into a confederation, I take it your sister was among those who preferred to—"

Another roar of thunder prompted Goran to stop in midsentence. The three rangers exchanged startled looks. *A roar, yes, but was it truly thunder?*

The Sylph yanked his bow over his head and drew an arrow. Diri did the same while Dyl slipped the enchanted net from his shoulder and began to scan the trees. None said a word. All listened for the sound to repeat itself, the sound that chased all thoughts of politics and family from Goran's mind.

The sound did recur—a mighty roar filled with menace and rage.

A distinctively *feline* roar.

The Sylph had heard its like before. He'd heard such a roar on his first solo ranging, when he met Daniel Boone on a Carolina mountaintop. He'd heard it during his final visit to the Sylph village on the Knob, and again during his final confrontation with Atta Yellow Jacket. It had been the Pukwudgie who perished that day in the shadow of Hanging Rock. Was some monstrous feline about to claim another victim?

There was another scream, long and throaty. It came from upriver, not downriver. *Is there more than one feline monster here?*

Goran's legs sensed the monsters' approach before his eyes did. When he first stepped into the shallows of the Illinois River, the water reached halfway up his calves. Now it surged to his waist, then nearly over his head. Struggling not to be toppled, the Sylph took a couple of side steps, then launched himself into the air. Water was still pelting his body, though its source wasn't the surging river—it was a driving rain from what had a moment before been a cloudless sky.

"Behind you!" Diri shouted. Then something hard struck the back of Goran's legs, knocking him head over heels. Disoriented, he found that his initial attempt to stay aloft merely propelled him downward. Only when his head and shoulders crashed into the top of a pine tree did Goran come to his senses, allow his feet to rotate below his head, and flap his wings to arrest his momentum.

Alighting on a branch, Goran turned his attention to the ground below. What he saw chilled him to the bone. Dyl and Diri were standing back-to-back in the river, each facing a sinewy adversary with the furry face and paws of a cougar, a scaly body a dozen human feet in length, and a long copper-colored tail snapping over each horned head.

It was one of those whiplike tails that had knocked him into the trees, he realized. When the two monsters roared again, their jaws open wide, their aquamarine eyes sparkling with energy, Goran recognized the descriptions he'd heard from Dela and other rangers.

Water Panthers.

Goran's companions answered the monsters with fierce cries of their own. Diri had already shot one arrow and was fitting a second to her bowstring. Dyl held his trident in one hand while whirling his shell-lined net with the other. Goran watched the young ranger hurl the enchanted weapon at an advancing Water Panther. Then, without waiting to see if Dyl had struck home, the Sylph jumped off the pine branch, drew the nock of his own arrow to his chin, and released.

He aimed for a tuft of brown fur atop the monster's head, between its short bison-like horns. The arrow flew wide, merely grazing one of the Water Panther's white-tipped ears and plunging into a patch of ground made muddy by the sudden squall.

The rain lessened then, its force replaced by swirling winds. It was hardly rare for magical monsters to manipulate the weather, whether consciously or unconsciously. At the Battle of Yorktown, Goran had seen a Sea Serpent perform the feat on a grand scale. Water Panthers were much smaller and, presumably, capable of much less destruction, he reasoned. Though the Sylph found no comfort in that, remembering how a grizzled Gwragedd Annwn ranger had once described them: *exceedingly dangerous, especially when they hunt in pairs*.

The monster Goran had missed emitted a hideous shriek. He quickly figured out why: Dyl's attack was more accurate. Both front paws were entangled in the net as the Water Panther thrashed and thumped its paws, trying to free them. Lightning flashed in its angry eyes.

From behind Goran came the growls of the other monster, interspersed with Diri's taunts and grunts. Trusting the more experienced ranger to fend off her attacker for the moment, the Sylph reloaded and swooped closer to the ensnared Water Panther, hoping to finish it off with a shot at close range. Dyl had the same thought. Shouting in exultation, he thrust his trident forward with both hands and propelled himself toward the Water Panther with frog-like kicks.

There was a blur of motion in Goran's peripheral vision. Instinctively, he flinched, recalling the wallop to the back of his legs. The Water Panther's undulating tail didn't hit him, however, nor did it hit Dyl. Instead, the coppery tail wrapped around the blue-skinned ranger's narrow waist and jerked him out of the river.

Goran shot his second arrow. The bronze point struck the roof of the monster's mouth and erupted just above its nose in a spray of sparks and blood. Immediately reloading, the Sylph inclined his wings into a banking turn. He heard the strangled cry of the wounded Water Panther and turned his head to seek out another vulnerable spot. What he didn't expect to see, and what prompted Goran to drop his bow and arrow hastily to the ground, was Dyl's body twisting through the air just a few feet below him.

Executing a sharp turn, the Sylph beat his wings to pick up speed as he hurtled toward the flailing form of the young ranger. It was a race to see whether his grasping hands could reach Dyl before the latter's head smashed into the ground.

Goran won, albeit barely.

Grabbing the young man's leg, he kept Dyl from colliding with the ground—but he couldn't keep both rangers from careening into a nearby oak. The shock of the impact made Goran cry out in pain. The *sound* of the impact, the snap of bones breaking against the tree trunk, made him cry out in concern, for the sickening crunch didn't come from him. It came from the cracked rib cage of his companion, now slumped to the ground.

"Dyl!" the Sylph shouted. "Do not move. I will bind your chest with a—"

"No, leave me! Help Diri!"

Of course, what was I thinking?

Alone, the grandmaster couldn't long withstand the joint assault of two Water Panthers. Goran spotted his discarded bow and arrow on the ground, scooped them up, and took off. The monster they'd fought had freed one of its paws from Dyl's net and now advanced on Diri from behind. Her own arrows must have severely wounded the other monster, for it neither pounced on the grandmaster, gored her with its horns, nor attacked her with its prehensile tail. Instead, the beast staggered back and forth in the water, shaking its head as if trying to dislodge something from its ears.

Surmising that the sleep magic embedded in Diri's arrows was taking effect, Goran chose the nearer monster as his target. Flying past its wildly gesticulating tail and hovering above its scaly back, the Sylph aimed for the ribbon of neck separating its feline head from its first dorsal scale. The arrow flew true, sinking into the monster's flesh and delivering another dose of sedative magic.

A sharp grunt from Diri drew Goran's attention. Her mouth clenched in determination, the grandmaster was backing away from the second Water Panther, one hand holding a slender knife and the other pressed against her thigh. Blue blood trickled from the wound, which Goran guessed was made by the monster's horn when Diri had attempted to finish the battle with her blade.

"I am coming!" With a great sweep of wings, the Sylph passed over the head of his initial antagonist and charged the one now menacing the wounded woman. His bowstring twanged. The Water Panther hissed, and Goran spotted the fletching of his arrow sticking out of its right foreleg. He saw the fletching of other arrows, Diri's arrows, protruding from the monster's head, chest, and legs, but he didn't halt his charge. He didn't reload. With one fluid motion, he drew his own knife and slashed as he flew by the Water Panther's massive jaws.

Blood didn't trickle from the monster's throat—it spurted. The Water Panther managed a final, furious gurgle before it fell forever silent.

The other Water Panther still had not. From deep within the surviving monster's throat came another rumble of thunder, of frustration, of... *anguish?* Goran felt pricks on his neck, as if someone were jabbing him with needles.

Ever since the Oneida woman Polly Cooper revealed herself many years ago at Mount Vernon to be a Tlanuwa, a shape-shifting Thunderbird, he'd known some monsters were thinking, feeling creatures. So why did it surprise him now that the Water Panther would mourn the death of its hunting companion?

No, not its hunting companion, Goran realized with a start. *Its mate.*

The rumble rose in volume and pitch until it became a forlorn howl. A panicked scream. Then a roar, longer and more terrible than before. From the swirling fury of clouds above its head erupted vengeful bolts of blinding light. One soon found its target, splitting Goran's bow in two, knocking him roughly to the ground, and scalding his shoulder and chest with angry flame.

The Sylph tried to stand up, to sit up, to crawl away, yet his numb arms and stunned legs refused his commands. He managed only to lift his head. He saw the Water Panther stalking toward him, the point of Goran's arrow still visible about halfway between its black nose and aquamarine eyes. Its gait was slow and ungainly, the creature evidently attempting—and so far succeeding—to fight off the effects of sleep magic. Coming up behind the monster, and moving even slower, was a limping Diri with the knife still clutched in her shaking hand.

There would be another fateful race that night, a race between the wounded monster and the wounded woman. It was one the Water Panther seemed destined to win and Goran, to lose. His hands groped fruitlessly for his own blade. He closed his eyes and conjured a mental image of Dela, bound and abandoned in some unknown Elfish dungeon. Only he could find her. Rescue her. Love her.

Move! he commanded his aching limbs.

Again, they defied him.

Then the Water Panther's unforgiving roar became a plaintive whine. Goran's eyes snapped open. It was as if he were looking through a Shimmer wall into a place where time was moving more slowly than the Blur but far less slowly than a Folk realm. He watched the ranger Dyl, wielding his mighty trident despite his cracked ribs, slowly drive its three bronze blades deeper into the side of the monster. He watched it slowly buck and shiver. He watched the young ranger's mouth slowly form a triumphant smile. He watched a copper-colored tail slowly wrap itself around Dyl's throat and lift him off his feet. He watched the dying Water Panther, with a final burst of power, fling Goran's savior against the scales bristling like a row of sharp axeblades along its back.

He saw Dyl join his foe in death.

"No!" he heard Diri shout. "It cannot be!"

Yes, it can.

"You—you did this!"

I suppose I did...Dyl came along to help me. I led him to his doom.

From beyond Goran's field of vision came a dull thud, then the sound of scuffling feet. He heard grunts and curses, some from Diri and some from another voice. Summoning all his strength, the Sylph flexed an arm to raise his head and shoulders higher above the ground. Coming toward him was the grandmaster of the Gwragedd Annwn, her progress impeded not only by a pronounced limp but also by the struggling form she dragged behind her.

"It was *she* who summoned them," muttered Diri, panting from pain and exhaustion. "It is *she* who will pay."

When they got closer, Goran's eyes widened at the dark-green clothes and pointed ears of the grandmaster's captive. *An Elf ranger! Have we finally found one of their villages? Perhaps even the new seat of Prince Veelund?*

He felt hope splash over him, salving his wounds, renewing his vigor. He pushed himself to a sitting position. "Where is she?"

The Elf responded with a cough that spattered her tunic with drops of dark liquid. It was then that Goran noticed the hilt of Diri's blade in the Elf's abdomen. The Sylph thought of Dyl's mangled body and felt no pity. "Where is she?" he repeated.

"Where is…who?"

"Veelund's hostage, the Water Maiden named Dela."

The Elf shook her head. "You will never find her."

"Then you *do* know where she is," Diri snapped. "Speak and earn mercy."

"Too late," the Elf insisted. "She is no more."

"You lie!" Goran struggled to his feet, his pain forgotten in the intensity of the moment. "She must be close. Your ambush did not keep me from her. Neither will your lies."

The Elf snarled. "I am Thekla the ranger. I do not lie. You are too late."

Goran stumbled forward and grabbed Thekla's chin, jerking her face up so he could stare into her verdant eyes. "Tell me where to find her."

"I know not where her body is buried."

"She is not dead! I *know* she is not!"

The Elf ranger sneered. "I know better. It was my arrow that killed her."

Of all the bestial roars that had reverberated along the banks of the Illinois River that day, none was more savage or heart-rending than the roar that issued from the mouth of the Sylph ranger who slumped, utterly defeated, to the muddy ground.

Chapter 9 – The Mission

March 1836

I WILL NEVER GET USED to this.

Har repositioned himself once more, attempting to stay upright by clamping his legs harder against the flanks of the horse—and without having to put his arms around the human.

The leering face of the Elf ranger Roza came to mind. During the Creek War, they'd spent months together traveling with General Jackson's army. Initially irritated by her sarcastic banter and flippant attitude, over time Har came to appreciate her prowess and courage. He even saved her life once. She repaid the debt by helping Goran and Dela rescue the Dwarf from captivity at Spirit Forest. In the end, though, Roza had placed her loyalty to Prince Veelund above her friendship with Har. When the time came, neither admiration nor gratitude stayed Har's hand.

When the time came, he took her life.

That didn't keep Har from appreciating lighter moments. Watching him reel awkwardly on a horse, Roza had once doubled over with laughter. "The Tower totters!" she'd said between giggles. "But will it fall and shake the earth?"

Now, I totter again. And if I fall, there will be no one to ridicule me.

The trail from Gonzales to San Antonio was far from deserted. Har had traveled its entirety in the company of James Bonham, the young courier whose horse the Dwarf commandeered as his mount. Bonham didn't possess the Sight, however. As far as Har could tell, neither did any of the other humans—English-speaking Texians and Spanish-speaking Tejanos—they encountered during their seventy-mile ride. None could resist his concealment spell. None saw him bouncing around uncontrollably on the back of Bonham's horse.

My dignity may survive the journey. But will I survive what comes next?

~ ~ ~

Sam Houston was certain the Duendes were responsible.

Or so he had told Har back in Nacogdoches. In November, the Texas revolutionaries elected Sam commander in chief of their new army, such that it was, but then spent months second-guessing his decisions and ignoring his commands. Some hotheads even devised a reckless scheme to ride south and loot the Mexican town of Matamoros—a scheme that, of course, turned into an utter fiasco. Frustrated, Sam returned to Nacogdoches to negotiate a treaty with the local Cherokees. That's where Har caught up with his friend after investigating rumors of winged fairies along the Texas coast.

"In order to win, we must act together," Sam said. "United we stand, divided we fall. Santa Anna knows it, too. That's why he sent those fairies among us, to sow division."

Har shook his head. "You have that backward, my friend. If the Duendes are responsible, it would not be at the behest of a human—he would act at *their* behest. Besides, you know as well as I no fairy magic is needed for humans to follow bad leaders or lose their nerve. You admit most Texians have no experience with warfare. Why expect them to obey your command when they cannot understand its purpose?"

"The purpose is clear enough—defending Texas!" Sam spread a rough-drawn map on the ground and pointed with a quivering finger. "Santa Anna was sure to march against us, winter be damned, and with vastly superior numbers. I told Stephen Austin and the provisional government months ago that the only defensible line went from Gonzales down through Goliad to the coast. San Antonio de Béxar is too far inland."

"Yet they insisted on holding the town."

The general sighed in exasperation. "I thought Jim Bowie, at least, had better sense. When he and his men left for San Antonio, they were supposed to destroy the old mission and bring the garrison and guns back to Goliad."

Sam concluded the only way to save Texas was to call another convention, formally declare independence, and get the new government to confirm his authority over the armed forces. As for Har, Sam asked him to look for signs of Duende influence, reminding him the four fairies they'd previously encountered in Nacogdoches had been keenly interested in human forts.

The Dwarf agreed—but only to gathering intelligence. Although he wished his friend well and deplored Santa Anna's outrageous acts, the Dwarfs of Grünerberg had taken no side in the conflict. And while he understood the rebels' grievances, were not most newcomers to Mexico? Were not many in violation of Mexico's laws themselves, by crossing the border illegally or bringing slaves into the territory? Still, the possibility that a Duende confederation was manipulating events in Mexico, America's sprawling and often unstable neighbor, merited investigation. There also remained the tantalizing rumors of flying fairies in the territory. Might Veelund have his own human puppets in Texas, and might following one of their strings lead Har to Dela?

Recalling his disastrous misjudgment of the Prince of Elves made Har wince. *I am no deep thinker, gifted strategist, or clever diplomat, but I can still be a loyal friend.*

So, he'd set off in search of forts. The only one in the territory "truly worthy of the name," in Sam's words, was the old Presidio La Bahía in Goliad, the place the Texians called Fort Defiance. Har went there first but saw no Folk. Now he would look for rangers in San Antonio de Béxar, where Bowie and some one hundred and fifty defenders were surrounded by Santa Anna's vastly larger army. The rebel "stronghold," which lay across the San Antonio River from the town proper, consisted of a roofless chapel and a few ramshackle buildings enclosed by low walls of adobe, timber, and stone.

Even its defenders didn't give it a lofty name like Fort Defiance. They called it the Alamo.

~ ~ ~

Perhaps James Bonham would have slipped past the Mexican lines without Har's magical assistance. The Dwarf admired the young man's bravery and resourcefulness. Back in Goliad—where Bonham had delivered a request for reinforcements from the Alamo's acting commander, William Travis—some of the Texians tried to dissuade Bonham from going back. Har was watching from the shadows when one man warned Bonham he'd be "throwing away his life" by returning to the Alamo. "Buck Travis deserves an answer," Bonham snapped before spitting contemptuously into the dirt.

Recognizing a man after his own heart, as well as a fast way to San Antonio, Har had sung a concealment spell and pulled himself up on Bonham's horse. First they headed north to Gonzalez, where Bonham secured a letter from another Texian commander promising reinforcements. Then they galloped west, evading Santa Anna's patrols to reach the Alamo on March 3.

Har soon found the one member of the garrison who saw right through his magical disguise. "Was wonderin' when one of you lot would show up," said David Crockett, clapping the Dwarf on the shoulder as the two peered over the south wall at the Mexican lines.

Har knew his longtime friend would be at the Alamo. He'd also heard Crockett refused an officer's commission, allowing the less experienced Jim Bowie and William Travis to share command, though the former had fallen deathly ill and left "Buck" Travis in charge.

"I looked forward to seeing you again," Har allowed, "but why would *you* be expecting *me*?"

David offered him a wan smile. "Last night makes the third time I heard one of them magic songs waftin' over from the enemy camp. Figured there's a fairy out there. Also figured Sam would send one *our* way."

"The general had his suspicions." *And I hoped they were groundless.* "Any signs of unrest or panic here?"

"No more than you'd expect." David removed his coonskin cap and wiped his forehead with its furry tail. "We know what we're up against. Santa Anna's got thousands of men. Last night was different, though. The men weren't scared. Plumb tired, more like. The sentries could barely keep their eyes open."

A sleep spell! "Did the Mexicans try to—"

"Shot a mess of cannonballs at us, sure enough, but didn't attack." David grinned again. "Least not in force. I did spot one runner—fast little feller. Tried to make it all the way to the old mission. Young Betsy sent him packin'." The former congressman gave the stock of his hunting rifle a playful pat.

A Duende ranger, perhaps? Why expose yourself when you could send charmed humans instead? Har pointed to the gun. "I thought its name was Old Betsy."

"Naw, left her back in Tennessee. Got me a Young Betsy now."

"The garrison is fortunate to have a Sighted human on watch."

David looked at him with bleary eyes. "Even the Sighted's got to sleep sometime. Best tend to that, now you're here."

~ ~ ~

While his friend slept, Har studied the position and its garrison. The fortifications were more impressive than he'd been led to believe. If a winged ranger such as Goran were to fly overhead, he'd describe the layout as a human letter *L*, with the old Alamo mission itself forming the far east end of the horizontal bar. The long western walls were twelve feet high and three feet thick. The rebels placed their two biggest cannons, each hurling eighteen-pound balls, at each corner. Har judged the weakest points to be the partially ruined north wall and a gap where the previous Mexican garrison had thrown up a rough palisade of sharpened cedar posts. It was there Har had found David Crockett, whose Tennesseans had volunteered to defend the Alamo's most vulnerable spot.

Although Har initially kept to the shadows, he grew less cautious as the day wore on. None of the others showed any signs of having the Sight. They ranged widely in age, dress, and equipment. Some were ill-clad youths with anxious expressions on their smooth faces. Others were grizzled, buckskin-clad hunters with matted beards, hardscrabble farmers with tattered blankets drawn over shivering shoulders, or townsmen in faded suit coats and mud-spattered cravats. Most spoke in English, though their accents marked them as hailing from all over the United States as well as England, Scotland, Ireland, and, to Har's surprise, his own native Germany. Others still were Spanish-speaking Tejanos in work shirts and leather trousers with wide sombreros or flat-brimmed poblano hats on their heads. Through overheard conversation, Har learned the most prominent of them, former San Antonio Mayor Juan Seguín, had recently left to recruit more Tejanos.

Although surrounded by Santa Anna's ever-growing army, the Alamo's defenders seemed surprisingly optimistic. Bonham, the young courier, bore a letter promising reinforcements from Goliad and Gonzales. The rebels also expected Seguín to return any day with additional recruits. When a well-rested David Crockett resumed his post on the palisade, a great cheer revealed the former congressman's popularity—and how much his presence reassured the men their cause was just and destined to prevail.

Watching David's return from a nearby horse pen, Har decided to cross the plaza and resume their conversation. He stopped short when he heard stiff boots crunch across the cold ground. A moment later, a tall man in a frayed brown coat stomped into view. "Mister Crockett," he drawled. "A word, sir."

"My pleasure, Colonel Travis." The Tennessean led the commander to the horse pen, winking at Har as he passed. Then the Dwarf heard loud clangs from the occupied town across the river.

"Hear that, Crockett?" asked Travis, scratching his reddish whiskers with a long-fingered hand. "Our enemies ring the cathedral bell. They're celebrating."

David shrugged. "Some festival I don't know about?"

"Celebrating their reinforcement!" Travis shot the Tennessean an exasperated look. "Maybe a thousand fresh troops."

"I understand many brave souls are headed our way, too."

"That's what Bonham's letter promised, but I have my doubts," Travis said. "The spirits of our men are high, though they have much to depress them. Where are our recruits from Goliad? From Gonzales?"

"Might be out there figurin' a way to get past the Mexicans. They'd be fools to face them long lances of Santa Anna's dragoons in the open field."

Travis nodded. "My thoughts precisely. We need more men on these walls, not out wandering the countryside."

"And maybe all *they* need's a guide to bring 'em in. Wouldn't mind stretchin' my legs a spell."

"Nice of you to volunteer." For the first time, Har saw the harried commander of the Alamo crack a smile. "But the legs you stretch ought to have iron shoes. Our reinforcements might be a good ride away."

~ ~ ~

There is no such thing as a good ride.

The Tower was again tottering on the back of a horse, though this time he gladly held on to David Crockett's waist to keep from slipping off. They had left the Alamo just after nightfall, riding north where the besieging forces were thinnest and then turning east toward Gonzales.

In addition to Har, two other Texians rode with David. Both expressed surprise the party made it past the Mexicans so easily, but David knew better. "That's the second favor you did me in the space of a day," he told Har as their horse slowed to a walk along a narrow creek.

"You are my friend, one I do not wish to see come to harm, though the wisdom of attempting to hold the Alamo escapes me. Sam insists it would better to pull back and—"

"Sam's got it wrong!" David's voice bore no trace of its usual geniality. "Santa Anna must be stopped here and now. Seen many a tyrant in my day, but he's the worst. Mighty big principles at stake. Liberty. Decency. The right of folks to govern themselves."

"If that is the case," the Dwarf replied, "why not find a safer place to stand up for them? Why not shorten your supply lines and lengthen your enemy's?"

"*If* that's the case?" David sounded offended. "You been listenin' to Santa Anna's lies? That Texians and newcomers like me started the trouble? Sure, there are all sorts fightin' this here war. Some more noble than others, and a few who ain't noble at all. For the most part, though, they're fightin' for the same things our pas and grandpas fought the British for. If it was all about gettin' land or makin' fortunes, there'd be plenty safer ways than takin' on the whole Mexican army."

Did I offend truly him so much? "Sam does not question your principles—he shares them. He only questions the strategy."

"Travis says San Antonio's the gateway to the rest of Texas, and I believe 'im. We can hold the Alamo. We just need more men."

Their horse stopped at the water's edge to take a sip. The other two humans' mounts did the same. The Texians heard none of David's conversation with Har, of course. Spellsong took care of that.

"That's Salado Creek," said the Tennessean in a more amiable tone. "If a column did ride out from Gonzales, they're probably camped a few miles ahead at the ford on Cibolo Creek. Best push on."

Har inclined his head. "I follow your lead, my friend." *Given my epic history of blunders, my advice is probably faulty, anyway.*

David spurred their horse across the shallow brook. "Yep, sure was some pretty singing back there. Right inspirin'. So long as your spell holds…" He let his voice trail off in what both men knew was an unspoken question.

The Dwarf answered it by singing a jaunty song he'd heard many times since his journey westward with Sam Houston:

We are a hardy free-born race
No man to fear a stranger.
Whate'er the game we join in chase,
Despising toil and danger.

David chuckled and joined in:

And if a daring foe annoys
Whate'er his strength or forces,
We'll show them that Tennessee boys
Are alligator-horses.

They reached the Cibolo ford by midnight. Just as David had predicted, more than a hundred men were camped next to the creek, most Texians from Gonzales or newly arrived volunteers from the United States. A few were Tejanos. One introduced himself as Carlos Espalier. "Captain Seguín sent us back to San Antonio de Béxar," the slender youth explained, "but we ran into a patrol."

"Got to slip in from the north," David said. "Best get back before we lose the night."

He handed a packet of letters from Colonel Travis to one of the Texians, who took off toward Gonzales while the others returned along the same trail David's party had followed. Har renewed his spellsong, plucking the strings of his scheitholt as he sang to strengthen the magical effect. It would do no good, however, if any Mexican soldiers they encountered possessed the Sight. In that case, the reinforcements would have to rely on the cover of darkness—and on the canny leadership of Har's old friend.

It was shortly after they recrossed Salado Creek that one of the scouts, young Carlos Espalier, rode into view. "Lancers," he reported breathlessly. "Dead ahead, less than a mile."

"Let's get around 'em," said David. Crossing the San Antonio River, the men worked their way slowly south, eyes peeled for Mexican scouts. Presently, they came upon a loop in the tree-lined river, from which more than one Texian whispered about seeing glints of light.

"Bayonets." David pointed over the river. "The fort's about eight hundred yards that way, past them cottonwoods and mesquites. Let's go while it's still dark."

The moment Har had dreaded was here. He'd be no longer searching for a lost friend or protecting another from harm. If he helped Crockett and the others fight their way into the Alamo, he'd be taking sides in a new war, the implications of which he didn't fully understand.

What was that?

It wasn't the sight of shadowy movement or moonlight reflecting off gun metal. Har *heard* something, a loud voice coming from the old millhouse on the far bank of the river. A Mexican picket? Another Texian volunteer hoping to join their mad dash to the Alamo?

No. The language wasn't Spanish or English. It was Folktongue.

David heard it, too. "Duende?"

Har nodded. "A ranger singing a revelation spell. Soon, you will be visible to your enemies."

The Dwarf glanced from David's worried face to the determined faces of the other recruits, who had no inkling of the magical enemy awaiting them. Har's war, it may not have been, but he couldn't bring himself to abandon these men to their fates. Then came a new idea: Perhaps if the Alamo was sufficiently reinforced, Santa Anna would think twice about storming it. Perhaps prolonging the siege, and converting it into a standoff, could lead to a negotiated settlement instead of a bloodbath.

It was a slender hope, one Har grabbed as it were a lifeline tossed into a raging sea. Opting not to try to overcome the Duende's counterspell, the Dwarf sang the first words of a fear spell. Dismounting and pulling his battleaxe from his pack as he sang, Har jerked his head at David. The Tennessean understood: Har could only weaken the resolve of so many enemy humans for a short time.

"Let's go!" David yelled, waving his rifle.

His men responded with a chorus of shouts and a harmony of hoofbeats. They surged southward in three ranks, most also clutching rifles, but some Texians brandishing flintlock pistols or broad-bladed knives and Tejanos brandishing an assortment of muskets, sabers, and horn-handled Belduque knives.

Har didn't follow David's men. He bore east, as fast as his stout legs and stocky frame would allow, until he reached the bend in the San Antonio River. To his right, situated against the near bank, was an artillery battery. A quick glance confirmed the success of his spellsong. While a few Mexicans were firing muskets, most were huddled together and arguing, trying to decide whether to fight or flee.

They weren't his primary target, however. As Har gazed across the stream to the millhouse, its doors flew open to reveal its lone occupant: a burly Folk ranger with a blue stocking cap on his head and a gray battleaxe in his hands.

Har grimaced. *The one called Kitu.*

The other ranger stopped singing. "You are far from kith and kin, Dwarf!" he shouted.

Har paused his own spellsong. "You threaten one of my friends, Enano!"

Kitu scowled. "Only a fool would befriend a human."

"And only a fool would break his blade against the Tower!"

Har wasn't sure his boast could be tested—for all he knew, the river was too deep here to cross—but at least he'd distracted Kitu from hindering David Crockett's desperate charge.

It soon became clear the other ranger wouldn't settle for exchanging insults. The Enano stepped into a small boat and launched it into the water. Though he didn't bother rowing or steering the little craft, it somehow drifted unerringly toward the Dwarf.

The river seems intent on testing my boast, as well.

Har didn't wait for the boat to touch shore. Bellowing a spell to conceal them from human eyes, he charged into the shallows and swung his axe. Kitu parried with his own weapon, shoving Har sideways and giving the Enano time to jump into the water himself.

There is nothing elegant about a duel by battleaxe. Each combatant repeatedly swung his double-bladed weapon at his foe's head, chest, or abdomen while the other either blocked or dodged the attack. It was a contest of strength and balance, the larger Har the Tower enjoying an advantage in the former, the nimbler Kitu showing him up in the latter.

It was all Har could do to keep the Enano at bay, so only sporadically did the sounds of the human battle nearby catch his attention. He hoped David's outnumbered men could make it to the Alamo before daybreak removed their cover of darkness.

"You grow tired, Dwarf!" Kitu barked. "Soon, you will sleep for the last time!"

He is right. Har's limbs felt like lead weights. *Time to try something else.* "Neither of us need die tonight. Why not talk?"

"I have nothing to say. You have nothing worth hearing."

Har stumbled back a step. "If I could but know why you Enanos—"

"*Duendes*!" Kitu's eyes flashed with fanatical fury.

"—why you *Duendes* aid the dictator Santa Anna. Perhaps we could come to some understanding."

"Our humans are but means to an end. As yours are to you."

"I came here to help a friend, and to find another long lost to me," Har said. "I mean your Folk no harm."

The Enano ranger curled his lip. "We guard the Unity that makes us strong. We serve the Throne that sends the seekers. No one, human or Folk, may stand in our way."

"The seekers? What do you—"

"No more words!" Rushing forward, his eyes gleaming in triumph, Kitu aimed his blow at the chest of a foe he deemed too tired to fight.

It was the very impetuosity the Dwarf sought to provoke. Lurching leftward, Har swung his axe in front of his chest, then finished the move with just his right hand extended toward the Enano barreling past him. The blade struck the back of Kitu's thigh. He neither cried out in pain nor dropped his weapon, proving himself no newcomer to combat.

Neither was Har the Tower. With practiced efficiency, he yanked his axe free, spun on his heel, and swung again. The Enano's own turn was a split second too slow. Har's axe took him in the right shoulder, then slashed open his broad chest.

His axe took Kitu's life, as it had once taken Roza's.

Struggling to catch his breath, Har turned his senses to the larger battle. He heard guns firing, blades clashing, horses whinnying, men grunting. Har straightened and looked across the river. Many figures moved among the sparsely spaced trees and bushes.

Willing his muscles to overcome their exhaustion, Har stepped into the little boat and used his axe as a paddle. Soon, he was running toward the battle. There were bodies lying on the field, most moving but a few deathly still. Some wore the light-colored trousers and blue-and-red coats of Mexican soldiers. Others were Texians. The cloud of dust ahead told the story: A good number of David's men made it past the Mexican lines. Most of the reinforcements had, however, been forced to retreat.

Har guessed the latter would return along the Gonzales trail until they found a safe place to camp and await another chance. As for Har, he knew his proper place was far from safe. As the first rays of dawn streaked the sky, he headed back to the Alamo.

~ ~ ~

"Did you see her?"

It was the last question Har had expected when he found an excited David Crockett reloading his gun near the south wall.

"I do not know—"

"The fairy!"

Har shook his head. "The ranger was male, not female. He will never sing again."

"Not back at the river—right here!" David thrust the ramrod down the muzzle. "While I was tyin' up my horse, I saw her comin' out of the chapel. A little woman. Tried runnin' her down, but she was too quick. Then I shed my chivalry and took a shot, only Young Betsy let me down."

Another Duende ranger? "Which way did she—"

Har needn't finish the question, for David began running toward the wooden palisade. The Dwarf trotted after him, catching a fleeting glimpse of a small shape darting behind a distant bush. Perhaps even at such a range, Young Betsy might have recovered her reputation, but a blast of a Mexican battery spoiled David's aim. Moments later, the thud of a cannonball against the wall prompted them to duck. When they looked back at the bush, there was no sign of movement.

Har pointed at the ruined chapel. "What was she doing in there?"

"Can't say. Not much of value inside. And if she'd set fire to the powder magazine, we'd know already."

Not if the fire in question were unnatural! Har hopped off the crate and headed for the door of the mission, his friend right behind him.

The roofless structure was about seventy feet long and sixty feet wide. At the far end, on a raised platform, were three cannons and their crews guarding the eastern approaches to the fort. To Har's left were two small chambers. He entered the first, where gunpowder was stored. Close inspection revealed no enchanted device, and when David questioned the defenders, they reported nothing out of the ordinary.

Puzzled, Har poked his head into the other chamber. It contained barrels of food and other supplies. None appeared to have been tampered with.

As the two exited the chapel, the human pointed to an enclosure just across the plaza. "Gonna look in on Jim Bowie in the hospital. He's pretty bad off."

The Dwarf grunted in assent and glanced back at the old mission. *What am I missing? And how many more Duende do we face?*

~ ~ ~

When David resumed his post after dark, he insisted the Dwarf take a rest. Har went back into the mission and found a shadowy spot in the corner. His eyes wouldn't stay closed, however. They kept staring across the floor at the supply rooms.

Why else would the ranger have come in here? He couldn't think of a reason. As dawn painted the interior of the mission in shades of amber, Har searched the powder magazine again to no avail. He searched the other room. Still, nothing seemed out of place. The Dwarf stomped in frustration.

And jerked in surprise.

Har stomped again. His boot should have made a dull thud against the stone, yet it didn't. The sound was hollow.

He knelt to inspect a large slab set into the floor. Tracing its edges with stubby fingers, Har discovered soft soil. Using a handaxe as a wedge, he gained enough leverage to raise the stone half an inch, then more. Soon he'd lifted the slab perpendicular to the floor, discovering two large handles carved into the opposite side. Using them to move the slab aside, he found a wooden ladder descending into a stygian unknown.

A hidden chamber? Har was sure he'd found what the other ranger had been looking for—and he was also sure she hadn't found it herself, since the dirt around the slab had been undisturbed. He reached into his pouch for the enchanted flints and stave that formed the field equipment of all experienced rangers. Soon, his lit torch revealed a dozen rungs of the ladder extending down to a rough floor of gravel and dirt.

Har was about to explore further when two sounds drew his attention. One was the sound of feet running toward him, the other of singing voices.

The third sound was loudest. "Har, you in here? Come quick! They're bewitchin' the men!"

They?

Hurriedly, the Dwarf slid the slab back into place and ran from the supply room, nearly colliding with David Crockett. "That fairy's back, I reckon, and she's got company!"

When the two emerged, they found nearly all two hundred defenders of the Alamo congregated in the plaza. Colonel Travis stood atop a gunnery platform, addressing the men. Only Har and David seemed to hear the voices *outside* the fort, voices singing low, leaden notes and slow, somber words. And only Har could decipher both languages.

"Our fate is sealed," the taciturn commander of the Alamo told his men in English. "Within a very few days, perhaps a very few hours, we must all be in eternity."

Your courage fades, a setting sun that jealously withdraws its beams, sang the Duende rangers in Folktongue.

"This is our destiny, and we cannot avoid it. This is our certain doom."

Your cause a race already run, a twilight's end, a dusk of dreams.

"I have deceived you long by promise of help. In deceiving you, I also deceived myself."

Its bleak futility confess, a hidden, bitter truth relate.

"We have no hope for help, for no force that we could reasonably have expected could cut its way through the strong ranks of these Mexicans."

Alone, forgotten, powerless, abandoned to a gruesome fate.

David turned to the Dwarf, eyes wide. "Why's Travis speakin' this way?

We got fifty men in yesterday. More are comin'. There's no reason to give up!"

"It is the magic speaking." Har grimaced. By himself, he had little chance of counteracting the Duende spell. He could also think of no other option but to try.

So, he sang.

Har had nothing like Dela's talent for courage spells, but he poured into his song feelings he still possessed in abundance. Grim determination. Surly defiance. A bull-headed stubbornness. He could sense the emotion welling within him, pooling into words, gushing from his throat, animating the pudgy fingers he drew over the strings of the scheitholt he'd pulled from his back. Har could sense its power washing over the Texians and Tejanos in the plaza.

He could also sense it wouldn't be enough.

Then Har saw something completely unexpected—something that filled him with wonder, with relief, with hope. Har saw wings.

The winged figure hovered above the old mission for an instant, then soared over the plaza and past the west wall. While continuing to sing, the Dwarf dashed to the wall and peered through a hole. He watched the slender figure glide over the San Antonio River. The flier landed on a tree, and began to sing.

That is, *he* began to sing. It was a male voice blending his own mood magic with Har's. Whether the voice belonged to his friend Goran Lonefeather, however, the Dwarf couldn't yet be certain. *But it could be Goran.*

From behind him came the voice of Buck Travis, louder and more forceful than before. Har spun around to see the colonel striding down the ramp of the platform and whipping out his sword as if to strike a foe.

"Let us resolve to withstand our adversaries to the last," Travis shouted, "and at each advance to kill as many of them as possible. And when at last they shall storm our fortress, let us kill them as they come! Kill them as they scale our walls! Kill them as they leap within! Kill them as they kill our companions! And continue to kill them as long as one of us shall remain alive!"

Har felt queasy. He'd done his best to combat the Duendes' fear spell. With the help of the flying ranger, he appeared to be succeeding—but at what cost?

"My choice is to stay in this fort and die for my country, fighting as long as breath shall remain in my body," said Travis. Then he drew a long thin line in the dirt with his sword. "I now want every man who is determined to stay here and die with me to come across this line. Who will be the first? March!"

"I am ready to die for my country!" said a Texian, stepping across the line. Others followed, initially in twos and threes, then in larger groups.

The Dwarf met the eyes of David Crockett, standing among the throng of whooping men. The Tennessean sighed and nodded, as if to confirm Har's unspoken realization.

I may only have given these men the courage to be slaughtered.

~ ~ ~

The magical duel continued off and on throughout the day. When the Duendes sang their mood spell, Har countered with a courage spell—and was quickly joined by the flying ranger. When the Duendes stopped singing, the Dwarf headed back to the chapel to investigate the underground chamber. Every time he began to descend the ladder, however, the Duende spell resumed and Har had to respond. The only way to save David and the others, he reasoned, was to combat the Duende spellsong, stiffen the rebel resolve, and trust that reinforcements were on the way from Gonzales or Goliad.

The behavior of his ally outside the walls left Har puzzled. The flier shifted positions many times—perching sometimes in treetops, other times on roofs or belfries in the town beyond the river, but never within the Alamo compound itself. If it was Goran, why didn't he come inside? If not Goran, who else would be helping him?

Har did get a chance to tell David about the underground room, but the Tennessean felt no freer to investigate than the Dwarf. Mexican artillery pounded the Alamo throughout the day, suggesting an ever-present risk of imminent attack. David stayed with his Tennesseans on the palisade.

The situation changed shortly after nightfall. First, the Duendes fell silent. Then the Mexican guns followed. When after several minutes neither form of attack resumed, Har began walking the perimeter of the fort, hoping to communicate with his ally. He saw no sign of the flier.

Frustrated, the Dwarf found David leaning against a wall. "We need to find out what lies beneath the mission."

David shook his head. "Can't leave my post. What if there's an attack?"

"That is why we *both* must go."

Confused but trusting his friend's judgment, David followed Har into the mission and helped move the stone slab. When the human's foot touched the first rung of the ladder, Har held up a hand. "I go, you stay. If they attack, signal me and I will return."

After David nodded, Har lit his torch and started his descent. What would he find below? An old supply chamber? An abandoned water cistern? A trove of treasure, like something out of a human's fairy tale?

It proved to be none of those things. What the Dwarf found was no room at all—it was merely the start of a passageway that stretched south as far as his torch allowed him to see. *Who would dig a tunnel here? And where does it lead?*

At first he walked briskly, holding the torch one hand while running the other along the side of the tunnel, thinking that if it took him below the river, he could tell by the dampness of the walls. Then Har had second thoughts. After all, he could be mistaken about the stone slab being undisturbed. Perhaps the female Duende already knew about the tunnel.

Perhaps she already used it.

Drawing one of his handaxes, Har moved more cautiously down the passageway. If she *had* used the tunnel to get into the Alamo, for some purpose yet unknown, he didn't want to bumble into her or some other enemy.

Even if Folk used the tunnel, humans had certainly dug it. Har could tell by its high ceiling and irregular shape. When Folk excavated, they employed not just pick and shovel but elemental magic that carved smoother, more elaborate structures from the earth. Folk also used a mixture of magecraft and spellsong to shield underground habitats from the prying eyes of humans and the encroachments of all others.

After many minutes, and many hundreds of steps, Har halted. He'd gone a long way and found nothing. If he kept going, that might take him out of range to hear his friend's signal.

"David!" he called over his shoulder. There was no response.

Just as Har turned to retrace his steps, the flickering torchlight fell on a wall a few paces ahead. Part of it was missing! He rushed forward and found a large section had fallen in, revealing another passageway beyond. Unlike the tunnel he'd been traversing, its walls were smooth to the touch.

Magecrafted.

Pulse racing, Har crawled through to explore the new corridor. He saw no sparks, felt no wind or pricks against his skin. Whatever Shimmer wall had once guarded the place was gone. After fifty paces, the passageway opened into a circular chamber. Along its curved walls were seven stone columns extending from a floor of tightly fitted planks to a high ceiling.

A ceremonial center? A guildhall? Har couldn't tell, for any furnishings or other objects that might reveal the room's function had long since been removed. Only the great four-sided columns remained.

Har approached one for a closer look. Each of the column's four surfaces was covered in carvings. Some depicted Folk rangers in mantles, capes, and loincloths interacting with similarly dressed humans. Others showed Folk warriors, hunters, and mages combatting a wide variety of monsters, from hideous giants and enormous birds of prey to reptilian creatures with the heads of dogs and cats. Still others depicted what appeared to be scenes of guildmasters teaching apprentices and grandmasters meeting in council.

On the front surface, just above eye level, was a strip not of illustrations but of letters carved into the stone. Har held his torch high and read the inscription in Folktongue:

Douse the spark, drown the flame
That dares to blaze against the night.
Heat to cold, pride to shame,
From steamy haze to clearest sight.

The stanza of a spellsong, presumably, but one he'd never heard before. Glancing around, he noted bands of Folktongue inscriptions on the other six columns as well. *Additional spellsongs, perhaps? Or more stanzas of the same one?*

A faint popping sound interrupted his speculations. Instantly on alert, Har turned to face the opening. As far as he could tell, it was the only way in or out of the chamber. He stood there, motionless, straining his eyes and ears. After about a minute, he heard the sound again.

This time, he recognized its import. Someone far away, perhaps David Crockett, had fired a rifle.

Though tired from the events of the previous day, the Dwarf did his best approximation of a sprint as he barreled down the corridor, reentered the human-created tunnel, and returned the way he'd come. He heard no more gunshots, and when he reached the ladder, his friend wasn't there.

The Dwarf scrambled up and drew the stone slab into place. It was then he heard another sound, one that brought a groan from his parched lips. It wasn't the report of artillery, small arms fire, or the battle cries of soldiers. Nor was it the sound of the Duendes resuming their mood spell.

They'd changed tactics. The Duendes were now singing a sleep spell. And by the looks of the Alamo's defenders when Har emerged from the chapel, it was working. A few were already curled up on the ground, fast asleep. Others were stumbling along unsteadily or sitting with their backs against a wall, seemingly in a daze.

"Thank God!" yelled David Crockett from the palisade. He was shaking one of his snoozing Tennesseans. "Might be fixin' to attack!"

Har nodded and pulled his scheitholt over his shoulder. A moment later he was countering the Duende magic with a spell of his own, one designed to heighten the humans' alertness and determination. Shortly after that, and to his immense relief, he heard the now familiar voice of the flying ranger joining him.

While continuing to sing, Har strode to the west wall, the one facing the Mexican-occupied town of San Antonio. His ally's voice came from that direction. Soon, he spotted a small figure as it rose from a treetop and flew toward the Alamo. Was he finally deciding to join Har within the fort? The Dwarf felt another wave of relief.

The feeling abruptly disappeared, replaced with alarm, for Har glimpsed the shape of another winged figure against the starry sky. It was chasing the first. It was swifter. It was gaining. Then Har heard the twang of a bowstring and saw the first flier jerk in midair.

Goran! Har screamed, but only in his head. The rest of his body kept singing and playing, even as he watched the second flier catch up with the first. There was a brief struggle. The wounded ranger jerked again, then fell, twisting and spinning.

Deprived of assistance, Har felt the power of his counterspell diminish.

Several humans he'd managed to rouse began to slip back into a magically induced slumber. While he yearned to climb over the wall and discover whether his ally was dead or merely injured—and whether the ally was indeed his best friend—Har resisted the temptation. He knew his magic couldn't last for long against two Duende spellsingers.

And when enough of the garrison was asleep, he knew Santa Anna's army would attack.

~ ~ ~

At it happened, Har the Tower—singing his counterspell from a gunnery platform on the west wall—wasn't the Alamo's only defense against magical assault. Another was the dogged determination of David Crockett. As minutes became hours, the Tennessean walked the length and breadth of the fort, poking sleeping men awake and exhorting drowsy men to their feet. Their other defense, one the Duendes eventually concluded they could never fully overcome, was the sheer number of rebels inside.

Many times, Har had discussed the decreasing potency of spellsong with Goran, Dela, and other rangers. All agreed temperamental magic was less effective in the Blur than they'd been taught to expect. Americans were especially resistant, it seemed, though Har had never heard a satisfactory explanation for it. Texians weren't Americans any more, strictly speaking, and the Tejanos never had been. Still, for whatever reason, the Duendes were incapable of putting them all to sleep.

Nor, in the end, did it prove necessary.

Just before sunrise, the Duende spellsong abruptly ceased. Before Har and David could do any more than exchange questioning looks, a rocket exploded above the fort. For an instant, its walls and all that stood, sat, or lay within them were revealed in a flash of yellow. It darkened to fiery orange, then blood red. "*Viva la Republica!*" cried a voice dangerously close to the west wall. "*Viva Santa Anna!*" answered another voice south of the palisade.

"They're here!" David yelled. A few other defenders took up his call or shouted their own warnings. To his left, Har spotted Buck Travis sprinting toward the battered north wall, carrying a shotgun in one hand and waving his sword with the other. "Come on, boys!" the colonel shouted. "The

Mexicans are upon us, and we'll give them hell!"

Then came the cacophony. Bugles blared. Cannons roared. Muskets barked. Rifles spat. Blades clanged. Men whooped, and groaned, and breathed their last breaths. Everywhere he looked, the Dwarf saw Texians and Tejanos confront the uniformed Mexican soldiers who'd climbed over or picked their way through the crumbled walls.

For an instant, Har's indecision returned. It was one thing to help stave off the Mexican attack in the hope of a peaceful resolution, however unlikely, or to protect his friend. It was quite another to help kill Mexican soldiers. Besides, there was another outside the wall who might also need his protection. Another friend, perhaps—though Har prayed it had not been Goran Lonefeather—or at least a fallen ally to whom he owed a debt.

Then three sights drove indecision forever from Har's mind. First, he witnessed two soldiers in blue coats and gray trousers fire at a Texian trying to surrender. Next he saw a white-uniformed grenadier drive his bayonet into the back of a wounded, helpless Tejano. The truth struck the Dwarf like a blinding light: There had never been any chance of saving these men. Whether they fought or surrendered, they would die. Santa Anna wanted their deaths more than he wanted the Alamo.

The third sight that transformed Har the Tower from watcher to warrior was of David Crockett standing before the palisade, his coonskin cap askew, his forehead painted red, swinging the butt of his rifle at the head of a foeman—while two other Mexicans charged him from behind.

"Look out!" Har cried, but he did more than that. His handaxe found the throat of one assailant. His battleaxe would have found the other had David not spun and drove the blade of his hunting knife into the charging man's breast.

"Pull back to the church!" David yelled, leading the way across the crowded courtyard. Six Tennesseans followed him. Har brought up the rear, making retreat possible with a hastily sung illusion spell.

David surely knew their cause was lost and figured they'd purchase their lives more dearly in a defensible position. Har knew something even more important about the old chapel, something his friend did not: that it offered more than just a chance for glory. It offered a chance for escape.

As the others barricaded the entrance with sandbags, Har yanked David's arm. "I found a tunnel. A way out."

"Where does it lead?"

"I do not know, but there is an abandoned Folk village beneath San Antonio. Many places to hide. And perhaps a passage to the surface."

"Show me!"

They dashed to the storage room and shoved the slab aside. David gazed into inky blackness. "How will we see down there?"

Har pulled out his torch. "I will place it at the foot of the ladder." He lowered himself into the passage and scrambled down as quickly as he could. When he reached bottom, he lit the torch and looked up.

To his surprise, David was still there. "Wasn't that fairy woman lookin' for the tunnel? And maybe that village of yours?"

Har recalled the room with the seven ornately carved columns. "Could be. Make haste, now! Call your men!"

"She's in league with Santa Anna." The human clenched his jaw. "Can't let her find it!"

The Dwarf dropped the torch and grabbed the first rung of the ladder. Even before he heard the heavy slab scrape the floor, he'd guessed what his friend had in mind. "No! Your life is—"

"— my life, to spend as I wish," David insisted, his grim smile still visible through the narrowing crescent of space. "Besides, most men are remembered as they died, and not as they lived."

"I will not see you die!" Har insisted.

"True enough," David agreed, "but don't worry about me. I am with friends." Then the stone dropped into place.

Har kept climbing, intent on forcing the lid and rescuing David, whether the human liked it or not. When he reached the top and pushed against the slab, however, he found it immovable. His friend must have piled other objects atop the lid before rejoining the other defenders. Again and again, Har drove his shoulder against the stone. It refused to budge.

Reluctantly, Har climbed down and picked up the torch. Then came the sounds of voices, and of heavy objects striking or dragging across the floor above. Had David reconsidered and led his men to the only safe way out of the Alamo?

No.

Har turned and ran, his bouncing torch casting shadows along the floor of the tunnel, for the voices were speaking Folktongue.

~ ~ ~

Many minutes later, when the Dwarf reached the junction with the narrower Folk passageway, he heard the faint footsteps that signified pursuit. By sacrificing his last hope for escape, David Crockett had purchased a significant head start for his friend.

I must make the most of it—whatever that may be.

The safest course, he knew, was to follow the original tunnel as far as it would take him. Presumably the humans of San Antonio had dug it for a reason, likely as an escape route in case Indians attacked the mission. If so, it probably led to a building in town, or even one of the other missions in the vicinity. Once he reached the surface, he might be able to find the fallen fairy who'd rendered him aid and, if possible, return the favor.

Nevertheless, Har kept hearing David's resolute words in his mind. *She's in league with Santa Anna. Can't let her find it!* Har knew what "it" meant: the abandoned Folk village, not the tunnel. There must be something there the Duendes wanted, something of great value. He was but one ranger facing two enemies, at least. Still, he had the element of surprise—and, perhaps, one other edge.

I am no deep thinker, gifted strategist, or clever diplomat, but I am a Tower. I can take a punch—and punch back harder.

The Dwarf scrambled through the hole. He could have proceeded into the circular chamber to stage his ambush, but Har chose to stay at the mouth of the passageway. Its tighter confines better suited his purpose. He doused the torch and waited in darkness. Soon he saw the flickering lights of Duende torches, and their approaching voices became distinct enough for him to interpret.

"I hear the old crone lasted three hours before the rack loosened her tongue," said a female voice.

"A crude human device, to be sure," answered a male, "but not without its uses."

"Though her tongue be loosened, it spoke more riddles than answers. We know only the location of the treasure, not its size or shape."

"Aya said we will know it when we see it."

So, the yellow-haired one isn't with them. Har took comfort in that. When he had met the Duendes in Nacogdoches, the Xana woman struck him as the most dangerous. And he'd already eliminated the most powerfully built one, the Enano ranger Kitu.

"Look there!" the female exclaimed. "This must be it!"

Har tightened his grip on the battleaxe. Bright torchlight cast a shadow of the corridor's opening against the far wall. He would get no more than a couple of swings. He had to make them count.

And he did. The first slashed the back of the first figure to pass through the opening.

The second swing of his axe took another in the chest as he tried to enter.

"Ambush!" screamed the female voice.

"There could be others ahead!" warned the male.

I face more than two Duendes, then. The thought sprung to mind even as Har leapt through the opening, intent on taking advantage of their confusion.

The twang of the bowstring warned him just in time to duck. The whistling arrow passed an inch above his stocking cap and continued its flight down the tunnel. Snorting like a bull, Har charged forward, brushing aside the winged fairy and knocking the bow from his grasp. Before the Dwarf stood the slight dark-haired form of Oina. She held no blade, no bow, no weapon of any kind, only her wooden flute. She made no effort to block his charge. She merely stepped aside and spoke a single word.

"Shoot!"

Iron teeth flashed wicked smiles. Iron throats belched smoke and shot. The Tower shook. Pain stabbed his shoulder and hip. *I face more than two enemies, yes, but not all are Duendes*. Har saw flickering torchlight reflected in the shiny bayonets of bewitched Mexican soldiers. Then the Tower toppled.

~ ~ ~

He was still alive. That was Har's first surprise when he regained consciousness. The second was that the only pain he felt was from musket wounds in his shoulder and hip. The Duendes had apparently left him for dead, not bothering to have their humans stab him to make sure. He lay there motionless for a time—"playin' possum," as David would call it—listening for voices or footsteps. He heard neither. His enemies were long gone.

Groaning, Har rose to his knees, revealing a smear of blood on the ground and comparable stains on his jerkin, tunic, and trousers. His wounds burned, his hands and feet felt numb, his ears rang, and Har found it difficult to keep his eyes focused. Wincing and wheezing, he managed to force himself to his feet, only to lose his balance and fall against the wall of the tunnel.

They had good reason to leave me for dead. I soon will be.

His mind told him that was true. His heart didn't argue the point, not really, but it did lay claim to defining the term "soon."

I must survive long enough to discover why my killers came here. And whether my friends have joined me in death.

Ripping strips of cloth from his tattered cloak, Har bound his hip and shoulder wounds as best he could. Then he relit his torch and walked—or, more precisely, stumbled—into the lower-ceiling corridor that led to the chamber. The columns were still there, seemingly intact. If the Duendes had entered, they had left no sign and hauled not so much as a stone away.

How long Har shuffled, limped, and sometimes crawled his way along the tunnel to the Alamo, he couldn't say. When he reached the ladder, it took nearly all his remaining strength to drag his aching body up the rungs. If the Duendes had left this way, they made no effort to block the exit. Even in his weakened condition, Har was able to move the slab and clamber into the storage room.

He knew the battle was long over, and that Santa Anna had prevailed. What Har hadn't expected was to find the mission deserted. He lumbered into the plaza. It was nearly sundown. All around him were blasted buildings and crumbled walls. In the fading light, he could see countless stripes and tracks in the dirt. The Mexicans had apparently removed all the weapons, supplies, and casualties from the fort. Weren't they even going to occupy the position they'd fought so hard to take, that the rebels had fought so hard to defend? Har could scarcely believe it. Had he and his friends come here to die for no purpose?

My friends!

A wave of nausea made him double over and retch. His knees buckled. Still, the mighty heart of Har the Tower refused to surrender to his mortal wounds. Not yet. He had to find out what happened to David, and to the winged fairy. Both answers lay outside the Alamo.

Har stumbled to the west wall. Peering through the cracks in the rubble, he spied several squads of soldiers grouped around bonfires. Some poked the flames with sticks and bayonets. Others were dragging what appeared to be logs onto the fires.

Har sucked in a ragged breath. *Those are not logs. They are corpses.*

Dead Mexicans would be receiving Christian burials, he knew. The soldiers were burning Texians and Tejanos. If David Crockett had perished during the battle, his remains were already among the ashes piled around the bonfires or would soon be there. And if David had been taken alive, Har had every reason to be believe the human's fate was the same. The Dwarf had witnessed the massacre of Alamo defenders suffering from grievous wounds or holding up white cloths of surrender. Santa Anna had ordered no quarter be given to the rebels of Texas.

Whispering a prayer for his fallen friend, Har next directed his attention to the spot by the river where the winged fairy had plummeted to the ground. Slowly, laboriously, he picked his way through the rubble and trudged across the field. Between coughs, he sang the first few bars of a concealment spell, though he knew it wouldn't matter if Duende rangers were nearby—and probably wouldn't matter even if they were gone.

Har was done for. All he wanted to know now was if his best friend was done for, too. It didn't take long to find out, though Har never found the body of his fallen ally.

What he did find in the bushes by the river were several items clearly belonging to the flying ranger. Perhaps the Mexicans had discovered the body, deemed it that of a Texian boy who'd tried to escape, and discarded his unfamiliar equipment before dragging the corpse to a bonfire. One of the items was a ranger's kit that could well have belonged to Goran. It contained several strips of dried meat, two unused torches, a roll of parchment, a water flask, another flask containing a darker liquid, and a small ocarina fashioned from horn.

It wasn't his friend's, though. Goran played a flute, not an ocarina. And the Sylph would have had no need for the other items the Mexicans had tossed aside: a small backpack with crisscrossing straps and two thin pieces of translucent material.

Goran Lonefeather had no need for artificial wings. Har's ally had been an Elf.

The Dwarf's reaction wasn't surprise at the realization, nor curiosity about its implications. The image that sprung to mind, as it had during his initial ride to the Alamo, was the bittersweet memory of his erstwhile friend, the Elf ranger Roza. She'd worn artificial wings like these during the battle for Spirit Forest. Back then it was Har serving in a besieging army, and Roza in defense of a stronghold. She hadn't been wearing wings when Har killed her, though. She'd given them up to join the doomed garrison in the final melee. She'd given up hope and accepted her fate.

So had Har the Tower—until he experienced another memory of Roza, a memory of when she'd helped him escape.

Reaching into the Elf's pack, Har pulled out the flask with the dark liquid and held it up. The pale rays of the setting sun make its contents sparkle and swirl. Removing the cork, he downed half the liquid in one greedy gulp.

~ ~ ~

The healing potion took effect almost immediately—dulling his pain, restoring vitality to his extremities, making it easier for Har to breathe. Still, he knew its two doses would give him only a few hours of respite. The potion couldn't heal his injuries entirely. Har resolved to use the time to make his escape.

Returning to the Alamo, he first rebound his wounds with greater care. Then he ate the meager rations scrounged from the Elf's pack, supplementing the meal with corn and beans stolen from the cookpot of a snoozing soldier. He had to build up his strength. He had to get to Sam Houston, to let him know he'd been right about the Duendes. To reach him meant first surviving the seventy-mile journey back to Gonzales.

Har decided to visit the Mexican army's camp for supplies before setting out. When he reached the west wall, however, the Dwarf halted in his tracks. He saw some two dozen torches bobbing up and down across the field. Many times that number of Mexican soldiers were approaching the fort. There were no more bodies inside to burn, so Har drew the obvious conclusion: they were coming to complete their destruction of the Alamo.

He thought quickly. With their intentions thus diverted, it would be easier for the Dwarf to steal supplies, take one of their horses, and flee. As it had before, however, the fierce loyalty of Har the Tower challenged his rational faculty.

My friend died defending this place, his heart insisted. *I nearly did, as well. I will not let them destroy it!*

Sam Houston is your friend, too, and needs your help, his mind replied. *Besides, you cannot hold off so many humans for long.*

This time, his heart yielded. Sighing, Har turned and walked back into the ruined mission—then spun back around, his mind and heart now united in a common realization, devoted to a common purpose.

I still do not know why the Duendes came to this place. I will never know if I let them destroy it.

Har's eyes now blazed with intensity, and he let the sensation guide his magic. Yanking out his scheitholt and plucking a chord, Har began to sing an illusion spell. He allowed himself to grieve the death of David Crockett and the rest of the garrison. He allowed his grief to transform into resolution, into anger, into vengeful fury. He pictured the defenders' corpses pulled unceremoniously from the newly hallowed ground of the Alamo and stacked like firewood, reduced to fuel for Santa Anna's unholy funeral pyres.

These were the images Har saw in his mind as he sang. The approaching soldiers, intent on carrying out the orders of General Antonio López de Santa Anna, saw something else entirely. To their un-Sighted eyes, what materialized in front the Alamo mission was a row of six unearthly figures, enormous and terrifying. Their yellow-orange eyes smoldered. Clutched in their claws—for they were too monstrous to have human hands—were glowing swords that drew circles of flame high above their horned heads.

"*Diablo*!" breathed one soldier.

"*Demonio*!" screeched another.

The Mexicans halted, faltered, panicked. Their officers tried in vain to urge them forward. Then a general in a fancy white uniform rode up to the front of the column, dismounted a fancy white horse, and waved his fancy sword over his fancy plumed hat. In response to his stentorian commands, some of the soldiers began to shuffle forward again.

Har let his thoughts wander further afield—to his shameful betrayal by Prince Veelund, his humiliating confinement at Spirit Forest, the pitiful suffering of his friend Goran, and the continuing captivity of Dela the Water Maiden. His righteous anger became blinding hatred. Fire became conflagration.

Then another shape appeared within the Alamo, a gigantic shape looming high over the crumbled walls of the mission. Its oblong head began with a screaming mouth full of coals and ended with a tall tuft of flaming hair. Its hands—there were at least two of them—held spinning balls of fire.

"Leave my house," warned the screaming mouth, "and never return!"

It was all too much for the Mexicans. Some slumped to their knees and cowered, praying for deliverance. Others broke and fled, including the man in a fancy white uniform who no longer wore a fancy plumed hat on his now shaking head.

When all the soldiers were gone, their childhood superstitions now transformed into lasting fears, a drained but determined Har the Tower strode forth and strapped himself to the fancy white horse as best he could. He knew the potion's effects would fade, that in his weakened condition it would be a very difficult ride to Gonzales.

So be it. I may totter.

But I will not fall.

Chapter 10 – The President

April 1836

IT WASN'T SUPPOSED TO BE like this. Not after the delegates had declared independence, written a constitution for the new Republic of Texas, and voted to confirm General Sam Houston as commander in chief.

All that did was give them someone to blame.

The weary general emerged from his tent and swept his eyes across the ragtag army camped on the west bank of the Brazos River.

It wasn't supposed to be like this. The garrisons at San Antonio de Béxar and Goliad were to fall back and merge with Sam's army, giving him enough men to strike Santa Anna in force. Instead, some two hundred brave men had stayed behind at the Alamo, fought, and been butchered. And some three hundred and fifty men had stayed behind in Goliad, gotten caught, and been butchered.

Their deaths gave us martyrs. I'd rather have live soldiers.

Sam mopped his brow and thought of the man sleeping in his tent. No, it sure wasn't supposed to be like this. Suspecting the president-general of Mexico had Duende allies, Sam had hoped for magical assistance of his own—but his Nunnehi friend, Tana Song Snake, was in the Indian Territory. Of Goran Lonefeather and his search for Dela, he'd heard nothing. The only fairy to arrive in Sam's camp was Har the Tower, gravely wounded and delirious, ranting about mysterious foes and underground cities.

I didn't need another infirm man to care for. I needed a spellsinger.

Sam stepped onto the bluff and watched the crew of the steamship *Yellow Stone* stacking cotton bales to make room on the deck. Otherwise distracted, he took no notice of the approaching footsteps until the messenger was behind him. "Mister Rusk's here."

Wheeling around, Sam glared at a portly young man in a tattered hat.

"What was that, soldier?"

The youth gaped for a moment, then jerked a dirty hand toward his eyebrow in a clumsy salute. "I…I mean, *General* Houston, sir, the secretary of war's here."

Sam nodded, then rolled his eyes as the boy fled down the hill. *Shouldn't beat up on him. This "soldier" was probably chopping wood or slopping hogs a month ago. Even after weeks of drilling, I command less an army than a pack of semiwild animals.*

As for Thomas Jefferson Rusk, now trudging up the hill to see Sam, a month ago the attorney from Georgia had been just one of dozens of delegates at the Texas Convention. Now the interim president of Texas, David Burnet, had made Rusk his secretary of war.

And, I suppose, my superior. Is he here to confer, give orders, or replace me?

~ ~ ~

"President Burnet says to retreat no farther. The country expects you to fight."

"The country?" Sam exploded in irritation. "You passed half the country on your way here, didn't you? They may want *us* to fight, but all they care about is flight."

Secretary Rusk said nothing. He didn't need to. Both men had witnessed the multitudes of panicky settlers, rickety wagons, and snorting livestock streaming out of central Texas. Some called the exodus the "Runaway Scape." Sam himself had helped set it off several weeks ago when he arrived at Gonzales, got word of the Alamo disaster from survivors (including Har), and urged all the residents of the area to follow his small army eastward, to the banks of the Brazos. While the evacuation kept civilians and supplies out of Santa Anna's clutches, Sam thought it might also convince displaced Texians and Tejanos to join his army. Fewer than expected did so, and some proved only temporary recruits. Resentful of Sam's relentless drilling, or perhaps just disenchanted with his refusal to hunt for Santa Anna, they slipped away from the army to rejoin the Runaway Scrape.

"Pulling back to the Brazos made sense," Rusk allowed, "and you insisted you had no intention of crossing it. You blamed deserters for spreading rumors to the contrary, but I can see men clearing the deck of that steamship to turn it into a ferry. Does that make *you* a deserter now?"

Uncertain of Rusk's intentions, Sam thought it best to interpret his question as a joke. "I've been sorely tempted to desert, especially at dinner time. With all the head of cattle stomping by, you think we'd get a mouthful of good beef."

"Or maybe a mouthful of something else?" Rusk pressed.

Already flushed with frustration, Sam's cheeks turned a darker shade of red. It was obvious what the secretary of war meant. Many critics thought their commander in chief had lost his nerve and was trying to find it at the bottom of a liquor bottle.

It's a lie! he wanted to yell.

It *was* a lie. Whatever mistakes he may have made since the start of the war, resuming his worst habit wasn't one of them—but would Thomas Rusk or anyone else take the word of a drunk?

No.

Sam had to find a better way than angry denials to convince Rusk to trust his judgment. *Fairy magic would sure come in handy about now*. He thought again of his friend in the tent, feverish and weak. Sam had never fully recovered from his own wounds suffered twenty-two years earlier at Horseshoe Bend. He owed it to Har to leave him be, to let the Dwarf try to heal.

"I have every intention of keeping Santa Anna on this side of the Brazos," Sam said calmly. "That's why I sent the two companies under Wiley Martin and Mosely Baker to guard the river crossings."

"Which just so happened to get two of your angriest critics away from the army," Rusk pointed out.

True enough, but if I learned anything from Crockett's campfire tales, it's that shooting when the partridges line up in a pretty row is a handy way to save on gunpowder. Sam thought sadly of the former congressman, another fallen friend.

"They're angry, yes," Sam allowed, "but anger is not enough. It was Odysseus who defeated Troy, not Achilles."

Rusk's eyes narrowed. "What's that?"

"The timeless wisdom of Homer, captured in the very first lines." Sam smiled and began reciting:

Achilles' wrath, to Greece the direful spring
Of woes unnumbered, heavenly goddess, sing!
That wrath which hurled to Pluto's gloomy reign
The souls of mighty chiefs untimely slain;
Whose limbs unburied on the naked shore,
Devouring dogs and hungry vultures tore.

"I did not travel here for a poetry lesson, sir," Rusk interjected. "This is a council of war."

Sam felt as if the other man had slapped him across the face. *A slap I well deserve. Did I expect to impress him with my memory? Beguile him with my oratory?*

He tried a different tack. "The river's rising. If our camp floods, we'll have to relocate west to the open prairie, where Santa Anna can encircle us, or else get our men across to the east bank for safety. Just keeping our options open."

Rusk looked skeptical. "President Burnet says your only option is to fight."

"We *will* fight—when we're ready, on ground we choose. I have kept the army together under most discouraging circumstances. You can be sure I'll only cross the Brazos to act with more effect against the enemy."

"I am sure of little these days," said Rusk in a weary voice. "Neither David Burnet nor I have anything resembling your military training, I grant you. What I know of war comes from stories I've heard from men like my father-in-law. He fought in the Creek War, as you did, though his most fabulous tales were of his grandfather's exploits during the Revolution."

"Oh?" Sam seized the opportunity to build rapport. "My father also served in that war. What was his name? The grandfather, I mean, not your father-in-law."

Rusk grinned. "Both men had the same name: Benjamin Cleveland."

"The militia colonel at Kings Mountain?"

"The very same. You've heard of him?"

Kings Mountain! Sam had learned much about the battle from elderly Tennesseans and Carolinians who'd fought there, as well as from David Crockett's account of his father, John, serving in Isaac Shelby's regiment and Goran Lonefeather's own account of the fairies and monsters involved. When they were last in Washington together, Sam and David had even talked about Kings Mountain with the author of a book about it, a John P. Kennedy, and another writer named Poe.

Inspiration struck. Sam recalled the tale of Shelby, Cleveland, and the other American commanders charging up Kings Mountain from all sides. *Perhaps it's not fairy magic or epic verse I need to accomplish my task.*

"I'd be pleased to hear those Kings Mountain tales of yours, sir," Sam said. "The way I heard it, the British major, Patrick Ferguson, let himself get surrounded. Is that what happened?"

~ ~ ~

Several days later, after the Mexicans had moved past Baker's position and prepared to overwhelm Martin at the river crossing, Sam issued the order he wasn't supposed to issue. He ordered the army of Texas to retreat across the Brazos.

Secretary of War Thomas Rusk, standing at his side, watched approvingly as the steamship *Yellow Stone* ferried its first cargo of soldiers to the east bank of the river. "I know it's necessary, Sam, but David Burnet will have both our heads."

"I am more concerned about President-General Santa Anna than Interim President Burnet." The general turned to an aide. "Send word to all regiments. They are to congregate at Donoho's farm, about three miles east of here."

As the aide scurried off, Rusk threaded his fingers together. "Then what? Do you concentrate our forces in case they come right at us?"

"Defeating the republic's sole remaining army would bring our rebellion to a sorry end," Sam agreed, "though we can't be certain of their next move. Whatever it is, we best counter it from a position of strength. I still have some aces up my sleeve."

"The Twin Sisters, you mean." It had been Rusk who'd informed Sam that the two donated cannons were on the way from Ohio—and that they already bore the nickname the Twin Sisters.

The imminent arrival of the guns would aid his plan, yes, but Sam opted not to tell the secretary of war the rest of it. If Sam still deemed the army of Texas too outnumbered or green to risk in open battle, he'd keep retreating eastward—over the San Jacinto River next, then the Trinity, even as far as the Sabine River that divided Texas from Louisiana. Such a retreat would act as his version of a Trojan horse, a trap to stretch Santa Anna's supply lines and pull Mexican conscripts further away from their homeland. And if Sam knew Andrew Jackson—and he figured he knew the man better than anyone else did—America's president would have American troops waiting just over the Sabine with orders to use any pretext possible to assist the Texian cause.

Despite their budding friendship, however, Sam wasn't sure Thomas Rusk would endorse such a plan. He reminded himself that Odysseus used not just cleverness, but guile to prevail.

Sam tried not to dwell on the fact that on his way home to Ithaca, Odysseus got every other member of his crew killed.

~ ~ ~

The Twin Sisters arrived just as the *Yellow Stone* was ferrying the last troops to the east bank. After Baker's and Martin's detachments arrived at the rendezvous point, the army was nine hundred strong, newly supplied—and just as resentful as before. Sam had already threatened to arrest and execute deserters but soon realized any attempt to carry out the sentence would only make things worse.

While the men ate their supper, he kept himself busy by directing several recruits to gather scrap iron and broken horseshoes for the blacksmith to make into grapeshot for their new cannons. Sam even pitched in at the forge, determined to demonstrate his dedication.

Exhausted and covered in sweat and grime, Sam trudged back to his tent to check on Har. Soon, he heard footsteps approaching. "Uh, mister?" said a thin, reedy voice in what Sam recognized as an Irish accent. "Can ya help me?"

The skinny lad waiting outside the tent looked no more than sixteen. "Look here," he said, shaking an old flintlock at Sam.

"What do you think you're—"

"Had to bring me da's gun," the Irishman continued. "Not been fired in years."

Having stifled his initial impulse to curse, Sam now struggled not to giggle. "Sure looks it," he said appraisingly, "but why bring it to me?"

The sallow-faced youth looked surprised. "Ya be the blacksmith, aye? The other lads said take it to the blacksmith. Can't ya fix it?"

Sam smiled, both at the new recruit and the prank being played on both of them. "I expect I can."

The youth headed off into the night.

Sometime later—long after Sam had removed the lock, cleaned it, fitted it back into the old rifle, and lay down to rest—he was awakened by someone nervously clearing his throat outside the tent.

That'll be my customer. "Be right with you, son." Sam slipped on his boots and scooped up the repaired rifle.

The young man looked paler than before. "I…uh…Mister General, sir, I be sorry. They said ya was a blacksmith. Had no idea that—"

"My friend, they told you right—I *am* a very good blacksmith." Sam gave the lad a searching look. "What's your name, private?"

"Lane, sir. Walter Lane."

Sam worked the rifle's lock. "She's in good order now, Lane, and I hope you're going to do some good fighting with her."

The lad gulped and took the gun. "Do me best, sir."

Returning to his tent, Sam kicked off his boots again and lay down, feeling better than he had in days. It was not his destiny to get much sleep that night, though. No sooner had he closed his eyes than stomping hooves roused him.

This time, two riders waited outside his tent. One was a black man on a mule. The other was Thomas Rusk on a horse. "Here's a ferryman from downriver, General Houston," the latter explained. "He says the Mexicans forced him to carry them over the Brazos. Also says Santa Anna sent him with a message for you."

"That so?"

"Yes, sir." The man removed a folded paper from his coat pocket.

The message was in English. Sam read it aloud: "Mr. Houston, I know you're up there hiding in the bushes. As soon as I catch the other land thieves, I'm coming up there to smoke you out."

"Land thieves, are we?" Rusk snorted. "That such a lawless dictator would be brazen enough to—"

"The president-general gave you this himself?" Sam asked eagerly.

The ferryman nodded. "May I go get somethin' to eat, sir?"

Dismissing him with a wave, Sam fought yet another urge to laugh.

"What is it, Sam? What's made you so giddy?"

Sam clapped him on the shoulder. "Go tell the officers to get ready to march."

If the secretary of war resented getting orders from a general, Rusk gave no sign of it. He merely looked confused.

"Hurry, man!" Sam insisted. "Time is now our bitter enemy."

As he watched the man gallop off, Sam recalled another line from Homer: *"Bold is the task, when subjects, grown too wise, instruct a monarch where his error lies."*

I no longer need to spring my Sabine River trap. Santa Anna's built a Trojan horse of his own. Now we've got to figure a way inside it.

~ ~ ~

His head throbbed. His bad shoulder ached. His bad hip burned. His empty stomach growled. By all rights, the two-mile ride south from Harrisburg should have left him exhausted, grumpy, and desperate for the relief, however fleeting, of a stiff drink.

As Sam Houston passed the last stand of trees and spied a group of Texians about to cross Buffalo Bayou, however, he felt better than he had in weeks. His mount had a lot to do with that. The gray stallion was a magnificent animal, sleek and swift. A mount fit for some knight-errant of old, a sharp contrast to the skinny ponies and broken-down carthorses Sam had ridden lately. Following Homer's lead, he'd named the stallion Xanthus after one of the immortal horses of Achilles.

He's worth every penny of the three hundred dollars I didn't pay for him.

Sam first spotted Xanthus during the Runaway Scape, which took him by the farm of an old friend. It was the friend who owned the beautiful stallion—and to whom Sam wrote a promissory note.

If I survive what's coming, it won't be hard to scare up three hundred dollars. If not, I won't need to.

At the moment, he was inclined to optimism, and it wasn't just because Sam was riding a proper general's horse. After weeks of hard drilling and tedium in their camp on the Brazos, his men had initially found just as much to grumble about when Sam suddenly ordered them to strike camp. Many suspected another ignominious retreat. It was only when they reached a fork in the road that they learned otherwise. A left turn would take the army northeast to Nacogdoches and relative safety. A right turn would take them southeast toward the republic's temporary capital, Harrisburg, and possible danger.

"Columns right," Sam ordered. The men cheered.

Still, many doubted his intentions. Some had even taken the left-hand road with Wylie Martin's company, preferring to escort civilian refugees to Nacogdoches rather than follow any more orders from their drunken coward of a general.

They just don't understand. Santa Anna's letter changed everything.

The president-general had foolishly told Sam exactly where the Mexican army was headed: to capture David Burnet and the interim government. Intent on capturing Burnet at Harrisburg, Santa Anna had raced ahead with only a few hundred soldiers, leaving the bulk of the Mexican army behind. Burnet slipped away at the last minute. When Sam reached Harrisburg and learned Santa Anna was continuing the chase, he did the same. Finally, they had a chance.

If we can catch Santa Anna in time.

"Ho, there!" he called to the Texians on the riverbank. "Where's the ferryboat?"

"Ain't much of one," said a grizzled farmer. "Raft of scrounged timbers. Just got them Twin Sisters loaded when a plank broke. Take a while to replace."

"Ladies always take more time to get ready than menfolk do," Sam replied, "but in my experience, it's worth the wait."

There was an explosion of laughter. "Just wait till Santa Anna gets a look at them Sisters!" the farmer exclaimed.

"I look forward to making the introduction." Eyeing a stretch of open ground, Sam beckoned to a lieutenant. "If we're to wait, let's make the best of it. Send word to assemble the men."

Whether eager for information, hungry for inspiration, or curious about their commander's sobriety, the soldiers of Republic of Texas soon filled the gap between the river and the woods. Sam scanned their faces—some excited, others grim, a few panicked, and more than a few openly disrespectful—and found two of the latter among his officers. Colonel Sidney Sherman, commander of the Second Regiment, flashed the general a mocking smile. And standing in front of a company of Tejanos was their captain, Juan Seguín, the former mayor of San Antonio. Keeping his sharp eyes averted, Seguín's lips curled into a sneer.

Sam couldn't really blame the man. Concerned the Texians might mistake Seguín's recruits for the enemy, Sam had originally ordered them to stay behind in Harrisburg to guard their supplies. After Seguín challenged the order—Tejanos had as much reason to hate the dictator Santa Anna as anyone, he'd insisted—Sam changed his mind, but Seguín still felt affronted.

Sam raised his hands. "Gentlemen, if you please."

Most of the crowd paid him no heed. They continued to whisper, converse, or argue.

Now is not the time for soothing words, Sam admonished himself. *You have stepped onstage. Play your part.* He tried to recall every stirring line from every speech he'd ever heard or given. Then he let his mind fix, like a compass needle pointing north, on the immortal words of a long-dead poet.

"Warriors of Texas!" he shouted. "Our moment of glory has come!"

That quieted the men.

"Today, we are in preparation to meet Santa Anna," Sam continued. "The army will cross, and we will meet the enemy. We go to conquer. It is our only chance to save our beloved Texas. The enemy is cruel. He sweeps over our wide land, and tramples afoot our lives and our liberties. He cannot be defeated by words sweet as honey. Only sour lead and bitter iron can bring an end to his tyrannies.

"The odds may be against us. Some may perish, but for what greater cause than liberty may we spend our lives? What greater bliss may we feel than to be forever honored, forever mourned? It is our place to fight. It is Heaven's to give success. I feel the inspiration in every fiber of my being. Trust in the God of the just and fear not!

"The wretch who trembles in the field of fame meets a fate worse than death: eternal shame. Brave men need no miraculous sign to draw their swords. They need no omen but their country's cause. You serve me most by serving your country best. And soldiers, you'll serve your country best by charging at the foe with these words on your lips: Remember the Alamo! Remember Goliad! Remember La Bahía!"

A young man pushed his way to the front. Sam recognized him as Walter Lane, who'd mistaken him for a blacksmith. "Remember the Alamo!" repeated the scrawny youth.

"Remember Goliad!" yelled Thomas Rusk, thrusting his fist into the air.

"Remember La Bahía!" cried Juan Seguín, now meeting Sam's gaze and offering a curt nod.

Hundreds of hearty shouts later, Texians and Tejanos were thronging the shore, calling for the ferry or trying to coax their reluctant horses across Buffalo Bayou. Sam sighed in relief and turned away. His eyes sought out his own mount, tied to a nearby tree. Xanthus was bucking against the tether, as if even the gray stallion had been stirred to resolute action by the speech of his master.

Sam wished he had as much confidence in his own words as his audience did. He knew something they didn't. If Santa Anna had any nonhuman allies, the only possible protection for the army lay weak and helpless in the back of a supply wagon.

Not for the first time, and surely not for the last, Sam longed for a taste of liquid courage.

~ ~ ~

Blam! Blam!

Watching from a low rise, Sam grinned with satisfaction at the Twin Sisters' handiwork. Two terrified Mexican privates were dragging a wounded captain across the field, leaving behind dead horses and a busted crate of ammunition.

While keeping the bulk of his tired army among the oak trees lining Buffalo Bayou, close to where it flowed into the San Jacinto River, Sam had stationed his two cannons just beyond the cover of the forest. Santa Anna took the bait, advancing his own cannon and its crew far enough to take potshots at the rebel guns. So far, the rebels exhibited better aim.

"Keep firing!" Sam ordered, but his men needed no such urging. A company of Mexican infantry emerged from their own forest cover, the tails of their blue coats flapping above gray trousers as they sprinted across the field. Before they came within two dozen paces of the Texian position, however, the Twin Sisters flashed their teeth again. Three Mexicans fell, bitten by grapeshot. The rest fled.

Colonel Sherman trotted up next to Sam. "Let's go cut 'em down!"

Sam shook his head. "We don't yet know their size and strength. It would be folly to—"

"I came here to fight, not hide in the trees," Sherman snapped.

Wishing he'd ridden Xanthus up the hill rather than leaving the gray stallion back in camp, Sam sat up as straight as he could on the borrowed pony—and frowned when the effort still left his eyes several inches below those of Colonel Sherman.

"You came here as an officer, not a bushwhacker," Sam replied, keeping his voice level.

Sherman merely glared at him, but Sam could hear nearby Texians murmuring and cursing. *Don't you see Santa Anna dangling his own bait?* Sam wanted to shout. *That he* wants *us to dash out into the open where he can blast us with canister and countercharge us with lances and bayonets?*

They didn't see anything of the sort, though. Few had significant military training. Most had never seen battle. Sherman was a good example—a scant three months ago, he'd been a manufacturer of carpetbags in Kentucky. Now he was a colonel, having recruited and led the volunteers who brought the Twin Sisters to Texas.

Nudging his pony into a walk, Sam left Sherman fuming and approached the Texians closest to the cannons. "Be patient, men. You'll get your crack at them. We—"

Boom!

Boom!

His attention fixed on the grumbling soldiers, Sam failed to take note of the second boom, the fainter one. It was only when a hailstorm of iron struck the surrounding trees that he realized the sound came from across the field. And it was only when his pony suddenly lurched, tossing Sam unceremoniously from the saddle, that he realized the Mexican cannon had claimed at least one casualty.

"General Houston!" exclaimed one of the volunteers, a ruddy-faced man in loose-fitting pleated pants and a bright-yellow waistcoat. He rushed forward to help Sam to his feet. "Are you hit?"

"Not bloodied, only soiled," Sam said, brushing dirt from his trousers.

"She wasn't so fortunate, sir," said the soldier, whose long black hair was swept back from a pronounced widow's peak. He pointed to the crumpled form of the pony. She had a gaping neck wound. Her frantic wheezing suggested damage to lungs or windpipe.

Without another word, the soldier placed the muzzle of a pistol against the pony's head and pulled the trigger. Her suffering ended.

Sam closed his eyes. "I appreciate the gesture. May I ask your name, private?"

"Lamar, sir. Mirabeau Napoleon Lamar."

Sam's eyes jerked open. "A distinctive name. Do you come from Huguenot stock or—"

"They're pulling back," Colonel Sherman interrupted, threading his horse through the trees and pointing at Mexicans laboring to wheel their cannon into the distant forest. "Let's go grab that gun!"

"Too dangerous," Sam insisted. "By the time our infantry run such a distance, they'll form up and—"

"Not on foot, Houston," Sherman snapped. "Got lots of riders here, fifty or more. I'll lead the charge."

"Bravely go to meet the foe!" Sticking his newly reloaded pistol into his belt, Mirabeau Lamar spun around and mounted his own horse. "I will gladly follow you."

Sam ground his teeth. "Riflemen on horseback aren't proper cavalry. Not like lancers."

Sherman turned away. "One courageous American is worth half a dozen cowards."

Some twenty mounted Texians were already congregated on the forest's edge. Others were coming. Sam was rapidly losing control of the situation.

"Count me in."

Thomas Rusk rode past the general and took his place next to Lamar. Catching Sam's eye, the secretary of war gave a brief nod.

Sam relented. "You may proceed with a *reconnaissance*, Colonel Sherman, but keep to the trees and take care not to get too close. By no means should you engage the enemy."

Only Sam could have heard his own final sentence, however. Sherman, Lamar, Rusk, and the rest had already galloped away.

As foolhardy as their venture was, Sam felt a twinge of envy. He was thankful it was the pony, not the stallion Xanthus, who'd been shot out from under him. At the same time, he wished Xanthus were close by.

Relegated to footsoldier, Sam scrambled forward, determined to see what the reconnaissance would reveal. There was, however, no reconnaissance. Blithely ignoring his orders, Sherman exited the trees and charged directly at the Mexican cannon. The others followed, whooping as they leveled their guns and fired.

None of their bullets struck home. Sam watched with frustration as the Texians reined their horses to a halt, slipped off their saddles, and began to reload. Then he watched with dismay as dozens of Mexican riders—true cavalrymen in red-and-green uniforms and shiny black caps—emerged from the trees, lances trained on the startled Texians.

"They're gettin' swarmed!" shouted a man on Sam's right.

"Let's go help 'em!" another suggested.

"You will do nothing of the kind," Sam insisted, wishing he were still mounted and thus more visible to his men.

From those near enough to hear him came a chorus of curses. It was the men out of earshot who posed a bigger problem. Dozens were already dashing into the open field, brandishing rifles and muskets as they yelled, "Remember the Alamo!" and "Remember Goliad!"

Sam rushed after them. "Get back here! Countermarch to the rear!"

"Countermarch yourself," muttered a passing Texian, an ugly look on his grimy face.

The rampant disobedience could have made Sam hot under the collar. It didn't. Instead, the back of his neck went cold. Feelings of helplessness and futility made him shiver. He was witnessing the twilight of his command, the dusk of the revolution.

Then, from across a field of foolhardy fanatics and courageous fools, came a scene that grabbed Sam's attention. His new friend Thomas Rusk, having dismounted to reload, was swinging his rifle like a club as Mexicans attacked from all directions. Sam braced himself for the inevitable when a streak of brown and yellow intervened. Riding straight at the Mexicans, Mirabeau Lamar fired his rifle at one and poked at another with its smoking muzzle. "In freedom's cause!" he yelled.

Unnerved by Lamar's impetuous charge, the enemy riders drew back. Seeing his chance, Rusk remounted and beat a hasty retreat. His rescuer made to follow, then Lamar abruptly changed course. He saw the same thing Sam did: a Mexican lancer bearing down on the prostrate form of a Texian who'd fallen off his mount.

With a wince, Sam recognized the unhorsed man. It was Walter Lane, the young Irishman the other recruits had tricked into thinking his general was a blacksmith. The prank had been a lighthearted episode in a grim saga. Tears welled in Sam's eyes. *Now Lane's tale will end in tragedy.*

Again, he failed to predict the plot twist.

Mirabeau Lamar yanked the pistol from his belt and fired. The lancer cried out in pain and jerked his horse to the left. Lamar brought his own horse next to the young Irishman still struggling to stand. With one fluid motion, Lamar slipped an arm around the spindly lad and pulled him onto the horse's back. The two galloped toward the Texian lines, accompanied by loud cheers.

To Sam's astonishment, the cheers were coming not from the retreating Texians, but from the Mexican cavalrymen no longer pursuing them. *They know a hero when they see one,* he reflected.

Whether his thought triggered it or not, the dull ache in Sam's bad shoulder became a sharp pain. Two decades ago, it had been *his* daring exploits that impressed both sides at Horseshoe Bend. Was that man long dead? Judging by the events of the past few minutes, neither side of the current war saw in Sam a hero capable of inspiring loyalty or fear.

~ ~ ~

It was midafternoon of the following day when the soldiers of Texas marched into attack formation. Behind them was Buffalo Bayou. Astride his magnificent stallion Xanthus, General Sam Houston gazed across the field that stretched along the south bank of the San Jacinto to the Mexican camp. It was a sea of green, dotted here and there by bright-colored islands of springtime blossoms.

Win or lose, we will soon paint this field in red.

Sam glanced to his left where his infantry stood in two ranks, guns loaded, spirits high, their mettle largely untested. At the extreme left, near the confluence of the San Jacinto and Buffalo Bayou, was the volunteer regiment led by Sidney Sherman. Before yesterday's cavalry skirmish, Sherman had been disagreeable and disrespectful. After Sam had dressed him down in public for precipitating a near disaster, Sherman became infuriated and vengeful. Still, Sam knew he couldn't demote the popular colonel on the eve of battle.

What he *could* do was promote another popular man. Turning his head, Sam saw Texian horsemen moving through the clump of trees on the extreme right of his line. At their head rode Mirabeau Lamar, now *Colonel* Lamar. Also on the right, and closer to Sam's position next to the Twin Sisters, were Captain Juan Seguín and his Tejanos, with playing cards thrust into their hatbands to distinguish them from the Mexican soldiers camped across the field.

When at noon Sam assembled his officers to confer, they'd expected him to advocate another cautious day of maneuver. Instead, Sam proposed to attack. He'd finally backed his foe into a corner, with Santa Anna's retreat blocked by the San Jacinto. If Sam waited, other units of Santa Anna's dispersed army might find their way here to reinforce him.

Besides, yesterday's indecisive skirmish had answered a question only Sam knew to ask: whether Duendes accompanied Santa Anna. If they had, then surely Sam would have heard their spellsong or seen its adverse effects. He hadn't. With Har the Tower still recuperating in a supply wagon, though, Sam couldn't count on such good fortune to last.

He nodded to the farm boy who'd first brought him news of Thomas Rusk's arrival. The chubby lad smiled eagerly and lifted the pole in his hands. From it flew their army's only battle flag. It depicted a Roman goddess with a "Liberty or Death" ribbon streaming from her upraised sword. Then Sam nodded at Walter Lane, the lad Lamar had rescued. The young Irishman began a steady beat on the old drum bouncing from a tattered leather strap. Sam drew his sword and kicked Xanthus into a walk.

"Trail arms, forward!" he cried.

Some eight hundred Texians and Tejanos awakened battle-ready that morning. Some eight hundred men now strode or rode forward at Sam's command—though motivated more by a burning desire to avenge their fallen friends and countrymen than by a firm confidence in their commander in chief.

When they came within range of the Mexicans' makeshift barricades of brush and saddlebags, the Twin Sisters announced their arrival with thunder. Next came a rumble of rifle and musket blasts from the Texians and Tejanos.

"Reload!" their officers ordered.

"Hold your positions!" Sam added.

After their first volley, however, all semblance of military discipline went up in a cloud of black powder. With scattered shouts of "Remember the Alamo!" and "Remember Goliad!" and "Remember La Bahía!" and other, cruder imprecations, the warriors of Texas hurled themselves at the thin line of Mexican sentries, the inadequate line of Mexican barricades, and the ragged line of Mexican soldiers roused from afternoon siestas to face their enraged enemies.

Sam spurred Xanthus into a gallop, waving his sword. The afternoon sun glinted off its steel surface and cast flashes of light in the eyes of friend and foe alike. He spotted a white-coated officer and resolved to add at least one Mexican to the casualty list himself.

Then, much as the pony had the day before, Xanthus suddenly lurched to one side. Unable to arrest his momentum, Sam few from his saddle and twisted in the air, landing on his bad shoulder. Grunting in pain, he scrambled awkwardly to his feet and searched the ground in vain for his lost sword.

Hooves pounded the ground behind him. Sam wheeled and discovered Juan Seguín on a white mare. Clasped in one gloved hand were the reins of a bay pony. "A general must have a steed," he said.

I have one, Sam was about to insist before his eyes fell on the motionless form of Xanthus a few paces away. *So much for my glorious career as a paladin on his warhorse. At least Xanthus met his end swiftly, without suffering.*

"You have my gratitude, sir," he said, accepting the reins. Seguín tugged the black brim of his hat in salute, then raced away.

Sam decided to employ the pony not in charging at the enemy—he was now unarmed, after all—but in surveying the state of the battle. It began only minutes before, yet it looked as though few Mexicans remained in sufficient numbers to put up a resistance. Some had fallen during the initial attack and lay as motionless as Xanthus on the plain of San Jacinto. Other Mexicans stood in small groups, disarmed and distraught, newly taken prisoners of war. Here and there Texians and Tejanos still pitted knives and gun butts against Mexican swords and bayonets.

Spotting a group of volunteers who'd taken to hooting and shaking hands, Sam turned the pony in their direction. "Form up, men. The victory's not yet won."

Whether they would have paid him any heed, Sam never found out. Something struck his left ankle. It shattered. Yelping in pain, Sam nearly tumbled again off his latest mount. His vision blurred. His ears began to ring, drowning out the triumphant shouts, low curses, and agonized cries of those around him.

Some minutes later—though how many, he couldn't tell—Sam found himself surrounded by Juan Seguín and other officers. "Can you hear me?" Seguín asked.

Sam nodded, the ringing in his ears having subsided. "How goes the fight?"

"There is no more fight, least not here," said another officer.

"Have the men assemble by company," Sam said between labored breaths. "There may yet be Mexican reinforcements on the way."

"They're in no mood to listen," the wary officer replied.

The flame in Sam's eyes matched the one consuming his wounded ankle. "An army marches on orders, not moods!" he snapped. Breaking away, he rode to a group of exuberant Texians singing a bawdy song. "Form up," he barked.

They made no answer.

"Parade, men," Sam ordered. "Parade, I say!"

The song just got bawdier.

"This is your commander speaking. Gentlemen. Gentlemen! I demand that you cease that racket!"

Only one of the Texians stopped singing. He turned his head and yawned.

The burning in Sam's ankle grew hotter, as if the wound were reasserting its claim on his attention. Sam surrendered to it. "Men, I can win victories with you," he muttered, "but damn your manners."

~ ~ ~

Sam was right not to declare victory prematurely. At the cost of just nine dead and a couple dozen wounded, the army of Texas had killed more than six hundred Mexicans and taken another seven hundred captive. None was named Santa Anna. Somehow, the president-general of Mexico had slipped away.

Moreover, thousands of Mexican soldiers remained somewhere north and west of the river, armed and dangerous. And it wasn't just Santa Anna who was unaccounted for—his brother-in-law, General Cos, had also eluded capture. If either Santa Anna or Cos reassembled the remaining Mexican forces and hurled them against Sam's disordered, overconfident army, disaster might still follow.

"I will go after them," said Har the Tower, suppressing a cough.

Raising his head from his pallet, Sam studied the gaunt face of his formerly robust friend. "You'll do no such thing. I've already sent men out to find them."

"They lack my talent for—" Har began, until the next cough proved irrepressible.

"They may lack many talents," Sam said, "but they have the advantage of being able to stand without fainting."

The Dwarf shook his head. "And should they encounter Duende rangers?"

"We must pray they do not. So far, Santa Anna's fairy allies appear to have deserted him."

Har sighed. "Fewer nightmares plague my sleep of late. As they fade, my memories of the recent past grow clearer. My clash with the Enano ranger, for instance. Before our final battle in the river, he called Santa Anna 'but a means to an end' and spoke of 'the Throne that sends the seekers.' I know not what he meant, but I am convinced it must have something to do with the Folk ruins I discovered beneath San Antonio de Béxar."

"It was odd of him to call Santa Anna's seat of power a throne," Sam observed. "The man's more of a dictator than a president, yes, but no one calls him king."

"I am not convinced that—"

Har stopped in midsentence. Sam knew why. He heard the same sound the Dwarf did, a sound he'd been dreading for weeks. *Spellsong.*

Sam sat up straight, ignoring the pain in his ankle. "Must see if my gun's loaded. Har, are you strong enough to—"

Now it was Sam's turn to halt in midsentence. The expression on Har's face wasn't alarm, resolution, or fear. It was elation.

"Rest easy, my friend! More friends are coming."

The tent flap parted. Sam didn't recognize the first small figure who entered, though his eyes went wide when he realized the import of her pale-blue skin and dark-blue hair. "The Water Maiden?" he inquired eagerly.

It was the lithe figure following her into the tent who answered. "A Water Maiden, yes," said Goran Lonefeather, returning Sam's gaze with haunted eyes, "but not the one you mean. Meet Grandmaster Diri of the Gwragedd Annwn."

Har had lurched to his feet in his excitement. "What of Dela?"

Goran slumped, his broad wings of gold-tipped feathers retracting against his small form, and locked eyes with his longtime friend. It seemed to Sam the two had an hour-long conversation in the space of a few seconds. Har's great shoulders slumped, too.

Then Sam understood. *I will never meet Dela the Water Maiden.*

It was Diri who broke the silence. "I am pleased to make your acquaintance, General Houston, though not as pleased as you will be to hear our news."

"Oh?" Sam was preoccupied by his friends' tragic loss. "You have news for me?"

The Sylph seemed to welcome the change of subject. "While making our way here, we happened upon your men searching a marsh. Flying overhead, I spied a Mexican cowering in the tall grass, surmised he was their quarry, and revealed the soldier's hiding place to them. Their prisoner is now entering your camp."

"We hold hundreds of prisoners already," Sam said. "I suppose we can handle one more."

Goran's mouth formed a wry smile. "I suggest you handle his case personally. He says he is Antonio López de Santa Anna."

~ ~ ~

Having sung a concealment spell to shield themselves from the senses of—as far as they knew—all but Sam Houston, Goran and Diri ushered Har away for a lengthier conversation. Then the man identified by multiple prisoners as the president-general of Mexico was seated on a box next to Sam's pallet, which now lay beneath the sheltering branches of a mighty oak.

The prisoner was trim and striking, with a prominent nose, black hair, and high forehead. Though he wore a pair of tattered trousers and a simple blue jacket, his imperious manner marked him as a man used to gaudier attire. Deciding not to initiate the interview, Sam merely turned on his side and grinned at the prisoner.

After an uncomfortable silence, Santa Anna spoke first. "I place myself as your disposal."

"In what condition, sir?"

"As a prisoner of war," the man replied. "The conqueror of the Napoleon of the West is born to no common destiny. He can afford to be generous to the vanquished."

"Generosity to the vanquished?" Sam recalled the gruesome tales from Har and other survivors. "You should have remembered that, sir, at the Alamo."

Santa Anna's eyes narrowed. "I acted properly on that occasion. The history of warfare records many such cases. When the besiegers vastly outnumber the besieged, it is the duty of the latter to yield so lives are not unnecessarily lost. When forced to suffer such losses, the besieging force is within its right to take revenge. Did not the troops of the famous Duke of Wellington do the same to Napoleon's allies in Spain?"

"The outrages at the Alamo were not the vengeful acts of wayward men," Sam replied, struggling to keep his voice level. "They were soldiers acting on your authority."

"As were the Alamo's defenders under the authority of your wrathful Colonel Travis. He refused to surrender. They paid for his pride with their lives."

Sam frowned. *"Wrathful" Colonel Travis. Does he know of my fondness for Homer? Why would he want to goad me to anger?* Sam could think of no good reason, but decided it suited his own purpose to keep his temper in check.

"May I point out, sir, that Colonel Fannin *did* agree to surrender—and he and his men fared no better at Goliad."

At that, Santa Anna blinked and looked away. It was as though a mask had slipped, revealing a nervous face beneath, but the moment didn't last. It was a haughty president-general who replied. "My subordinate had no authority to accept Fannin's surrender. I will so instruct him the next time we meet."

"Do you deny responsibility for the massacre at Goliad?"

"The Congress of Mexico has permitted no quarter be given to rebels. I am but a servant of the government."

Sam resolved to remain calm. "You *are* the government yourself, sir. It was your overthrow of the constitution that obliged us to form our own state and take up arms in defense of our liberties."

"Pirates and traitors need no excuse to take up arms," Santa Anna retorted. "As for your so-called government, your David Burnet is no president, though he calls himself one. It is to you I surrender, and in whose hands the fate of our great nation rests."

"We are two nations now."

The prisoner pursed his lips, then gave a brief nod. "I tire of blood and war, and have seen enough to suspect our two people can no longer live under the same laws. I would treat with you as to the boundary between us."

Sam's smashed ankle again felt afire. "I do not possess the authority to settle that question."

One eyebrow shot up Santa Anna's high forehead. "Perhaps not yet, General Houston. As I said, the conqueror of the Napoleon of the West is born to no common destiny. Today I call you general, but someday soon I may call you president."

Sam rolled on his back and closed his eyes. It occurred to him that for the first and perhaps the only time, the two men were in full agreement.

Chapter 11 — The Breach

August 1838

"'TIS BUT A LUBBER'S TALE," Bull insisted.

In frustration, Gez yanked his stocking cap down over his ears, as if trying to block out his friend's skepticism. "There is more here than some scribbler's flight of fancy! How can you deny it?"

The two sat in the captain's cabin, Bull in his sturdy chair and the Kabouter on the table with the leather-bound book open in his lap. It was the second time Gez had read the story aloud that night, and one of many such readings he'd performed since the *Courser* reentered the South Pacific on its latest whaling trip.

It had been the Kabouter's idea to buy the book, back on Nantucket. Its bright-red cover caught Bull's eye in a shop window, but being at best a rudimentary reader, he had lost interest upon discovering it had three hundred pages of stories and poems but only eight pictures.

"Such tales conjure pictures in the *mind*," Gez had scolded him, handing the shopkeeper a stack of coins and cocking his head to read the book's title: *The Gift: A Christmas and New Year's Present for 1836*. "A welcome companion on our next voyage, I say."

The shopkeeper had nodded amiably. "You a sailor, lad?" Thanks to spellsong, most humans saw Gez as a freckle-faced youngster, not a bearded fairy.

"Cabin boy." Gez pointed up at Bull. "To Captain Stormalong of the *Courser*."

"Captain Stormalong, eh?" The shopkeeper winked conspiratorially at Bull. "Old Stormy of the sea chanty? Why, you're a skilled teller of tales yourself, lad."

Now, in the present, Bull felt inclined to repeat the observation.

"Ya tell it well," he allowed, whittling a whalebone, "but the story's just a lark."

Gez jabbed his finger at the book. "Listen to this part, again, on page eighty-two: 'About an hour ago I made bold to thrust myself among a group of the crew. They paid me no manner of attention, and, although I stood in the very midst of them all, seemed utterly unconscious of my presence.' An apt description of a concealment spell."

"No fairy in the tale."

"We Folk rangers are not the only wielders of such magic. Many monsters cast spells, though not always by intent."

"So it's a monster tale?"

"Not necessarily." Gez stroked his beard thoughtfully. "I know not what real event this story, this 'Manuscript Found in a Bottle,' is meant to depict. What I am sure of is, its author is at least partially Sighted."

"Said the other writer was, too. Mister Irvine."

The Kabouter chuckled and flipped to the contents page, turning it around to show his friend. "Mister *Irving*, you mean. Who is to say the book cannot contain two authors with Sight—Washington Irving *and* this Edgar A. Poe?"

~ ~ ~

Bull relished the feel of sea breeze against his whiskers, once jet-black but now dappled with gray. No matter how many times he came on deck, the sensations filled him with intense satisfaction. The sight of three masts of square-rigged sails billowing in the stiff breeze. The sounds of three dozen crewmen laughing, singing, playing games, or grunting with exertion. Mingled smells of wet canvas, salty sea, and boiled blubber.

The *Courser* had left Nantucket just nine months ago, but the voyage had already proved more successful than their previous thirty-month journey. The latest catch, a sperm whale taken just north of the Juan Fernández Islands, yielded not only many casks of oil and spermaceti but also two great lumps of ambergris from its intestines. Highly desired by perfumers, chefs, and apothecaries, they'd earn Bull and his crew a small fortune.

When he'd first spotted the blow, Bull nursed the same hope he always felt when the *Courser* happened on a sperm whale: that it might turn out to be Mocha Dick, who'd once robbed them of two kills. Gez insisted the mysterious Mocha Dick was an intelligent monster. Bull wasn't so sure. He'd seen many strange things, and Gez was living proof that magical creatures were real. Yet something within Bull insisted there was more to know about the white-skinned monstrosity—and that only by finding him again would Bull learn the full truth.

The latest spout of mist had come from a normal whale, however, as did all the blows the crew had spotted and chased in the years since their encounter with Mocha Dick.

"Afternoon, cap'n," said Morgan, the second mate. He was inspecting the work of two recent additions to the crew. The greenhands looked anxious enough without drawing the attention of their famous Captain Stormalong, so Bull merely nodded and continued on his way.

"Storm a-brewin'.'"

The first mate, Gunnar the Norwegian, pointed to a bank of gray clouds.

"Maybe," Bull replied. "Best check the lashin' in the hold. Don't want spilled casks."

Gunnar grinned. "Orcus already below, cap'n."

Bull nodded back. His men knew what to do without prompting. *If any whaler on the high seas has a crew as skilled as mine, I'll eat my hat.*

The captain stepped to the rail and studied the distant clouds. They made him think of the story Gez had read him. Its first-person narrator, never named, took passage on a cargo ship sailing from Batavia. First, a terrible storm swept all but two men off the ship. Then it forced a near collision with another craft, a ghostly black galleon. The narrator was hurled into its rigging, tried but failed to communicate with an elderly crew who couldn't see him, and was driven inexorably along with the galleon to the South Pole, all the way chronicling his adventures on scraps of paper. He managed to stuff them in a bottle and hurl it into the icy sea before the ship was sucked to the bottom of a mighty whirlpool.

As did all sailors, Bull enjoyed colorful tales. They helped make bearable the long stretches of inactivity at sea. He couldn't decide if he liked this Poe story, however. It had no hero, no villain, no savage battle to save a maiden or win a treasure. Still, one line stuck out, thanks in no small part to the way Gez had delivered it. Bull tried reciting it aloud:

"I went as passenger—having no other inducement than a kind of nervous restlessness which haunted me like a fiend."

It was then the fiend appeared.

Something lightning-quick broke the water's surface, that is.

Why Bull deemed it a fiend and called all hands on deck, he couldn't say. Was it the fin of a great whale, perhaps Mocha Dick himself? Or was it some other denizen of the deep? It moved too fast to tell. But that it posed a threat, Bull was immediately—and inexplicably—certain.

"Lower away!" Gunnar yelled.

The captain barreled across the deck to where sailors were lowering his own boat. To them, this was just the start of another whale hunt. To Bull, it felt like the reverse—like *they* were the ones being hunted. *Only we will not flee. We will not tire. We are the kind of prey who fight back.*

"Why do you gnash your teeth?" asked Gez, hopping into the boat. "What is wrong?"

Bull made no answer as the boat shot way from the *Courser*. He was transfixed by another blur of motion in the distance, a light streak over dark waves.

Gez sucked in a breath. "If it is the monster, you must resist his magic. Resist the rage that controls you."

Am I in magic's grip? Bull was a man of action, not introspection. Still, what he was experiencing wasn't like the irrational hatred he had felt during their prior encounter with Mocha Dick. It was something else, less emotion than instinct, less blind fury than intense awareness of mortal peril.

"This…ain't that." Bull struggled to find the words. "Be ready!"

Despite his warning, neither man proved ready for what happened next—for what arced through the salty spray and struck the center of their boat. Bull and Gez, seated aft, were hurled into the air, as was Bayani, the harpooneer, who'd been at the bow. What struck the whaleboat cleaved it in two, and now the same weapon was winding itself around a screaming Bayani as he twisted awkwardly in midair.

The red tentacle squeezed until the Filipino stopped screaming.

Hitting the water with limbs akimbo, Bull fought the impulse to expel the air from his lungs in a roar of frustration. Instead, he let himself sink a fathom or so, then drew his rigging knife and kicked hard to propel himself at the thick stalk easily discernible in the blue water. When he was just inches from it, the tentacle jerked quickly away—but Bull's huge arms moved quicker. One grabbed and pinned the writhing stalk between forearm and bicep. The other plunged his sharp blade into the slimy red flesh.

Dark liquid squirted from the wound. Bull stabbed over and over, clinging to the tentacle like a rider on a bucking horse. No longer able to see in the inky blackness, his lungs aching for relief, Bull was about to let go and swim for the surface when his foe saved him the effort. With a final yank of herculean strength, the thick red stalk dragged Bull through the water and flung him at the sky.

Gulping a mouthful of air before landing, Bull swam a few strokes underwater and then resurfaced, intent on locating his crew, the other boats, and the tentacled creature. That it was a cephalopod, some octopus or squid of enormous size, Bull had no doubt. Any experienced whaler would have seen its like before, though usually in the form of partially digested food in the belly of a sperm whale. Sometimes the men would catch small squids or cuttlefish in their fish nets, which made for a welcome change of taste. Judging by the width of the tentacle that smashed his whaleboat, however, this squid could rend with ease even the stoutest of nets.

It wasn't the sight of ten impossibly long tentacles jutting from the water that made Bull doubt his initial identification of the beast. Nor was it the speed and power of those arms as they flailed against the lances and hatchets of the men in the three surviving whaleboats. Nor was it Bull's fleeting glimpse of an impossibly massive body just beneath the surface, a crimson form sheathed in a cylinder so hard and shiny that it more resembled the carapace of a lobster than the mantle of a squid. It wasn't even his more fleeting glimpse of two enormous eyes illuminating the water with a golden glow.

No—the sight that made the captain think again was the terror-struck face of Gez the Kabouter, kneeling on a piece of wrecked whaleboat and singing in an uncharacteristically reedy voice.

A rope snapped tight in Bull's mind. Even since the *Courser* had rescued Gez and the three Dutch sailors so many years ago, Bull had assumed they were stranded by a hunt gone bad, by an encounter with a great whale like Mocha Dick, though Gez never said as much. The fairy never spoke of the incident. Now Bull knew why.

This was no mere squid. It was a magical monster of humongous proportions, and Gez had seen such a monster before. He'd watched it destroy a ship and most of its crew.

I won't let my friend see that again. With mighty strokes and powerful kicks, Bull cut through the waves to the nearest whaleboat. "Ahoy there!" he bellowed.

Gunnar spotted the approaching captain. Handing his hatchet to another sailor, the stout Norwegian tossed a tow line. "No *blekksprut*!" the wide-eyed man shouted. "No squid!"

"Aye." Bull snatched the rope and drew himself to the side of the boat. "'Tis a monster."

Gunnar nodded. "It be Kraken!"

Kraken! The same name had already sprung to Bull's mind, a name from fairy stories. It wasn't what you'd expect to hear from a sober-minded seaman and his still more sober captain. *Unless he was the legendary Captain Stormalong, colossus of the high seas, whose best friend happened to be a real-life fairy.*

He grabbed Gunnar's shoulder and pointed. "Fetch Gez."

By the time the Kabouter climbed onto the whaleboat, Bull had a plan. "Can ya bewitch it?"

The fairy dropped dejectedly to one of the thwarts that served as seats for the oarsmen. "Its will is too strong to confuse or elude. And singing solo, my mood spells are but the bites of a flea."

"What of the other song? The go-home one?"

"A summoning spell?" Gez looked pensive. "I might turn the monster away briefly, but it would soon move out of my limited range and return."

Bull's whiskers bristled. "We'll stay in range."

"You cannot mean to harpoon the beast! This is no whale. It will not soon tire."

"Me neither."

Gez jumped to his feet. "This is a foe no human ship has ever bested!"

"It never met the *Courser*."

~ ~ ~

In the end, it wasn't Bull's confidence that persuaded Gez but the futility of every other option. The Kraken wasn't going anywhere. Having presumably tasted the flesh of the unfortunate Bayani, the creature craved more. Armed only with thin blades and short hatchets, and clearly unnerved by their foe's unnatural appearance, Bull's men were no match for the Kraken unless it could be severely weakened by fatigue. Nor could they be sure the *Courser* would be a sufficient refuge against the gigantic monster.

Bull ordered the other boats to head for the creature's cylindrical body, evading its arms as best they could. He also ordered the crew still on the *Courser* to lower the spare, adding a fourth boat to the hunt.

Standing at the bow of Gunnar's craft, Bull batted aside one of the Kraken's tentacles with the oaken shaft of his harpoon. "Almost there," he announced.

Gez groaned. "This is madness."

"Be ready to sing."

Recognizing the iron point of the harpoon would likely bounce off the monster's shiny shell, Bull kept his attention trained on the base of the tentacle, a broad bulge of pink flesh just below one of its great yellow eyes. A glance to starboard confirmed that Morgan's boat, approaching from the other side, was almost as close to the head. The boat of Orcus, his third mate, wasn't far behind. The men were anxious—some truly terrified, Bull realized—but they revered their captain and followed his lead.

Just a few more seconds, he cautioned himself. *Two lines drag heavier than one. Three, heavier still.* Bull couldn't be sure the Kraken would respond to harpooning like a typical whale, by bolting away. He was counting on Gez's spell to prod the beast, and he was counting on their harpoons and tow lines to hold—though if the creature dove too deep or proved too strong, they'd need to cut their ropes quickly or be dragged under.

The whaleboat rolled suddenly to port. "Stay the course!" Bull shouted.

"Aye, cap'n," Gunnar replied in a shaky voice.

The captain chanced another sideways glance. The other boats were closing. The moment had come. Lifting the harpoon, Bull rocked back on one foot and pitched the weapon with all the force his mighty thews could muster.

It struck home, burying the iron hook deep into the base of the tentacle before its wooden pole fell away. A loud whoop from another boat signaled that at least one other missile had found its target. Then, from behind Bull, came the first note of the Kabouter's spell.

As always happened when he heard Gez use summoning magic, strange images flooded Bull's mind. White-crested waves gave way to blue shallows, then indigo waters, then darker depths. Uncomfortable warmth became cozy cold. For an instant, Bull felt a powerful urge to dive into a welcoming sea.

It was the grinding sound of the uncoiling rope against the loggerhead that broke the trance. "Brace yourselves!" Bull warned.

To no purpose, as it turned out. Not because his crew were able seamen with many kills to their names, and not because the force of the monster reaching the end of the tether had wrenched the tow line from its fastenings or snapped it in two.

The Kraken had, indeed, sped away from the whaleboats, propelled by great blasts of water shot from a funnel above its glowing eyes. Unlike a whale, however, the monster didn't maintain a consistent course. Instead, rippling the broad fin that extended from its carapace, the Kraken executed a turn with each stream of water from its funnel. Bull watched with dismay as its latest change of direction dislodged both harpoons from its flesh.

They were for snagging whales, and even then they didn't always stay hooked. *Guess no one ever thought to make a harpoon for hunting Krakens.*

Given his men's inadequate weapons, Bull's only hope of subduing the monster had been to wear it out. Now, it was dashed. "Back to the *Courser*!"

Gez resorted again to trying to confuse the monster, so he managed only a shrug in reply. Bull understand his message anyway. They'd been fortunate to lose just one sailor in the battle. It would take a great deal more luck for all four boats to make it back to the ship.

Their luck ran out almost immediately. One instant, Morgan and his crew were rowing toward the *Courser*. The next they were twisting in the air, surrounded by the jagged shards of the boat flung into the air by a flick of the Kraken's tentacle. All fell into the water save Morgan himself, his anguished cry cut short by the thick cord of flesh and sinew that closed on his neck.

Bull snorted. His face was so flushed with rage that he half expected smoke rather than breath to come out of his nostrils. The loss of his second mate, so soon after the loss of Bayani, was more than he could stand. Feeling the impulse to dive in after the monster, Bull's hand dropped to his knife.

Another hand closed on his. "Resist," Gez said, his voice strangely quiet. "You *can* this time. The anger is not meant for you."

Before Bull could reply, he and the Kabouter were knocked sideways by a wall of water. Seizing the gunwale to right himself, the captain saw another impossibly large shape pass their boat. Unlike the smooth, shiny carapace of the Kraken, its hide was pocked with scars and bristled with the rusty remnants of countless battles against whalers doomed to disappointment or death.

If Bull uttered such a description aloud, he knew, Gez would have corrected his choice of word. It wasn't *its* hide pocked with scars. It was *his* hide.

Like a giant bolt from an outsized crossbow, Mocha Dick streaked across the water. His barnacled head struck the trunk of the other monster with a loud crack. Although the newcomer's eighty-foot body was longer than the Kraken's, the latter appeared to be made of denser stuff. The force of the impact drove the cephalopod back a few feet but didn't crack its armored mantle. When two of the Kraken's red tentacles whipped around the snapping head and twisting fluke of Mocha Dick, Bull marveled that anything could make the White Whale look small.

Gez rapped his knuckles on the gunwale. "What did I tell you? No mindless beast is Mocha Dick!"

Bull turned to the other sailors. "Make for the ship. Put yer backs into it!"

"What?" The Kabouter was aghast. "We cannot let him fight our common foe alone!"

"No help to give." Bull took his place at an oar. "No more men die today."

"And what of Mocha Dick?"

"He is no man."

"For which you should be *thankful*!" Gez rapped the boat again, this time clenching his fist in frustration instead of excitement. "One need not be a man to be a friend."

A thunderous crash drew their attention back to the battle. Mocha Dick had somehow escaped the Kraken's clutches and vaulted clear over it, landing on the far side. As Bull and Gez watched with rapt attention, the White Whale caught one of the Kraken's flailing arms in his teeth and clamped down. Other tentacles snaked around Mocha Dick. The two behemoths, locked in mortal combat, slowly sank from view.

Only then did the full import of the Kabouter's words register in Bull's mind.

"You *are* one of my men, just like Morgan or Bayani," he insisted. "And my friend."

Gez stamped his foot. "We cannot just leave him to his fate."

"We can. We must."

~ ~ ~

After much hard rowing, they reached the *Courser* and scrambled aboard. As the men winched the whaleboats back into place, Bull shouted up to the spotter halfway up the mainmast. "Any sign of 'em?"

"Nay, cap'n, but a gale's upon us.'"

"Oh?" Bull glanced up at the sky. It was clear. The bank of dark clouds once on the horizon had dissipated. The wind was mild.

"Big waves yonder!" the spotter replied, pointing in the direction they'd just come.

Gez yanked the captain's sleeve. "It is not the wind that—"

Bull broke away and headed aft. He'd already guessed what the Kabouter would say. Dashing past the mizzenmast, he muscled the helmsman aside and took the wheel. "Weigh anchor!" he shouted.

Not all his crew had been on the whaleboats. Not all had seen up close the tentacled monster that killed Bayani and Morgan or the barnacled monster that attacked it. All were, however, men of the *Courser*, skilled sailors who served the legendary Stormalong. They didn't need to know the peril they faced—they needed only his command to spring into decisive action.

When the first wave hit, the ship was already underway. It barely rocked the *Courser*. Bull glanced at Gez, who flashed a relieved smile. The second wave struck with even less effect. There was no third.

Still, something was wrong. Bull heard the wooden bones of the *Courser* creak. He felt them strain against an unseen force. Try as he might, he couldn't turn the wheel. Though three masts of sails billowed in the wind, the ship's momentum slowed, then stopped.

Gez dashed to the rail. "No sign of the Kraken!"

"What of Mocha Dick?"

The Kabouter shook his head.

What happened next defied all expectations. The *Courser* began moving again—moving *backward*, not forward. Bull nodded to the helmsman to take the wheel and leaned far over the stern rail, trying to spot the well-muscled tentacles he was certain must be wrapped around the rudder and hull.

"I see it," said Gez in a shocked voice.

"Where? I can't—"

"Not beneath us. *Behind* us."

Bull's eyes followed the fairy's pointing finger. Far in the distance, there was a whirl of motion above the water. The intervening expanse of sea looked oddly flattened and striped in blue and white, as if the dark troughs and white caps of the waves formed a fabric stretched from both ends.

The captain turned to Gez. "Magecraft?"

"Not as such."

Then the flat swath of ocean turned concave, bulging downward along its vertical axis—and Bull understood. The *Courser* was caught in an unnatural current, as if upstream from a gigantic waterfall, but no fairy mage had crafted it.

"Hard to starboard!" he told the helmsman, though he knew it would be pointless.

Faster and faster the ship skated across the glassy surface, stern-first, unable to shake the grip of the powerful current. Bull felt the *Courser* list to port, slightly at first but then so much that the spotter on the mainmast had to throw his arms around it to keep from falling into the sea.

That's what might have happened to Gez had Bull not grabbed his cloak as the Kabouter slid past. "Lash yourself!" he shouted over the roar of rushing water, pointing to a bit of line dangling from a cleat.

Gez fumbled with the rope, his hands shaking, then tied it to his belt. Reaching up to grasp the rail, the Kabouter traversed it, hand over hand, until his lips were close to Bull's right ear. "I have seen this before, long ago."

"I know. On your doomed Dutch ship."

The Kabouter nodded. "Before the end, there is a truth I must speak."

The *Courser* was no longer headed directly backward. It had turned sideways, its tilt more pronounced. Bull could see blue and white stripes now forming concentric circles around the vortex at its center.

"I know that, too," he said. "You would speak of the monster."

The captain could see it clearly now at the bottom of the vortex. Expelling jets of water from its twisted funnel, the Kraken was rolling over and over like a barrel, its tentacles forming a rigid red circle of suction, its glowing eyes forming an indistinct streak of gold just above its spinning mantle. Bull noticed that one of its arms was missing half its length, however.

At least the White Whale went down fighting.

"Not the Kraken, Bull. I speak of another."

As if on cue, the craggy head of Mocha Dick, now crisscrossed with dark stripes, pierced the surface of the whirlpool a few dozen feet behind the ship. Bull gaped. Was this the lifeless corpse of the Kraken's erstwhile foe, swept into the vortex along with the soon-to-be-lifeless crew of the *Courser*?

No.

Blood oozed from the sucker marks on the monster's head and body. The great red eye of the White Whale moved in its socket until it found the captain. The two stared at each other for what must have been only a few seconds, but to Bull it felt like an eternity. Then Mocha Dick disappeared into the water.

What passed between the two wasn't an exchange of words. It couldn't have been. Yet somehow, Bull understood what the other had told him.

He knew what to do.

"Fetch me harpoons!" His order was directed at no one in particular. It didn't need to be. "And tow lines!" There was a chorus of ayes, followed by stomping sounds and clanks of metal on wood. Bull felt a tug on his sleeve. He turned to face an exasperated Gez.

"You would strike at Mocha Dick again?" the fairy demanded. "To what purpose?"

"To save us all."

Gunnar was the first to reach them, bearing two sturdy harpoons. Bull saw the Kabouter's question mirrored on the face of the first mate, but the Norwegian didn't voice it. He handed the weapons to his captain. More sailors arrived with coils of rope. At Bull's direction, they secured them to the ship and attached the other ends to the irons.

"All hands brace!" Hefting a pole in each hand, Bull stepped to the rail and waited.

Of all the watchers on the *Courser*, he alone was unsurprised by the miraculous breach—by the sight of the great White Whale leaping from the spinning wall of water and soaring over the lip of the maelstrom toward the open sea.

In that instant, Bull felt all eyes upon him. The hopeful eyes of the startled crew. The reproachful eyes of Gez at his side. The baleful eyes of the Kraken below. And the doleful eye of Mocha Dick.

One of Bull's harpoons struck home, burrowing deep into the White Whale. The other dealt the hide only a glancing blow, but still served its purpose by becoming tangled with a rusty hook that might have been planted in Mocha Dick a year ago, or a hundred.

So great a leap the monster took, and so swiftly he swam after crashing into the water that within seconds, the ropes were no longer coiled. When the lines went taut, jerking the *Courser* out of the water, it felt as though Bull's ship sprouted fins and fluke of its own and breached itself into the open air.

The crew hadn't known what to expect. Still, they obeyed their captain and braced themselves, so no one tumbled from the deck as the *Courser* cut through the top of the whirlpool, landed on the level water with a crash, then skipped twice as if flicked by the hand of a playful giant.

Bull had thought only of escaping the vortex. He hadn't considered when and how to disengage, and what might happen when they did. Being pulled stern-first at significant speed, the *Courser*'s sails were flapping and rending in protest. The rudder was likely ruined. Drawing his rigging knife, Bull placed its sharp blade against the nearest rope.

"Not yet," Gez whispered. "Look back."

When he did so, Bull withdrew the knife. The danger had not yet passed. A high arc of water was all he could see of their pursuer, but it was enough.

On and on they fled, the grimly silent bulk of Mocha Dick and the creaking, squeaking bulk of wood and canvas and metal that bounced along behind him. With the ship now aright, her crew distributed themselves across her deck and riggings, taking their stations for what might come next. Bull and Gez were among those who made their way to the bow to observe their pursuer. Gunnar stayed behind with the helmsman, awaiting the command to free their monstrous steed.

The command didn't come when the Kraken began to fall behind them, nor when the monster stopped altogether, its writing tentacles drawing angry scarlet shapes in the sky. It didn't even come when the last visible claw of the Kraken disappeared below the horizon. Bull waited many minutes more before ordering the lines cut.

As the men of the *Courser* worked frantically to repair the damage and get her ready to sail again, the captain and his cabin boy kept a constant vigil. They watched fearfully for any sign of the Kraken's return, as they watched hopefully for any sign of the White Whale.

They watched in vain.

~ ~ ~

It was weeks later, during a visit to Floreana Island in the Galapagos, that Bull and Gez discovered what befell Mocha Dick. They heard the story directly from the first mate of the whaling ship that encountered the White Whale shortly after he parted ways with the *Courser*. The whalers had just killed a calf and harpooned a cow when Mocha Dick intervened. After a lengthy battle, the exhausted creature finally met his end at the points of their lances.

"It was not that final battle that fatally sapped his strength," Gez confided when they got back to the ship. "It was rescuing us that did him in."

"Can't know for sure," Bull insisted, though he persuaded neither of them.

Sleep eluded the captain. First he tossed and turned, then he paced the floor of his cabin, his troubled mind restaging over and over the *Courser*'s clash with the Kraken. He second-guessed every decision he made. He resented the loss of time and equipment. He grieved the lives lost to no good end. And he remembered the great red eye of Mocha Dick staring into his, and their wordless conversation before the White Whale's final breach—before the monster's mighty leap from the vortex.

By morning, Bull reached a decision. Whether to rid the high seas of a terrible menace or avenge the loss of his two sailors or, God help him, to avenge Mocha Dick himself, Bull would do whatever it took to find the tentacled demon of the deep again.

For the greater breach had been wrought by the Kraken—a breach of justice, of the natural order, of the honor of Captain Stormalong and his dauntless crew. The wound had cut deep, and Bull was determined to close it for good.

Chapter 12 – The Race

November 1839

NO MATTER HOW MANY PEOPLE he met in Santa Fe, Manuel Antonio Chaves never stopped feeling like a visitor. The bustling territorial capital bore little resemblance to the humble village where he'd grown up. It would never be Cebolleta. It would never be home.

So when Manuel entered the barn, he wasn't just relieved to take refuge from the cold night air. Another source of relief was waiting in the corner stall—one of three companions who'd come north with him from his uncle's hacienda in Albuquerque.

Manuel pulled out a key and unlocked the stall. For several minutes, he nuzzled and rubbed the flank of the sleek black stallion. "I know you will not fail me, Malcreado. You never have."

"Nor have I!"

His second companion from Albuquerque stepped out from behind a haystack. Manuel had mistakenly thought Román Baca was off looking for his supper. Smiling, he beckoned the youngster closer.

"That is true, vaquerito," said Manuel, using his favorite nickname for his half-brother. "I have never seen so clean a stall, or so well-groomed a racehorse."

Román's round face beamed. "All ready for tomorrow!"

I know what you desire, Manuel mused, *but there is too much at stake.* He reached down to tousle Román's thick hair and tried to remember what it was like to be a little boy living in the shadow of a popular older brother.

~ ~ ~

In Manuel's case, he'd initially idolized his brother José, following him around Cebolleta like a devoted puppy. But José had shown little interest in little Manuel, preferring to ride with the older boys or flirt with the older girls.

Rejected and hurt, Manuel turned for companionship to his brother Pedro. That Manuel and Pedro shared little in common but their resentment of José became evident as they grew older, however. Manuel had channeled his envy of José into hard work, discipline, and constant drill, determined to prove himself the equal of his eldest brother. In Pedro, similar envy produced dissimilar results. He had spurned manual labor and disdained physical exertion. Instead, Pedro spent his time eating, drinking, gossiping, and—once he grew to manhood—dabbling in the turbulent frontier politics of New Mexico.

When Santa Anna placed an obnoxious stranger named Pérez in charge of the territory, Pedro had ingratiated himself with the new governor—even though Pérez displaced Pedro's own uncle, Mariano Chaves. Later, when high taxes and other heavy-handed policies of Governor Pérez provoked a peasant revolt, Pedro switched sides to join the revolutionaries. And when prominent landowners subsequently banded together to put down the peasant revolt, Pedro changed sides again, helping make one of his fellow turncoats, Manuel Armijo, the territory's new governor.

Armijo was himself a Chaves relative—a cousin of Mariano, and thus of Manuel and Pedro. Manuel did his part to help place the new governor in power, getting his first taste of soldiering in Armijo's army before moving to Albuquerque to help run the hacienda of Mariano Chaves. Still, neither Manuel nor his uncle fully trusted Armijo, who was rumored to have amassed his personal fortune primarily through sheep rustling. They simply preferred order under Armijo to the disorder of revolution. Pedro Chaves had, as usual, chosen a different course, becoming one of Governor Armijo's closest advisors.

And, no doubt, one of the biggest bettors against Malcreado.

Against me.

~ ~ ~

"Took him out today," said Román, offering the black stallion a slice of apple. "He never ran faster."

Manuel chuckled. Though charming, his little brother was utterly transparent. *He wants to ride Malcreado tomorrow. To prove himself a worthy brother to Manuel Chaves.*

Over the past six months, Malcreado had won every major horse race in New Mexico, from Taos in the north to Albuquerque in the south. That made Manuel and his magnificent stallion the talk of the territory—which hadn't gone over well with its vain governor. When Armijo had proposed a race between Malcreado and his own Victorio, Manuel eagerly accepted. Even after Armijo had second thoughts, proposing a wager so far beyond Manuel's means that it was clearly meant to scare him off, Manuel raised enough money to match the bet.

If Malcreado wins tomorrow, I can buy my own ranch. If he loses, I will be ruined.

Though the stakes might have terrified a lesser man, Manuel felt only excitement. He'd watched Victorio run. The governor's white horse was fleet of foot, but unsteady and poorly trained. Armijo hadn't spent years honing his senses as Manuel had. The overconfident governor wasn't aware of Victorio's weaknesses.

I hear what is silent. I see what is invisible. I know what is hidden. "I know you will not fail me, Malcreado," Manuel said aloud.

"And I?" Román hung his head, not daring to meet his elder's gaze. "Will you not let—"

"Just take care of him, vaquerito. Make sure he gets a good night's sleep."

Appearing to take Manuel's words as encouraging, the boy produced a couple of blankets and folded a pallet for himself on the hay-strewn floor.

It occurred to Manuel that only one occupant of the stall would likely be well rested by morning. Excitement would keep Román up all night.

If I displace the boy's hope with disappointment, he still won't get any sleep. The truth can wait.

~ ~ ~

When Manuel Chaves returned after breakfast, he wasn't alone. He brought the third of his companions from home, the rider he'd chosen for Malcreado—though the rider wasn't happy about it.

"He is *your* horse," said Aki. "You should be the one to ride him to victory."

"You know why I cannot," Manuel insisted. "Governor Armijo stands at the finish line with the judges. They cannot be trusted. If I am absent, they will not let Malcreado claim victory, no matter how fast he runs."

Aki scoffed. "You really think they will let a *Navajo* claim victory?"

"You are no Navajo."

One of the two skinwalkers Manuel had met four years ago at Turquoise Mountain, Aki had since spent every spring and fall with Manuel, first in Cebolleta and then at his uncle's hacienda in Albuquerque. The two had become close friends, the shape-changing monster mastering the language, skills, and horsemanship of a Mexican vaquero while the human learned more about the clever Aki, his powerful wife, Shash, and how two magical beings managed to live undetected among the Navajo.

Manuel tried to imagine how the governor and his entourage would react if they witnessed Aki shed his human skin to reveal his true form of Tieholtsodi, the Water Monster, with his long furry body and great horned head. The image brought a smile to his lips.

"This is no laughing matter," Aki said. "The judges will know only that an Indian races the governor's man."

Manuel's hand shot to the knife at his belt. He flicked it open, relishing the glint of the morning sun off its newly polished blade. "I will see honor prevail, one way or the other."

"You would threaten the governor of New Mexico?"

Shrugging, Manuel returned the navaja to its sheath. "I do not fear him, or his pack of lickspittles."

"Perhaps you should. Danger surrounds you. For the last time, I beg you to call off the race."

"Too late for that. The wager is made. I would lose everything."

"No, *life* is everything—and that, you would save."

"I do not just speak of losing the bet, Aki. I would lose that which is dearer than life itself: my honor."

The two friends exchanged wordless stares. Manuel could guess what was going through the other's mind. Aki lived in constant fear of being discovered, either as a skinwalker by his Navajo neighbors or as prey by the two-foot-tall hunters he called Nimerigar, the "People Eaters." For Aki and Shash, every day of life was a precious gift.

Manuel loved life, too, but so had the Indian boy Pahe, whom Manuel had treated abominably and who'd nevertheless refused to leave Manuel behind at Canyon de Chelly. Pahe—really a skinwalker like Aki and Shash—had done the honorable thing. He'd paid with his life. Manuel refused to believe Pahe's sacrifice was in vain.

As if by mutual agreement, the two let the matter drop and entered the barn. When Manuel unlocked the stall, he was surprised to find his half-brother fast asleep. Only when the horse whinnied and stamped his feet did Román Baca open his eyes.

"Man…Manuel? Is it close to dawn?"

Aki helped the unsteady lad to his feet. "The sun has long since emerged to greet the day, my young friend."

Román's face reddened. "My chores! Malcreado must be hungry! I should have—"

"Yes, you should." Manuel tried to look stern.

That made the boy sound desperate. "I…I am sorry, brother."

Aki clapped him on the back. "Do not worry, lad, there is still time to do your chores. You do not have to miss the race."

Román glanced up at Manuel, then at Aki. When the import of the latter's words struck home, the boy's face fell. If he were riding Malcreado, there'd be no question of him missing the race.

~ ~ ~

In the end, both Manuel and Aki had misjudged Governor Armijo. There would be no chance of his handpicked judges cheating Aki of his victory.

"I will not stand for it!" the governor thundered. "I agreed to a race with my cousin, not his servant!"

"Aki is no servant," Manuel replied. "He is my friend, and a fine horseman."

Pedro Chaves, sitting on a barrel next to the governor, waved a languid hand. “My brother’s judgment has long been faulty where Navajos are concerned.”

Manuel glowered at him. “I might say the same about you.”

“Why do you not ride Malcreado today, brother?” Pedro shot a sideways glance at Armijo. “Are you afraid?”

“Manuel is never afraid!”

Román Baca’s outburst took everyone by surprise, Manuel included.

“He is the best rider in the territory,” the lad continued, “and Malcreado, the fastest horse in all of Mexico!”

“Hold your tongue, boy.” Armijo turned back to Manuel. “As I said, I proposed a race between kinsmen. If you do not ride, I must hold you forfeit.”

Struggling to maintain his composure, Manuel forced himself to grin. “And if *you* do not ride, are you forfeit?”

“That was not our agreement. I never race, as everyone knows. My nephew Juan rides Victorio. There will be a contest of cousins today, or none at all.”

“Very well,” Manuel said. The delighted expressions on the faces of Pedro and Armijo confirmed his suspicions: with Manuel in the race, there would be no credible witness on hand to prevent the judges from ruling in favor of Victorio.

“We *will* have a contest of cousins today,” Manuel went on. “Román will ride Malcreado.”

Pedro shot to his feet with surprising alacrity, given his girth. “You cannot be serious!”

“The boy is barely out of diapers,” Armijo scoffed. “You might as well forfeit.”

“Not at all.” Manuel placed a hand on Román’s quivering shoulder. “He is a fine horseman. No one knows Malcreado better.”

The governor exchanged looks with Pedro and the judges. There appeared to no logical objection to the idea, yet Manuel could tell the men were still trying to think of one.

He decided to deny them the chance. “Come, Román. We must saddle our champion.”

~ ~ ~

Most of Santa Fe turned out to watch the spectacle. There were well-tailored officials and businessmen, ladies in frilly dresses, ranchers and farmers in plainer attire, vaqueros in mud-spattered chaps and wide-brimmed hats. Aki took his place among a throng of Indians on the other side of the track, while Manuel wedged himself between Armijo and the judges. A steady stream of men approached the governor, holding up cards or stacks of coins to bet on Malcreado defeating Victorio. In each case, Armijo nodded his assent. He looked amiable, even giddy.

Two vaqueros in tattered vests stood at the starting line, each holding the reins of a racehorse. Victorio was a beautiful animal, Manuel had to admit, but he was no Malcreado. Tall, majestic, dark mane waving in the breeze, the black stallion was a well-sculpted statue come to life. There was no finer horse in New Mexico. His owner liked to think there had *never* been, that Manuel had already accomplished something remarkable, something that would have impressed José—and made him envy his younger, scrawnier brother.

Younger still was Román Baca. Nervously adjusting the chin strap of his flat-brimmed hat, Román glanced across the field at Manuel, who flashed a reassuring smile. When the boy stood next to the great black stallion, it made him look like a toddler.

"Get ready!" One of the vaqueros handed Malcreado's reins to Román. Juan Armijo took the reins of the other. The riders mounted their steeds—in Juan's case, with a dramatic flourish of a long-fingered hand. Román's stubby-fingered ones were balled into white-knuckled fists.

A hush fell over the crowd. Even Pedro, who'd been filling the governor's ears with the latest gossip from Mexico City, went silent. Manuel sucked in a breath and held it, his confidence in Malcreado warring with his doubts about his young rider.

Bang!

Smoke trailed from the muzzle of the vaquero's pistol, but Manuel scarcely noticed. His eyes were locked on his stallion. One instant the massive bulk of Malcreado stood patiently at the line, sunlight glinting off his sleek skin. The next, he was an indistinct streak of black in a cloud of dust. An instant more, and Malcreado was a horse length ahead of Victorio.

Relief released Manuel's held breath. He drew in another, then shouted at the top of his lungs, "Ride the lightning, Román!"

The boy couldn't have heard him. The spectators were yelling, too, urging on one rider or jeering at the other. Still, as Malcreado rounded the first turn, Román's head and torso pressed flat against his mount's crest and withers, Manuel caught a fleeting glimpse of the triumphant smile on the boy's round face.

I know how you feel.

If Malcreado's lead held up, Armijo's handpicked judges couldn't possibly rig the outcome. Manuel chanced a brief glance to see how the governor was taking it. To his surprise, Armijo was neither yelling instructions at Juan nor cursing his misfortune. He wasn't even watching the riders make the second turn. Instead, the governor's head was turned toward the crowd, as if trying to spot someone.

Pedro was not so easily distracted. "Come on, Victorio!" he cried, desperation creeping into his voice. "Make your move!"

It was Malcreado who picked up speed, however, and negotiated the third turn nearly three lengths ahead. The crowd saw which way the wind blew. Those who'd wagered against the governor were cheering. Those who'd bet on Victorio were booing.

Again, Manuel glanced at Armijo. The governor was watching the riders now, but there was no frustration or anger written on his face. The man seemed, at most, mildly curious. Manuel wondered if the man was so fabulously wealthy that the prospect of losing hefty bets didn't faze him.

At the fourth turn, Malcreado was more than four lengths ahead. A few seconds more and it would be over. Fifty yards more, and it would be Manuel who possessed great wealth and esteem.

The black stallion stumbled.

Time seemed to stand still. It felt as though a fiery hand reached down Manuel's throat to clench his heart. Had the horse slipped on a loose stone? Had he been tripped?

Malcreado stumbled a second time, but that didn't slow him. The horse careened wildly instead, no longer under any semblance of control by his suddenly terrified rider. The third stumble deflected Malcreado rightward, sending him flying. Somehow, Román Baca managed to leap free before the horse hit the ground less than a foot from a fencepost.

Galloping hooves told Manuel that Victorio had shot past his erstwhile competitor. Shouts from Pedro and the governor's entourage told him the race was over. Stunned silence from the crowd told him Armijo had won his wagers. Still, Manuel had eyes only for Malcreado. Hopping the fence, he ran to the fallen horse, trying to recall all possible injuries and treatments.

Approaching from the other side, Aki was obviously thinking along similar lines. "Any broken bones?"

It took but a brief look into the dark eyes of the horse to render the question irrelevant, for those eyes didn't look back at Manuel. They never would again.

~ ~ ~

"I'm sorry!" Malcreado's final rider shivered as if it were the dead of winter.

To Manuel, however, all was aflame. *What did you do to my horse?*

"I don't know what happened." Román's tears rained in torrents.

Manuel saw only dry, unending desert. *I was a fool to trust a sniveling boy.*

"It was an accident." Aki placed a comforting hand on his shoulder.

Manuel felt a knife plunge into his chest. *I have lost everything.*

It wasn't just his savings and the enormous debts he now had no means to repay, though those were bad enough. He'd lost what was dearer than money. As Aki led a stunned Manuel and a whimpering Román from the track, they'd been hissed at, cursed at, and even threatened by the unruly crowd. Many had bet heavily on Malcreado. When Armijo had eagerly accepted their wagers, they'd assumed he was being recklessly overconfident. Now they suspected Manuel had conspired with his cousin, the governor, to fix the race. They'd call him a swindler, a cheater.

I have lost my reputation. There is nothing left.

"I am sorry!" Román crawled across the floor he had slept on the night before. "Forgive me, brother!"

Manuel jerked away and gave the wall a swift, pointless kick. "Be glad it is not you who feels the point of my boot."

"See reason, my friend," Aki said. "This was no fault of the rider. A sudden illness must have—"

"I left Malcreado in *his* care. I gave a serious job to a silly child."

"You blame yourself, then?"

Manuel fumed. "I trusted the boy I thought he was. The boy *I* once was. That boy would not overfeed a horse, or let him drink dirty water."

Román sobbed. "I would never—"

"Malcreado is dead!" Manuel jabbed his finger at the boy. "Crying will not bring him back. Talking will not restore my good name. Forgiving you will pay no debt."

Aki bowed his head. "Are you sure of that?"

His friend's question took Manuel by surprise. He was saved from answering by a knock on the barn door.

"Is there anyone there?" asked a deep voice. "I seek Manuel Antonio Chaves."

Although the voice didn't sound familiar, and spoke with a foreign accent, Manuel figured he must be a creditor come to collect—the first of many, no doubt. He opened the door. "You have found him."

Whatever people say, none may call me coward.

The man in the doorway was sallow-faced and spindly, dressed in a threadbare suit and dirty cravat. "You are he, the owner of Malcreado?"

"His former owner. His corpse now belongs to the earth."

The stranger cast a furtive glance over his shoulder. "I have come on urgent business."

Manuel sighed. "You only *think* it urgent, sir. The debt will remain unpaid."

"That is why I have come." The man pulled the door closed behind him. "I guessed you might be here."

"How did you know—"

Manuel cut his own question short when the man visibly started and backed away. Turning, he saw Aki and Román approaching from the corner stall. Then the realization struck Manuel like a club to the head. He pointed to his half-brother. "You recognize the boy."

The visitor grimaced. "Yes."

"You have been here before."

The man nodded.

Manuel took a step toward Román. "You let a stranger in the barn? How could you be—"

"The boy is blameless," said the visitor. "I saw the boy. He did not see me."

Aki put his hand on Román's trembling shoulder. "Because he was asleep, I take it?"

"Yes, but not by choice."

Manuel and Aki exchanged puzzled looks.

"My name is Philippe Auguste Masure," the man continued. "As you can tell, I am no native of Mexico. I am Belgian. I have lived and practiced in Santa Fe for eight years."

"Practiced?" A sour taste came to Manuel's mouth.

"Medicine, sir. I am a physician."

The taste turned bitter.

"My practice has not been, uh, lucrative of late. So when a patient made me a business proposition, I felt compelled to consider it. He had much money riding on the race. He asked me to take certain steps to, well, to make sure he won his bet." Masure paused, seemingly reluctant to explain further.

Manuel didn't need him to. "Poison."

Again the man nodded, keeping his eyes averted.

"And Román?"

"A common anesthetic. I soaked a rag in it, tied it to a pole, and waited until the boy closed his eyes for a moment. Then I passed the pole through the window and held it under his nose. Did no lasting damage, I assure you. Once he was fast asleep, I entered the barn and, uh, well—"

"No lasting damage, you say." Manuel clenched his fists so tightly, the nails dug into his palms. "You killed my Malcreado. And his rider, my little brother, barely escaped injury himself."

"I meant him no harm, but what choice did I have?"

"What *choice*?" Rage narrowed Manuel's eyes to tiny slits. "You could have refused your gambler friend's 'business proposition.' You could have said no."

"One does not say no to the governor of New Mexico."

Aki bounded forward. "Armijo made you do this?"

Manuel raised a hand to cut off the doctor's reply. "No one *made* you. The governor offered to pay for your services, did he not?"

Masure blanched. "I…I was promised a thousand dollars, but if I had—"

"So the unpaid debt you spoke of, it is not mine." Manuel unclenched his right hand and dropped it to the handle of his knife. "It is his."

The doctor gulped. "The governor paid me three hundred. When I asked about the rest, he called me a 'damned rascal and a bad citizen.'"

The flick of the navaja startled the doctor, who gulped when the long blade clicked into place. The lamplight reflected in its surface made Manuel smile. "My cousin does occasionally tell the truth."

Masure fell to his knees and laced his fingers beneath his chin, as if in church. "He ordered me out of the territory, on pain of death! What am I to do?"

"You can run," Manuel began, "though if you hide until tomorrow, you may find flight unnecessary."

Neither the doctor nor Román took the meaning of his words, but Aki did. "Surely you do not mean to confront the governor, knife in hand."

"Confront him?" Manuel shrugged. "That would be pointless. I will simply kill him. You do make a good point, though. It would be wrong to dirty Lionclaw with his blood. My bow will serve me better."

"*Mon Dieu*!" Masure wailed. "You will fail, his soldiers will kill you, and he will have me killed for revealing his scheme!"

Manuel smiled. "Then you should pray my aim is true."

~ ~ ~

The crescent moon threw dark shadows across the central plaza of Santa Fe. Some of the shadows were short and wide, cast by adobe walls. Others were tall and thin, cast by the trimmed evergreens lining the courtyard. One shadow was unlike the others. It was short, thin, and moving.

If Armijo followed his usual schedule, he'd emerge just after midnight from the Governor's Palace north of the plaza, headed for the gambling den down the street. If Manuel had his way, his cousin wouldn't live to place another crooked bet.

Slinking past the chapel on the south side of the plaza, Manuel found a hiding place behind a juniper bush. Armijo would walk within a dozen feet of it. Even a novice archer would have a good shot of hitting the governor from there.

And I am no novice.

Manuel knelt and slipped the bow over his shoulder. Drawing an arrow from his quiver, he ran a finger along its osprey-feather fletching and fitted the nock to the string. Then he focused his attention on the palace across the plaza. If the governor followed his usual schedule, Manuel wouldn't have long to wait.

Though I will wait all night, or as many nights as required, to see justice done.

A few minutes later, a short, thin shadow bobbed along the dark ground of the courtyard. This time Manuel was its observer, not its cause. He knew in an instant it couldn't be Armijo. The gate of the palace remained closed. And no one could mistake the governor for thin.

Working his way around the bush, Manuel sought to keep his eye on the running figure without revealing his own location. His attention otherwise engaged, Manuel only learned of the approach of the third figure when a rough hand closed over his mouth and another pinned his right arm to his side.

Squirming in the attacker's viselike grip, Manuel dropped the bow and attempted to draw his knife.

"No." The voice was low and raspy. "It is I."

Recognition caused Manuel to relax a little. The other did the same. Twisting around, Manuel gave Aki a reproachful look. "I made myself clear," he whispered. "This is my task alone. The only aid I need from you is to conduct Román safely to my uncle in Albuquerque."

The skinwalker gave a quick jerk of his head. "I did not come to take a life. I came to save one."

"You doubt my prowess?"

"Against one man? No, but against a dozen?"

The brisk night air turned suddenly frigid. Manuel looked over Aki's shoulder, then glanced right and left. The moon now cast many moving shadows.

An ambush!

Of course Armijo had realized his despicable deal with Philippe Masure wouldn't stay secret for long, least not from Manuel Chaves. Of course he'd known his impetuous cousin would seek revenge. The governor had bet on that impetuosity, just as he'd bet on the doctor's poison. "How much am I worth?" he asked.

"The governor is offering five thousand dollars to whoever brings him your head."

"A small fortune, eh? My reputation seems to have recovered a bit."

Aki raised an eyebrow. "This is no time for humor. Your enemies are closing in."

"Why do they do the bidding of such a man? He admits his own guilt."

"Not at all. Armijo calls you a sore loser, and a traitor for threatening the governor's life."

Manuel smirked. "I'll do more than threaten it, once we dispose of his assassins."

"That will gain you nothing. All of Santa Fe will be hunting for you."

"Then I will—"

"You will run, my friend, or you will die. Some believe Armijo's lie. Others only fear him, or regret betting against him."

The shadows in the plaza were no longer skulking around in silence. Manuel heard boots striking stone and men speaking in low tones. Soon, they would find him. Even if Aki was right, was it already too late to heed his advice?

The shape-shifter seemed to read his mind. His reply, however, came not in words. Aki smiled and leaned forward, placing his hands and knees on the sandy ground. His face and form began to ripple, as if melted to liquid and buffeted by strong winds. Even before the points of two twisted horns erupted from Aki's head and the loincloth fell away from his elongating trunk of glistening fur, Manuel had picked up his bow and risen to his feet.

The hunters would chase their fleet-footed quarry across the length and breadth of Santa Fe this night. And they would never catch him, which is why they'd never know Manuel Chaves was long gone.

~ ~ ~

Days later, Manuel learned the fate of his friend.

The brown mare that had carried him along the trail was no Malcreado, to be sure, but she was swift and sure-footed. She was also the only possession of consequence left to Manuel, other than the clothes he wore and the weapons he bore. Riding east from Santa Fe, he happened on a group of traders and volunteered to accompany them as far as the recently established settlement of Las Vegas on New Mexico's Gallinas Creek. From there, they'd keep following the trail east and north until they crossed into Texas on their way to the trading cities of Missouri.

Where Manuel would go from Las Vegas, however, he hadn't decided. He only knew he couldn't venture back to Santa Fe, or to Albuquerque or Cebolleta, at least not for a long while. Even the political influence of his uncle, Mariano Chaves, wouldn't be enough to shield him from the vengeful grasp of Governor Armijo, though Manuel was reasonably sure his little brother would be safe back on the hacienda in Albuquerque. Taking Román there was the task he'd originally given Aki. Assuming the skinwalker had survived his encounter with the assassins, he'd surely be on his way there with the boy.

Which was why Manuel was so startled when another brown mare sidled up next to him on the trail and its rider spoke. "How far is it?" Aki asked.

"What are you doing here? Where is Román?"

"Your second question is the only one I need answer," said his friend. "Your uncle Mariano arrived in Santa Fe shortly after I won my nighttime race with Armijo's assassins. I entrusted your brother to his care, borrowed one of his horses, and rode in the direction I guessed you would choose."

Manuel inclined his head in gratitude. "You might have journeyed back home to your Shash."

"She will know why I did not." Aki gestured to the trail ahead. "How far is it?"

"To Las Vegas? A couple of miles, at most."

Aki shook his head. "You are only passing through that town. I speak of your destination."

"I do not have—"

"How far is it to this Missouri?"

Chapter 13 – The Muddy

AM I BLIND?

Although she could feel her eyes moving in their sockets, all was blackness.

Am I deaf?

All was stillness. She could sense her heart racing, but it was a vibration within, not a pounding without.

How long she lay in blackness and stillness, she didn't know. A moment? A lifetime? From somewhere in the darkness, in her mind, a soft voice spoke against the latter. She had no memory of eating or drinking. Without sustenance, survival was impossible.

Am I dead?

Her inner voice protested feebly, then fell silent. That she was able to ask the question was no refutation of it. Perhaps this was what it was like to be dead. Eyes that cannot see. Ears that cannot hear. A body capable of only a semblance of life, of sensation without perception, of subject without object. Such a body would have no need for food or water. Such a body might imprison a soul forever.

Then came the sound. *Tap. Tap. Tap. Tap.*

It grew louder. *Clomp. Clomp. Clomp. Clomp.*

There was a series of clicks, then a long creak. A shaft of light stabbed the dark. It stung her eyes.

"It is time," said a different voice.

She found her own. "T-t-time?"

"Come with me."

"W-w-where?"

"Runa."

Is that a place?

"Come on, she is waiting."

So Runa is a name. It was an obvious conclusion, yet its realization thrilled her. She wasn't blind! She wasn't deaf! She wasn't dead! And for at least some questions, there were answers!

Her next realization, however, extinguished this small ember of hope.

Runa is a name. Everyone must have a name. So, what is my name?

She waited for the inner voice to reply. She waited in vain.

Who am I?

~ ~ ~

The room was large and square, its walls crowded with shelves. Runa sat across the cluttered table, her thin eyebrows shot halfway up her high forehead. "You retain no memory of our previous conversation?"

"None."

"Perhaps that is for the best." Runa stood, signaling the guards to exit.

"I do not—"

"Look around the room." Runa gestured to the shelves. "Tell me what you see. Tell me what you recognize."

"I see books and scrolls. Flasks and bottles. Artwork and handicraft."

"Interesting. You readily recognize objects and their functions. Pick a book and read its title aloud."

The closest book wasn't on the shelf. It lay on the table, its leather cover inscribed with ornately crafted letters. "*Songs of Two Rivers*."

Runa's small eyes flashed. "No trouble reading, either. Your command of our language appears completely intact."

"*Our* language? Then you and I are of the same—"

"The same Folk? Hardly." Runa held up a bony hand. "I am an Elf of the Black Forest. Compare the color of my palm with your own."

Runa's palm was a pale pink. The other was blue.

"What kind of Elf am I?"

"You are no Elf at all," the grandmaster sneered.

"Then what is my—"

"You *were* a ranger of Water Folk, the Gwragedd Annwn in the tongue of the humans you herded. You name was Dela."

The Water Maiden blinked in confusion. *Dela.* The word meant nothing to her. "Is it not still my name?"

"The one named Dela was an enemy. She was a prisoner and I, her jailer. She is no more. You are now a specimen and I, the scholar. You, a subject—I, your tester. You have no need of a name."

I may have no recollection of this place, this Runa, or my own identity... but I know I am a person.

The grandmaster pointed to the jumble of books, scrolls, and devices on the table. "What you and I do here is more consequential than you could possibly imagine. To recover the lost knowledge, to explore the boundaries of spellsong—we craft the very key that will unlock the past and secure the future."

Every person has a name. My name is Dela.

"It was not my intention to wipe your mind's slate clean," Runa continued. "We did not realize the significance of the colored lines in the painting. Now we know. The memory of one insignificant specimen is a small price to pay for such a breakthrough."

Insignificant specimen. The phrase jolted Dela. "*You* removed my memories?"

"Well, not all, it seems." Runa leaned forward. "You recognize objects. You speak and read Folktongue. What of your profession? Do you remain a spellsinger?"

"I do not understand the—"

"Cast a summoning spell!"

The grandmaster's unexpected command yielded an immediate response. The words sprinkled Dela's lips like a morning dew. The melody bubbled from her throat like a woodland spring. Effortlessly, unerringly, the Water Maiden sang of a place that, as far as she knew, she'd never been. A dark, dank place nestled deep within a dark, aromatic forest. A place that she *knew*, somehow, felt like home to the only other person in the room.

"Remarkable." The Elf sat back and stroked her pointed chin. "Only memories tied to your personal identity and experiences are gone. Your tacit knowledge and skills appear intact."

Dela stopped singing. "I recall the spell, but not its purpose. What do I summon?"

"A Black Forest Elf," Runa replied, "though I am already here."

"So that is why the spell failed."

"No, it failed because I am Folk and your face is bare." The grandmaster picked up a quill and dipped it in a vial of murky liquid. "Tacit knowledge, you retain, as I said, but key facts elude you. Are they lost forever or only submerged?"

"I cannot say whether—"

"Be silent." Runa was scribbling furiously. "I need no speculation from my specimen. Only further testing will reveal the answer."

"I am not a specimen. I am Dela."

The Elf scowled. "You are my *specimen*, for which you should be grateful. If not for me, you would be the lifeless corpse the rest of my Folk believe you to be."

When Dela heard the phrase "lifeless corpse," an image sprung unbidden to her mind. It was fuzzy, indistinct, as if seen through a coarse-woven cloth. There was a face coming toward her, a leering face tapering to a point at the chin. *Runa.* Behind the grandmaster was a large shape painted on a wall of stone. Straight legs. A breechclout. Outstretched arms. A face partially covered by a long-nosed mask.

The mental image made the Water Maiden wince. She felt a burning sensation in her shoulder, another at her breast. "I was…I was…"

"What is it?" Runa had returned to her writing. "Stop your babbling. I must finish my notes."

"I was…slipping away."

"Ah." The grandmaster no longer sounded annoyed. "You recall your dying breath, perhaps."

"Dying breath? Do you mean I am—"

"Were you always such a simpleton? Of course you are not dead. We thought you were at first, when brought to my chamber for…study."

Dela was barely listening to Runa. She was trying to bring the gauzy memory into focus.

"Imagine our surprise when you jerked and coughed up blood. I administered a healing potion and bound your wounds. Prince Veelund believes his prize of war perished in the pits of Cahokia. Only my guard and I know the truth, and I have sworn her to secrecy. How else can I conduct my experiments without interference?"

In an instant, it was as though the cloth covering the inner eye of the Water Maiden was ripped away. Dela saw clearly the blood-covered arrowhead rising from her chest. She saw the grandmaster, the painting behind her. And she saw another face—not leering like Runa's, but flashing a reassuring smile. It was a familiar face, framed by a strong chin and wavy hair. She knew its every wrinkle and contour. She felt the urge to touch the face, caress it, pull it down toward her.

The instant proved fleeting. The cloth reappeared, thickened, obscured the image. It faded away.

Quill in hand, the grandmaster looked eager. "Describe what you remember."

Try as she might, Dela couldn't bring it back. "Nothing. The memory is gone."

"Fascinating." Runa scribbled. "And useful."

"How can a lost memory be useful?"

The grandmaster rolled her eyes. "Not the *effect*, foolish woman. The *cause*. I thought banded agate from Indian Creek would suffice to focus the spell. It was a mistake—though a fortunate one for me, it turns out, whatever misfortune it brought you."

Dela could of nothing to say. Still, the look of utter bafflement on her pale-blue face produced a response.

Runa turned and snatched something off the shelf behind her. When she held it up to her face, the Water Maiden gasped in recognition. The shield-shaped mask was made of hammered copper. Embedded in its eyeholes were two round crystals, and in its forehead a colorfully striped stone. An oddly shaped horn protruded several inches from the nose. Attached to the sides of the mask were oblong rocks, from which miniature versions of the mask, carved of shells, dangled over Runa's pointed ears.

Dela was sure she'd seen the mask before. When and where, she couldn't say.

"I thought only the design mattered." Although the Elf still held the mask to her face, her words didn't sound muffled. "I should have realized the materials mattered, too. Their scarcity. Their thaumaturgical properties."

"I do not understand what—"

This time, no preemptory challenge or curt retort cut Dela off—it was a chorus of shouts from the corridor. Runa shot to her feet as the door burst open. "What is it?"

"Intruders!" said the guard who'd conducted Dela from her cell. "Pierced the Shimmer at the west gate!"

"The Dwarf king has found us at last." Runa wheeled to grab two daggers off the shelf, slipping each into a sheath inside her robe.

"No, Grandmaster." The guard was panting. "Not Dwarfs. Not even Folk."

Runa's eyes widened. "No time to return the specimen to her cell. Bind her wrists."

~ ~ ~

It was only the second passageway Dela remembered traversing—and this time was a very different experience. When the guard had led her to Runa's chamber, they'd been alone in a rough-hewn tunnel. This time, the three sprinted along a downward-sloping corridor lined from floor to ceiling with wooden planks and brilliantly illuminated by mounted torches. There were other Elves in the passage, too, some headed down the tunnel like Runa's party and others retreating in the opposite direction.

"How many invaders?" Runa asked the guard as they ran.

"At least two, I hear."

"With most of our guildmasters accompanying Prince Veelund's expedition to the southern colonies, we are short of rangers." Runa stopped to let two gray-haired Elves in ragged cloaks totter by. "A duet must suffice."

Though Dela heard their words, she lacked the context to make much of the conversation. Thus, she wasn't prepared for the sight that met her eyes when the three entered an enormous cavern. More than a dozen Elves were already there, thrusting bronze-tipped spears or loosing bronze-tipped arrows at their two foes. One was a giant clad in strange tight-fitting clothes of leather and cloth. He towered so high above the defenders that the flat-brimmed hat on his head nearly touched the top of the cavern. Gripping a long club of wood and metal with two hands, the giant swept it back and forth among the Elves, knocking one warrior against the wall and forcing the others to dodge or duck.

The other foe didn't stand on two trousered legs—it crawled on four furry ones. More than twice as long as the giant was tall, the dark-brown monster lowered its horned head and charged the Elves, two of which narrowly escaped being impaled.

Runa and the guard drew no weapons. Instead, they began to sing. The monster snapped its oblong head in their direction, glaring at the rangers with bestial eyes that glowed bright blue. Their other target, however, paid the spellsingers no heed. Slamming the metallic end of its club into an Elf, the giant man opened his giant mouth and bellowed three words.

"Resist, my friend!"

They were in a language other than the Folktongue with which Runa had interrogated Dela. Yet the Water Maiden understood the words. She understood that the towering man, and presumably the furry monster, were intelligent. That they were companions. And that their enemies were her enemies.

Her captors' attention fixed elsewhere, they failed to perceive Dela's first backward step. The second and third also went unnoticed. Soon, she was running back along the tunnel they'd descended, praying the intruders would keep the Elves occupied long enough for her to find some means of escape. It gave Dela no pleasure to abandon her inadvertent rescuers to their fate, but she could think of no way to assist them with her hands securely bound. Nor could she rule out the possibility that other Elves, perhaps multitudes, would soon arrive and overwhelm the giant and monster, with or without her attempt to balance the scales.

Racing along the corridor, Dela tried desperately to recall the layout of her prison and failed. She kept running up the tunnel, trusting her fate to two logical guesses. First, if the complex was underground, fleeing upward offered the best chance of finding an exit. And second, Dela ought to get as far away as she could from the woman who'd robbed her of her memories.

For many minutes, she encountered no Elves rushing to the battle. At the next bend in the tunnel, however, she ran headlong into a burly spearman. Both struck the floor hard.

"Invader!" shouted the Elf, mistaking Dela for one of those who'd "pierced the Shimmer," whatever that was. He reached for his dropped spear.

The Water Maiden reached it first. Kicking the man in the shoulder to keep him at bay, she fumbled with the shaft until her bound hands found a secure grip. Then she drove the butt of the spear into the Elf's temple, knocking him senseless.

Scrambling to her feet, Dela braced the weapon against the tunnel floor and rubbed her fetter against the blade. The rope parted. Looking down at the fallen Elf, she noticed for the first time that he wore a pack secured to his back by crisscrossing straps. Extending from the pack were two thin panels of translucent material. Something about the apparatus seemed familiar, though Dela couldn't recall its function.

~ ~ ~

So that *is what they mean by the Shimmer.*

She stood at the mouth of the tunnel and looked down at the grassy field below. It wasn't what she had expected. She'd thought she'd been imprisoned underground. She'd never guessed the Elf colony lay inside an enormous mound of earth and stone—and that, as large as it was, it couldn't possibly have contained the sprawling colony without the use of sorcery that either shrank its inhabitants or made the hill bigger on the inside than on the outside.

Adding to Dela's bewilderment was the glistening membrane over the mouth of the tunnel. She could see through it, but the effect was to render the blurry world outside unintelligible to her. The grasses that covered the mound and the field beyond it were waving so rapidly, Dela couldn't distinguish the individual blades. Assuming at first a storm was raging outside, she discarded the notion when she saw the cloudless sky. Then a small object flew at an impossible speed, forming an indistinct blue streak across her field of vision. Two more streaks followed, one red and the other gray.

Did she dare venture out to such a bizarre world? Dela saw no alternative. Remaining in the mound meant falling back into Runa's clutches.

The Water Maiden thrust the spear at the shimmering wall. It bounced off. She tried again, this time pressing the bronze point against the wall and pushing vigorously. The effort produced only a few reddish sparks. Setting down the weapon, Dela reached out with her hands. When they encountered the transparent wall, it felt as though she pushed against a strong wind.

No wonder Runa and the others were so surprised by the incursion of the giant man and the horned monster. The Elves considered themselves safe behind their impassable barrier. *They must use magic to open it*, she thought, *perhaps even the spellsong Runa spoke of.* Dela tried singing the summoning spell the grandmaster had provoked from her. The barrier remained.

She was about to return down the tunnel and seek another exit when a streak of brown caught her eye. Something was rapidly approaching from outside. The Water Maiden retrieved the spear and backed up against the wall, flattening her body as best she could to avoid detection.

At that angle, she could no longer see through the Shimmer. When a shadow fell across the floor, however, she knew a large figure now stood on the other side of the magical barrier. A moment later, a shower of sparks told her the figure was emerging.

Dela was ready. When the arm and face of the Elf came in sight, she sprang at him, touching her spear to his side at a point just below a leather strap. Like the other Elf, this one wore a backpack from which two gossamer panels protruded. Each was attached to wrist and elbow by small, faintly glowing ropes.

This time, Dela conjured their purpose from her murky mind. *Wings. They allow Elves to fly.*

"Do not shout!" she warned.

The shocked Elf nodded his assent.

"How did you pass the barrier?"

"The security song."

"Sing it or die."

He choose wisely. His reward was unconsciousness.

After stepping through the temporarily open barrier, Dela paused to consider her next move. The Elves would pursue her. Though Runa hadn't explained the nature or extent of her experiments, they were obviously important. And they were just as obviously harmful to the Water Maiden.

How to evade pursuit was less obvious. Not knowing how to operate the artificial wings, she didn't steal them from the Elf—she destroyed them. Her enemies would be airborne, however, giving them an advantage. Moreover, Dela couldn't remember her people. She didn't know where or how to find them.

As she surveyed her surroundings, which included other grass-covered mounds, a distant ribbon of water caught her eye. *A creek!* The grandmaster had called her people Water Folk. Dela felt the bubbling brook beckoning to her. She scampered across the plain, threaded her way through a forest of trees, and jumped into the creek. The water came up to her knees. As she followed it north and west, the water rose to her waist, then her shoulders. When the creek led her to a river, the water closed over her head. It flowed across her limbs and torso. It salved her bruises. It washed over her doubts. She was still in danger, she knew, but she no longer felt alone.

Swimming *down* the river would be faster—but her pursuers would know that. Dela turned against the current and began a steady stroke. Soon, she reached a confluence and chose the left fork. It proved to be a muddy river, though the press of silt and sand against her skin felt more like a caress than an impediment.

At first, Dela glanced over her shoulder every few strokes, intent on spotting any fliers chasing her. Her attention so engaged, she missed the threat ahead until she was almost upon it.

"Look, Absalom," cried a shrill voice. "That ain't no fish!"

"It's a little girl!" someone else replied.

Dela submerged and kicked hard, passing rapidly beneath the boat despite the strong current pushing the thick water against her. She heard the slap of paddles and decided to stay under as long as her lungs allowed—which, she was gratified to discover, was quite a while. When at last she surfaced and cast a backward look, the two giants in the boat were nearly out of sight. They'd spoken in yet another language she recognized without knowing why.

For many hours Dela maintained her pace, swimming along the surface most of the time and diving into the muddy depths whenever she heard voices. All the people she encountered were giants, most fishing or hauling cargo. To her relief, she spotted no Elves. To her disappointment, she spotted no blue-skinned Folk, either.

Her aching arms and legs insisted Dela stop to rest. She resisted as long as she could, intent on putting as much distance as possible between her and Cahokia. It was only when her exhausted body could barely make headway against the current that the Water Maiden turned her face to the shore and found a secluded place to lie down among the weeds.

Still, it wasn't secluded enough. She awoke to a flutter of wings a few feet above her.

Chapter 14 – The Raid

July 1840

THE CABIN ON THE BLUFF wasn't much to look at: a single square room, only fourteen feet a side, built of rough-hewn logs and roofed with cedar shingles. It was the view—of the sparkling bay and the sandy shores surrounding it—that justified the owner's description of his summer retreat as a "fairy region."

Or so his human friends thought—they didn't get the joke. They didn't know about the colony of fairies who lived at the base of the bluff. Nor could the other humans have spotted the three fairies, shielded by spellsong, now plodding up the slope to the cabin.

Not much to look at, and hardly a suitable residence for a former president. A wry smile parted the lips of Goran Lonefeather. *Still, it suits Sam Houston just fine.*

"Are we certain he is alone?" Diri produced a handkerchief and mopped beads of sweat from her forehead. The ranger wasn't yet accustomed to the sweltering summers. She'd spent most of her life in Wales before joining her Folk's migration to America. After a falling out with the Gwragedd Annwn of Tennessee, led by her sister Gwyla, Diri had accepted Sam's invitation to resettle the rest of her Folk in Texas. They chose the waters of Galveston Bay as their new home, digging caverns and grottos under the bluff at Cedar Point, the same place the new republic's first elected president had built his own summer home.

"Sam told me Margaret would be at her mother's house in Galveston," said Har the Tower, whose beaming face reflected his delight at being on the surface again. Although no more bred to thrive in the steamy weather of Galveston than the others, Har never shared his fellow Dwarfs' love of confined spaces. He liked the cold, damp grottos of the Cedar Point colony even less than the cold, dry caverns of his own Folk. Whenever Grandmaster Diri sent out rangers to forage, hunt, or bear messages, Har volunteered to go along, almost always coming back with juicy stories and a fresh catch of succulent fish.

Goran nodded to the Dwarf. *Everyone grieves in his own way*, the Sylph reminded himself. The loss of Dela had left a great emptiness in the hearts of both men, and they threw themselves wholeheartedly into Diri's colonization project as a way to fill it. Over time, Har found joy in new friendships among the Gwragedd Annwn as well as excursions into the Blur. For Goran, however, joy was impossible. He settled for the distraction of toil and the fulfillment of duty.

When they reached the bluff, there was no need to announce their presence. The cabin door flew open, revealing a tall human clad in trousers, moccasins, and a rumpled shirt tied loosely at the collar with a dark cravat. "Welcome, friends!"

Despite his now familiar hulking form and cleft chin, the Sam Houston who greeted them scarcely resembled the tired, often melancholy man Goran had grown to know during their stay in Texas. Sam's two years as president had been turbulent and frustrating. Frequently at odds with the Texian Congress and shocked by Andrew Jackson's unforeseen opposition to American annexation—Texas would upset the balance of slave states and free states, he explained—Sam resorted to a combination of connivance, bluster, and inebriation to make it through his term. Not surprisingly, this won him few political victories or friends. Mirabeau Lamar, whom he'd promoted to an officer on the eve of the Battle of San Jacinto, proved to be as headstrong a politician as he was a warrior. Elected vice president at the same time Sam was elected president, Lamar had befriended the former interim president, David Burnet, and led the political opposition to Sam in the very capital named after him, the town of Houston.

Sam had even fallen out with his friend Thomas Rusk, who served as his secretary of state but didn't share Sam's confidence that a lasting peace could be made with the Cherokees of Texas. Limited by the constitution to a single term, Sam was forced to watch Mirabeau Lamar succeed him as president, repudiate his policies, move the capital from Houston to the inland town of Austin, debase the republic's paper money, lay a dubious claim to half of New Mexico, intervene in a Mexican civil war, and then make war on the Indians of Texas—with General Thomas Rusk at the head of the army that killed many of Sam's Cherokee friends and drove the rest north into the Indian Territory.

Goran had witnessed few of these events himself. After accompanying Diri back to Tennessee and returning with her Gwragedd Annwn settlers, the Sylph spent two months behind Shimmer walls, helping build and organize the Cedar Point colony. Outside, in the Blur, years passed. It was only through Sam Houston's periodic visits to the colony and updates from Har that Goran learned of his human friend's travails.

Which had clearly lessened of late.

"We were delighted to hear of your marriage, President Houston," said Diri, holding out her hand.

He kissed it with a dramatic flourish. "Just Sam now, little lady, and thankfully so."

Har clapped the human playfully on the shoulder. "Why not let us see this Margaret Lea Houston of yours? We could have come in human guise."

"Well, to be honest," Sam admitted, "I'm not sure she isn't Sighted—and I'd rather keep a few secrets to myself. Margaret already knows pretty much everything else about me."

"And married you anyway?" Har feigned surprise. "I never thought to see you an old raven caged up."

"You'll find no lovelier cage on either side of the Mississippi." Sam pointed to a small bench against the wall, then leaned back on a piano wrapped in canvas. "First laid eyes on her when I visited Alabama last June on business. By summer's end, we were engaged."

Har and Diri sat on the bench. Seeing too little space for his wings, Goran remained standing. "We have made much progress since you went back to Alabama for your wedding. The colony contains guildhalls, storehouses, and living quarters for a hundred settlers."

"At least that many Gwragedd Annwn are already en route," Diri added. "We expect the first shipload to arrive in Galveston any day now."

Har cleared his throat. "I was delighted to find you back home the other day, Sam, and to pass along your invitation for us to visit your cabin."

"Raven Moor." The human swept his eyes around the room. "Not much to look at yet, but when we get it fixed up, that's what I mean to call it."

The Dwarf cast a sideways glance at the Sylph. "Perhaps we will see

Raven Moor in all its finery one day, but I believe it may be time for Goran and me to—"

"To leave Galveston?" Sam's genial smile disappeared. "I agree. You must go."

The three fairies exchanged startled looks. "President Houston, if we have done anything to—"

The human's arched eyebrow prompted Diri to start over.

"*Sam*, I know your invitation to settle here applied only to my Folk, but Goran and Har—"

"That's not it." The former president shook his head in frustration. "Mirabeau Lamar has poked his head in another hornet's nest. All of Texas is likely to get stung."

The Dwarf nodded. "You speak of the Comanches."

Goran had heard the story after Har's last ranging. The Comanches lived as a number of distinct tribes within a great oval swath of territory called the Comancheria, bordered by the Cheyenne lands to the north, the Indian Territory to the east, New Mexico to the west, Apache tribes and the breakaway Mexican Republic of the Rio Grande to the southwest, and the major population centers of Texas to the southeast. The Comanches were both facile negotiators and fierce warriors, often raiding their southern neighbors for horses, supplies, and captives. When Sam led Texas, he sought to conciliate the Comanches. President Lamar had chosen a different course, however, vowing "total extinction" of all Indians living in lands claimed by Texas.

Lamar's officers had invited Comanche leaders to San Antonio to negotiate the return of captives. When a group of Comanche men, women, and children arrived with only one prisoner as an opening bid, the Texians tried to take them all as hostages. In the resulting melee, more than half the Comanches were killed. In retaliation, the Indians tortured their remaining captives to death.

"The Comanches will surely ride south seeking more revenge," Sam warned. "Blood will flow."

"Is Lamar truly to blame?" Har inquired. "From what I understand, Comanche raids have gone on for generations."

"That's just it—I don't blame him, at least not wholly." The human's voice rose in intensity. "Lamar's decisions are wildly irrational, even for him. Someone else is pulling his strings."

"Whose puppet do you think he is? The Americans? The Mexicans?"

The former president spat out his answer. "The Duendes."

"What motive could they have to provoke war with the Comanches?" Goran asked.

Sam snorted. "The recovery of Texas, of course. With our men distracted, and with Santa Anna once again leading Mexican troops in the field, they could march north and—"

"Mexico's leaders are themselves distracted by the revolt of their northern states," Diri pointed out. "Until they put down the insurrection, how could they think of reconquering Texas?"

"Santa Anna is a vainglorious madman," Sam insisted. "I put nothing past him."

Har looked pensive. "What do your suspicions have to do with Goran and me?"

The human shrugged. "I think I'm right, but I'm willing to be proved wrong. I humbly request that you investigate. Go to the capital. Observe President Lamar and the Congress. See if they've been bewitched, or if there are Duende about."

"That was…not what I had in mind." Har glanced again at the Sylph, who knew perfectly well what the Dwarf was thinking. Convinced Goran's tortured soul could never find peace among his lost love's blue-skinned Folk, Har had repeatedly hinted they ought to journey north to seek an audience with the Sylphs of Niagara Falls or search for Goran's long-lost brother, Kaden, along the shores of Lake Ontario.

Har is not wrong, Goran had to admit. *I should stay here no longer.*

Although it was clear Diri appreciated his help, life among the Gwragedd Annwn proved excruciating. Every time a Water Maiden smiled, Goran saw the beguiling face of his Dela, forever frozen in a mask of death. Every time a Water Maiden sang or laughed, Goran heard Dela's sweet voice, forever silenced.

Time to move forward, not backward. Time to find a future without her.

"We will do as you ask," Goran announced. He met Har's gaze.

The Dwarf approved.

~ ~ ~

As it happened, the two friends didn't make it to Austin.

It was in Bastrop, a settlement on the Colorado River, that Goran and Har first saw the stranger. The slender fairy waded into the shallows of the river to fill a flask. Dressed in a blue tunic and gray stockings, he was certainly no ranger of the Nunnehi or some other native Folk. Watching from a forest on the opposite shore, Har cupped his mouth with a meaty hand. "Duende?" he whispered up to Goran, perched on a high limb.

The Sylph was about to reply when another motion drew his attention. The humans he and Har had shadowed on their way to Austin, a trio of merchants riding up from Houston, jerked up from their own wading in the water. A few moments later, Goran heard galloping hooves.

Humans best us in at least one way: their superior hearing.

The other fairy reacted to the sound as well, stepping out of the river and moving his lips in what Goran guessed was spellsong. He and Har did the same, reinforcing concealment spells as they watched the Folk ranger pick up a pack and spring behind a bush.

The rider soon came into view. The traders rushed forward to meet the Texian. "You come in from San Antonio?" one asked.

"Not that far." The rider slowed to a stop. "Got a message for Ed Burleson."

"We were meeting Colonel Burleson in Bastrop," the trader said. "Maybe we can help."

The rider tipped his hat back. "Just give 'im the news and I'll head back. Tell 'im the raiders got slowed up on the San Marcos. Waterin' all them stolen horses."

"Mexican bandits causing trouble again?"

"Nah, ain't you heard?" The rider spat on the dusty ground. "Comanches. Hundreds of 'em. Raidin'. Killin'. Burned Linnville near to the ground, but we'll get even."

Goran glanced at Har, who sighed in frustration. Neither was surprised to hear Comanches had come south to avenge the massacre in San Antonio.

"We'll pass along the message," the trader promised.

The rider's eyes narrowed. "That's a one-man job. The rest of y'all comin' back with me, right? Need every man we can scrounge up."

The trader and his fellows exchanged wary looks. "Well, you see, we only just arrived in Texas and don't have much experience with—"

The frenetic high-pitched melody that grabbed the humans' attention was instantly recognizable as a mood spell. The Sylph leapt from the limb and flapped his wings, intending to confront the spellsinger.

Only then did realization come: the mood spell wasn't a solo. Goran heard several distinct voices. Caution overruled curiosity. Returning to the cover of the forest, Goran joined Har in scanning the surrounding countryside. A moment later, the Dwarf knocked softly on the trunk to get the Sylph's attention, then inclined his head. Two Folk rangers were walking along the river toward the human riders, one singing and the other playing a small harp. In response, the spellbound traders remounted their horses, muttering curses and swearing vengeance against the Comanches.

"Sam was right," Har whispered. "Duendes *are* stoking the fires of war."

Then, from behind him, two more voices join the chorus. Goran turned to study the plain beyond the forest. He saw no one. Then he lifted his eyes—and his blood ran cold.

He looked at Har. "Not Duendes."

The Dwarf's eyes followed his pointing finger and went wide. The figures gliding down to the river were readily identifiable.

Elves.

~ ~ ~

Their thirty-mile trek from Bastrop felt like thirty thousand miles to the impatient Sylph. With his powerful set of feathered wings, Goran might easily have outpaced the two Elf fliers, but that would have left the Dwarf behind. More importantly, Goran and Har couldn't afford to get ahead of the humans. That Texians from Bastrop, Gonzales, and other communities were trying to converge on the retreating Comanches was obvious. Precisely where battle would be waged was not.

Despite hanging well back from his quarry, Goran twice came close to being discovered—once when an Elf flier stopped to hover in midair, adjusting the straps that held his artificial wings in place, and a second time when one of the Elf rangers seated behind a charmed human rider happened to glance behind him. In both instances, Goran ducked behind trees to escape detection. As for Har, the mule he'd commandeered from a farmer was shielded from human eyes and ears but not from Elfish ones, so the Dwarf stayed far behind the column, using the distant form of the Sylph to stay on course.

When the travelers reached the confluence of two creeks, however, there was no more need for pursuit. Well over a hundred Texians were watering their horses or milling around on the banks. Goran spotted a nearby thicket and descended to it. A few minutes later, Har arrived and dismounted.

"Did you see the Comanches from the air?"

Goran shook his head. "Must be farther upstream."

"And the Elves?"

The Sylph pointed to a low hill where several small forms were congregated. "Conferring about the coming battle, no doubt."

The Dwarf stroked his yellow beard. "I care not for the Elves and their schemes, but what are we to do? Though their intervention may explain President Lamar's misdeeds and his people's rage, Texians have just grievances against the Comanche raiders."

"Moreover, we are just two against at least five foes," Goran observed.

"They are Elves." Har's eyes were steely. "Double their number and perhaps the odds shift against us."

Seeing no hiding place from which to eavesdrop on the Elves, the Sylph focused on the Texians. Casting an illusion spell on a passing rider, Goran posed as a fellow volunteer and learned that the nearby waterway was called Plum Creek. He also learned the Comanches and their Kiowa allies had made off not only with thousands of horses and pack mules carrying loot, but also with several Texian, Mexican, and African captives. The human relayed stories of Indians seeming to come of nowhere and taking the settlements by surprise despite prior warnings of raiders.

"Sounds like the Comanches are the ones with magical help," Har mused. "Could the Duendes be responsible?"

Goran frowned. "There is much we do not yet understand."

More volunteers arrived, white settlers as well as a dozen friendly Indians wearing distinctive white armbands. With their numbers approaching two hundred, the Texians decided to ride north. They were accompanied by three Elves on horseback, two in the air, and—unbeknownst to any of them—a Dwarf on a mule and a Sylph on the wing.

~ ~ ~

They'd traveled about nine miles up Plum Creek when the first shots rang out.

From high above the creek, Goran had already seen the distant cloud of dust revealing the location of the Indian caravan. Though he resisted the impulse to fly ahead for a closer look, Goran could see the pursuers were rapidly overtaking the raiders, whose speed was hampered by the heavily laden mules and the presence of hundreds of women and children, native and captive, among the Comanche and Kiowa warriors.

Seeing the Elves dart forward to overfly the developing battle, Goran flashed a signal down to Har and took off after them, intent on rescuing any noncombatants caught between the vengeful settlers and their equally vengeful foes. As he grew closer, the Sylph could pick out whiskered Texians in wide-brimmed hats firing pistols and long guns from horseback and war-painted Indians in buffalo-horn headdresses firing bullets and arrows back at them. He also found riderless horses, pack mules, and crates of trade goods abandoned by the raiders and now swarmed by dismounted, whooping Texians.

There will be no decisive battle here, Goran concluded. *Just a contest over who goes home with the most plunder.*

A high-pitched cry from west of the creek caught his attention. Goran swooped leftward, and an infuriating sight met his eyes. The five Elves spotted earlier were advancing with weapons drawn—two by air, three by foot—on a group of women and children huddled in a patch of grass and bramble.

Pulling his bow over his head, Goran nocked an arrow and dove at the closest Elfish swordsman. One of the captive women, an elderly Mexican with a shawl drawn over her shoulders, jerked her head so dramatically that the Elf noticed, whirled, and managed to catch Goran's arrow in his upraised shield. With no time to draw another arrow, Goran rotated his body and made momentum his weapon, striking the Elf's buckler with his boots and driving the swordsman to the ground.

Beating his wings to gain altitude as he reloaded, Goran heard the thud of wood on wood and the clank of metal on stone. Had Har the Tower already arrived and hurled his massive bulk and sharp battleaxe into the fray? Or were the Elves' innocent victims trying to defend themselves? He angled his wings into a tight half-turn and looked for a new target.

This time, the sight that met his eyes astonished the Sylph. In his haste, he'd misjudged the encounter entirely. The Elves had indeed advanced with weapons drawn. Their prey had, however, proved far from defenseless—and they weren't all human.

The "children" were, in fact, four stoutly built Folk armed with clubs, spears, and bows of their own. Their dark-red faces displayed menacing scowls, revealing rows of yellow teeth filed to sharp points. Their long, intricately braided hair bounced wildly as they moved. They battled furiously with two Elves while a third, the blue-clad flier, hovered overhead. The fourth Elf, the swordsman Goran had struck, was struggling to his feet and an Elf flier lay crumpled on the ground, a flint arrowhead sticking out of her back.

"The Nimerigar have allies!" the swordsman warned his companions. "Sylphs fight at their side!"

"He is no ally of ours," grunted one of the red-faced rangers, her necklace of interlocked bones rattling as she parried a sword with her spear. "The winged ones left the Hunt long ago."

Goran was about to reply when he heard another high-pitched cry issued by neither Elf nor Nimerigar. The cry, really more of a screech, came from the Mexican woman's mouth, which was really more of a beak.

The captive—if, in fact, she'd ever truly been one—dropped her shawl and stooped over, stringy gray hair blowing in the breeze. As if by mutual agreement, the Folk rangers paused their battle to watch what happened next. The woman's thin legs grew thick and leathery, her five-toed feet becoming four-taloned ones. Her arms flattened against her body and hair, all of which flowered together like a liquid and then congealed into multicolored wings. Her narrow, wrinkled face flattened into a white-feathered face, apple-shaped with two black, baleful eyes separated by a long, curved nose.

"Lechuza!" the bone-necklaced Nimerigar yelled to her companions. They answered not with shouts of alarm, but cheers of delight.

The Lechuza, now resembling an enormous barn owl with a vaguely humanoid face, straightened and spread her wings. Goran couldn't tell whether the monster planned to attack the Elves, the Nimerigar, or merely flee. Still, he was inclined to help her. After all, the Lechuza's transformation suggested she might be intelligent, like Goran's old friend Polly Cooper, the shape-changing Thunderbird.

In keeping with the events of the day, however, the monster did the one thing he didn't expect: with a vicious squawk, she leapt into the air and flew straight at Goran.

Astonished, the Sylph only barely dodged the monster's outstretched talons, which raked the air just inches above his left shoulder. Surrounded by dangerous enemies, Goran saw no recourse but to beat his wings hard against the hot summer air and streak away, hoping the monster and Folk rangers would ignore him in favor of closer antagonists.

After a few moments of rapid flight, he dared a glance over his shoulder. The Folk had, indeed, resumed their skirmish, five with hand weapons and one Elfish bowman hovering in the air, trying to get a clear shot at the Nimerigar. As for the Lechuza, she hadn't followed Goran—she flew in the opposite direction. The Sylph smiled and watched her retreating form shrink to a speck. Hers *was* an act of intelligence. The Lechuza couldn't have known Goran meant her no harm. She'd counted on the others' mutual hatred to give her a chance at escape, and on her ability to defeat the one aerial adversary who had no allies.

There remained the problem of the other captives, though. Goran retraced his flight path, determined to get them out of harm's way. The three women still stood in the tall grass, two white settlers and a black girl. As he drew close he saw another Elf fall, crushed by a heavy club, while one of the Nimerigar fell to the ground, bleeding profusely from a slashed throat. Of the remaining combatants, the flying archer posed the greatest threat to his plan, so Goran loosed his own shaft while the Elf's attention was fixed on the melee below.

Alas, the arrow flew wide of the target, serving only to alert the Elf. He spun and shot back at the Sylph, also ineffectually. Then the two fliers dropped their bows and drew knives, seemingly destined for an aerial duel to the death.

It never got that far.

First, the Elf's two remaining companions cried out in anguish, each mortally wounded by Nimerigar weapons. Then the sound of stamping hooves signaled the approach of dozens of riders—so many, in fact, that the Folk couldn't be confident their spellsongs would ensure their concealment or safety.

It took only a split second for the surviving Elf to make his decision.

Spinning around, he adjusted a control on his pack strap and shot away, first toward the setting sun and then turning to the north. As for the Nimerigar, two of them turned and scampered away from the approaching Texians. Their leader tarried, however, rattling her necklace in frustration.

"No other may claim our prizes!" she announced, glaring up at Goran. Then, before the Sylph could guess her intention, the Nimerigar picked up a bow and quiver discarded by a fallen comrade. Her first arrow pierced the breast of the black girl.

"No!" shouted a horrified Goran as he hurtled toward the Nimerigar, oblivious to the risk posed by the ranger's reloaded bow.

The second arrow didn't streak up at him, however. It took another woman in the throat.

"Stop!" the Sylph demanded.

The Nimerigar didn't. Her third missile struck the remaining captive in the chest. Much to the surprise of all three observers, the arrow bounced off something hard beneath the woman's pink blouse.

The fiend will loose no more arrows, Goran swore to himself.

He was right—but his blade never touched her flesh. A rifle barked, and its bullet knocked the Nimerigar on her back. Strengthening his concealment spell in low tones, Goran rose into the air and looked down. The Nimerigar's wide, wild eyes stared back at him, though they did not see him.

"Did ya see what that Comanche crone did?" A young Texian in a blood-spattered coat passed beneath the Sylph, followed closely by two settlers. "She deserved what I gave her!"

She did, but her victims deserved so much more.

The humans dismounted and rushed to the unharmed captive. Goran headed in the same direction, hoping that perhaps the other two had miraculously survived. His hope proved forlorn. The first arrow had pierced the black girl's heart, killing her instantly. It took only seconds for the second woman to bleed out from her throat wound. Goran hovered for a moment, whispering a silent prayer and trying to convince himself their deaths weren't his fault.

"Goran." Har's voice washed over him like a warm bath. The Dwarf stood a dozen feet away, holding his mule's reins in one hand and his battleaxe in the other. Its edge was streaked with red. "Met an Elf back there. He wielded an enchanted blade."

Goran glided to the ground. "And?"

"It was a short meeting. What happened here?"

The Sylph hung his head. "Discovery. Death. And much else that remains shrouded in mystery."

Strengthening his own concealment, the Dwarf strode toward the fallen captives. Goran followed. After a few paces, Har stopped so suddenly that Goran nearly ran into him.

"What is it?" the Sylph demanded.

The Dwarf's only response was to point. Goran dashed past him and gasped. The two women still lay where they'd fallen in the tall grass—but their bodies were no longer human.

The one with the arrow in her throat now resembled a huge ape, at least eight feet in length, with dark fur that gave off an almost unbearable stench. As for the other, her shape wasn't even humanoid. The reptilian head, thin forelegs, stubby hind legs, and exceedingly long tail made her look like a miniature version of a wingless, bipedal dragon. The Nimerigar's arrow protruded from her scaly chest.

Why did they not transform and try to escape, as the Lechuza did? Goran wondered.

It took only a moment's reflection to answer his unspoken question. *Because they no longer remembered they were monsters.*

Chapter 15 – The Lament

April 1841

THE SHALLOW CREEK TURNED SHARPLY to the right just before reaching the Shimmer.

Dela thought of the only other creek she remembered, the one she'd used to escape the Elf colony at Cahokia. That creek, also shallow but full of silt, led to an even muddier river. By contrast, the water of this creek was remarkably clear. It wound its way east until it reached the great salt marsh that was now the Water Maiden's home.

Humming the entrance spell learned from her hosts, Dela held her borrowed spear above the waterline and kicked hard to thrust herself forward. Her skin tingled. She glanced up, watching the puffy clouds that drifted lazily in the blue sky become a swirl of gray and white stripes. The blazing, seemingly stationary sun became a glowing orb that crawled slowly but inexorably across a shimmering dome.

As a ranger, she must have entered and exited the Blur hundreds of times, or so Dela's new friends assured her. She recalled only shards and shadows of that former life, however, so crossing the Shimmer still thrilled and unsettled her.

"Any new threads, child?"

Wazi didn't appear to have moved since Dela left for her swim. Given the slow passage of time inside the Shimmer, Wazi probably hadn't. Clad in a deerskin skirt and mantle fastened at her left shoulder, the old woman reclined in a high-backed chair on the edge of the salt marsh. Water lapped the cottonwood legs of the chair as well as Wazi's dangling feet.

"None." Dela cast aside the flint-tipped spear and ran her fingers through long, wet hair, brushing it back over bare shoulders. "Or at least no threads of memory thick enough to follow."

Wazi shifted in her seat. "I have heard rangers talk about the workings of spellsong. Even some Sightless humans recover memories in time. That may yet happen to you."

"I am no human. What Runa did to me may differ greatly from what your spellsingers do to humans."

The old woman blew out a raspy breath. "Hope will do you no harm, child. It has already granted you refuge."

"For which I am truly grateful." Dela extended a blue hand to grasp the other's brown one.

"And now," Wazi wheezed, welcoming the Water Maiden's assistance in rising from the chair, "we should rejoin the others."

"Has the council made its decision? I meant what I said. I will gladly help your Folk find a new home."

"Your offer is appreciated, though you have no debt to repay." The old woman smiled. "All Folk are welcome among us. It was ever thus in Quivira."

"Now you must leave it behind."

"Leave Quivira?" Wazi shook her head. "No, child. This island is not Quivira. There have been many such places. High cliffs. Rushing streams. Caverns carved deep in the ground. Quivira is not a place—it is a way. Quivira is wherever the Mialuka make our home."

Then the old woman spread her wings and flew.

~ ~ ~

It was only a few hundred feet from the edge of the marsh to the rows of conical tents that constituted the village of the Mialuka. Still, it proved too far for Wazi's ancient wings to manage. She fluttered weakly to the ground and walked the remaining distance on foot, clutching Dela's proffered arm for support.

From outside, in the Blur, the island in the center of the salt marsh looked too small to house even the tipis of Quivira, much less the wider complex of pens, gardens, and grasslands that surrounded them. Though Dela had seen something similar during her escape from Cahokia, realizing the Elves' elaborate network of underground chambers and tunnels lay within a single earthen mound, she still marveled at the wonders Folk could perform with magecraft.

Wazi was just such a mage, the aged chief of the Lightning Clan. As she had explained to Dela during their many conversations, all speakers of Folktongue belonged to guilds, societies, or clans aligned with their capacity to wield magic.

Those who exhibited the greatest capacity for absorbing and wielding elemental magic became mages. Others, like Dela and Runa, had bodies entirely resistant to elemental magic. This allowed such rangers to journey in safety outside the protection of Shimmer walls and to wield a very different power, temperamental magic. It wasn't shaped with hands or crafted with tools—it was played and sung. All other Folk possessed a capacity for magecraft somewhere in between that of mages and rangers. Some became warriors or hunters. Others learned to cultivate living things or craft inanimate ones.

Dela must have known all this during her former life, memories of which remained tantalizingly out of reach. After Mialuka scouts had carried the exhausted, half-starved Water Maiden to Quivira, she'd relearned much Folklore from Wazi, along with the history of the Mialuka.

For many generations, the winged Folk had made their home in the hills and mountains of Virginia and the Carolinas, hunting the monsters that threatened the local Indian tribes and warring incessantly with an indigenous Folk of lake and stream, the Yehasuri. Finally, the chiefs of the Mialuka, including a then-young Wazi of the Lightning Clan, decided to move their Folk westward in search of more game and fewer enemies. They found the former but not the latter, encountering such bellicose Folk as Pukwudgies in the Ohio valley, Kowi Anukasha in the woodlands of Alabama and Tennessee, and Paissa along the Great Lakes.

Rather than shed more blood, the Mialuka tried the way of peace. As winged fairies, they could offer much to potential allies—but the Folk nations they encountered saw only more competitors for scarce resources. So, the Mialuka continued their migration, crossing the mighty Mississippi and making their way to the high plains.

It was there, on a sunbaked prairie, that they found another desperate Folk seeking safety and sustenance. Called Teihiihan, the "Strong Ones," by local Indians, this small band of stout, wingless fairies either couldn't remember the original name of their Folk or chose not to reveal it to the Mialuka. All they would say is that they were refugees from a terrible catastrophe in the far south, and that they'd run so short of stored magic that most of their number had died or gone mad in the Blur.

The Mialuka had welcomed the refugees with open wings. The two groups built a new Shimmer-shielded home of hide tents and grass domes on the bend of a nourishing river, calling it Quivira. The Teihiihan were skilled trackers and fierce warriors, skills that complemented the unparalleled mobility and perception of the winged Mialuka. Together, the allies found enough monster game—primarily canines in the grasslands and reptilians in the rivers, along with the occasional avian, bovine, and cervine quarry—to sustain Quivira's Shimmer walls for many Folk years, along with valuable humanwares from nearby tribes.

As always, though, nothing stayed in the same in the ever-shifting Blur. The local Indian populations were driven off or shrank precipitously for unknown reasons. The diminishing stock of monsters on the desolate plains forced hunting parties to journey longer and longer distances from Quivira to find game. Some never returned.

At the increasingly contentious councils of Quivira, Mialuka chiefs repeatedly proposed a search for a new home. Teihiihan chiefs flatly refused. They'd lived through one horrendous trek across a forbidding wilderness. Rather than risk another, they came up with a radical alternative. Reasoning that monsters survived in the Blur while also retaining the capacity to store and use elemental magic, the Teihiihan proposed an attempt to gain the same combination of abilities by eating the flesh of monsters—especially those exhibiting any inkling of intelligence.

Horrified at the suggestion, the Mialuka forbade the killing of the few bedraggled beasts still remaining in the pens of Quivira. At first, the Teihiihan grudgingly complied. Then, after a particularly docile River Serpent went missing, several young Teihiihan warriors were caught with gnawed bones and other evidence of a grisly feast. Sentenced to exile, the laughing warriors boasted that the Blur held no more terror for them. Whether the criminals had truly gained the ability to survive beyond the Shimmer, the Mialuka never learned. Attempts to carry out the sentence sparked a short but bloody civil war, after which the rebellious Teihiihan departed by transport spell with most of Quivira's remaining monsters and supplies. Facing no other recourse, the Mialuka fled northeast to build a new village within the great salt marsh.

"How can your Folk be confident of finding yet another place with sufficient game?" Still holding Wazi's slender arm as they walked to the council lodge, Dela glanced at the nearby monster pen and spied a single scrawny Hellhound lying on its side, its formerly red eyes now glowing a faint orange. The sight made her shudder.

"It is not confidence we share," said the old woman. "It is hope. What else is there, in the end?"

~ ~ ~

The council had, indeed, decided to leave.

Assembling the remaining population in the central square, Wazi flew to a beam stretched across two poles. Although high chief of the Mialuka, she'd chosen not to preside over the council's deliberations, since it was her proposal the other chiefs debated. Now that they were agreed, Wazi accepted the responsibility of informing their people.

"All is as it ever was," the gray-haired woman intoned. "Our Folk stands strong. Our Folk soars high. Our Folk survives."

"Our Folk survives," the people of Quivira repeated in unison.

Glancing around the square, Dela studied the few wingless fairies interspersed with the Mialuka. Not all Teihiihan had rebelled against the council. Some were just as revolted as the winged fairies at the notion of eating intelligent monsters. Others had grown too close to the Mialuka to leave. A few even intermarried with them.

This last revelation hadn't shocked Dela, though she couldn't explain why. To be sure, the two peoples differed starkly—it wasn't just the presence or absence of wings. The Teihiihan were shorter and stockier. Their skins were darker red, their teeth more yellow than white. While the Mialuka wore their hair straight and lightly adorned with small beads and shells, the Teihiihan shaved their heads in intricate patterns, wove their remaining tufts of hair into long braids, and wore elaborate headdresses of feather and hide matching the thick bands around their arms and legs. Yet here they were, Mialuka and Teihiihan, slender fairies of the air and squat fairies of the earth, standing side by side to face an uncertain future together.

Are the Gwragedd Annwn so openhearted? Dela wondered. *Are my own Folk so brave?*

The high chief began to sing. The people of Quivira joined her. The Water Maiden had heard many songs during her stay, but none so often as this one. Wazi called it "The Great Lament," explaining that Mialuka rangers had written the piece by adding their own evocative lyrics to a traditional Teihiihan melody, a gesture of respect and solidarity. Though repaid with ingratitude and treachery, the Mialuka continued to revere the song as a musical tribute to their epic quest, adding a final stanza to depict Quivira's civil war and its aftermath.

The Water Maiden closed her eyes and sang the song she now knew by heart:

Sing of when, sing of why,
And sing of what may never be.
Barren land, clouded sky,
A home consigned to memory.

Trekking west, path unknown,
With little but a stubborn hope.
Never trod, never flown,
So through a darkened landscape grope.

Rays of light, faith renewed,
New nations found, new friendships sought.
Wasted word, futile mood,
And countless wars we never fought.

Fields of grass, vast expanse,
More wanderers met on the plain,
Fleet of foot, fierce advance,
Stout allies in our new domain.

Silent sun, starry eyes,

Mute witnesses of deeds below,
Frantic search, dwindling prize,
The seeds of violent discord sow.

Danger grows, no defense,
From desperate minds come ghastly schemes.
Thinking beasts, innocents,
To nightmares turn our noblest dreams.

Acrid words, bitter blood,
The hunters now become the prey.
Mournful tune, teary flood,
A great lament we sing today.

~ ~ ~

A short time later, four parties of rangers set out from Quivira, each in a different direction. Those headed north and south were bound for places where they'd previously found monsters. Those headed east and west were tasked with finding a suitable site for resettlement.

Dela volunteered to join the westbound party. Wazi told her of a great river the humans called the Arkansas, which began in faraway mountains and drew on many tributaries as it wound its way east to the Mississippi. Perhaps somewhere along the river system, they'd find just the right spot for a new Quivira.

Or perhaps a Water Folk was already settled there. *My Folk.*

The party consisted of Dela, two Mialuka rangers, and a Teihiihan loyalist named Shka. Though even shorter and squatter than the average Teihiihan, Shka was surprisingly speedy on his two heavily muscled legs, though of course neither wingless fairy could match the pace of the Mialuka soaring overhead. The three rangers of Quivira did share one thing in common: their preference for the bow, a traditional weapon for both Folk. While Dela tried to master the weapon, her archery skills remained rudimentary. A spear felt more natural in her hands. She borrowed another for the ranging, a thick shaft fitted with a shoulder strap and topped by a jagged triangle of flint.

After two days' travel, they reached a wide river flowing northeast. Dela guessed it was the Arkansas. She volunteered to follow it upstream, suggesting the others continue westward in search of one of its tributaries, the Pawnee River.

"You will fly faster without me stumbling along behind you," Shka told the Mialuka. "I will go with Dela."

That wasn't what the Water Maiden had in mind. Although Shka had been a congenial travel companion, Dela longed to submerge herself in cool water. With the Teihiihan ranger plodding along the riverbank, she'd have to restrain her swimming speed and surface often to stay in contact with him. Given everything the Folk of Quivira had done for her, however, Dela didn't want to seem ungrateful.

"You are most welcome, Shka."

It was an overcast afternoon, gray clouds nearly blotting out the late-spring sun. Coming up for air after a lengthy swim, the Water Maiden found it had begun to rain. The shower sculpted tiny pits and gentle ripples across the surface of the Arkansas River.

"Dela!"

In response to Shka's guttural shout, she spun and jerked the spear over her head, expecting to find her companion contending with some snarling beast. She saw only the pudgy man jogging along the riverbank, an apologetic smile on his wide face.

"Tarry...please," he grunted between pants. "I will...catch up."

Trying not to show her annoyance, Dela gave a curt nod and make a show of studying the narrow strips of vegetation along each side of the river and the silvery fish darting among the reeds.

"Your speed is impressive." Shka slowed to a walk. "I thought only finned or web-toed Folk swam so fast."

Dela whirled in the stream. "You have known other Water Folk?"

"Yes, when I was a lad." The Teihiihan ranger waded into the shallows, relishing the coolness of the water against his tired feet. "While crossing a southern river, we encountered a Folk called the Paakniwat. Slight in body they were, much like the Mialuka, but with the hands and feet of frogs."

"Was their skin like—"

"Nothing like mine." Shka saw Dela start and shook his head. "I do not speak of color. They had copper *scales*, not copper skin."

The Water Maiden tried not to let her disappointment show. “You mentioned ‘finned’ Folk.”

“Yes.” Shka drew an arrow and pretended to tighten its fletching, though Dela guessed he just wanted an excuse to avert his eyes. “Merfolk. Generally they have upper bodies like yours or mine but the lower bodies of fish, though I was once heard a grandmaster talk of a Folk from the frozen north with tentacles instead of—”

The arrow struck Shka in the right leg. Even as he was falling backward into the mud, however, the ranger fit the drawn arrow to his bow and let it fly.

Dela reflexively swept her arms upward, which had the effect of driving her body below the surface of the river an instant before another black-fletched arrow shot past. Then her legs took over, propelling the Water Maiden rapidly through the water in the direction from which the arrows flew. She heard muffled voices ahead.

We face more than one foe, she realized.

Dela gritted her teeth and leapt from the river, gripping her spear tightly. Three stocky archers were running through the grass. Each was in the process of reloading his bow while bellowing in rage. A fourth was sprawled behind them, an arrow sticking out from his dark-red chest.

Well done, Shka!

Then the import of what she saw struck Dela like a thunderbolt.

They are Teihiihan, too.

Ducking into a roll to dodge their next volley, the Water Maiden chose the closest archer and closed the remaining distance with a bound. The man parried her first thrust with his bow. Rather than jab at him a second time, Dela swung the spear at the ranger’s stubby legs, knocking him sideways.

Then something hard struck the side of her head.

Stunned, Dela sank to her knees. Unable to bring her eyes into focus, she groped desperately for her dropped spear.

“Finish her!” demanded a gruff voice.

“No, she may prove useful,” said another.

“They killed Dza-de. No mercy.”

“The traitor is already dead. Dza-de is avenged.”

A rough hand grasped Dela’s hair and jerked her head back. “Blue skin. Never seen her like before.”

A dozen curses, most learned during her stay in Quivira, sprang to Dela’s mind—but it was only a question that sprang to her lips.

"You are Teihiihan. Why kill your own kind?"

"Our own kind? Bah. Teihiihan serve. We rule. Teihiihan cower. We fear nothing."

The broad face that bent down to hers was twisted into a sneer, baring a set of yellow teeth filed into sharp points.

"Teihiihan? A servant word. Now we bear our true name. We are Nimerigar!"

Chapter 16 – The Surrender

May 1841

"THE GOVERNOR MUST THINK ME a fool."

Their spirited conversation, conducted in Spanish, drew little attention. News of the Mexican merchants' arrival from Santa Fe, the first such caravan of the trading season, spread quickly through the bustling city. Discerning businessmen in calf-length frock coats, eager shopkeepers in sweat-stained work shirts, curious ladies in low-waisted dresses, lean young trappers in buckskin leggings—all had crowded into the cramped confines of the popular store on Olive Street. They came to inspect the furs, pelts, fleeces, buffalo robes, and other trade goods brought from New Mexico or to arrange an inspection of the caravan's fine mules.

One reason no one took note of the three men speaking Spanish in the corner was that there were so many other conversations happening in so many other languages. St. Louis was a polyglot city of more than sixteen thousand. They included English speakers from the east, French speakers from the south, German and Gaelic speakers from across the ocean, and Spanish speakers from Mexico and the Caribbean, along with visiting Indians conversing in their own tongues.

So when Mariano Chaves snapped at his nephew to pipe down and listen, the only other person in the store who noticed was their mutual friend, the one who'd accompanied Mariano on his journey to St. Louis.

"You are right to be suspicious, but your uncle speaks wisdom," said Aki, wearing his false human skin to disguise his true form as the monster the Navaho called Tieholtsodi. "Governor Armijo faces bigger problems than a seventeen-month-old accusation of cheating at horses."

"The president of Texas demands most of his attention," Mariano added. "Mirabeau Lamar makes no secret of his desire to claim all of New Mexico east of the Rio Grande for his new republic."

"Texas is nearly bankrupt and has no real army," Manuel scoffed. "Even our foolhardy cousin Armijo is more than a match for Lamar and his rabble."

"What of the United States?" Mariano leaned closer to his nephew, who stood behind a wooden counter. "We hear talk of Texas annexation. Perhaps Lamar only does the bidding of the American president. William Henry Harrison is no stranger to wars of conquest."

Manuel shook his head. "You have not heard. Harrison died weeks ago. The Americans have a new president, a Virginian named John Tyler, and his hold on power is uncertain."

While Aki looked taken aback by the new information, Mariano was unfazed. "Whether Armijo's concerns are justified is immaterial. He has them—and seeks allies to counter a possible invasion."

"Am I to be his *ally* now? The man he cheated? The man he wanted dead?"

"Governor Armijo has already rescinded that order."

"So I can serve in his army? Was I so impressive a warrior during his rise to the governorship?"

Mariano sighed. "You are a skilled marksman and rider, yes, but it is more than that. You are a natural leader, Manuel. You remain popular in the capital. And during your time here, you have become a man of influence. Armijo values your knowledge of the Americans. Their politics. Their interests in Santa Fe."

Although he missed his family, Manuel had to admit, his exile in St. Louis had proven far from disastrous. After some initial setbacks, including a failed partnership with a dishonest Cuban, he found profitable employment with the Spanish merchant whose Olive Street shop Manuel managed. Trading in lumber, fruit, livestock, and goods imported from Santa Fe, Manuel had restored his finances and made many valuable acquaintances.

Of greater personal significance to him—though unknown to all but Aki—was what Manuel had learned during his exile about the magical world existing beyond the perception of most humans. Shortly after the two friends first arrived in St. Louis, they'd visited an ancient Indian site east of the city and spotted a tiny man walking between two grassy hills. Convinced he was one of the Nimerigar, the "People Eaters" feared by shape-shifting monsters, Manuel rushed at the fairy. At first, the little man responded not by drawing a sword, but by singing. When his song proved ineffectual—only later did Manuel figure out singing was the way Folk cast their magic spells—the fairy turned and fled. Easily outpacing his diminutive quarry, Manuel's hand had just reached his billowing cloak when the fairy sang another spell and seemed to run directly *into* an earthen mound.

Strange sensations followed for Manuel and for Aki, who'd grabbed his friend's arm. Their skins felt pricked by tiny needles. The bright light of the shining sun dissolved into the dim light of a dozen torches. And instead of confronting a single People Eater, Manuel and Aki faced half a dozen armed fairies across a cavern that looked far too large to fit inside the mound. One fairy fired a strange-looking bronze gun at Manuel, missing him. Manuel fired back and didn't miss. Meanwhile, Aki shape-shifted and charged, scattering the others with great sweeps of his horned head. After a fierce skirmish, during which the Folk managed to bewitch Aki with their magic song, Manuel noticed one spellsinger exiting through same wall they entered. Recognizing a chance to escape, he seized his friend's tail and lurched backward through the shimmering barrier, knocking the fairy senseless with a parting swing of his musket.

On their way back to town, Aki explained to Manuel that the fairies in the mound differed much in appearance, clothing, and weapons from the Nimerigar. Just to be safe, though, Manuel insisted Aki return to Santa Fe with the next trade caravan, posing as a native guide. Manuel had steered clear of the mounds ever since. Nevertheless, he'd spotted other fairies during his time in Missouri—some dressed, like the mound dwellers, in archaic clothing from the Middle Ages, while others wore breechclouts, mantles, and leggings like Indians.

Now, Aki had come back to St. Louis to add his voice to Mariano's. "Your little brother Román misses you. As does the rest of your family."

Not all, I'll wager. While Manuel only fumed silently, the others heard his unspoken objection.

"Your brother Pedro is rarely in Santa Fe these days," Aki explained. "When not in Cebolleta, he undertakes trade missions south to Chihuahua."

"I need you in Santa Fe, nephew," Mariano added. "We all do."

Manuel scowled. "I will not go home to defend Armijo."

"The real question," his uncle replied, "is whether you will go home to defend New Mexico."

"I cannot do that if the governor has me jailed or killed."

His uncle sighed. "I know you cannot trust Armijo, but you can trust me. I promise he will not harm you, and you know whether my promise amounts to anything or not."

~ ~ ~

It did, of course. So, when the merchants left St. Louis—their wagons and mules loaded with cloth, garments, cutlery, and other trade goods—Manuel Antonio Chaves was in their company, riding a fine young palomino acquired in Missouri. He'd named the stallion Malcreado after the champion Armijo had stolen from him, though his coat was bright gold instead of jet-black.

During the eight-week journey to Santa Fe, Manuel learned more about conditions back home. Like their counterparts in other Mexican states, the leading citizens of New Mexico deplored the instability and violence plaguing their country. Although they didn't join the recent rebellion by other northern states, the demise of the short-lived Republic of the Rio Grande brought a new wave of infuriating taxes and impositions from Mexico City. At the same time, the intrigues of President Lamar and his grasping Texians threatened not only New Mexico's territorial integrity but also its increasingly lucrative trade with the Americans in Missouri.

When the caravan reached Santa Fe, Mariano suggested they spend the night at a cousin's house, then head on to Albuquerque the next morning. News traveled fast in the capital, however, so a summons soon arrived for Manuel to report to the Governor's Palace. Flashing a wry smile, Manuel nodded and picked up the fine Hawken rifle he'd brought from St. Louis.

"You will not need that," Mariano assured him, "for I will accompany you."

Manuel refused to go without his gun, but it was all for naught. When they arrived at the adobe structure on the north end of the city plaza, guards insisted Manuel leave his rifle outside. Seeing no alternative, Manuel did so, taking no small comfort from what remained carefully hidden in his boot.

If your tongue proves forked, Armijo, Lionclaw will cut it out.

The governor greeted them warmly. "Manuel Antonio Chaves, my kinsman! It has been too long."

"It has," Manuel muttered.

"And Mariano, my friend. Your company is always welcome."

The older Chaves inclined his head. "I hope it is clearly understood Manuel has come with a promise of—"

"—a fine supper, and he shall have it," the governor broke in. "There is news to share, and urgent matters to discuss. I always welcome wise counsel. Whose is wiser than that of my honored cousin?"

"From which direction comes your news?"

"It is a threat from the east," Armijo said, though he looked more elated than threatened. "Ruffians from Texas invade our territory to burn, slay, and destroy all in the path."

"So, you *do* expect me to fight in your army." Manuel ignored Mariano's reproachful glare.

The governor rolled his eyes. "I already have an army of soldiers."

"Then what would you have of me?"

"Your knowledge of English, and of the ways of these American devils."

"I am to act as interpreter?"

"And aide-de-camp, when it comes time to treat with them."

The governor seemed strangely nonchalant about the Texians. For the first time in weeks, Manuel found the need to focus his mind with same silent recitation he'd used since childhood. *I hear what is silent. I see what is invisible. I know what is hidden.*

"What do you know of their true intentions?" he asked.

Armijo smiled. "Less than I will know after you question my prisoner—but let us sup first."

~ ~ ~

No wonder he never races his own horses.

Manuel tried not to stare at the governor but found it hard to keep his eyes averted. Armijo looked absurd at the front of the column, riding a stubby-legged mule and wearing a dress uniform a size too small for his portly frame. That he'd ventured out himself at the head of some fifteen hundred regulars and militiamen should have made it obvious he expected no pitched battle with the Texians. However, most of the officers and soldiers sent from Mexico City knew Armijo only by reputation. They seemed impressed.

Whatever else one might say of the man, he was skilled at self-promotion.

Manuel had by now interviewed several prisoners taken from the Santa Fe Pioneers, the name the Texians gave to their expedition. By all accounts, it had gone wrong from the start. After leaving Kenney's Fort, near Austin, the group of some three hundred merchants, officials, teamsters, and armed escorts—including an artillery company—got repeatedly lost, suffered Indian raids, and ran short of provisions. The prisoners insisted the expedition was no invasion, that its commercial intentions were genuine and its leaders empowered only to "offer" New Mexicans the "opportunity of participating in the Texas government," as one Texian put it.

Armijo dismissed their claims as a deception. Manuel gave them little credence as well, but not because he thought the captives were lying. They seemed genuinely to believe much of New Mexico rightfully belonged to Texas and would be better governed from Austin than from Mexico City.

During his time in St. Louis, however, Manuel had come to appreciate how lucrative trade along the Santa Fe Trail could be—and how much cash-strapped Texas stood to gain by taxing it.

A cloud of dust revealed the approach of mounted men. Manuel soon discerned the distinctive red coats and plumed caps of Mexican regulars interspersed with the varied dress of other riders.

"More prisoners!" Armijo announced with satisfaction. "We must be closing on the invaders."

There were five captured Texians, three on horseback and two afoot. One of the riders—a slightly built man wearing white pants, a gray uniform coat, a blue cloth cap, and a nervous smile—dismounted and walked straight to the governor. "In your debt," he said in broken Spanish. "We are American traders from Red River with—"

Armijo moved with surprising alacrity, grabbing the collar of the young man's coat and yanking his shocked face close. "Texas!" Armijo spat, pointing to the lone-star insignia on the captive's buttons. "Do you take me for a fool? Do you think I cannot read? No merchant travels in a Texas military jacket."

One of the other prisoners spoke up. "We *are* Texians, sir," he said in English, "but we have only peaceful intentions. Trade. Cooperation. Formal relations between our governments. Captain Lewis and the other soldiers are merely escorts to safeguard our passage through the wilderness."

The governor turned to Manuel, who quickly translated. "Tell them we already know the scheme of the renegade president they serve," Armijo replied. "Tell them that while their crimes merit death, mercy may yet stay my hand—if they renounce their lies."

As if to punctuate the point, one of the mounted officers behind Armijo, a tall man with long hair and hollow cheeks, slowly drew the sword from his scabbard. The Texian officer named Lewis gulped, his face as white as his trousers.

~ ~ ~

"He had them shot?"

A moment earlier, Manuel Antonio Chaves was enjoying the cool breeze and admiring the cool moonlight dancing across the cool surface of the Pecos River. Now he felt, and saw, only fire.

"Right in the middle of the square, for all to see." Aki shook his head in frustration, flinging drops of water from his long black hair. The skinwalker had just scurried downstream from the village of San Miguel to the main Mexican force camped on the Pecos.

"Coward!" Manuel spat. "I distrust the Texians as well, but those two were not soldiers."

Aki looked grim. "If Armijo has merchants blindfolded and shot in the back, what fate awaits Captain Lewis?"

"Even he deserves better than summary execution. Were there no objections from the regulars?"

"Not that I heard, though some looked disgusted when the sentence was carried out."

That is something. "The militia officers from Santa Fe and Albuquerque will listen," Manuel said. "If I can get enough of the regulars to see reason, perhaps we—"

"There you are, Manuel!" Governor Armijo strode confidently along the riverbank, followed by two officers and a sallow-faced Captain Lewis. "Send your servant away so I may give you instructions."

Manuel glared. "I have told you before. Aki is a friend, not a servant."

"What you choose to call your Indians is up to you." The governor motioned Lewis forward. "Whose ears may hear my words is up to *me*."

Aki rendered their exchange moot by hurrying away.

"What would you have of me, uncle?" Manuel asked. "Am I to translate for you and Captain Lewis?"

Armijo smiled. "We have already come to an understanding."

"Oh?"

"The captain will return east, across the Gallinas River, to parley with the invaders. He needed no interpreter to learn what fate awaits those who resist us. He needed only his own eyes."

So Armijo made Lewis watch his companions die. Manuel studied the pathetic-looking young captain. "Nor will he need an interpreter to deliver such a message."

"Still, you will accompany him." The governor's tone was matter-of-fact. "You are a persuasive talker, and you know something of these Americans. Make sure Captain Lewis fulfills his end of the bargain. Make them see the wisdom of surrender."

"On what terms?"

"That they submit immediately and give up their arms. Then they will be conducted out of New Mexico, never to return."

That sounds...reasonable. "They will ask about their captured men. Are we to return the corpses to them?"

Armijo's lips curled. "That will not be necessary. Word of their fate will be enough."

Manuel glanced again at Lewis, whose eyes were as big as dollar coins. "If the Texians learn what happened to their traders, distrust and anger may lead them to fight, not submit."

"Then I leave the matter to you and Captain Lewis." Armijo turned away. "Say what you must. Unless they lay down their arms, more blood will flow."

~ ~ ~

When Manuel, Aki, and Lewis made contact with the latter's unit several days later, the Texians had already crossed the Gallinas and encountered a forward detachment of Mexicans near the village of Anton Chico, nestled in a bend of the Pecos. As Aki scouted the perimeter, Manuel and Lewis forded the river. Two men rode out to meet them, each wearing a faded coat, threadbare waistcoat, and dirty cravat.

"Lewis!" exclaimed one of the Texians. "God, man, we feared the worst!"

The captain cleared his throat. "I, uh, I am well, sir. Commissioner William Cooke, may I present Manuel Antonio Chaves, the governor's nephew and confidential secretary."

"You may speak your own tongue, sir," Manuel hastened to add. "I know it well from my days in St. Louis."

"Can it be you ply the Santa Fe trade, Don Chaves?" the other man asked. "Commercial opportunity is what brings us here. I am José Antonio Navarro of San Antonio de Béxar."

"You are an…ally of the Texians, Don Navarro?" Manuel failed to mask his surprise.

"I am a *Tejano*, an elected member of Congress," said the man testily, "and duly commissioned by President Lamar to establish peaceful relations with the people of New Mexico."

Manuel sighed. "I fear our government will *not* honor that commission, Don Navarro."

"So we see." Cooke gestured to the hundreds of Mexican troops on the other side of the river. "Our journey has been most trying, sir, and I will not deny our supplies run short, but the men of Texas are not easily cowed. Your former president learned that lesson at San Jacinto."

"Just as your people should have learned a lesson from the Alamo," Manuel replied. "Defiance in the face of overwhelming force earns only death."

"Overwhelming force?" Cooke shook his head. "Our numbers are comparable, and you will find Texians fight like demons."

"You do not understand. Governor Armijo has yet to arrive. He heads an army many times your size."

Cooke turned to Lewis, who nodded in confirmation. "What would you have of us, then?" the commissioner demanded.

"Your surrender, sir."

Navarro sneered. "If your governor takes inspiration from your disgraced former president, how can he be trusted? All of Texas knows what truly happened at the Alamo. All of Texas knows what 'terms' Santa Anna offered the victims of the Goliad massacre."

The man's suspicious were not without foundation, Manuel had to concede, yet the only apparent alternative to surrender was a battle that would take many lives. He also thought it best not to correct Navarro's reference to the "disgraced" Santa Anna, who—Manuel learned during his short stay in Santa Fe—was angling to return to power in Mexico City.

He chose his next words carefully. "I am Manuel Antonio Chaves. From my home village of Cebolleta on the western frontier to the thriving cities of the Pecos and the Rio Grande, and even in far-off St. Louis, my name is known and respected. The offer I carry is of an honorable peace. Lay down your arms. We will provide food and supplies. Your persons and property will be respected. You have my word that I will do everything in my power to ensure you are conducted safely back to the border of your country."

Navarro inclined his head. "We do not question your word, Don Chaves, but you are not in command. How can we be sure your uncle will honor such an agreement?"

It was then that Lewis spoke up for the first time. "He gave me his personal assurance."

Cooke touched Navarro's arm just as the latter was about to reply. "Captain Lewis, you didn't ride out from our column alone. Where are your companions? Is the governor holding them prisoner to compel you to speak on his behalf?"

Manuel grimaced. *I will not lie to cover up Armijo's crimes.* "It is not necessary that you—"

"The others are safe," Captain Lewis blurted out. "The governor will honor the terms of the surrender. You have my word as an officer, a Mason, and a Texian."

Shocked into silence, Manuel stared at the young man's anguished eyes and twitching throat. Why would Lewis lie about the fate of the other captives? Was he a coward trying to save his own skin? Had Armijo promised him a reward for delivering the Texians into his hands? Or did Lewis simply agree that surrender was their only option but, unlike Manuel, was willing to say anything to accomplish it?

If I contradict Lewis now, that will destroy the credibility of us both. The Texians will never lay down their arms.

There was nothing left to say.

~ ~ ~

Whatever Captain Lewis's motivations, his answer proved decisive. Cooke and Navarro accepted the terms. After making sure the first promise was kept—Manuel personally supervised the delivery of meat and flour to the famished Texians—he rode out from camp under a sky painted orange by the setting sun. Aki had not yet returned from reconnoitering the Texian position. It was a task that shouldn't have consumed the better part of a day. Manuel feared something was amiss.

Hours after the gibbous moon rose to flash its cryptic smile, he reached a wide creek that fed the Pecos. Thinking it was just the sort of waterway Aki would find congenial, he directed Malcreado to follow its winding path into the brush.

The song sliced the night air like a sword.

Manuel had heard its slash before, though he hadn't felt it. He'd witnessed a fairy use such a song to bewitch Aki during their skirmish in the Indian mound. Now he was hearing it again, not hundreds of miles away in Missouri but here in his own country.

Aki is in danger!

Manuel drew the loaded Hawken rifle from his saddle, yanked its back trigger to cock the hammer, and spurred his palomino to a gallop. The closer he got to the source of the song, the more its keen edge dulled into a blunt pressure against his body. Soon, it felt like an invisible lasso drawn tight by an unseen vaquero.

My friend is in danger!

Though he kept a firm grip on his reins and rifle, Manuel was determined to break free of the unseen constriction. He willed himself to imagine a second set of arms sprouting from his torso, sinewy and swift. They grabbed the invisible lasso and yanked. Its fibers stretched, and squeaked, and broke.

Then he spotted Aki. The long-trunked Water Monster crouched in the shallow creek, snarling and shaking his horned head. A pointy-eared spellsinger stood in the grass beyond, his thin lips forming a perfect circle, his arms holding a bronze musket, his finger on the trigger. Another figure hovered overhead, a diminutive archer drawing back his bowstring to shoot.

It was impossible to tell at such a distance which way the winged archer was aiming. The gunman was, however, clearly aiming at Aki. Without hesitation, Manuel raised the rifle to his shoulder and tapped its front trigger.

The magic song ended abruptly. Then Manuel heard the whistle of an arrow and the thump as it struck home.

He felt no sting. His eyes only for Aki, he leapt from the saddle and landed with a splash in the creek, intent on discovering how badly the monster was wounded. Moonlight glinted off his blade. Lionclaw would dig out the offending arrow—after it tasted the blood of its shooter.

Aki was, however, unharmed. Freed from the spell, the Water Monster thrust his head up and roared. Manuel looked up as well and saw a small form silhouetted against the night sky.

Crash!

Manuel and Aki spun around, finding a little man floating face down on the surface of the water, an arrow protruding from his back. He was shaped and dressed like the other fairy, except that he wore small pack from which protruded two thin crumpled objects that might once have been wings.

When the two friends returned their eyes to the sky, they saw only the grinning moon.

~ ~ ~

The ride back took a long time, during which Aki, now back in human form, related his tale of spotting the spellsinger near the Texian position, shaking off the fairy's initial spell attack, chasing him downstream, and then succumbing to a mood spell strengthened by the second fairy's voice.

It was midmorning when they reached the camp and discovered the now unarmed Texians sitting in groups within an old sheep corral, their hands securely bound with ropes and thongs. Manuel dismounted, signaled to Aki to lead the exhausted horse away, and approached a line of Mexican officers on the porch of a small house. "What is the meaning of this? We promised to respect the persons and property of these men."

"The renegades received no such promise, as far as I know, nor do they deserve one," said one of the officers, whom Manuel recognized as the gaunt-faced man who'd threatened Captain Lewis with his sword. "Mexico is no weakling to be bullied by such as these."

"Only a bully would truss up defenseless men and abuse them so."

The officer stiffened. "I do not answer to you."

"Hold on, Captain Archuleta," said another officer. Manuel recognized him as Miguel Pino, whose father had once represented New Mexico in legislature of Spain. "This is the governor's secretary, Manuel Chaves. He negotiated the Texian surrender."

"So what?" Archuleta replied. "If Armijo himself were standing before me, I'd still say the same thing."

The door to the house, which had been slightly ajar when Manuel arrived, now swung open so violently that it banged. "Say it now, then!" demanded Governor Armijo as he entered the porch, followed by other senior officers.

Archuleta looked unperturbed. "I would say we must make an example of the invaders, Your Excellency. Do their crimes not merit the ultimate punishment?"

"Ah." Armijo stroked his whiskers thoughtfully. "And you, Lieutenant Pino, what would you have me do with them?"

Pino's eyes flitted to Manuel's. "Carry out the terms of the surrender, sir. Honor requires no less."

Captain Archuleta glowered at the lieutenant, who mumbled something under his breath. The senior officers behind Armijo also began arguing. Only when the governor removed a handkerchief from his waistcoat to mop his furrowed brow did Manuel finally understand what was happening. Armijo had evidently ordered the Texians stripped of their possessions and tied up in the corral. He'd probably ordered their summary execution, as well. Some of Armijo's officers objected, however, in an unmistakable challenge to the governor's authority.

Was Armijo only pretending to consider their views? Or might he bend to the will of a majority of his officers? Manuel considered all that he knew of the man. One description stood out more than any other: coward.

He wants to repudiate his own terms of surrender. He wants to massacre the Texians, but lacks the nerve to act against prevailing opinion.

"You certainly have the courage of your convictions, uncle!" Manuel announced in a loud voice that silenced all other conversations. "I have heard you say good leaders listen to the counsel of others. Now, in your wisdom, you have left the fate of your captives in the hands of your officers!"

This time, it was Armijo who was left with nothing to say that would not impeach his own credibility. His icy expression warmed Manuel's heart.

~ ~ ~

The debate began after supper and lasted much of the night. The abode walls of the house were thin enough that the men tied up in the corral must have overheard it. They must have heard Armijo and his lackeys argue passionately for immediate execution. They must have heard Manuel and others argue just as passionately for the terms of the agreement to be carried out, that the Texians be conducted safely out of New Mexico.

Finally, the exhausted governor called the question. By a single vote—his own—Manuel Chaves prevailed. The Texians would live, though Armijo still refused to grant them liberty. Instead, he ordered they be taken to Mexico City as prisoners of war.

The governor stormed out of the house in a rage. After a prudent delay, Manuel exited as well, not enraged but also far from satisfied by the partial repudiation of the terms. Finding Aki waiting by the river with Malcreado and another saddled horse, Manuel mouthed a silent "thank you." The two left immediately for Santa Fe.

They hadn't gone far when a rustle of leaves caught their attention. Snapping his head around, Manuel spotted moving branches in a nearby tree. Then something leapt from the foliage.

Aki held up his hand. "It could be just a bird taking—"

It wasn't. Both men saw slender legs dangling from the body of the flier, legs clad in light-green breeches fastened at the knee and thrust into shoes of brown leather. Manuel yanked out his rifle.

"Hold!" The approaching fairy held up his hands to show them empty. "I am not your enemy!"

"You lie!" Manuel retorted. "We have fought little winged men like you before!"

"No, you fought Elves—as have I." Now hovering overhead, the fairy gazed down at them with a reassuring smile. "I am no Elf. I am a Sylph. My name is Goran Lonefeather."

Chapter 17 – The Monster

October 1841

ALL GAMS ARE THE SAME.

Bull knew what was coming. He'd experienced enough shipboard visits to know their choreography, just like his Irish sailors knew their jigs and reels.

At the start of a gam, the host captain would welcome his counterpart aboard his whaler, boasting about its speed, its crew, its latest kills. Then he'd invite his visitors to dine in his cabin, feasting on fresh fruits and vegetables, poultry, or fish, even as the common sailors made do with salt pork and hardtack. When the meal was done, the captain would produce a deck of tar-stained cards and offer to play whist, cribbage, or high-low jack.

Here in the cabin of the *Zone*, a three-masted bark out of Nantucket, the mates had just cleared the table. "Care for a game of whist?" asked their captain, a thin-faced Rhode Islander named Edwin Hiller.

Absolutely not, Bull wanted to snap.

"Aye, let's play," Bull actually said, stroking his gray-tipped whiskers. Over the years, he'd found that the longer a gam lasted, the looser the other captain's tongue became.

Hiller tittered nervously, glancing at the other two men in the cabin. His first mate, Munroe, was a scrawny Scotsman with a bushy red beard. The *Zone*'s second mate, Orley, was a big bear of a man. His prodigious appetite kept his mouth full throughout the meal, though he apparently had nothing to say when his mouth was empty.

"I'd normally challenge you and your first mate, Captain Stormalong," Hiller began, "but as you're alone, I suppose Orley here can serve as your—"

"Ain't alone." Bull jerked his thumb toward the fifth occupant of the cabin.

"Your *cabin boy*?" The captain of the *Zone* guffawed. "I think you'll find Orley a better whist partner."

"Think not," Bull replied, glaring at Gez to keep him from objecting to the insult. "Good boy. Whip-smart."

Hiller sighed. "Very well. You *are* my guest. That'll be all, Orley."

Clearly disappointed, the hulking officer rose. When Bull stood up to nod his farewell, however, he made Orley look more like a cub than a bear.

Gez scrambled to take the second mate's place. Hiller regarded him with disdain. "Should I review the rules for the boy's benefit?"

"No, thank you," said Gez, snatching the deck and giving it a practiced shuffle.

Hiller's dark eyebrows shot up. "So, Captain," he said, watching the Kabouter's deft card-handling. "I understand you've just arrived in Tahiti. Having a profitable voyage?"

"Yep," Bull lied.

In point of fact, he'd kept his men so busy chasing rumors of Krakens over the past three years that their whale hunts were mostly afterthoughts or fortunate accidents. Moreover, after Bull had renovated the *Courser* to accommodate cannons and carronades—as well as a dozen extra crewmen, marines recruited from four different navies—the ship had less room for storing oil and spermaceti. When last in Massachusetts, the sale of the *Courser*'s wares produced barely enough money to resupply the ship. Still, most of Bull's sailors had stayed with him. They had their own score to settle with the Kraken, after all. And there was no richer life for a mariner than to sail with the legendary A. B. Stormalong.

"Well, I've been stuck here for weeks," the captain of the *Zone* complained. "Outbreak of smallpox. Half my men were down for the—"

He jerked in surprise when Gez slapped the shuffled deck down on the table.

"Uh, yes, I suppose I should deal." Recovering his composure, Hiller nodded to the visiting captain. "Cut?"

Bull frowned. *I'd rather cut firewood with a dull hatchet!* he wanted to shout. *I'd rather cut a dozen tentacles off a dozen Krakens than play another blasted game of cards with the likes of you.*

He said none of that, of course. Bull merely tapped the deck with a meaty forefinger.

"Wasn't just on the *Zone*, you know." Hiller began dealing. "The *Almira* was here for weeks. Captain Tobey had to hire Tahitians to restock because his men were too weak. The *Almira* only left port yesterday."

"How odd," said Gez, trying to sound like the naïve boy he resembled. "Captain Stormalong insisted everyone on the *Courser* be inoculated against the pox before we left Massachusetts."

"Mind ye tongue, laddie," snapped Munroe, the first mate. "The pox dinnae concern ye."

"True enough." The Kabouter suppressed a smirk. "I was inoculated."

"Captain Hiller," Bull interjected, determined to get on with the real reason he'd agreed to the gam. "Heard strange tales up Honolulu way, about a terror of the sea. Some call it a Kraken. Ever heard such?"

He'd posed this question dozens of times, in seaports, coastal villages, and ship-to-ship gams from the North Atlantic to the South Pacific. The captains, sailors, and merchants Bull queried answered in one of two ways: Either they laughed off talk of Krakens as nonsense, or they gleefully passed along colorful stories and preposterous rumors they'd heard from others while denying any personal experience with the beast.

Edwin Hiller did neither. He didn't respond to Bull at all. Instead, the captain of the *Zone* tossed his unplayed hand on the table and grimaced at his first mate. "Put 'em up to this, Munroe?"

"Nae, cap'n," the Scotsman insisted. "Musta haird it elseweer."

Gez placed his own cards down, though more carefully than Hiller had. "Heard what?"

"Nothing of consequence," said an irritated Hiller. "Fanciful chatter by a callow youth who doesn't know when to stay silent."

"A sailor on the *Zone*?"

"Fur mair 'en two yars," Munroe said. "Nem's Peter."

"Peter *Williams*," Hiller finished. "Signed on in Nantucket. A greenhand, to be sure, but better than some. Peter's loyal, at least, which is more than I can say for many. Ungrateful wretches. You know the type, Captain."

Bull *didn't* know but nodded anyway. "This Peter's spreadin' Kraken stories?"

Hiller frowned. "That's just it. He's no chatterbox. Mostly keeps to himself. Peter didn't soak up a fish tale from some old salt. He claims to have seen a sea monster himself, during our last hunt."

Gez and Bull exchanged excited looks. "How long ago?" the Kabouter pressed.

"Aboot a month," Munroe said.

"Took a black calf off the coast of Tubuai," Hiller explained. "Peter's never been much use with spade or knife. So, while the others cut in, I put him up in the crow's nest spotting for sharks. Says he saw a huge form break the surface, shiny and red, with writhing arms."

Munroe shrugged. "Jus' a cuttlefish."

"Or a squid, aye, but he won't stop talking about it. I won't have him making the *Zone* the butt of jokes from here to the Bay of Islands!" Hiller's fist struck the table so hard, his cards bounced. One flipped face up—the nine of diamonds.

The first mate jerked back as if the table had burst into flames. "Curse o' Scotland!"

His captain rolled his eyes. "You and your primitive superstitions. Captain Stormalong, I trust you will not think ill of me for the delusions of my crew."

Bull thought ill of Edwin Hiller, all right, but not because of his sailor's talk of a Kraken or his mate's irrational fear of a playing card. Bull just didn't like this captain of the *Zone*. The man hadn't bothered to inoculate his sailors against smallpox, always a prudent precaution. And Hiller's complaints about loyalty made Bull suspect he'd so mistreated his crew as to make them mutinous. *Or perhaps some already tried to mutiny, but young Peter didn't join in.*

"Got no ill will for you," Bull lied again. "Mind if I meet this Peter?"

Hiller's eyes narrowed. "Why waste your time?"

"A hobby of the captain's," Gez added quickly. "Stormalong has a legendary reputation of his own, you know, so he is naturally curious about how such fanciful stories get built up from nothing."

Munroe had backed up against the wall, still staring at the nine of diamonds and mumbling. Recognizing there'd be no whist game, Hiller reluctantly agreed to call Peter Williams to his cabin. As Bull sat back to wait, it occurred to him that while this shipboard visit had started like all the others, it ended with a surprise.

Maybe all gams ain't the same.

~ ~ ~

Peter Williams wasn't the "callow youth" Bull expected. A tall, well-built twenty-year-old with dark skin and close-cropped hair, Peter was reserved to the point of timidity and stammered while repeating his story to the imposing captain of the *Courser* and his precocious cabin boy. His words sounded sincere, however, and Peter's description fit the Kraken in every respect. Although it had been many weeks since Peter spotted the beast—and it would take at least a week to reach its last known location, off the coast of Tubuai—Bull had his first solid lead in more than a year.

The men of the *Courser* could tell their captain was excited and correctly surmised it had to do with the Kraken. They could also tell his excitement was tinged with annoyance, and correctly surmised its cause was following closely behind the *Courser* as it sailed south from Tahiti.

"Slowin' us down." Bull groused.

"The same wind fills our sails and his," Gez chided, not bothering to look up from the newspaper he was reading. He sat on a barrel next to the mizzenmast.

Bull stood nearby, his back turned, his sepia eyes fixed on the foremast of the ship trailing them, the *Zone*. "Only wanted Peter." It pleased Bull to imagine that if he glared long enough, Edwin Hiller's sails might burst into flame.

Gez chuckled. "And Captain Hiller could not help wondering *why* you wanted a greenhand for your crew. I keep telling you to learn self-control."

"You also say 'show my true colors,'" Bull replied. "Which is it? Can't do both."

"Oh, I do not know about that." This time the Kabouter looked up, regarding his captain thoughtfully. "There is more to you than meets the casual eye, my friend."

Bull had spent years trying to make sense of such cryptic comments. *Waste of time*. "Mister Williams!"

The young sailor dropped the mop he'd been pushing and hurried across the deck. "Aye, cap'n."

"You know Hiller. How long'll he follow?"

Peter glanced at the other ship. "Long as he sees profit in it."

"Ain't after whales. Told 'em that."

"He does not believe you," Gez said. "He sees all this talk of a monster as code for some big, lumbering bull."

While Bull refused to reward his mocking friend with even a faint smile, Peter didn't get the joke at all. "The tale of Mocha Dick fascinates Captain Hiller. Talks of it often."

"So if another great whale meets its end, Hiller wants a hand in it." Gez rose from the barrel. "Captain Stormalong, I submit your problem will take care of itself. Either Mister Williams leads us to—"

"Not Williams."

Bull and Gez exchanged puzzled looks.

"Not my real name." The young man stared at his feet. "I'm Peter Van Wagenen. That's the name my mama chose."

The Kabouter inclined his head. "Very well. Either Mister *Van Wagenen* leads us to the Kraken, from which Hiller will likely flee, or we will have a long and fruitless hunt—and, soon enough, a solitary one."

~ ~ ~

For all his experience, Gez had failed to foresee a third alternative.

When the *Courser* and *Zone* reached Tubuai, Peter guided them to where he'd spotted the tentacled beast. An extensive search revealed no sign of it. The search did, however, net two whales off the northeast coast of the island, followed a few days later by two more. Although the crews of both ships were exhausted, the resulting bounty of oil and baleen left them delighted. For his part, Captain Hiller concluded that fortune smiled on the legendary A. B. Stormalong—and that the longer he remained in Old Stormy's company, the more money he'd make.

Hoping to discourage his unwanted ally, Bull headed northeast, toward the sparsely populated Paumotus islands. Unfortunately for his plans, but fortunately for everyone else, their streak of successful hunts continued. And so the *Zone* followed along, week after week, as the *Courser* passed the islands and entered the open sea.

Half a dozen times, Bull was tempted to put the matter bluntly to Hiller: Sail the other direction or suffer a broadside from the *Courser's* impressive array of guns. The *Zone* had only a single bow-mounted cannon, a precaution against pirates—but it never came to a firefight.

Every time, Gez talked Bull out of it.

"Only a scoundrel would fire on a fellow countryman," said the Kabouter, leading the way to the cabin after Bull's latest tirade on deck.

"Not my 'true colors,' you mean."

Gez nodded. "The *Courser* flies a hero's flag, not a villain's."

Bull plopped onto a chair and produced a walrus tusk from his pocket. Drawing his rigging knife, the captain began to carve. Though Hiller's continued presence frustrated him, their regular sequence of hunts *had* given the crew of the *Courser* multiple opportunities to practice close-quarters tactics for battling the Kraken. Each whaleboat was crowded with three extra men—marines armed with long halberds and short pistols. Against whales they were largely superfluous, though sometimes an axeblade rather than a lance finished a hunt. Against a tentacled monster, however, the marines would be invaluable.

Bull's other tactic for battling the Kraken—broadsides from the *Courser*'s lower row of heavy cannons and upper row of lighter carronades—was harder to practice. He couldn't afford to use up his limited inventory of powder, ball, and grapeshot. Still, much of his crew had previously served on naval vessels. They knew their way around guns. When the time came, they'd do their duty.

If the time comes. Bull dug in with the point of the knife, channeling his frustration into the yellowed surface of the ivory.

They'd journeyed far, far past Tubuai. Had it been too long since Peter sighted the Kraken? Had he truly seen it? Not for the first time, Bull entertained a still more disquieting thought: Even if the young man *had* seen a Kraken and they caught up with it, how could they be sure it was the same beast that killed Morgan and Bayani? After all, no one could say how many Krakens there might be the world.

I'll know, Bull insisted to himself. *Somehow, I'll be sure*.

And he was.

The scrimshawed tusk dropped to the floor. For only the second time in his life, Bull felt his insides twist into a knot. Invisible needles pricked the back of his neck. He wasn't afraid—as far as he could remember, Bull had never experienced that emotion—nor was he angry. He'd experienced that emotion too many times to count. No, this was neither fear nor rage. It was the feeling of being watched, being studied, being assessed.

Being stalked.

Bull bolted for the door.

When he reached the deck, followed closely by Gez, the first mate was waiting by the hatch. "About to call ya, cap'n. Spotted to starboard. Could be the—"

"'Tis," Bull agreed.

"Red deevil." Gunnar blew out a breath. "All hands ta stations!"

The men of the *Courser* scrambled to their prearranged posts, though none could yet see the quarry. Some stood ready at the sails while others headed below to man the guns. All knew their captain's battle plan: First, they'd batter the monster with ball and shot, hoping to slay it outright or greatly degrade its strength and mobility. Once it was sufficiently weakened, they'd launch whaleboats and move in for the kill.

Though their captain couldn't see the Kraken either, Bull knew it was close. He could feel its attention. Its hunger. Its contempt. He glanced around the deck. Gunnar, Orcus, his sailors, his marines—all were at their stations, their faces painted with streaks of anxiety and determination, their eyes trained not on their captain but on the stretch of ocean between the *Courser* and the *Zone.*

Bull followed their gaze. Far in the distance, something red and shiny broke the waterline. It was out of range of the carronades, but not the other guns. Gunnar realized that too. "Fire starboard guns!"

As they blared, Bull felt a sudden irrational urge to hurl himself over the rail, following the path of the cannonballs to attack the Kraken with his bare hands. Whether their first barrage struck home, he couldn't tell. Perhaps it would be the second barrage that cracked the creature's thick carapace, or the third. That it would crack was, he judged, a certainty.

The *Courser* turned, then fired again. The heavy missiles from the port-side cannons struck the surface, sending a spray high into the air. After it receded, Bull saw tentacles twisting frenetically above the waterline. Had they already wounded the Kraken? He fought the impulse to order his men into the whaleboats. *Not yet. This is no whale. It's a creature of shell, sinew, and sorcery. We must weaken it further before we can kill it.*

Again, Gunnar steered the ship closer to their prey. Again, Bull hurried across the deck to keep it in sight. As he passed the mainmast, he glanced up and spied the small form of Gez standing on a spar next to Peter Van Wagenen.

The starboard cannons fired again. Soon, the *Courser* would be close enough to blast the beast with grapeshot. As the round shot hit the water, Bull saw the long tentacles jerk, then flail the water fecklessly. They'd surely hit the beast that time! "Keep it up, men! Carronades, prepare to fire!"

Then, just beyond the writhing stalks, Bull saw glimpses of flesh, cloth, wood, and glinting metal.

Curse him!

"Cap'n!" Gunnar shouted. "The *Zone* has launched boats!"

"I know. Cease fire!"

Perhaps Edwin Hiller wasn't so craven after all. Or, at least, his avarice exceeded his cowardice. Though Hiller clearly didn't know what sort of prize awaited them in the water, he was intent on claiming his share of it.

Or more than his share, if the man can get away with it.

~ ~ ~

The *Courser*'s whaleboats sliced rapidly through the choppy water, propelled by stout oars and the stout men who pulled them. The lead craft outpaced the other three, its speed seemingly enhanced by the fury of its boatsteerer.

"I ask you once more—turn back!" Gez stood next to Bull in the stern. "Convince Hiller to pull his boats back, too. The Kraken remains too much of a threat to face with hand weapons."

"It'll get away," Bull insisted. "And Hiller won't listen."

"You cannot know unless you try."

The captain rolled his large eyes at the Kabouter, then returned his attention to the sea ahead. Hiller's men stopped rowing their whaleboats, which now formed a ragged line. Had they finally realized their quarry wasn't a whale and lost their nerve? Then it occurred to him there was no line of wriggling tentacles between Hiller's boats and his own.

Has the Kraken already fled?

What happened next supplied a grim answer to Bull's unspoken question.

Up rose a mountain from under the distant whaleboats, a mountain formed of sea and flesh and evil. Its watery plateau struck the boats' keels and hurled their occupants into the air. A moment later, what lay beneath caught some of the failing sailors with pliable arms and others on its rigid carapace.

Hiller's men were babbling, bawling, screaming. Stormalong's men were grunting, cursing, shouting. Gez was singing. Only Bull and the Kraken were silent, the former by choice and the latter, he assumed, by nature.

Bull steered his boat at the closest tentacle. It held two sailors in separate coils. Nodding to one of the marines to swap places with him, he grabbed the man's long-shafted halberd. He'd often practiced with the archaic infantryman's weapon—cutting with its axeblade, yanking with the hook that protruded from the back of the blade, stabbing with the spike at its top.

When he reached the harpooneer thwart, Bull stopped and looked up at his target. Oddly, the two sailors from the *Zone* were still struggling and blubbering in the coils. During their first encounter with the Kraken, it had squeezed the life from Bayani within seconds and finished Morgan almost instantaneously.

Why are these sailors still alive?

Puzzled, Bull looked over his shoulder at Gez. The Kabouter, still singing, could only shrug. It was then Bull realized the Kabouter was casting a spell not on the Kraken, but on the men of the *Courser*. A courage spell. Bull studied the faces of his men. Each returned his gaze with blinking eyes and nervous smiles. They weren't as terrified as Hiller's men, but none looked as determined as the sailors had back on the *Courser*.

Then the explanation came to him: *terror magic*.

Bull had witnessed the effects of magic before. During his first encounter with Mocha Dick, the White Whale intensified the hatred felt by Bull and his crew, making them act recklessly. And during their first battle with the Kraken, his men were more anxious at the sight of it than he'd expected—though, for some reason, the monster's terror spell hadn't worked on Bull. Now, the Kraken seemed to be radiating stronger magic than before, perhaps in response to being shot at. If not for the Kabouter's counterspell, fear might have completely overwhelmed Bull's men, as it had the men of the *Zone*.

Again, however, the captain of the *Courser* felt no terror. He felt only righteous anger. He drew strength from it, feeling it course through his veins and nourish his muscles.

As his boat passed under the waving tentacle, Bull swung the halberd with all his might. The blade chopped deep into the slimy stalk, releasing the two sailors as it recoiled. Spinning the shaft of the weapon in his hands, Bull reached out as far as he could and swung the halberd, trying to snag the base of the tentacle with its hook.

On the fourth swing, it caught. The boat lurched to port as the stalk jerked back. Trusting the men behind him were ready, Bull held the haft of the halberd with an iron grip and braced himself against the side of the craft, forcing it to skip along the surface of the sea after the retracting tentacle.

Whether because of the Kabouter's courage spell or their captain's example, his men *were* ready. While a couple remained at the oars, the rest attacked. Two marines swung halberds at the tentacle. A third jammed the muzzle of his pistol into the monster's flesh and pulled the trigger. The remaining sailors stabbed with lances and boarding knives.

Intent on keeping their target close, Bull clung to the poleaxe. Through the choppy water, he could see the base of the tentacle where it merged into the fleshy trunk of the Kraken. Then his eyes wandered to the lip of its protective shell. The first thing he noticed thrilled him. There was a large round indentation in the carapace—and extending up and down from it, a large crack. The *Courser*'s guns had struck home!

However, the second thing Bull noticed chilled him. The round indentation in the shell was surprisingly shallow, the chitin-like substance within it noticeably pinker and shinier than the carapace surrounding it. Though the implication seemed impossible, Bull couldn't deny that it looked like the cannonball wound, dealt only minutes before, had already begun to heal!

Is anything truly impossible when magic is involved?

Bull looked left and right. All around were sights and sounds of battle. He saw his second mate, Orcus, standing at the prow of another boat and jabbing the water with his lance, trying to reach the Kraken's unshielded flesh. Other men of the *Courser* filled their mouths with curses and their hands with blades and guns. Even some of Hiller's crewmen, apparently regaining their nerve as they came in range of Gez's spellsong, had clambered aboard an intact boat and rowed into the fray, swinging at passing tentacles with hatchets and oars.

Though their ferocity and unity of action should have heartened Bull, he remained suspicious. The Kraken still seemed to be holding back. Was it merely playing with them, like a cat with a mouse? Were its wounds so grievous it lacked the strength to fight aggressively? Or was it planning to—

"Harpoons!" Bull ordered at the top of his lungs. "Don't let it dive!"

He let go of the halberd and looked over his shoulder. One of his sailors was already fitting the iron shaft of the harpoon into its pole. Seizing the weapon eagerly, Bull pitched it at the base of the tentacle. His aim was true. Only a short distance away, Orcus hove his own harpoon through the hide of the monster with a triumphant yell. Whether the other boats managed the feat, Bull couldn't tell. Then the whine of his tow line against the loggerhead confirmed that if they hadn't, the opportunity was now lost.

The Kraken was fleeing, all right—and fortunately for its human hunters, the beast chose a horizontal path away from their boats rather than diving straight down, which might have forced them to cut their ropes to avoid being sucked into the sea.

"Brace!" Bull bellowed, eyeing the rapidly diminishing coil of tow line. His men crouched low, grasping the sides and thwarts of the boat. Still singing, Gez narrowed his eyes in concentration.

As the rope went slack and drooped, so did Bull's hopes to tire the beast. Just as before, the Kraken used its fin to execute a sharp change in direction. Its sudden right-angle turn dislodged both harpoons.

And the monster was headed straight for the *Courser*.

"Follow!"

Bull soon recovered the tow line and harpoon. He glared in frustration at the latter, clearly incapable of a solid grip on the agile monster. Behind him, oars slapped in a steady rhythm, driving the whaleboats rapidly through the water.

Not rapidly enough. The shipkeepers—the mechanics, greenhands, and other crewmen left behind when the rest went hunting—lined the rail of the *Courser*. Most were motionless, watching the approaching behemoth with wide, panicked eyes. A few were scrambling down hatches in a frantic search for refuge.

"Too far." An exhausted-sounding Gez stopped singing and fumbled for his canteen. "Too many."

Bull groaned when he saw unmanned guns. He cursed himself for removing their best gunners—and their only spellsinger—from the ship. *Fool! You no longer captain a whaler. You captain a warship!*

When the Kraken reached the *Courser*, it didn't use its flinty carapace as a ram as Bull had expected. Instead, it reached five tentacles under the keel and snaked the others up the starboard side. Grabbing and then casting aside several frightened sailors, the monster soon found the leverage it sought. Red stalks wrapped around the foremast, mainmast, and mizzenmast. Another seized the bowsprit.

"Faster!" Bull called back to his rowers. It was all so clear in his mind. The glistening body of the beast was halfway out of the water, covering multiple gunports. *If we could but fire a couple of broadsides at such range! Not even this spawn of Hell could survive!* Unfortunately, they remained too far away, and the resumption of Gez's spellsong had yet to free the shipkeepers from the grip of the Kraken's magic.

Crack!

The pull of the massive cephalopod proved too much for the bowsprit. Waving the broken shaft in the air with an upthrust arm, the Kraken kept crawling up the ship with the other three. Would the thicker masts hold its weight? To Bull, it hardly seemed to matter. Either the monster would reach the deck and have its way with the crew or the *Courser* would lose its masts, rigging, and sails, leaving it unable to move, turn, and fire.

Boom! Boom! Boom!

A chunk of carapace shattered and fell into the churning water, along with the joint and upper trunk of a tentacle. The rest of the severed arm went limp, letting go of the mizzenmast and flopping against the side of the *Courser*.

A raucous cheer from behind Bull jolted him out of stunned astonishment. All was not yet lost! Somehow, enough shipkeepers had overcome their fear to operate the carronades. Through the opening left by the Kraken's missing body, he could see movement behind one of the smoking guns. Was it his men reloading the short-range guns?

Boom! Boom! Boom!

This time it was the cannons that fired. The monster shuddered, losing its grip on the mainmast. As its twitching body slid down the side to reveal part of the gun deck, Bull spotted an unexpected face peering over the muzzle of a cannon: Peter! Of all the men of the *Courser* and the *Zone*, he'd never have expected young Van Wagenen to be the one to exhibit such willpower and ingenuity.

The captain's whaleboat was now only two dozen feet from the ship. The others were close behind. "Get ready!" Bull shouted, hefting his pole-axe. "It's close to done for!"

Crack!

Had the creature's sole remaining hold put too much weight on the *Courser*'s foremast? Bull looked up. No, the foresails still fluttered in the breeze. He returned his attention to the hulk of flesh and shell clutching his ship. Selecting the base of a flailing tentacle as his target, Bull swung the halberd. He grunted his satisfaction as it dug a large cleft.

The report of pistols, the clang of metal on shell, and the thud of metal on flesh told him other *Courser* men had also entered the fray. Gez stepped aside, allowing an axe-wielding marine to join Bull at the bow of the boat, then resumed his courage song. Soon its lilting melody would further weaken the monster's control of the men on the ship. If they could reload and fire the guns again, the Kraken might be done for.

Then two sounds reached Bull's ears—two fateful sounds that drove all thoughts of impending victory from his mind.

Crack!

This time, his eyes found the source of the sound. Using the broken bowsprit like a pike, the Kraken had smashed it into the side of the *Courser*. Although the entry hole was above the waterline, Bull judged by the angle that the spar had likely punched a second hole in the hull.

"Bull!"

The Kabouter's yelp redirected his attention yet again. Whirling, Bull saw the tentacle curled around Gez's chest yank him high above the boat. The arm constricted, silencing the fairy's next attempt to cry out.

The sea was green. His friend wore blue and gray. All Bull could see was red.

He'd sworn vengeance against a monstrous foe. He'd spent years chasing it. Now it threatened his only true home in the world, the *Courser*, and his only true friend. The sight of the Kabouter twisting helpless in midair enraged Bull. His nostrils flared and burned, each breath seeming to draw in more fury from the surrounding air to feed the flame. He felt the fire singe his whiskers. He felt his clothes smolder and melt. His whole body was aflame.

"No!" he snorted, letting the poleaxe fall from his stubby grasp and shrugging off his coat.

"No!" he bellowed, stamping his now bootless feet so hard, they nearly passed through the bottom of the boat.

"No!" he roared, closing the distance between his boat and his friend with a single bound. Grabbing the Kraken's thick stalk with two huge, hairy appendages that used to be hands, Bull ripped it in half like it was made of paper. Then he snatched the suddenly liberated Gez and cradled his tiny frame as they plummeted to the sea.

Down they sank into the murky depths. Keeping a firm grip on the Kabouter, Bull spun to face the *Courser*'s keel and kicked with two brawny legs that were no longer contained within the tattered remnants of his pantaloons. They shot rapidly through the water. Though Bull felt no pressing need to replenish the air in his now capacious lungs, he knew Gez would soon drown. His next mighty kick brought them to the surface.

They were surrounded by bobbing boats and shrieking men. Deprived of the Kabouter's protective spellsong, the sailors succumbed to the terror magic of the monster—which still clung, with surprising vigor, to the foremast and horse-shaped figurehead of a sinking ship.

Bull seized a nearby oar and drew it in until he felt the oarlock. First lifting Gez into the whaleboat, he pulled himself aboard. Three sailors huddled on the other side of the boat. One was Gunnar.

"Help 'im," Bull ordered, pointing to the seemingly unconscious Kabouter. "I'll row."

The first mate merely stared with wild eyes.

"Help 'im!" the captain repeated. "Or grab oars. Must reach the ship!"

There was, however, only one human left on the boat. Gunnar was on his knees, shaking and whimpering. The other sailors had leapt overboard.

"Get up!" Bull knew his anger at the cowering Norwegian was unfair, that the man lacked resistance to the sea monster's magic, but he couldn't help it. Unless he could rally Gunnar and some of the others to spring into action, the battle—and the *Courser*—would be lost.

"B-Bull." The fairy's voice was weak, little more than a whisper. "Look."

The captain glanced from Gez's pointing finger to the bottom of the boat, where the late-afternoon sun cast a distinct shadow on the groaning planks. In it, he saw hulking shoulders spaced too wide to be those of a human. He saw a neck as thick as a mast. And he saw the outline of a shaggy head topped with two curved horns.

"Tr-true c-colors." The Kabouter's parched lips formed a slight smile.

~ ~ ~

The *Courser* was lost.

It might have been done for anyway, even if the colossal cephalopod were not adding its considerable weight to a craft already carrying casks of oil, drowning men, and a hold rapidly filling with seawater. The monster was loath to release its prize, however, and Bull saw no way of challenging its hold on the ship. Most of the crew were dead, dying, or trapped below deck. He caught a fleeting glance of Peter Van Wagenen try to force his way out of a gunport before a walloping tentacle brought the brave lad's efforts to a swift and final end.

The surviving sailors wanted no more to do with the fearsome Minotaur shouting at them from the only intact whaleboat than they did with the fearsome Kraken. Some treaded water or floated on shards of wrecked boats, seemingly resigned to their fate. Others paddled away from the sinking ship, though not nearly fast enough to escape its undertow.

Determined at least to save the wounded Gez and whimpering Gunnar, Bull grabbed an oar in each hairy hand and rowed toward the *Zone*. Though he expected Captain Hiller to panic, the *Zone* had continued to circle the battle rather than flee it.

When Bull got close enough, he discovered the reason. Their captain was missing. Hiller had been in one of the *Zone*'s whaleboats when the Kraken rose up beneath them. Though his craft survived, Hiller had broken a leg. When Bull reached the drifting boat, he found the captain alone, helpless, and groaning.

He had no love for the man, and Hiller's impetuous assault had brought disaster. Still, Bull couldn't just leave him behind. He reached over and lifted Hiller with ease onto his own boat. Then he resumed his rowing.

Gez's every breath was labored. The Kraken's tentacle had crushed his ribs and, probably, vital organs. Still, he retained enough vigor to sing. After they boarded the *Zone*, Gez cast both courage and memory spells on its crew. In their eyes, he was a frail cabin boy, not a wounded fairy. Bull was a giant human with anguished eyes, not a gigantic Minotaur with dark, bulbous eyes veined with crackling streaks of orange. And the harrowing ordeal that had resulted in the injury of their captain and the loss of their companion ship, the *Courser*, was a desperate battle with a great whale, not a doomed battle with a many-armed monster.

Bull stood at the rail, unable to avert his eyes from the only remnant of the *Courser* still visible, the top of the foremast. When it disappeared beneath the waves, he looked down at Gez's prostrate form. "It's gone."

"And the Kraken, too?" Altering the memory of the *Zone*'s crew had sapped even more of the Kabouter's waning strength.

The captain shook his shaggy head. "Gone, but not dead. I can feel it."

Gez opened his mouth to reply. All that emerged was a raspy cough.

Bull squeezed his eyelids together. "I can *feel* it—one monster to another."

~ ~ ~

The *Zone*'s surgeon was one of its few crewmen to die in the battle, so neither Gez nor Captain Hiller received proper medical attention. It was no hard task to set and splint the latter's broken leg, but infection had set in and the man was running a high fever. Although command of the *Zone* should have fallen to its first mate, Munroe, the Scotsman and his fellow officers insisted Bull skipper the ship until Hiller returned to duty. None apparently wanted to make any decisions their prideful captain would later resent. Moreover, much of the *Zone*'s crew had heard tales of the legendary Captain Stormalong and relished the bragging rights of serving, however briefly, under his command.

As for Gez, Bull forced some broth down his throat and kept him comfortable, but the Kabouter's internal injuries proved severe. He was only intermittently conscious. Bull had so many questions—about his true identity and what Gez had previously known or guessed—but his friend was in no condition to answer. Unless Bull could find a physician soon, Gez wouldn't survive.

After determining their approximate location, Bull set a southerly course toward Pitcairn Island. Concerned his magical disguise would dissipate during Gez's frequent slumbers, he spent most of his time in the captain's cabin, trying to will himself back into human form. It was only when Hiller's cabin boy burst in with urgent news that Bull could gauge his success.

The boy's eyes went wide. "Wha-what are you?"

Bull groaned and grabbed the dark-blue labels of his borrowed coat in an attempt to cover his exposed chest—a pointless gesture, though, for he could find no hat big enough to cover the horns on his head.

"I mean, uh, sorry," the young stammered. "For a moment I thought I saw—"

"Saw what?"

"Nothing, cap'n. Eyes playing tricks on me."

Bull sighed in relief. Though robbed of his ship, his crew, and quite possibly soon his friend, there was at least one thing over which he'd regained control. "Why are you here?"

"Oh, right. There's a ship ahead."

~ ~ ~

This gam didn't start at all like the others.

When Bull came aboard the *Acushnet*, a whaler out of New Bedford, he brushed aside a dinner invitation. "Need your surgeon, not your vittles."

"Are you ill, sir?" asked the captain, Valentine Pease.

"Not for me. Injured captain and cabin boy."

"Of course," Pease replied. "He'll row over. In the meantime, we can retire to my cabin for a hand or two of—"

"Rather stay on deck." Bull was too anxious to go below.

"Suit yourself," Pease snapped before stomping away.

Standing at the rail, Bull watched the surgeon and two sailors row to the *Zone*. After what seemed like an eternity, the two *Acushnet* sailors returned.

When the first reached the deck, Bull was waiting. "How is he?"

"Captain Hiller, you mean?" said the sailor, a scruffy-looking youth of average height—which meant he had to crane his neck to meet Bull's gaze. "Doc says he'll be fine."

"No. The other."

The sailor's suddenly haunted eyes flicked away to the setting sun. "Was already dead."

Bull had guessed as much. *Now I am truly alone*.

"Funny-looking little man, that one," said the sailor. "Friend of yours?"

"Aye."

"Another martyr to our *noble* profession."

Though Bull was consumed with grief and despair, the young man's sardonic tone managed to startle him. "What you mean?"

The sailor pointed to one of the crank-driven tubs of rope used to lift strips of whale blubber to the deck. "By heaven, man," he began, his voice level as if in recitation, "we are turned round and round in this world, like yonder windlass, and Fate is the handspike."

Ain't in no mood for poetry, Bull wanted to say. *And I ain't no man*.

He said neither. After a while, he said only one thing more. "The sea and me—we're done."

"I know exactly how you feel," the sailor replied.

Chapter 18 – The Cannibals

April 1842

HAR THE TOWER HAD SEEN many mountain ranges. As a young apprentice, he'd scampered over the snow-topped peaks of Saxony's Harz range and trekked eastward through the rolling hills of the Lusatian Highlands. Since coming to America, he'd helped his Folk create their new colony inside the Virginia mountain they called Grünerberg, explored the Blue Ridge from Pennsylvania to Georgia, and traversed the tree-covered Ozarks of Missouri and Arkansas.

Still, it wasn't until the Dwarf headed northwest from the Indian Territory, tracking signs and rumors of Nimerigar raiders, that Har saw mountains so tall, rugged, and shrouded in mist, they hardly seemed like features of a natural landscape. It was as if some staggeringly powerful Folk—or perhaps even the Maker himself—had magecrafted the peaks out of ice and stone.

The bone club struck Har in the small of his back.

He groaned, though more from shame than pain. Its author was, after all, scarcely half his height. *I deserve that. Daydreaming about misty mountains is what got me into this mess.*

A rueful grin on his grizzled face, the Dwarf allowed his eyes to return to the stunning red cliff on the other side of the valley. Tana had spoken of the far-western range as the "Rocky Mountains," which proved a pitifully inadequate description. In her defense, the Song Snake had never laid eyes on them. When Har and Goran had visited her village—itself secluded on a high cliff, though not nearly as high as the one Har now beheld—Tana shared all her Nunnehi scouts had learned about the lands to their west, as well as the machinations of Elf and Duende rangers and the depredations of Nimerigar raiders.

"You wear a fool's smile." This time, the club merely prodded Har's broad back rather than striking it. "Soon you will discard it forever."

How Har longed to whirl and seize the tiny club-wielder by the throat. Would it please him more to hurl his antagonist over the ledge, or to throttle him between two meaty hands? It was a delightful choice to contemplate. One such captor, or even three, would be no challenge for Har the Tower. Unfortunately, there were a dozen vicious Nimerigar on the trail. Their hands grasped bone clubs, flint tomahawks, or bows fashioned of cedar and horn. Har's hands were securely bound, and empty.

It was Goran who'd suggested they split up upon leaving the Nunnehi village. The Sylph had wanted to return to Texas and uncover precisely what roles Veelund's Elves and the Duendes of Mexico were playing in the new republic's turbulent politics. As for Har, he couldn't stop thinking about the two female captives slaughtered by Nimerigar rangers. Their seemingly human corpses had transformed into monsters before his astonished eyes. Had they really lived so long in human guise that they'd forgotten their true natures, as Goran suggested? And why had the Nimerigar ranger risked her own life—foolishly, as it turned out—to kill the captive monsters?

So, Har had volunteered to seek out the village of the Nimerigar. After following several false trails, Har happened upon a Comanche hunting party that included a warrior from the Arapaho nation, recently allied with the Comanches. Under the influence of spellsong, he told Har of a river valley in the far-western mountains where little people were said to reside. Although the Arapaho called them Teihiihan, the human's description fit well the Nimerigar: fierce warriors about two feet in height, dressed and armed in Indian fashion, stocky yet surprisingly fleet of foot, and dark red in complexion with small black eyes and pointed yellow teeth.

"Stop here!"

Har saw many yellow smiles. Four of his captors waddled past, weapons drawn, leering up at him. Their leader, a smirk creasing his aged face, slipped the club into his belt and checked Har's fetters. "Enjoy your last glimpse of sun, spy."

"I am no spy," the Dwarf protested. "I was merely a tracking a monster when your—"

"You are a poor liar."

He has me there.

After entering the remote valley, Har had been so distracted by its striking beauty that he stumbled into an ambush. Suddenly surrounded by rangers with nocked arrows and bristling spears, he'd deemed surrender the wisest choice. *There will be a better time to fight, against better odds*. Or so Har assured himself.

Two of his captors walked around a boulder and disappeared from sight. Then the Dwarf heard an unfamiliar spellsong. Har listened carefully to the melody, hoping to etch it into his memory for future use. *If only I were as quick a study as Goran or Dela*. He instantly regretted thinking of the Water Maiden. Closing his eyes, Har tried to concentrate on the task at hand.

His efforts were rewarded with another hard poke in the back. "Move."

Once through the Shimmer, Har followed the Nimerigar down a long tunnel until they reached a junction. "To the pens, Nibei?" one of the rangers asked.

"Not yet." Their leader, whom Har supposed was named Nibei, eyed the Dwarf with a bemused expression. "First, we go to the feast lodge."

"Surely the spy will not partake of—"

"A stupid question." Nibei shot his subordinate a withering look. "Sano is there. He will want to question the stranger."

Bearing right, the party soon arrived in a large cavern with a high ceiling. It housed several partial enclosures fashioned of poles, planks, and hides. Nibei led the way to the largest of the chambers, where two dozen Nimerigar sat in a circle around a large copper pot. While some ladled a thick stew into wooden bowls, the rest laughed and joked.

"Nibei!" A gray-haired man beckoned to the ranger. "What manner of game have you caught today?"

"The kind that may satisfy only your curiosity, Sano."

"Ah." He rose to his feet. Slighter of build than the others, Sano's hooked nose, angular features, and wide eyes brought to Har's mind the image of a bird of prey. "Short for a human, but too tall to be Folk."

"I am a ranger of Grünerberg, sir." Har announced, hoping to alleviate the Nimerigar's suspicions. "I was tracking a monster when your scouts—"

"Grünerberg, eh? So, you thinking Trolls have named your nest."

"I am no Troll. I am a Dwarf ranger. How else could I be speaking to you in Folktongue?"

Sano snickered. "Some monsters are very clever. It is a trait we have come to appreciate."

"Hear, hear!" shouted another Nimerigar. The rest clapped hands or banged spoons against bowls in approbation.

Har pressed on. "As I said, I had no intention of intruding. I was—"

"Where is this Grünerberg of yours?"

"Far from your domains, I assure you. In a distant place called Virginia. We pose no threat to you or your village."

"And you would have us believe you traveled so far from your home on a simple monster hunt?" The Nimerigar's smirk became a sneer. "You lie. You have come to steal our secret."

I am, indeed, a poor liar. "I know nothing of your Folk or its secret. I only—"

"*All* know the Nimerigar!" Sano was speaking more to his comrades than to him. "All humans and monsters fear our power! All Folk envy it!"

Those sitting around the cookpot rose to their feet, shouting, "Fear our power!" and "We are mighty!" Notably, only two of Nibei's rangers joined in. The rest looked away or exchanged fleeting glances.

Sano turned back to the Dwarf. "Today you come to spy. Perhaps tomorrow, your Folk will come to beg, or to fight. You will gain nothing. And when the walls fall, only we will remain!"

Har struggled to come up with a fit answer. Nibei saved him the trouble. "Shall I take the prisoner to the pens?"

Sano made no response. He'd joined the other Nimerigar stomping their feet in a frenetic rhythm.

"Come on," Nibei snapped, yanking the rope around Har's hands. They exited the cavern, retracing their steps up the passageway to the junction and then taking another tunnel.

From behind him, the Dwarf heard whispers.

"He is no better than before," said one scout.

"Madder, I judge," said another.

"Silence." Nibei's voice was icy.

After several sharp turns, they faced double doors barred by a heavy pine log. Even before four rangers hurried forward to raise the bar, bestial cries from the doors told Har what to expect in the next cavern. It was larger than the one they'd left, again subdivided by high wooden walls into separate chambers and illuminated by torches. He'd never heard of confining Folk prisoners in close proximity to monster pens. Given the evident cruelty of his captors, however, the practice didn't shock him.

While archers threatened the Dwarf, Nibei led him past a series of doors, each closed from the outside by a lattice of posts and ropes, until they reached a narrow door about halfway down. "When next I bring you before Sano, you best tell the truth," said the scarlet-faced ranger as he began untying the knots that secured the door.

Har sensed an opportunity. "How could this chief of yours could tell the difference? His mind seems—"

The bone club smashed against his throat and mouth. Instinctively, the Dwarf raised his arms. The sound of half a dozen bows flexing behind him warned Har against yielding to instinct.

"Guard your tongue if you would like to keep it." Nibei returned the club to his belt and began working on another knot. "Know this: We have little use for mute prisoners, and none at all for male slaves. You may extend your miserable life a short while with honesty and obedience, or I will end it now. These are your only choices."

Tasting blood from a cut lip, Har said nothing. His disagreement with the Nimerigar's arithmetic must have been evident on his face, however, for Nibei pointed back the way they came. "Escape? Never. I admit you are the browniest ranger I have ever met, but even you cannot batter your way through those barred doors."

He threw open the cell door and waved Har inside. "If you resist, we will move you to another pen, where your dreams of escape will perish by fang, talon, or claw."

Seeing no immediate alternative, the Dwarf complied. The cell was narrow and lit only from thin cracks in the walls.

"Have you come for me at last?"

The voice from the shadows was high-pitched but calm. The words were in Spanish, not Folktongue.

"Not yet," Nibei replied, "but soon the stewpot will be empty. When it is your time, you will not be able to hide your true form."

"If you were alone, I would gladly reveal it."

The Nimerigar drew back quickly. *Is he afraid of my soon-to-be cellmate?* Har wondered. *Should I be, too?*

The narrow door slammed shut. Har heard Nibei retying the knots. As his eyes adjusted to the dim light, the Dwarf beheld not one but two forms in the corner. One was a few inches taller than he, the other much shorter. Each wore a simple cloth shift cinched at the waist with a thong. *Two human females. An Indian mother and daughter?* Har held up his hands.

"Stay back," said the taller one, still speaking in Spanish.

Har blotted his bloody lip with a forearm. "I mean you no harm."

The other figure moved forward. "He is not one of you, Shash."

The smaller woman took another step into a thin band of torchlight shining through a crack. The light revealed a lock of dark-blue hair dangling over a heart-shaped face. It caressed a pale-blue cheek. It danced in blue-green eyes.

Dela. Har grimaced. The torchlight was conspiring with his tired eyes to mock him with a mirage.

Then it spoke. "Could he be…one like me?"

"Dela?" Har's whisper escaped aching lips, having originated in an aching heart. His mind insisted this couldn't be the Water Maiden. She was dead. The Elf ranger Thekla had confessed to killing her.

The blue-green eyes blinked in surprise. "You know me?"

"Dela!" Har lurched forward, bound hands outstretched, not yet convinced but desperate to touch her, to discover if the illusion was truly solid.

The Indian woman, the one called Shash, leapt between them, her body far taller and wider than Har first thought. Her hands were raised, fingers curled, unnaturally long nails reflecting the torchlight. Her eyes glared down at him with a fiery ferocity, their dark irises surrounded by crackling circles of yellow.

"Back away!" she snarled.

Har raised his bound hands to swat her away.

"No, Shash." The blue-skinned woman reached up to touch the other lightly on the hip. "I do not think he is dangerous. His face seems…familiar."

Lowering his hands, Har cleared his throat and struggled to find the right words. "Are you truly Dela? Of the Gwragedd Annwn?"

"I am, sir, or so I am told. Now, who—and what—are you?"

~ ~ ~

It took several hours for the captives to share their stories. Har was horrified by Dela's account of waking up in the Elf colony of Cahokia, robbed of her memories. He was confused by her account of a human and monster gaining entrance to the colony, thus making possible her escape. And he was intrigued by her account of life among the Mialuka of Quivira, which provided answers—however grisly and unsettling—to many of the questions he had about the nature and intentions of the Nimerigar.

The Dwarf also learned much from Shash's account of life as a shape-shifting monster among the Navajo as well as her capture by the Nimerigar. She'd been traveling to meet her long absent husband, Aki, in a town called Albuquerque when a dozen raiders ambushed and subdued her with enchanted weapons and spellsong. The journey north to the Nimerigar village had been long and arduous. Shash was on the point of losing hope and trying to provoke her tormentors into killing her when they were joined by another Nimerigar column bearing many more captives, including the Water Maiden.

It was from her that Shash learned not all Folk were vicious, half-mad cannibals. She had found an instant kinship with Dela, who—like Shash and Aki, though presumably for different reasons—could not recall large chunks of her past life. Shash resolved to protect her from the Nimerigar for as long as she could. Dela resolved to do the same for her new friend.

Har scratched his chin and glanced at Shash, who'd made that possible by transforming her hand into a claw long enough to slice the ropes binding his wrists. "Do these savages really believe they can make their bodies resistant to the Blur by consuming monster flesh?"

"They do, though there are disagreements. Some believe any monster will do. Others fear that if they consume the flesh of common monsters, of ones lacking intelligence, they will lose their minds as a result."

"That may well be." Har recalled the bizarre behavior of Sano and his companions. "I see much madness here."

Dela shook her head. Har found the gesture mesmerizing. He hadn't yet recovered from the shock of discovering her alive.

"There may be another explanation," the Water Maiden said. "I have thought much about what you told me, Shash, as well as what I learned from the Mialuka. Perhaps the eating of monster flesh confers only scant protection, if any. It could be their trips into the Blur, not their diets, that are robbing nonrangers such as Sano of their sanity."

Shash turned to Har. "That reminds me of a question Dela lacks the memory to answer. Why is it that you Folk rangers can live in our world without going mad or perishing?"

"It is likely related to our innate ability to wield spellsong but not magecraft, though I know little of such matters."

Dela furrowed her brow. "The Nimerigar *believe* in their gruesome practice. They believe it will not only avert their destruction, but make them the most powerful Folk in the world. And as far as we can tell, the only intelligent monster left in this cavern is Shash."

Har shot the changeling a quizzical look. Shash nodded. "Although we catch only fleeting glimpses of the others penned here, we hear their cries. We call to them in Folktongue, English, Spanish, Navajo, and other tongues. None responds with anything but bestial rage."

"Soon the Nimerigar will come for you," Dela said. "We must be ready."

"Ready to do what?" Shash stared at the floor. "I can transform and attack, but they will use magic to subdue me."

Again Dela shook her head. Har once more found it distracting. "We are spellsingers, too. I could not have managed it by myself, but with Har's help I can protect you."

Shash shrugged. "Their spells may not harm you, but their weapons can. They are many, and we are only three."

Dela crossed her arms. "I *will* fight for you."

Her show of defiance reminded Har of another prisoner in the hands of another Folk. A fool who'd trusted the word of a villain and was repaid with humiliation and torture. A fool whose friends never gave up, who searched for him, who fought for him at great peril to themselves. Har remembered Dela's spinning trident, slaying his captors, and Dela's gentle touch, treating his wounds.

"I will *not* let them take you," Dela assured Shash.

"You will not have to," Har assured Dela. "When they come for her, we will be ready."

"To fight?"

"Yes, and to escape."

Shash sighed. "We are only three."

This time it was Har who shook his head. "No. We will *all* escape."

~ ~ ~

Whenever the Nimerigar entered the cavern, Shash explained, they came in force: two archers, two warriors, two monster tenders, and three rangers. The latter used a combination of confusion and beckoning spells to keep the monsters pacified while the tenders either passed food and water through tiny flaps in the doors or used magecraft to draw elemental magic from the monsters to fuel the village's forges, workshops, and Shimmer walls.

It was Shash who first heard the Nimerigar unbarring the outer doors. It was Har, however, who realized the import of the footsteps they heard on the cavern floor. There were clearly more than nine Nimerigar approaching. "They have not come to feed or drain monsters," he warned. "They have come for Shash, and in large numbers."

Defeating nine armed enemies would be difficult. Overwhelming twice that many, at least, seemed impossible, but what other option did they have? If they didn't attack, their friend was done for.

As the Nimerigar approached, Har heard not only voices and footsteps but also snorts and shrieks from the monster cells they passed. He and Dela flattened themselves against the walls. When the door opened, the Nimerigar could see only Shash cowering at the back of the pen. "Do not take me!" she wailed. "I am afraid!"

"You should be," snapped one of the archers, "but your motives are transparent. If your companions do not show themselves, I will silence your sobs with an arrow to your throat."

Sighing, Har stepped into view, followed by Dela. "Do not shoot!" the Water Maiden begged.

The archer chuckled. "I will not need to." He stepped aside, keeping his weapon trained on Dela and allowing three Nimerigar rangers through the doorway. They began to sing, accompanying their spell by shaking long rattles fashioned of rawhide and wood. Within moments, Shash's face was slack, her eyelids half closed.

It was now or never. The discovery of the prisoners' obviously doomed ambush attempt had boosted the confidence of the Nimerigar. The Dwarf turned to Dela and gave a slight nod.

Their two voices sang the same note at the same time. Their second notes were powerfully discordant. Their third formed an even more powerful chord.

As Har predicted, their counterspell was unexpected. The Nimerigar rangers outnumbered them and were amplifying their own spellsong with instruments, so there was no doubt whose magic would prevail, and it would take only seconds for the Nimerigar archers to silence the Dwarf and Water Maiden forever.

It was the utter foolishness of Har's tactic, though, that made it unexpected. Its success didn't require defeating the Nimerigar spell. It required only that the spell be briefly interrupted.

What rose from the floor during those few precious seconds was no weeping woman. It was a whirlwind of fur, claw, and fury that knocked two Nimerigar spellsingers back so hard, their broken bodies cracked the doorframe and wall of the cell. The third ranger emitted only a panicked shriek before the swat of a massive paw crushed his skull.

The Nimerigar warriors congregated outside were also surprised—but far from defenseless. Three arrows flew into the chamber. One soared harmlessly overhead and sank into the opposing wall. The other two struck the Monster Bear. Roaring in anger, Shash crashed her immense body into the frame. The impact snapped the shafts of the arrows protruding from her shoulder and foreleg. It also snapped both doorjambs in two, allowing the Monster Bear to exit the cell but also causing the wood-and-hide roof to fall in behind her.

"Move!" Har shouted to Dela as he yanked a stone knife from the belt of a dead ranger.

The lithe Water Maiden was, however, already on the other side of the collapsed doorway, having scooped up a spear and darted beneath the legs of the Monster Bear. Spinning to her right, Dela parried the thrust of a Nimerigar lance and kicked out with her left foot, felling her antagonist.

With no way of getting through the doorway, Har the Tower found the crack Shash had put in the wall. Bellowing like a bull, he crashed through the weakened planks and found himself facing three startled Nimerigar who'd been rushing the Monster Bear from her rear.

One was Nibei. Alarmed that a Nimerigar spellsinger still lived, Har threw a quick punch. The ranger captain hit the cavern floor and remained there. Maintaining the initiative, Har wrenched a spear away from one of the remaining warriors. Holding it horizontally, the Dwarf rushed them both, pushing one back several paces and knocking the other down. A blow from the butt of the spear was enough to finish the fallen man.

The remaining warrior was, however, far more skilled than Har with such weapons. While the Dwarf blocked his foe's first thrust, his second attempt was too slow. Har felt the flint spearpoint sting his right thigh.

"Enough of this!" he yelled. Dropping his own spear, Har grabbed the haft of the other and pulled. Loath to release his precious weapon, the Nimerigar was lifted off his feet and catapulted over Har's head. Not bothering to see where the spearman landed, Har stopped only to pick up Nibei's discarded club before running away as fast as his wounded leg would allow.

Har the Tower was no coward. Indeed, he longed to turn around and join the melee with a weapon better suited to his talents, the bone club. That wasn't his plan, however. Even Har's great strength wasn't enough to ensure victory over such overwhelming odds.

What they needed was to *even* those odds.

Transferring the club to his left hand, Har stopped before a cell door and drew the stone knife. His first pass parted some of the strands of rawhide. His second severed the rope completely. Even before the door opened, Har resumed his run. Trusting that whatever occupied the cell would be more attracted to the sights, sounds, and smells of battle than to a single fleeing Dwarf, he hurried to the next door and began sawing at its thicker rope with the flint knife.

From behind him came an odd mixture of clicking and booming sounds. Glancing over his shoulder, Har saw the leathery back of a bipedal creature scampering rapidly in the opposite direction. Relieved, he returned his attention to the task at hand. The series of low-pitched bleats and grunts coming from this pen suggested its occupant was ovine. He cut through the remaining strands.

The door burst open and banged against the outer wall. When Har saw the twisted horns emerge, they were much higher from the ground than he'd expected. The monster turned out to be a bony, ram-headed humanoid about seven feet in height. Har flattened himself against the outer wall and sang a concealment spell. The creature turned away, issued a rumbling noise, and began a shuffling charge in the opposite direction.

Trusting his friends were implementing the next stage of the plan, the

Dwarf slashed the ropes of the remaining doors, freeing their occupants—which included another Devil Ram, two equines with webbed feet, and several creatures with the horns of antelopes, the bodies of rodents, and the multicolored wings and tails of pheasants.

Har reinforced his concealment spell and followed the beasts back to the battle. Though much weakened by captivity, the monsters were launching ferocious assaults on the diminutive bowmen and spearmen. Beyond them, he could see Dela and Shash, who'd resumed her human form, dashing toward the outer door.

The Dwarf tried to follow, but one of the obviously frustrated Nimerigar blocked his way. "There is no escape," he hissed. "You will pay for this with—"

A mighty blow from Har's club left his debt to the Nimerigar forever unspecified.

"Hurry!" Dela yelled. "It is as we feared!"

The two women had reached the double doors and were pushing ineffectually against them. Har rushed forward to help, but even the addition of his considerable strength made no difference.

"Back away, my friends." Shash's voice began as a request but ended as a growl.

Har thought he'd seen her true form. Now, he realized Shash must have limited the extent of her prior transformation to allow her to get out of their cramped cell. The woman bent over, her nose becoming a snout, her arms and legs thickening and growing light-brown fur. The Monster Bear's shoulder hump took form at the level of Har's astonished eyes. Then the lump rose three feet above his head, then six, then eight.

Even the high ceiling of the cavern would have been too low for the fully grown Shash to rear up on her hind legs, but that was never her intention. Barreling forward, the Monster Bear rammed her massive head into the doors. They exploded into a cloud of pieces, splinters, and dust.

If Har were not elated by their success, and overjoyed by the rescue of the Water Maiden, there might have been enough room in his heart for another emotion: envy. After all, he was usually the one who got to smash doors to smithereens.

Chapter 19 – The Shells

May 1842

HE DRAINED THE MUG IN one great gulp and plunked it down onto the table. "'Nother."

Though rain drummed loudly on the tile roof, the tavern keeper couldn't help but hear the booming voice. The proprietor was three feet shorter than his customer but nearly as wide. Tottering across the room, a half-filled bottle in his pudgy hand, he flashed the taciturn giant a nervous smile. "Fine vintage, no?"

Bull shrugged. He'd visited many taverns in his life. It wasn't to sample the wares, however. He'd entered taverns to sign on with ship captains—or later, when *he* was captain, to recruit crewmen. He'd come to drag drunken sailors back to his ship, or to get sailors from other ships drunk so they'd tell him what they knew of the Kraken.

He'd never before entered a tavern with the intent of getting *himself* drunk. And he'd still never accomplished the task.

Perhaps it was his size that made Bull resistant to intoxication. Or perhaps all monsters were immune to alcohol—he had no idea. It was one of the many questions plaguing him. The only person he knew who could answer them lay forever silent at the bottom of the sea.

Gez! Why didn't you tell all you knew? Didn't you trust me?

"Enjoy, señor." The tavern keeper's English was heavily accented, but passable. Bull had picked up a smattering of Spanish during his years at sea and told the man so, but the proprietor insisted on practicing his English. While most of his customers were Mexicans residing in town or on the surrounding ranches, Americans were hardly a rare sight in the modest pueblo of Reina de Los Angeles. Many were merchants or sailors, though an increasing number were settlers moving into the area from the northern settlements of the California territory, or from the United States.

In Bull's case, he'd traveled here from distant Pitcairn Island. That was where he'd taken the *Zone* as acting skipper while Edwin Hiller, her real captain, recovered from injuries suffered during their battle with the Kraken. Determined to get to the mainland—North or South America, didn't matter—Bull stayed on Pitcairn after the *Zone* sailed west to resume whaling. Finally securing passage on a ship headed north, he went ashore as soon as it reached the California coast, just off San Pedro Bay.

Without so much as a farewell glance at the cruel sea, Bull walked briskly into the pueblo of Los Angeles. He'd intended to stay only briefly in the town, which consisted of several dozen mud-brick houses, a church, and a few other public buildings, including the tavern. One night became two, however, then ten, then many more.

It wasn't that he felt instantly at home here. He just didn't know where else to go.

There was a flash of light in the window, followed a rumble of thunder. Bull sighed and lifted the refilled mug. The wine was sweet. His mood remained sour.

Bull looked around. Two young Mexicans conversed boisterously at a nearby table. A third ranch hand, tall and lanky, sat napping in in the corner, the brim of a sombrero pulled down to the chin. Most of the fifteen hundred residents of Los Angeles worked on cattle ranches, as these men did, or in vineyards and cornfields. Bull did some labor himself to pay his room and board, helping stretch cattle hides out to dry and stack them into bales for sale to visiting merchants.

I can work with 'em. Drink with 'em. But I ain't one of 'em. Never will be.

The tavern door burst open. In came a gust of wind, a veil of rain, and a man.

He was tall, though not so tall as Bull, and he was round, though not so round as the tavern keeper. His faded blue uniform strained at its seams to contain a thick neck and ample belly. As he made his way to the bar, his sword clanged noisily against his stocky thigh.

"'Tis a night for evil deeds!" exclaimed the newcomer, whom Bull recognized as Sergeant Gonzales, one of the other regulars. "Devils howl in the wind. Demons are in the raindrops!"

And monsters lurk in the shadows, Bull added silently.

The tavern keeper's eyes widened. "The renegade, sergeant? On the prowl in such a storm?"

"But of course." Gonzales removed his hat to shake it dry. "Nights like these serve his purpose. A man of true courage would face us in the bright sunshine of day rather than flit around at night like some errant moonbeam."

The other man shrugged. "Some say courage comes in many forms."

"I say they lie." The sergeant's lips curled in contempt. "The rogue chooses the coward's way. Let me but face the fellow for an instant—and I will claim a generous reward from the governor!"

Apparently deeming it best not to prolong the conversation, the proprietor filled a mug and placed it before Gonzales, whose scowl became a smile. He lifted it to his lips.

Bang!

Again the door flew open, this time with such force that it struck the wall and made the cupboard rattle. Two soldiers dashed in, muskets in hand. Beyond the doorway, Bull could see other uniformed figures fidgeting in the pouring rain.

"Close that door, Garcia!" Gonzales slammed down the still full mug. "What do you think you are—"

"Came in here!" stammered the one named Garcia. "The señorita told us!"

Startled, the sergeant glanced around the room. His eyes flitted from the tavern keeper to the two workmen now sitting silently at the table. Then his big dark eyes met Bull's bigger ones.

"You there!" Gonzales walked over. "You cannot be the one we seek, but I care not for your looks. What do you know of the manhunt, American?"

"Nothin'."

"We shall see." Gonzales turned to the soldiers. "Bring him to—"

"Sir, he is not the one," Garcia insisted.

The sergeant's nostrils flared. "I just said that, you fool, but the man we seek may—"

"We seek no man."

"What?" Gonzales quivered with rage. "I command here!"

Garcia and his fellow soldier exchanged puzzled looks. "We follow orders. The señorita said the Indian is in here."

"Indian?" The sergeant swept his arm wide. "Do any of these men look like Indians to you?"

"Sir?" Garcia gulped. "We seek the Indian *woman*."

Gonzales opened his mouth as if to reply, then shut it again when he heard the song.

Bull heard it, too. Everyone in the tavern appeared to hear it. The two soldiers glanced around anxiously. The sergeant's angry face slackened into a nervous one. The suddenly fearful proprietor backed against the far wall, followed quickly by the two previously talkative workmen.

The remaining two occupants of the room leapt to their feet. In Bull's case, he felt a mixture of excitement and apprehension. It was the first time he'd heard spellsong since the death of Gez. That meant Folk were nearby. *Do they mean me harm? Or might they possess the answers I need?*

It was the other person standing across the room who quickly drew Bull's notice, however. The figure, wearing a long poncho, was taller and lankier than Bull originally thought. The sombrero had fallen to the floor, revealing a brown face framed by long black hair and twisted into an expression of fear.

"There she is!" Garcia blurted.

"Seize her!" Gonzales ordered.

The Indian woman raised her hands and shook her head vigorously, rattling the red-shell earrings dangling from her lobes. "No hurt! No fight!"

Bull clenched his fists. Instinct told him to come to the defense of the terrified woman, but why should he? *What they do to each other ain't my concern. I ain't human. Never was.*

He watched the soldiers seize the woman and rush her out of the tavern. Just before the sergeant closed the door behind him, however, Bull glimpsed the back of another Indian woman in the courtyard.

No, not a woman, he corrected himself. *Too short*. The girl wore a feathered headdress and a mantle and apron woven of grasses and tree bark.

Bang!

The door slammed shut. Bull jerked, though not in response to the sound. It was in response to a sudden realization.

That ain't no girl, neither.

~ ~ ~

Although no one had ever used the word "stealthy" to describe Alfred Bulltop Stormalong, he had managed to avoid detection. It helped that after they left the pueblo, the soldiers marched north through the hills of San Rafael, then across a canyon into the San Gabriel Mountains. The rugged terrain provided Bull with trees, rocks, and ridges to duck behind whenever Gonzales and the others turned their heads or stopped to rest.

There were several such rests over many hours. Stormy night turned to placid morning, then cloudy afternoon. Unaccustomed to scampering over hills and hiking up slopes, Bull welcomed each chance to catch his breath. It was some minutes into the latest stop, on the bank of a narrow stream, before it occurred to Bull that the humans might not just be taking a breather. Working his way up the trail, Bull found a boulder large enough to conceal his massive frame and peered through a crack at the clearing beyond.

Gonzales deployed the squad of soldiers in a rough circle, each looking with unease into the surrounding brush. The captive, hands bound, stood in the center with the sergeant and the miniature woman Bull figured to be a fairy. He hadn't followed them to rescue the prisoner. His quarry was the Folk ranger. For all he knew, she might be the only other ranger he'd ever encounter.

Never mind.

The new voice came from the other side of the clearing. It was a male voice, strong and melodious, reminiscent of Gez. And the voice was clearly speaking in Folktongue, though Bull couldn't translate the words.

The female fairy responded in kind. A small figure appeared atop a ridge. Rather than climb down, as Bull had expected, the male ranger leapt into the air.

And didn't fall! To Bull's amazement, he sprouted wings and spiraled downward, like a vulture about to feed. In all other respects, the fairy looked like Gez—though he was thinner and wore clothes of green and yellow, rather than Gez's blue and gray.

As he neared the ground, the female began to sing. For a few moments, Bull found it hard to keep the two fairies in view. Their forms grew indistinct, the colors of their clothes and flesh fading until he saw only vague clumps of white light. Then, from deep in Bull's throat, came a rumble. At the same time, the clumps resolved back into distinct bodies. The rumbling sound reached Bull's broad lips. It escaped them as a low growl.

Had they heard him? Part of him didn't care. That part wanted to charge into the clearing, swat the rangers aside with furry arms, and gore the human soldiers with sharp horns. The rest of him, though, the reasoning part, counseled restraint. He knew nothing of the fairies or why they'd charmed the Mexicans into bringing the Indian here. And if he killed them all, he'd never learn what the Folk could tell him about his own existence, miserable though it may be.

About one of his characteristics, however, Bull was already informed. During their many years together on the high seas, Gez had spoken often about the varying effects of spellsong on monsters. Some possessed virtually no natural defenses against it. Others were highly resistant, perhaps because they were themselves capable of radiating temperamental magic. For still other monsters—having reflected on his own experiences, Bull placed himself in this category—the effects of spellsong were at least partially transmuted. Rather than having only their intended effect, spells intensify these monsters' normal emotional state.

Which was, for Bull, rage. Spellsong, any spellsong, made him angry. Powerful spellsong made him powerfully, irrationally angry.

After a while, he dared another peek through the crack. The newcomer stood in the center of the Mexican formation, talking with the female ranger. She held up a basket woven of coiled bulrushes. The winged man inspected it, then offered a small canvas sack for her to examine.

The male fairy pointed to the tall Indian. Although Bull could see only the back of the female fairy, she seemed to be arguing. If she'd brought the human woman to trade to the little man, why balk now? And what need would he have for a human female, anyway?

Whatever the disagreement, it went away when the newcomer produced a second sack. Nodding, the female turned her head to speak to the Mexicans. Three broke ranks and converged on the shivering Indian. While two seized her arms, the third reached his hands up to her ears.

"No take!" the woman shrieked.

What happened next must have consumed only seconds of time, yet it seemed to Bull like one of those fanciful stories Gez used to read him was unfolding before his astonished eyes.

First, the female fairy began to sing. She sounded frantic.

The soldier with his hands on the Indian's ears fell backward, groaning.

The Indian woman spun on one heel, making her skirt ride up and flatten into a horizontal whirl of reddish brown.

She spun so fast that the soldiers clinging to her arms were flung sideways, their bodies forming another bluish blur of motion above her waist, which was widening and rising ever higher above the stony ground.

The green-capped fairy assumed a fighting stance, brandishing a bronze-barreled gun.

Gonzales shouted in alarm, drawing a sword. His men turned inward and raised their muskets.

Fiery bursts filled the sky. Sparks rained down on the fairies, the Mexicans, and their would-be captive. Streaks of color, glistening like puddles reflecting the sun, passed between the combatants.

Many more diminutive figures materialized in and around the Mexican formation. Some held bows, clubs, or spears. Others stretched empty hands up at the sky. All were dressed much like the female ranger, in garments of bark and hide.

Another, much taller figure sprang from concealment not far from Bull's own hiding place and ran toward the fray, uttering neither challenge nor battle cry but a series of mocking laughs.

Then, as if all this wasn't enough to leave Bull flabbergasted, the entire tableau before him seemed to freeze in place, as if it were a portrait encased in a solid block of ice.

Standing on its hind legs at the center of the frozen scene was what the Indian woman had become: a gigantic creature with a bulbous head, curved tusks, and huge floppy ears that were a brighter shade of red than the red-orange fur covering most of its body. Its long trunk—*her* long trunk, Bull corrected himself—was wrapped around the throat of a soldier. Two more Mexicans were entangled by snakelike appendages extending from the beast's midsection.

Most of the Mexicans and fairies surrounded the creature while the rest had turned to face the stranger captured in midleap in the foreground of the scene. He was dressed all in black, from his flat-brimmed hat and cloak to his trousers and boots. One gloved hand gripped a rapier pointed at Sergeant

Gonzales. The other held the handle of a bullwhip, its thong in the process of uncurling.

The block of "ice" through which he viewed the scene was Shimmer. That much, Bull quickly guessed—it matched Gez's description. So, the people within the Shimmer bubble weren't actually frozen in place. They were moving, albeit very slowly from his perspective.

Bull stared at the battle in the clearing. It was so much to take in, to make sense of. While the shape-changing monster's spoken words signaled intelligence, Bull couldn't know whether that made her an innocent victim or a dangerous villain. The Mexicans were no friends of his, but neither were they foes. He knew the black-clad stranger not at all. And to Bull, the fairies were a potential source of information, nothing more.

That last realization proved decisive. If they departed, he might never find them again.

For his first few strides, he remained a giant of a man known on the high seas as Captain Stormalong. By his final strides, he was much bigger, much taller, and much more than a man.

When the Minotaur felt the tingle of magic against his skin, he half expected it to shove him backward. Gez had once told him Folk used spells to protect fairy places from invaders, but apparently this wasn't necessarily true for Shimmer bubbles conjured out in the open. Bull felt only a brief resistance, as if he were pushing against a strong breeze, then he was through. The ensuing bedlam left his senses reeling.

Bull's bulging eyes saw plainly the furry monster and her antagonists but not the lightning-fast movements of the swordsman. One instant, the man parried a soldier's bayonet. The next instant, a flick of his whip wrapped its end around the ankle of the winged fairy, who'd risen into the air. Then the black-clad man was upside down, balancing on the knuckles of his whip hand—which had yanked the flying man back to earth—while his boot struck the side of Sergeant Gonzales.

The Minotaur's ears, now fur-lined ellipses sticking straight out from a shaggy head, struggled to separate the confusing cacophony into the distinct grunts of fairies, the curses of Mexicans, the jeers of the swordsman, and the cries of the elephantine monster.

Now what?

Bull's indecision vanished when an arrow grazed his shoulder. His eyes found the archer—and widened when he realized his mistake. So far he'd seen the female ranger and her people only from behind, and at a great distance. These *were* Folk, it seemed, but of a different sort. They didn't have copper-colored skins. They had coppery *scales*. Their head ridges, wide mouths, and vertical eye pupils gave them a reptilian look, as did the webbing between their fingers and toes.

Bellowing with renewed rage, the Minotaur charged the bowman. A single stomp from his hooved foot snapped the latter's arm. Bull seized another fairy by his slimy throat and hurled him against the rocky ground.

"Bravo, señor!" The grinning swordsman wrenched his blade from the shoulder of a fallen Mexican. As he sprang past to engage another, Bull noticed the man's hat had been knocked off his head, revealing a tangle of curly gray hair.

"Fire, blast you!" shouted Sergeant Gonzales.

"We will hit our own men!" a Mexican replied.

Bull's eyes found the floppy-eared monster. She'd uncoiled her trunk, dropping one unconscious soldier, but still held two more in the sinewy tentacles extending from her waist. Snorting, she turned toward one of the unarmed fairies who stood on the edge of the Shimmer bubble, his palms facing upward. The monster lowered her head, tusks pointed straight at the little lizard-faced man.

His shriek interrupted the battle. One of the reptilian fairies, clad in a sealskin robe and headdress of black condor feathers, raised his spear and shouted a command. Instantly, the surviving members of his Folk disengaged and rushed to his side—including the female, who began to sing again.

Her spell seemed to have no effect on the red-furred monster or black-clad human. Bull, however, felt as though a thousand needles were stabbing his flesh. His anger surged to fury—beyond fury. It consumed him.

"Come!" the swordsman called to him in English, grabbing his forearm. "We must get out of—"

Blind rage, not conscious thought, directed the Minotaur's mighty thews as they sent the stranger flying backward. Showing remarkable agility, however, the man in black somersaulted and landed on his feet a dozen paces away.

"Thank you, my friend!" he exclaimed. "Now join me in safety!"

The surprising jubilance in the man's voice jolted Bull out of his obsessive ferocity. Rather than charge the fairies, he willed his body to turn away.

The swordsman beckoned. "Hurry. The spell is nearly done!"

The Minotaur didn't understand—he could still feel the ranger's magic tormenting him—but he tried to comply. He took a couple of steps, fighting a desperate impulse to wheel and attack the reptilians. Just as his resolve begin to crumble, another gust of air struck Bull in the face. Careening backward, he felt the wind pass *through* him. Gentle tingles replaced the sharp needles prodding his skin. Then they vanished.

He looked back. The clearing was empty. The fairies were gone. The Mexicans were gone. So was the female monster, though Bull could hear heavy feet stomping down the slope.

"Fortune favors us. They took Gonzales and his men along."

The man in black bounded past Bull into the clearing. He seemed to be searching for something in the tall grass. Bull joined him.

"There it is." The swordsman picked up his fallen hat, which had somehow avoided a trampling. Inside it lay a strip of sackcloth tied at one end, with two holes placed and shaped like eyes.

"Who are you?" Bull asked.

The man pocketed the cloth and donned his hat. He was of average height, for a human, with broad shoulders and a narrow waist. There was a similarly triangular shape to his face, which tapered from a wide forehead and high cheekbones to a pointed chin. It was clean-shaven, though the man sported a pencil-thin mustache.

"I am Don Diego Vega, caballero of California."

Bull frowned. His command of Spanish salutation was limited. "Don, uh, Don Vega, how did you—"

"Diego will do, my friend." The man bent and scooped up something else. "Amazing. You ever seen such a thing?"

He held two thin panels made of a translucent material, like rigid paper. They were connected with hinges to a central cylinder, though two of the hinges were broken and the cylinder cracked nearly in two.

"The winged man?"

"No longer winged." Diego began coiling the thong and fall of his bullwhip. "His fall was far from gentle."

"They took him, too."

"No." The caballero stowed the whip in another pocket. "The green-clad fairy slipped away during the battle."

"You sure?"

Diego smiled. "I possess many talents, my friend."

"Friend?"

"We are *new* friends, yes, but how better to become acquainted than to fight shoulder to shoulder in a just cause?"

"Which is?"

"Rescuing the Haphap, naturally." Diego's eyes narrowed. "Unless you knew no more of her true form than she did."

"I didn't."

"Could it be you were following *me* rather than the Haphap?"

"Didn't know you were here."

The caballero crossed him arms. "Then what brought—"

"Followin' the fairy woman."

"The Paakniwat, eh?" Diego shrugged. "I'd never have guessed you sought the likes of her."

"The Pak-what?"

"Pa-ak-ni-wat. That is what Indians call them. It means 'Children of the Water.'"

The Minotaur snorted. "They ain't children."

The caballero arched an eyebrow. "And what are you called?"

Alfred Bulltop Stormalong, once. Captain Stormalong. Old Stormy. Names I never chose. Names I never deserved. Names I hope never to be called again. "Bull."

"But of course," Diego mused. "Was that always your name?"

The swordsman vanished.

~ ~ ~

So did the grass, the clearing, the sky.

Bull no longer stood on a mountain slope in California. He stood on a poleboat on the Sandusky, thousands of miles away in Ohio. Bull was one of those poling the boat up the river, alongside another crewman of greater than average size. While both men stood on massively muscled legs, the arms of the other man were oddly short. His wide-set eyes, large nose, and weak chin made him look like a turtle. He wore a flat-brimmed hat tilted rakishly to the left.

"Cock-a-doodle-doo, son, that's ain't a mystery," the turtle-faced man snapped. "Yer folks musta known what ya was."

"Then how come I didn't?" Bull demanded.

"That's the way it is for us. Memory comes and goes. Don't bother me none—I figure there's plenty I done that's best forgotten. In yer case, ya coulda sprouted horns in your sleep. Gave yer folks the idea of callin' ya Bull, see?"

"Weren't really my folks, though, you say."

The other man spat. "Course not. Ain't neither of us from regular homes. Least not 'round here."

"Where, then?"

"Shoot—ain't ya ever heard that tale about the maze? Yer from 'cross the sea."

Bull fell to his knees, his head swimming. *I remember now! I found out who I was once before, decades ago. I had a friend. Mike Fink—that was his name. He was a monster, too. We went off to war together. Fought on a ship. How could I forget all that?*

"Greece!" Bull said aloud. "I'm from Greece!"

"Well, Crete, actually."

~ ~ ~

At the sound of Diego's voice, Bull opened his eyes. He was back on the mountain. The man in black was walking slowly away toward a line of canyon oaks. As before, he appeared to be searching for something.

Bull rose unsteadily to his feet. "What'd you say?"

The caballero stiffened. "I should not have disturbed your trance."

"My…trance?"

"You communed with the past, no? Regained a lost memory?"

"I guess."

Diego nodded. "A solemn moment. Deeply personal. My apologies for—ah, he *did* drop one!"

The man pulled a small object from the grass. Befuddled but intrigued, Bull moved closer to see what Diego held up to the light.

It was a concave seashell, red and disc-shaped. It reminded Bull of the earrings the Mexicans had tried to take from the Haphap. Then he understood. "The basket."

Diego nodded. "There is little the Paakniwat value more than Carbuncle shells. I was surprised to see them part with so many."

"What do they use 'em for?"

"Nothing, in truth." The caballero slipped the red shell into yet another pocket. "Their value derives from how *others* use them, humans and monsters. You see, Carbuncles are shields against spellsong."

This was a new concept to Bull. Gez had talked about humans with the Sight and how certain monsters possessed natural resistance to spellsong, but not about this. "So the fairies—"

"Confiscate every such shell they find, to hide away. An old Chumash man with the Sight once told me of a sea cave off the coast, beneath Santa Cruz Island, where the Paakniwat keep their great trove of Carbuncles."

"Why not crush 'em to dust?"

"I wondered that myself, but my Chumash friend did not know—or else declined to tell me."

Bull was confused. "You call him 'friend.' Why would he not trust his own kind?"

Now Diego looked puzzled. "I am no Chumash."

"I mean, another Sighted man."

"Oh, I see." The caballero grasped the clasp of his cloak and flipped it up, revealing the two round stays underneath that held it in place. Each was bright red. "You drew a hasty conclusion, my friend."

Carbuncle shells! So, they are what protected Diego from the fairy's spell. He is just an ordinary human! Bull's esteem for the brave man swelled.

"Though, I suppose I should call you not friend, but cousin." Diego tossed his hat aside and bowed dramatically. Now thoroughly confused, Bull offered no reply.

"You muttered earlier you must be from Greece," the caballero went on. "I told you it was Crete. Even beardless schoolboys know the tale of the hero Theseus who journeys to Crete to face the fearsome creature in the labyrinth."

"The creature was—"

"A man-bull like you, yes. Born to the wife of King Minos. The Minotaur."

Bull had heard the word "Minotaur" many times, long before he realized it described the kind of monster he was, but he never knew its origin.

"Well, the Greeks had another legend," Diego said. "It is less exciting, and thus retold less often. Still, it features its own monster—and its own hero, Amphitryon. To punish the people of Thebes for a great sin, the god Dionysus sends a giant beast to ravage their country. It falls to Amphitryon to save them, but he finds the task impossible. With divine magic, Dionysus made the creature too swift and cunning ever to be caught."

"Bad story," Bull said.

"It is not yet done," Diego replied, laughing. "Amphitryon conceives a plan. He befriends a man whose giant dog, Laelaps, was also a gift of the gods. Just as the first creature was destined never to be caught, the dog was destined always to catch what he hunted. The friend agrees to help Amphitryon. For time beyond measure, or so the story goes, Laelaps chases his monstrous prey across the countryside until Zeus, the king of the gods, takes pity on them both and casts them into the heavens, where they become the constellations Canis Major and Canis Minor, ever hunter and hunted."

On many a night at sea, Bull had gazed up at the stars while Gez pointed out constellations. These names sounded familiar, though he couldn't recall their patterns or see what the story had to do with the caballero.

"I spoke of hidden talents," Diego said, unclasping his cloak and letting it fall to the ground. Next, he dropped his sword belt and gloves. "One is an excellent sense of smell. That is why I know the flying fairy did not transport away with the others. He ran off with his precious bundle of Carbuncles."

Bull's big bovine eyes blinked with recognition. His big bovine heart skipped a beat. He'd left the pueblo and followed the Paakniwat into the hills to learn what she knew of monsters. She'd slipped through his stubby fingers, but his mission hadn't failed.

"I am keen to follow this grounded flier, to find out what he's up to," said the caballero who was no longer a man. "Care to tag along? You have much to learn from me, I suspect, and I from you."

There was nothing keeping Bull in Los Angeles. And the fairy's trail led eastward, over the mountains, a direction that would take Bull further and further away from an ocean he never wanted to see again.

He grunted his assent. “Should I call you Laelaps?”

“Heavens, no,” his whiskered companion growled playfully. “You have drawn another hasty conclusion.”

Then Bull understood. The other creature from the ancient tale would also possess an unnaturally strong sense of smell.

“I am the Fox!”

Diego’s words were in English, but this was one sentence Bull could readily translate into Spanish.

“Soy el Zorro!”

Chapter 20 – The Canyon

August 1842

THE DISTANCE BETWEEN THE NIMERIGAR stronghold and the Navajo village was three hundred and fifty miles—or so Shash said. Har the Tower had no reason to dispute her. He'd never been to her village. And Shash possessed an uncanny grasp of distance and direction, no doubt a feature of her true form.

In their flight from the Nimerigar, however, the three friends had traveled far more than three hundred and fifty miles. That was Har's doing, not Shash's. Though some Nimerigar appeared quite mad, a consequence either of their ghastly diet or of forays beyond the Shimmer by nonrangers, they remained dangerous. And others, such as the ranger Nibei, were certainly capable of tracking their quarry in the Blur.

So when Har, Shash, and Dela escaped the Nimerigar, the Dwarf had insisted they head north, not south. After many days of travel—and an encounter with something resembling the Roggenwolf that Har had once encountered back in Germany—the friends turned west, following a wide arc across grassy plains and mountain gaps. When finally convinced the Nimerigar weren't on their trail, they journeyed south through a territory populated by humans Shash called Utes.

Game proved plentiful, as were fish in the waterways they crossed. When they reached a stream the Indians called "the Old Man's River," and the Europeans had named the San Juan, Shash announced gleefully they were in Navajo territory. Her desire to be reunited with her husband, Aki, was touching. It also made Har uncomfortable, for he'd been unable to elicit even faint memories of Goran from the woman who loved him, Dela the Water Maiden.

The Dwarf knew little about maladies of the mind. He knew still less about how Dela came by hers. During their long trek, however, he *had* learned that filling gaps in her recall of abstract facts and practical skills was much easier than filling gaps in her recall of family and friends.

Dela lapped up eagerly whatever Har offered about monsters, humanlore, magecraft, spellsong, and the various Folk nations of America, including her own. Nevertheless, the Water Maiden's interest in the Gwragedd Annwn was general, not specific. Whenever he tried to tell her about her mother, Tesni, Dela found a way to change the subject. He surmised that her inability to remember her own mother felt too painful.

If that was true about Tesni, a difficult woman with whom Dela had a fraught relationship, Har figured it might be even more painful to learn of a romance with a man she couldn't recall. So as the Dwarf recounted the many journeys he and Goran had made in search of Dela, he simply described them both as her close friends. Amazed at their devotion, the Water Maiden repeatedly expressed gratitude and curiosity—but she asked no more about the Sylph than about Har himself. The Dwarf responded in kind, happy to tell her about Goran but just as pleased to share his own experiences, thoughts, and emotions.

It was the day after crossing the San Juan River, as the three followed a tributary creek into the heart of Navajo country, that their conversation returned to the subject of Goran. Dela was asking Har about his birth Folk, the Dwarfs of Germany's Harz Mountains.

"The highest peak in the range, the Brocken, has been our home for many generations," Har said. "Among Dwarfkind, only the village beneath Rügen Isle is more ancient, built shortly after the Arrival."

Dela touched his arm. "You mentioned this event before, this Arrival. What was it? When Dwarfkind first came to the German-speaking lands?"

"Not just Dwarfkind. It was when Folk of *any kind* first came into this world."

The Water Maiden was dumbfounded. "Have Folk not always been here?"

"No." Har exchanged glances with Shash, but the shape-shifter seemed just as surprised as Dela at the revelation. "We came here from another realm. That is why most Folk cannot long survive in the human world."

"The *human* world," Dela repeated. "Folk came from another realm, you say. What was it like?"

Har shrugged. "Our chronicles preserve few descriptions. All agree, however, that it was vastly different from this one."

"And the Shimmer?"

"Something we brought with us." Har scratched his beard thoughtfully. "Precisely how it works, I cannot say. Within its protection, Folk are safe. Time passes for us as it once did in our own realm, or so I was taught. Beyond the Shimmer, every year becomes a generation. By the way we reckon time, some two hundred and fifty years have passed since the Arrival. By human reckoning, it has been five *thousand* years."

The three friends halted on a low mesa overlooking the creek. "Har, you keep saying 'we' and 'us' and 'our.' Are Folk not divided into many nations, often in conflict?"

"There are many nations, yes, and many conflicts among them. Still, we all speak the same Folktongue, also brought with us to this new world. There are other similarities, too."

Dela nodded. "Such as the existence of rangers like us who sing spells and travel the Blur unscathed, and craftsmen who can bind magic to metal, wood, and stone. All Folk have such guilds, I take it, though names and customs differ."

The Dwarf turned to Shash. "What of the Folk who herd the Navajo? What names do they give their guilds?"

The shape-shifter, who largely retained her human form during their travels, shrugged in confusion. "I do not understand. Until I met Dela, the Nimerigar were the only Folk I ever knew."

Har raised an eyebrow. "Do you mean to say the Navajo give no names to the little people who populate their fairy tales?"

"I mean to say that there *are* no such tales. The Navajo tell many stories about their past, of gods and men, of magic and monsters. None feature little people, as far as I know."

Dela's eyes flashed. "Is this so uncommon, Har? Humans without fairy lore?"

"That is a question better posed to Goran. He has read widely on the subject. Indeed, I remember him saying that when you and he lived together on Iris Isle, he happened across an old book in the Sylphs' library chronicling human travelers from faraway lands. He—"

"What was that?" The Water Maiden pale-blue face had grown a shade paler. "Goran and I *lived* together?"

Me and my loose lips. Har ground his teeth in self-reproach. *She recalls nothing of him. I must not cause her more pain.*

"Well, yes," he began, "but you and Goran shared the house with his sister and father, so—"

"I was part of his *family*?"

"No, I mean—it was for a short time, while you searched for Goran's brother, Kaden. I did not mean to upset you."

She'd turned away. Her shoulders rose and fell rapidly, as if panting after a strenuous run. Har the Tower feared she might be sobbing and wondered whether he should explain further, change the subject, or take her hand in sympathy.

Paralyzed by indecision, he stood and watched. *As always, I play the oaf.*

"Har," she said after a time, keeping her back to him.

"Yes, Dela?"

"Why did you think your words would upset me? Is there something you are not telling me?"

Har's stomach lurched. "Well, I, uh, it must be hard not to remember certain…people."

"People who were important to me, you mean. People I was close to."

"Yes," the Dwarf agreed. "Like Goran. Like your mother."

"And like you, Har?"

"Of course."

The Water Maiden turned around slowly. Her heart-shaped face was moist, but drawn into a smile.

"I believe I see," she said. "You wish to spare my feelings."

Har nodded, feeling his insides unclench.

"You wish to shield me, protect me."

"Always."

She took his hand. "Which is why there are truths you have yet to share with me, truths it could cause me pain not to remember on my own."

The Dwarf squeezed the tiny hand in his massive one. "Dela, it is only that I—"

"Say no more. I understand. I think I understand more than you give me credit for."

Har chuckled softly. "I give you credit for many wonderful attributes, Dela, including an understanding that far surpasses my own."

"There!"

Shash's exclamation startled the Dwarf, though he welcomed the interruption. Still holding Dela's hand, he led her to the edge of the mesa where the other woman was pointing southward. He followed her finger and spotted a sharp left turn in the little creek they'd been following.

"*Ch'ínílį*," Shash breathed.

Dela looked up at her. "What?"

Shash grinned. "Navajo for 'Flowing-Out Place.' We are close."

"Close to what?"

"*Tséyi'*. The 'Place Deep in the Rock.' The Mexicans call it Canyon de Chelly. At this time of year, we will find many Navajo there."

"Including, perhaps, Aki?" Dela let go of Har's hand and threw her arms around the waist of her friend. "Your husband may be close. After all this time. After all you have suffered."

Har cleared his throat. "Shash, do you wish to go on alone? Dela and I can make camp while you look for—"

"That might be wise." The woman ran a shaking hand through her matted hair, then pointed leftward. "I can show you a trail up onto those cliffs above the canyon. I will join you there as soon as—"

"At your leisure, Shash," Dela insisted. "Har and I are in no hurry."

That's not what Har would have said. Though the journey to Texas would be another long one, he was keen to start as soon as possible. Words were never his strong suit. The longer it took to reunite Dela and Goran, the likelier Har would say something else foolish and upset her.

Shash was still pointing at the cliff. "Looks like you two will have company, after all. Must be a hawk's nest there."

Har and Dela glanced up. Two small forms sprang from the cliff and began to spiral toward the canyon floor.

The Water Maiden gasped. "Those are not hawks. I have seen their like before."

The Dwarf's hand dropped to the bone club tucked into his belt.

As have I.

~ ~ ~

From the cliff, the canyon floor resembled a rippling carpet woven from light-green threads of grass and light-brown threads of earth dotted with stitches of dark-green trees and brush. In the distance were clusters of what Shash called *hogans*, the round houses of the Navajo, though there were far fewer humans and herd animals than she'd led them to expect.

The doing of the Elves, no doubt.

Scowling, the Dwarf scrutinized the tiny figures at the base of the cliff. Three were visible—the two winged rangers had met another on foot—though he knew other Elves might lurk in the caves, crevices, or ridges overlooking the canyon.

Dela had just as much reason to hate Elves as Har did. They'd robbed her of freedom and memories, just as they'd robbed Har of freedom and dignity during his captivity in Spirit Forest. So he knew her advice against immediately attacking them was born only of caution. That didn't make the advice any easier to heed.

"What is their mission?" Dela wondered. "Scouting new locations for colonies?"

"Perhaps." Har's eyes narrowed. "Or their presence may involve human affairs. Though Sam Houston suspects Duende rangers encourage war between Texas and Mexico, Goran and I have reason to believe Elves are as much to blame. The Texians claim much of New Mexico as their own. Perhaps these rangers seek to further the Texian cause."

"Then why come here?" Shash demanded. "Why so far west of Santa Fe?"

The Dwarf glared down at the Elves again. "Perhaps they plan to trick the Navajo into attacking the towns, as part of a larger strategy to acquire the territory."

"That would bring disaster," Shash groaned. "Death upon death."

The very earth rumbled in agreement.

Or so it seemed to Har, nearly toppled by the trembling ground. Dela and Shash *did* topple, though fortunately they fell backward, away from the cliff. Widening his stance and bending his knees, Har kept his footing during the second tremor, and the third.

"Earthquake!" Dela scrambled to her feet.

"No," Shash snarled, still prone, her arms and legs thickening into furry appendages. "Worse."

What Har heard next took him completely by surprise. It wasn't the sound of grinding stone, falling rocks, snapping branches, running beasts, or screaming men. What came from behind them, from a faraway ridge, was a laugh—a deep, dull, mirthless laugh. Har felt the hair rise on the back of his neck.

"It comes!" The Monster Bear rose up on hind legs and stretched her front paws toward the sky.

"What comes?" Feeling strangely disoriented, Har glanced up at her shaggy face, now some twenty feet above his own.

She met his gaze with glowing yellow eyes. "The Flintskin. The Walking Mountain."

"Is this why the Elves have come?" asked Dela. "Do they hunt it?"

"If so, they are fools." Shash swayed as another quake struck the cliff. "Make ready. I will delay the Yeitso long enough for you to get away."

Dela hefted the spear she'd claimed during their escape from the Nimerigar. "Nonsense. We will not leave your side."

The Monster Bear grunted in exasperation. "You do not understand. Its armor is too thick, its blows too mighty, its spell too strong. Har, get her to safety!"

Its spell. Another deep, dull laugh filled the air. It filled the Dwarf's ears, then seemed to fill his mouth, his throat, his lungs. It suffocated him with a nameless fear.

But only for a moment. Har was no Sightless human or witless beast. He did not suffer terror spells. He *cast* them. Drawing the club from his belt, he thrust it into the air and stamped his heavy boots in defiance.

"I am Har the Tower, ranger of Grünerberg!" he roared. "You do not fight alone!"

"You do not fight alone!" Dela repeated, beating the butt of her spear against the rough stone of the clifftop in rhythm with Har's stamping feet.

Shash turned her snout up to the heavens and howled. Har couldn't tell whether she meant to express frustration, resolve, or hope. *Perhaps all three*.

The ground shook again. Looming over the ridge was an oblong shape, striped in vertical bands of brown and black like some enormous melon.

Neither the coloring nor the size of the Yeitso's head—at least a dozen feet in diameter—was its most remarkable characteristic. Har pointed at the shiny disc at the center of the giant's forehead. "Is that its eye?"

"No," the Monster Bear growled. "There are eye slits below. Through them the Yeitso sees, but poorly. It finds its prey primarily by sensing fear."

"Then we have the advantage," Dela replied. "It will sense no fear from—"

The next quake dislodged the sheet of rock beneath them. Guided by instinct, Har's hand shot out, grabbed Dela by the arm, and pulled her into a controlled fall away from the cliff. Shash tried to leap away as well, but the force of her massive hind legs against the cliff's edge wrenched it free from the ground and sent it flying. Only by digging her front claws into the stony ground did the Monster Bear avoid following the debris over the cliff.

"Shash!"

Dela tried but failed to reach her friend. It took Har several seconds to realize why: the Water Maiden was lying on top of him, struggling to escape his protective embrace. He let go, flushing in embarrassment. Dela scrambled forward and seized one of Shash's paws. Har took the other. Once the Monster Bear recovered her footing, they hurried away from the cliff's edge.

By this time, most of the giant's body was in view. Har gaped.

The Walking Mountain, indeed.

Until this moment, the largest monster he'd ever seen was the Sea Serpent that pro-British Pixies had tried to use against the French navy at Yorktown. As gigantic as it was, the Yeitso was bigger—seventy feet tall, at least, its oversized arms ending in massive clawed hands. Covering most of its body were rocky protrusions somewhat resembling scales.

The Flintskin.

The Yeitso's ragged mouth formed a sneer, revealing jagged teeth. Then it laughed.

Har saw Shash flinch. "You can withstand its spell?" he asked.

"I can," she growled. "I must."

The Dwarf had a spark of inspiration. Casting a sideways glance at Dela, he sang a melody and lyrics he'd heard many times before, in person and in his dreams. The Water Maiden's lips parted, smiled, and formed the same words. *Her* words, to *her* courage song.

The Monster Bear shot forward, corded muscles rippling beneath shaggy hide. With two ground-shaking strides, the Yeitso stood before them, its long arms dangling past its hips, its forehead disc reflecting the sun as flashes of multicolored light.

With a bestial cry, Shash charged into the giant's right leg. The Yeitso shuddered but did not lose its footing. Its right hand swung into the Monster Bear, who'd driven her claws through rocky scales and into flesh. The Yeitso's blow shoved Shash away—but she took a chunk of the giant's armor with her, leaving a bloody wound below its knee.

Dela sprinted forward, aiming her flint-tipped spear at the same spot. Har headed for the other leg, raising his bone club and wishing it were a battleaxe. The Water Maiden's thrust hit not her intended target, but the back of the Yeitso's flicked hand. It sent her flying, though Dela managed a half somersault and landed on her feet.

The Dwarf brought the club down hard on one of the giant's three wide toes. It responded with a yelp of pain, which made Har smile, and a kick of its foot, which made Har dodge. The second swing of his club, aimed at the heel passing above his head, was less successful. The bone head shattered against the Yeitso's tough hide.

With a dismayed groan, Har tossed the useless handle aside and frantically searched for something else to use as a weapon. The sound of heavy footfalls told him Shash was charging the Yeitso, while lighter, more distant footsteps told him Dela was circling around it.

A large rock caught his eye. Har picked it up and spun around—just in time to see the Monster Bear barrel into the Yeitso again, digging her claws into the hole she'd already made. The giant tried kicking to dislodge her, but Shash's grip was too tight. The Yeitso's oblong head bent low, laughing at the ursine monster clinging to its leg and bringing both hands together in an attempt to crush her.

The Dwarf aimed for the Yeitso's leering mouth. His throw went high. The jagged rock struck the scintillating disc at the center of the giant's forehead. The Yeitso's laughter ended in a scream, its hands rising instinctively to its face.

A sensitive spot? Har backed away, searching for another missile. That's what saved him from being crushed beneath the Yeitso's foot. As it was, the impact shook the ground and sent chunks of rock flying. One struck Har full in the chest, hurling him backward into a pine tree. There was a sharp crack.

Head ringing, vision blurred, Har ran frantic fingers along his chest. No, it wasn't a rib that was broken—it must have been the trunk or low branch of the tree. Struggling to rise, Har again relied on ears rather than eyes to reveal the state of the battle. Again, he heard light footsteps behind the Yeitso—Dela seeking an opportunity to strike. Again, he heard padded paws drumming a furious rhythm on the stony ground—Shash returning to the attack after being dislodged by the giant's stomp.

It was a *third* set of footfalls, also heavy and rapid paced but from a different direction, that alerted Har something had changed. He got to his feet just in time to see a hulking creature hurtle past him. It ran on two legs, not four like Shash, and its furry head and arms contrasted sharply with the white shirt and dark pantaloons that contained, though just barely, its broad chest and stocky legs. Lowering its head, the newcomer collided with the Yeitso's shin. A shower of yellow sparks bathed the ground.

No footsteps announced the presence of a second stranger but rather a strong, clear voice. "Take that, fiend!"

A black-clad man leapt gracefully from the top of the Yeitso's foot, into which he'd carved a deep gash with a rapier. "Courage, my friend! We have arrived!"

Har was nonplussed. "You have?"

The swordsman, who wore a black hat and mask, spoke no reply. Instead, he launched himself at the Yeitso's approaching hand, cape rippling behind him. Pushing off its long claw with his booted foot, the masked man used the momentum to soar over the same giant foot he'd wounded a moment before. Delivering a second slash, he landed some distance beyond the Yeitso. "That makes two!"

"No time for games," grunted the other newcomer, whose curved horns jutted from a shaggy head. The Minotaur—for that was surely what he was—punched a hairy fist into the Yeitso's ankle. "Get on with it!"

"Bull," said the swordsman excitedly, "here is another, like your friend! A Kabouter!"

Har exchanged astonished looks with the Minotaur. "No, he ain't," muttered the latter.

The swordsman didn't seem to hear the response. He'd already spun on his heels and launched a third attack, yanking hard on one of the Yeitso's rocky scales in order to propel himself over the giant foot, holding his rapier behind him like the tiller of a boat. Another shower of sparks hit the ground.

"Now you bear my mark, foul villain!" the swordsman proclaimed.

There was a clatter of metal on stone. Har looked down. A well-worn knife lay at his feet.

"Don't just stand there!" Bull bellowed.

Har understood. He picked up the Minotaur's broad-bladed weapon and ran past the bleeding foot of the Yeitso. He found the Monster Bear gouging her claws into the shin of the giant's other leg. A moment later, he spotted Dela jabbing with her spear.

"Who are they?!" Shash barked. "Can we—"

The Yeitso's hand struck her side, slamming the Monster Bear against the ground.

"Shash!" Dela darted forward, then careened sideways to dodge the giant's grasping hand. Though balanced precariously on one foot, she was able to thrust her weapon forcefully upward. Its flint spearhead cut a short but bloody groove along the Yeitso's palm.

The Water Maiden scrambled to the side of her friend, who lay unmoving. Trusting her to tend to Shash, Har returned his attention to the laughing giant. Twice it tried to stomp the snorting Minotaur. Twice it missed, causing the ground to tremble. As the Yeitso turned away, its weak eyes searching the ground for Bull, Har saw an opportunity. Hurrying forward, he stabbed the borrowed knife into the Yeitso's heel. Its steel blade cut another bloody wound, though the Dwarf had to back rapidly away to avoid the monster's kick.

He glanced over at Shash and was relieved to see her yellow eyes open and crackling with resurgent power. Dela and the swordsman were on each side of the Monster Bear. Meanwhile, the Minotaur delivered two more punches to the Yeitso's open leg wound.

So far the allies had been fortunate, hurting the giant while suffering no grievous wounds of their own, but Har knew their luck couldn't last. New tactics were needed. "The disc on its forehead!" he shouted. "The Yeitso screamed when I hit it with a rock."

"Intriguing!" the masked man replied. Transferring his sword to his left hand, he slipped his right beneath his cloak and pulled out a pistol. "Bull, draw his attention!"

"Whatcha think I been doin'?" Grunting in annoyance, the Minotaur lowered his head and charged the giant's other leg. When his horn struck its flinty armor, the Yeitso kicked sideways, causing Bull to spin around and lose his footing. Roaring with malicious laughter, the monster bent low at the waist, craning its neck to find the Minotaur and finish him.

"*Gracias*!" shouted the masked man. He cocked the pistol, tracked the path of the giant head, and fired.

His bullet was neither guided by enchantment, as were lead or bronze missiles from Folk firearms, nor impervious to magical defenses, as an iron blade would have been. Whether by luck or skill, however, his aim proved true. The bullet struck the corner of the disc. Multicolored shards fell from the forehead of the Yeitso, whose anguished cry confirmed the severity of the wound.

The masked man bent over to reload his gun. That's why the back of the giant's hand caught him unaware. Striking his back, it hurled him a dozen feet through the air.

Har began heading toward the injured man—then stopped short when another shot rang out. It couldn't have come from the dropped pistol. The next sound was even more unexpected: a rapid patter, as if someone were drumming a frenetic beat on the stony ground.

Another horned creature hurtled past, nearly knocking Har over. Unlike the Minotaur, this monster was long-bodied, rangy, and ran on all fours. Just before reaching the Yeitso, it seemed to lose its nerve and swerved away, fleeing down the far slope. This provoked more venomous laughter from the Yeitso, who tramped after its new prey with earth-rattling strides.

Roaring ferociously, a fiery-eyed Shash charged down the hill after the Yeitso, followed closely by Dela. Har wanted to join them but remembered their fallen ally. Scanning the cliff, he wasn't surprised to find the swordsman sprawled on the ground, one leg bent at such an angle, it must be fractured. What *did* surprise Har was that the man was no man at all. He'd yanked off his hat and mask, revealing a triangular face covered in reddish fur.

Another Roggenwolf? Some other canine monster? The Dwarf had no time for speculation. Though armed only with the Minotaur's knife, he ran after his friends, determined to do his part.

There was another louder gunshot. Har wheeled. A man strode forward, smoke trailing from the muzzle of a two-triggered rifle. He wore the clothes of a Mexican vaquero: flat-brimmed hat, tightly fitted jacket and trousers, cowhide chaps, and sturdy boots. He was a bit short for a human, though it occurred to Har he might be no more human than the gallant swordsman.

"Where is Aki?" the newcomer demanded as he began reloading his rifle.

"Aki?"

"The horned beast, Har. The Water Monster."

"He fled."

"Excellent." The vaquero grinned. "And the bear?"

"She renewed her attack."

"Understandable, though I wish she had not. Shash does not know the plan."

Only then did the Dwarf realize he'd addressed them by name. "How did you—"

The man cut him off with a shake of his head, then lifted the curved stock to his shoulder and fired. Har returned his attention to the battle. The giant had turned back toward their position on the cliff, to which Aki the Water Monster was scurrying. Bull the Minotaur clung to the Yeitso's bleeding leg, pummeling his fists into the gaping wound. Shash and Dela were assaulting the other leg with claw and spear.

"Just like the last time," the vaquero snapped. "Bullets cannot stop it, but if we can bring it close enough to—"

"The disc." Har pointed at the head. "It is the key."

"I tried that before, though perhaps at too long a range."

"The other man nicked the corner."

"We can do better." Thrusting his ramrod down the barrel, the vaquero bent his head back. "The forehead!" he yelled upward, as if pleading for divine aid. "The disc!"

The Yeitso was coming. With a defiant cry, Har ran toward it. The approaching Water Monster shook his horned head. "Wrong way!" he shouted. "Let him chase me!"

The rifle barked. Har glanced up to see another corner of the disc explode into a cloud of shards. Then a different missile struck the disc with a thump, an arrow fletched with feathers of blue and white.

The Yeitso's malicious laugh become a furious scream. It stumbled, causing Bull to lose hold of its leg. The bellowing giant took another stutter step toward the cliff, where the vaquero was frantically trying to reload.

Recognizing his own peril—the Yeitso's foot was overhead—Har turned and followed the Water Monster out of the giant's path. He heard another thump. Looking up, he spied the fletching of a second arrow sticking out of the disc, which now had a crack running top to bottom.

The vaquero lifted his rifle, only to have a giant hand knock it from his grasp. The heavy weapon hit the rocky ledge butt first, then bounced over the cliff. The Yeitso bent low, a triumphant leer on its grotesque face.

"Manuel!" the Water Monster cried in horror.

The vaquero named Manuel didn't cry out, however. He didn't despair, or panic, or attempt escape. His hand streaked to his belt, then out to the side. A long steel blade flicked out of a long horn handle. With one fluid motion, Manuel drew back the flashing blade and hurled it at the Yeitso's forehead. It struck the disc dead center and sank to the hilt.

The gargantuan head jerked back, as if yanked by an unseen hand. The Yeitso fell to its knees, its body twisted unnaturally. Then, twitching and shrieking, it pitched over the side of the cliff. Though it took only seconds for the body to reach the floor of Canyon de Chelly, silencing the giant forever, it seemed to Har that its dreadful shriek hung in the air for more than a minute.

Presently, the Dwarf glanced at the figure next to him. It was no longer a barrel-bodied monster with matted fur and horned head but a human, brown-skinned and black-haired. "Might you part with that?" Aki asked, pointing at Har's blue cloak.

"Of course." He unclasped the garment and tossed it to the shape-changer, who wrapped it around his waist.

By this time, the vaquero reached them. "Are you unhurt?"

Aki nodded. "And you?"

"No worse for wear, though I feel naked without weapons." Manuel turned to Har. "I take it you tracked the Elves here, as well?"

"No, their presence was unexpected." Har pointed at Aki. "Shash led us here in search of *him*, I believe."

"Ah." Manuel arched an eyebrow. "Can you introduce me to your brave companions?"

Har turned to see the swordsman—no, the sword-*Fox*—hobbling toward them, supported by the brawny arm of the Minotaur. "He knows no braver man than you, my new friend. I am Don Diego Vega, and this is Bull."

Manuel inclined his head. "Naturally."

"Aki!"

Shash no longer wore her monster form, either. Having donned the clothes cast aside during her transformation, the woman left Dela's side and ran ahead. Aki open his arms wide and drew her into a long embrace. Then he lifted the chin of his mate with a trembling hand and kissed her panting lips.

"Har."

Taken by the sight of the reunited lovers, the Dwarf hadn't noticed the Water Maiden walk up to him. "Dela," he began, "I am so glad you are—"

She interrupted him, but not with a word or gesture. Instead, the Water Maiden did something he couldn't have anticipated. Following the lead of her friend, Dela slipped her hands around Har's neck, pulled his face down to hers, and kissed him.

There was a loud clatter. They all turned to see Manuel's rifle and knife lying on the stony ground. A moment later, a figure alighted next to them, gold-tipped wings retracting against a shaking back.

It was Goran Lonefeather.

Chapter 21 – The Capital

October 1842

SAM HOUSTON LEANED FORWARD, RESTING his elbows on the table and threading his fingers to form a cradle for his smoothly shaved chin. There was so much to do, yet he couldn't keep his mind from wandering. At that moment, it wandered into Homer's depiction of the Trojan hero Hector entering the fabled palace of his father:

And now to Priam's stately courts he came,
Raised on arched columns of stupendous frame;
O'er these a range of marble structure runs,
The rich pavilions of his fifty sons,
In fifty chambers lodged: and rooms of state,
Opposed to those, where Priam's daughters sate.

Sam swept his eyes around the one-room law office that served, for now, as the presidential palace of the Republic of Texas. In addition to his table and chair, the only other piece of furniture was the threadbare couch beneath the north window. Across the room, logs crackled and burned in a small fireplace. There were no soaring arches, no marble columns, not even a shelf to house the books he'd brought up the Brazos River to Washington.

You knew it all along, Sam reminded himself. *Not a dollar in the treasury.*

Nearly two years ago, when he'd confided to Margaret his intention to seek the presidency again, she wasn't surprised. Marrying Sam Houston meant marrying ambition. Still, his wife requested two promises: First, that as he continued his congressional service in the remote capital of Austin and campaigned across Texas for the presidency, he'd let no drop of liquor touch his lips. And second, that he'd eke out enough of a living to preserve their "fairy land," their cottage of Raven Moor on Galveston Bay.

You knew what you were getting into, my love. As did I.

The former president, Mirabeau Lamar, had frittered away the republic's meager resources on foolish military adventures. Then he'd issued mounds of worthless notes, debasing the currency. In a bid to fix the problem by taxing trade along the Santa Fe Trail, Lamar organized a "business expedition" into New Mexico that more closely resembled an invasion. It ended in disaster, of course, with most of the men captured and imprisoned—and none other than Antonio López de Santa Anna returned to power in Mexico City.

A year ago, in the Texas Republic's third presidential election, public frustration brought disaster for Lamar's vice president and chosen successor, David Burnet—the same Burnet who'd so annoyed Sam as interim president during the war. Burnet's embarrassing defeat made Sam's victory taste even sweeter.

How soon it turned sour.

Sam smacked his parched lips and reached for his cup. As usual, a part of him longed for something much stronger than the water it contained.

That promise, I have kept.

He couldn't say that about other promises. Although he'd begun to placate the aggrieved Indians of Texas, for example, it proved impossible to redress the harm Lamar had done to his Cherokee friends. The republic's finances remained in shambles. Sam's entreaties to Britain, France, and the United States had yet to produce diplomatic pressure on Santa Anna to recognize the independence of Texas, or for the politically weakened administration of President John Tyler to annex it into the American Union.

Indeed, relations with Mexico had worsened during Sam's first year in office. While he vetoed congressional attempts to initiate all-out war—including a ludicrous bill to annex much of Northern Mexico—Santa Anna sent his army on multiple raids into Texas, twice capturing and briefly occupying San Antonio. The continuing conflict stoked widespread Texian suspicion and persecution of the Spanish-speaking Tejanos in their midst. Many of the latter fled into Mexico, including Sam's friend Juan Seguín, who'd once rendered the republic heroic service.

The latest missive from San Antonio lay on the table. It reported that some two hundred Texians had attacked a far larger army of Mexican invaders at Salado Creek and won a decisive victory. Still, the Mexicans happened upon a separate column of Texians, massacring dozens and taking the rest as prisoners. On balance, the events of 1842 bolstered Mexican morale at the expense of Texian prestige.

Still, Sam Houston *had* fulfilled one other promise: removing the capital from Austin, which was too close to the disputed border. Washington—a modest settlement a hundred miles east of Austin, on the Brazos River—was safer, though its buildings were few. In addition to the presidential "palace," the seat of government consisted of a presidential residence, a room rented by Sam and his pregnant first lady; a Department of State in what used to be a carpentry shed; a House chamber in a drafty barn; and a Senate chamber in a saloon.

As Sam refolded the letter, he heard something unexpected.

Washington had swelled to several hundred inhabitants, most serving in Congress or otherwise engaged in affairs of state. The newcomers were a boisterous lot—chatting, arguing, or negotiating during the day and boasting, joking, or scheming long into the night. Given the meager accommodations, their spirited conversations often spilled out into the dusty streets.

Except, at this moment, Sam heard no voices coming from outside. The *silence* was what surprised him, and what made the president of Texas reach for another item on the table—a loaded pistol.

What he heard next was less surprising: strange words and dulcet tones.

Spellsong.

A woman's face appeared at the window. It was freckled and full, with light-colored eyes narrowed in concentration and thin lips forming Folktongue words with a hint of a grim smile. Sam glanced quickly away, recalling that night in Nacogdoches seven years ago when he'd first encountered rangers of the Duende. They'd figured out he was Sighted. Only the timely arrival of Tana and Har had saved him from peril. He couldn't count on fairy assistance this time.

The door creaked open. Sam slipped the pistol beneath his coat and held the letter up to his face as if carefully studying it.

"Your pretense serves no purpose," said the female voice in English. "Nor does that weapon you hide. If I wanted you dead, you would be."

Sighing, Sam looked up. A Folk ranger stood in the doorway. Her emerald eyes were a shade lighter than her cloak, tunic, and trousers. Her drawn bow confirmed the danger she posed. And her pale skin and pointed ears confirmed she was neither Nunnehi nor Dwarf.

Sam decided on defiance. "I don't take kindly to threats."

The fairy returned his stare for a moment, then lowered her bow. "As I said, I did not come to kill you."

Carefully, Sam brought out the pistol and placed it on the table. "What would Duendes have from the president of Texas?"

"Surrender, of course." The ranger looked bemused. "And subjugation."

"You'll find that Texians will never—"

"I was told you were clever, for a human," she cut in. "I am no Duende."

So, Tana's last message was correct. It was a different Folk pulling Lamar's strings. Sam shrugged. "An Elf, then. Why are you here? You'll find no weakling like Mirabeau Lamar. My shield is stout."

"Save your bluster." The Elf ranger stepped into the room and closed the door. "Has it shielded your people from captivity?"

She knows about the latest Mexican raid on San Antonio. Sam jabbed an accusing finger. "You're as much as blame as Santa Anna. You Elves manipulated Lamar into attacking the Mexicans, didn't you?"

"He needed little encouragement. After all, he and most of your people believe all the lands east of the Rio Grande belongs to Texas. Do you not agree?"

Careful, Sam. "Well, I, uh—say, what's your name, little lady?"

The Elf scowled. "I am called Thekla."

"Please to make you acquaintance, Thekla. Now, about the lands east of the Rio Grande, the problem isn't the legality of our claim. It's making it at the point of a gun. The Mexicans of Santa Fe and the other towns were bound to resist, and Texas lacks the military might to prevail."

Thekla's scowl melted into something like a smirk. "Texas may lack the might, but does the United States?"

Trick an old cardplayer like me to show my hand? Not likely. "I am but the president of Texas, ma'am."

"A president who surely knows the future of his people lies in union, not isolation."

"Just what do you Elves want with me?" Sam allowed only some of the irritation he felt to show in his voice—and none of the fear. "You know you can't bamboozle me with spells."

"We suspected you possessed the Sight. Tonight, you prove it by resisting my spell. Still, I did not come here to 'bamboozle' you. I came to help you."

Sam sat back. *Do the Elves know of my friendship with Goran Lonefeather and Har the Tower, their avowed enemies? Do they know of the Galveston Bay refuge I provide their former foes in battle, the Gwragedd Annwn? If so, she's trying to deceive and manipulate me. If not, maybe I can do the same to her.*

"What would help me, ma'am," he said, "is money in the republic's treasury. Can you conjure some out of thin air?"

"I am a spellsinger, not a magecrafter, but I offer the next best thing. There is enormous wealth to be found in your western lands. I can help you find it."

"If I had a dollar for every charlatan or rogue who's spun such a tale, I could fund the government myself."

Thekla blinked. "I do not spin. I *am* willing to bargain."

"With what? Fanciful maps and empty promises?"

"No." If the Elf was annoyed by his ridicule, she disguised it well. "With valuable information. Are you familiar with the story of Cibola?"

"The legendary Seven Cities of Gold, you mean?" Sam guffawed. "Yes—and El Dorado and the Fountain of Youth and a dozen other places that never were. Do you take me for a modern-day Coronado eager to go on some pointless quest?"

Thekla pursed her lips. "No, I take you for a human. Even those with Sight can fail to see. Your myths and legends are often rooted in reality, though your tales preserve only thin slices of the truth."

"Do you mean to suggest there really *are* Seven Cities of Gold?"

"Seven places of great wealth, yes—places built and inhabited by Folk long before Europeans set foot in the New World. Most are in what became the colony of New Spain."

Sam couldn't deny being intrigued. "Including New Mexico, I take it. How many there?"

"At least one we know of, probably more."

"So, you don't actually know their locations." The president of Texas rose from his chair and put his hands on his hips. "I was right. You spread fables."

Unperturbed, Thekla lifted her green eyes to meet Sam's blue ones. "We have already found three of the seven cities: one within the United States, in Alabama, and two beyond the Rio Grande. We have reason to believe others lie within territory claimed by Mexico as well, though our search is hampered by the danger we face."

"Danger? You fear the Mexicans so much?"

She rolled her eyes. "No. The threat comes from the Folk who *herd* the Mexicans. They seek the same prizes we do—and if they reach them first, it will not be only Elfkind who suffer."

"You mean…the Duendes also seek the Cities of Gold?" Though Sam hesitated to trust the word of an Elf, her claim sounded plausible. It would explain the strange things the yellow-haired Aya had said during their confrontation in Nacogdoches. It would explain many reckless decisions of Santa Anna and other leaders of Mexico, decisions that had cost their unstable country blood and coin for little apparent gain. And it would explain why Elves like Thekla, who already held multiple strongholds throughout the United States, might venture into his territory.

Maybe neither Folk wants to plant new settlements in Texas, or truly cares which great power controls it. Maybe they just want to get their hands on whatever gold or other treasure may be found here.

"Why do you tell me this?" Sam asked. "What do you want?"

"A *bargain*." Thekla repeated the word with emphasis. "Mirabeau Lamar was a fool. Despite our assistance, he was never able to extend Texian rule over your western lands. We can help you succeed where he failed—and, more importantly, to join the United States when the time is right. Under its jurisdiction, your large and fertile territory will be rapidly peopled. It will be prosperous. It will be safe."

Easier said than done, Sam reflected, *especially with His Accidency, John Tyler, in the White House*. "And in return? Am I to be your Elf lord's pawn?"

"My liege, Prince Veelund, needs no more vassals. He only desires for Elfkind to thrive within a strong and united American nation."

"A nation with borders extended all the way to the Rio Grande, you mean, so your rangers can search in greater safety for the other Cities of Gold."

"To the Rio Grande, yes—and even to the shores of the western ocean."

Sam's eyes widened. Over the course of his political career, he'd heard much talk about American expansion. During their service together in Congress, for example, he heard his Tennessee friend James Polk speak of spreading "the benefits of our republican institutions" across the continent and of the commercial promise of the British possessions in Oregon and the Mexican dominions in the Californias.

Sam found merit in such arguments, so long as American expansion could be accomplished without brutal conquest or the displacement of Indians. Now, Thekla's words made him wonder just how long the agents of Prince Veelund had been at work in the halls of American government. He'd heard enough about Veelund from Goran and Har to distrust the Elf intensely, but that didn't necessarily mean the prince's Duende rivals posed no threat to Texas, or that American expansion was unwise. Moreover, who was to say a devious puppeteer might not be made into a puppet himself? The wisest course appeared to be to play along, extract as much as information as he could, and then confer later with Folk rangers he really trusted.

With a dramatic flourish, the president of Texas lifted the tail of his coat and sat back down. "Pray tell me more, Ambassador Thekla."

Chapter 22 – The Homecoming

DELA LOOKED DOWN AT THE junction. One stream wound its way through the forested hills from the northeast. The other, wider waterway came in from the southeast, flowing around a narrow island just before it joined the northern stream. Wooden buildings lined the banks of the two forks. The human settlement here was once called Salt Lick. As it grew into a trading post and staging point for the barge trade down to Knoxville, the town adopted a more suitable name: Kingsport.

Or so she'd been told.

"Anything?" Har joined her on the ledge, pointing at the moccasin-shaped Long Island-on-the-Holston.

"No." She had no recollection of the place.

Of my home.

Feet shuffled on the rocky outcropping behind her. "They are waiting."

The Water Maiden didn't turn at first. She let her eyes linger on the picturesque river valley. The Dwarf did the same, though the cause of his reluctance surely differed from hers.

During their journey from New Mexico to Tennessee, Dela's initial excitement about reuniting with her Folk gave way to anxiety. Via message spell, the Gwragedd Annwn learned she was coming and that she'd suffered trauma during her captivity. Were they prepared to welcome home a woman with no memory of them?

They will be strangers to me—and I, to them.

Har insisted her fears were groundless. Unease about her homecoming wasn't why the Dwarf lingered at the cliff, though. It was unease about what might follow it.

Dela and Har turned to face the third member of their party. Goran

Lonefeather only had eyes for her. There was concern in those light-brown eyes, to be sure, but also a question. It was the same one Har had posed, though in the Sylph's case it was infused with so much emotion and hope that he dared not try to voice it.

She shook her head. He hung his.

~ ~ ~

Two rangers met them on the south bank of the Holston and escorted them through the underwater entrance into the village. They were the first Gwragedd Annwn she'd met. One was a head taller than Dela, slightly built, an engraved bow slung over his shoulder. The other was about her height and carried a three-pronged spear. It alone, the trident, looked familiar to Dela. Their faces did not. Nor did the damp corridor they traversed and the woven tapestries decorating its walls.

When they reached a large cavern, the smaller escort thrust her trident before Har's startled face. "Only Gwragedd Annwn may enter the council chamber."

The Dwarf grunted. "See here, I will go—"

Goran raised a hand. "You are mistaken. I have entered this chamber many times."

The blue-skinned archer nodded. "Indeed. That is why Grandmaster Gwyla instituted the rule."

Goran didn't so much as blink. "We have accompanied Dela this far. We will remain by her side."

"These two men are my friends," Dela insisted. Her statement had an intended effect—the rangers chose not to press the issue—as well as the unintended effect of making Goran wince.

He loved her. That much was written on his anguished face when she first recalled seeing it, at Canyon de Chelly, after the battle with the Yeitso. Dela had witnessed a joyful Shash greet her husband with a kiss. The sight of it brought a mixture of emotions crashing over the Water Maiden like an ocean wave: relief at the defeat of the monster, gratitude for her earlier rescue from the clutches of the Nimerigar, and even envy of Shash for having so devoted a mate in Aki. Yielding to a sudden impulse, and misinterpreting the Dwarf's feelings, she'd kissed him just as Goran alighted on the bluff next to them. In the next moment, she'd watched the shock on the Sylph's face turn to exhilaration, then outrage, then despair.

That's how she knew he loved her. What she didn't know—and what neither Goran nor Har would tell her—was whether she'd ever returned the love of the Sylph.

Were the two men being noble? Was Har too embarrassed by the kiss, and the fact that he hadn't pushed her away, to discuss the incident and its implications? Was Goran somehow trying to test her? Dela couldn't tell. And they wouldn't.

The chamber was crowded with Gwragedd Annwn. Six sat behind a table of twisted driftwood. Dozens more stood to the side, most in small groups but one standing alone. The woman wore a dark-gray shift and a silvery mantle draped over a rounded shoulder. A brooch and earrings fashioned of smooth gems and textured shells completed her costume.

"Mother," Dela correctly guessed.

"My daughter!" Tesni hurried forward, pulling the Water Maiden into an embrace.

"Welcome home, my dear," said one of the seated elders, a grim-faced woman with tightly braided hair. "Long have we worked and prayed for your rescue."

Har mumbled under his breath, too softly for Dela to make out the words. Slowly but firmly, she disengaged from Tesni's grasp. "You have my friends to thank for that," she said with a sweep of her arm. "Har, ranger of Grünerberg, and Goran, ranger of the Sylph."

"I am pleased to see you again, Grandmaster Gwyla," said Goran, unconvincingly.

"Your…assistance is appreciated." The elder gestured toward the other elders. "Now, we have much to discuss in council, and questions to pose to our newly returned daughter."

Har snorted. "That all you will say? After everything Goran did to save her—against your wishes, the way I heard it—you should be more gracious, woman."

"Mind your tongue, Dwarf," the grandmaster replied. "You are misinformed. I myself sent the Sylph in search of Dela, accompanied by rangers of the Gwragedd Annwn."

Har didn't back down. "I heard the tale from your own sister, leader of that expedition and now of your Folk's colony in Texas. Diri awaits answer to her many message spells, by the way."

Gwyla's glare was frosty. "The Sylph's service is now completed, as is whatever minor role you played."

"Minor role?" Dela couldn't remember her relationship to this woman but doubted it had ever been cordial. "Har is the one who discovered my location. At great risk, he infiltrated the village of my fiendish captors and effected my rescue. I would not be standing here but for him."

Once again, her statement—embellished for dramatic effect but correct in its essentials—had both intended and unintended consequences. It left Gwyla speechless, as Dela had hoped. Yet Har blushed and looked away. Goran blanched and looked down. Most surprising of all, her mother flashed a triumphant smile.

"My Folk and I will be forever indebted to you, Har," Tesni said. "You have brought my sole remaining child home."

Sole remaining child? Dela sucked in a breath. *Had I once a sister or brother?*

Her mother smiled. "You and the Dwarfs of Grünerberg will always be welcome here."

Dela noticed Goran's jaws clenching furiously. *My mother's gratitude is understandable. Why does it bother him so?*

"Thank you," Har said, "but it was Goran who decided we should investigate Folk activity in Texas, at the request of the human Sam Houston. It was Goran who first encountered the Nimerigar and sent me after them. Our escape from their pens required the help of a shape-shifter named Shash. And our salvation from a terrible giant was due to the courage and ferocity of still more friends. Many hands have brought Dela back to you, though more often than not at Goran's direction."

Tesni stepped in front of her daughter. "It was *his* direction that placed her in peril."

What? Dela looked quizzically at the Sylph. He was staring at her mother with an intense ferocity.

Har turned to the elders. "It was *your* decision, not Goran's or mine, to commit a Gwragedd Annwn warband to the siege of Spirit Forest. That is what led to Dela's capture. The Folk of Grünerberg and Long Island have fought shoulder to shoulder against our common foes. Are we allies still?"

Gwyla recovered her composure. "That is a discussion for another time. Now is a time for rejoicing."

Goran also regained his. "Veelund and his Elf host waste little time celebrating their victories, which are many. They plot and act to achieve conquest and domination. They would plant their colonies across the continent, from sea to sea, from frozen north to simmering south."

"So we have heard you say many times," Gwyla replied, "yet all we see are the broken bodies of our wounded and the lifeless bodies of our slain. These Elves you speak of, and the other Folk of the Great Alliance we fought during the war, they remain distant from our shore. Now you say they wish to move still farther away. Why should we not let them?"

"Because they will never stop!" Goran brought a quivering fist down on the council table. "Prince Veelund seeks to rule all the Folk and humans of America!"

Gwyla huffed. "Impossible. He lacks the numbers and the magic. Only a fool would attempt such task, but you portray him as a brilliant foe."

"That is no contradiction. Veelund may delude himself. His schemes may ultimately fail and yet cause great suffering."

"You are free to engage in such speculation." Gwyla stood up and gestured to the others. "We who lead our Folk are not. We must deal with the real and the now. It is the *Gwragedd Annwn* who lack the numbers to herd our humans and defend our domains. It is the *Gwragedd Annwn* who lack elemental magic and the monster game to replenish it. Let other Folk solve their own problems. We will tend to ours."

Har crossed his burly arms. "I asked you a question earlier. Do the Gwragedd Annwn of the Holston remain the allies of the Dwarfs of Grünerberg?"

In the silence that followed, Dela let her eyes linger on each person in turn. Har's craggy countenance conveyed suspicion and annoyance. Goran looked hot-tempered and impassioned. Gwyla wore a frigid mask of indifference. And Tesni looked back at Dela with weary, watery eyes.

"As I said, emissary." Gwyla's cold words matched her mask. "Now is not the time."

"It is my *daughter's* time." Tesni took Dela's hands in her own. "Your message spell sang of certain…wounds. Are they healed?"

The Water Maiden shook her head. "I am not sure they *can* be. On our way here, we visited the village of the Nunnehi. Their Medicine Clan treated me. I drank their elixirs and smoked their pipes. Still, my memories remain a jumble of discordant notes and silences."

Her mother turned to the Dwarf. "I am sure you meant well, Har, but this is a task for the Mages Guild. Only healers of the Gwragedd Annwn know how to treat their own."

Which is one reason I came here, despite my misgivings. Dela squeezed Tesni's hands. "I will place myself in their care, mother."

The fire went out of Goran's eyes. "And we will stay remain with you, as long as it takes."

"No." Tesni locked eyes with Gwyla. "The Dwarf may stay. The Sylph may not."

Why does she hate Goran so? Is it because she knows how he feels about me and disapproves? Or was it I who did something that upset her? Dela felt as though she were sliding down a slippery rock, unable to find the tiniest of seams to cling to.

The grandmaster sat back down. "In the matter of Dela's care, we defer to the judgment of her mother. Har, you are welcome to stay. Indeed, that will allow us to discuss other matters at the appropriate time."

The tall Dwarf glanced first at Goran, who'd turned away in disgust, and then at Dela. His eyes widened as his bushy brows shot up. Understanding the unspoken question, she gave a brief nod.

Har sighed. "Your invitation is gracious, Grandmaster Gwyla, but I have been too long absent from my home and duties. I journey to Grünerberg, with Goran. We leave Dela in the care of her family and Folk."

Do not go, she wanted to say to them, but did not. Har and Goran were her comrades in arms, no matter what else they'd been in her forgotten past. The Gwragedd Annwn—even her own mother—were still strangers to her. If any but the Elves themselves possessed the power to heal her mind, however, it would be her own Folk. She had to let them attempt it.

Thank you, she also wanted to say, but did not. She'd expressed gratitude for her rescue, many times, but if she thanked them now for letting her try to recover her memories, Goran might misinterpret her words. He might think that in accepting the hospitality of the Gwragedd Annwn, and its conditions, she was signaling a desire for distance from him. From his adoring looks. His eager words. His poorly disguised, increasingly desperate desire to restore whatever it was the two had been to each other in the past.

Would Goran, in fact, be misinterpreting my words?

Dela closed her eyes and said nothing more.

Chapter 23 – The Pivot

November 1843

HE'D SWORN NEVER AGAIN TO set foot on a boat. He kept that promise for many months, working odd jobs for room and board as he traversed vast deserts and trackless plains. Then necessity intervened. He reached a river too wide to ford.

So, he changed his oath. "I'll never set foot on a powered vessel," swore the wanderer as he stepped onto the poleboat headed for the east bank of the great Mississippi.

Then came more wandering. The soil of the heartland was rich and fertile. He lent his herculean strength to tilling it, unyoking the oxen to push the plow himself—when no one else was around—and smiling ruefully at the irony of it. Still, the solitude brought him no solace. After all, early on he'd traveled with a companion. Injured in battle, the man had been forced to stay behind to heal. The wanderer had pressed on alone. By the time the loneliness got to him, it was too late to go back.

Before long, then, the nomad left the plains and found his way to places where there were planks to hammer and wagons to load. Towns gave way to cities. St. Louis. Cincinnati. Baltimore. Philadelphia. In each he sought to lose himself, but even disguised he stood out from the crowd—in their eyes and, more importantly, in his own. The largest of all, New York, swallowed him for a time within its teeming masses. Hundreds of thousands of souls, toiling, striving, living, dying. Different in so many ways yet sharing a profound and inescapable commonality, a defining nature forever alien to the wanderer.

Humanity.

In the end, the city spat him out. He felt compelled to modify his oath again. "I'll never set foot on a sailing ship," he vowed as he boarded a steamship to cross the East River. Once in Brooklyn, he once more chose the direction of the rising sun, traversing the breadth of Long Island to Sag Harbor, a port he'd visited many times during his former life. The life he'd lived before he knew who he really was.

What he really was.

The whaling ships of Sag Harbor beckoned to him, like Sirens to his Odysseus—only, the Sirens were monsters seeking to bait the human mariner ashore, while the human-built vessels and their human crews in the harbor sought to bait a monster out to sea.

They failed. He resisted their song, though he did take passage on a steamship for the mainland. The wanderer headed further east, seeking it in the first place he'd called home, the tip of far-off Cape Cod.

But he didn't head there alone. And he never arrived.

~ ~ ~

"Like walkin' on the wind!"

The old man looked back at Bull with an expression of pure glee on his scarred face. They stood on one side of the tender car, leaning their heads out so they could see past the engine to their destination. Although Bull's *Courser* had sailed out of Nantucket, he was no stranger to the other great whaling capital of Massachusetts, the town of New Bedford. Its distinctive row of wharves—stretching down the west shore of the Acushnet River—had become a familiar sight during his seafaring days.

"Wouldn't say that," Bull answered. "Trains rattle and creak and crawl. Only ships ride the wind."

"I said *walkin'*, not ridin'." Chuckling, Bull's companion strode to the center of the car and tossed his shovel onto a stack of wood. "We walkin' up high, like we steppin' on clouds 'stead of earth. See?"

Bull rested his own shovel against the timber bunker. "No. Not the way you see."

"That's your awake head talkin,' Bull. Got to use your *dream* head. Heed ole High John, now!"

The name suited the fellow. He was tall, slightly built, and wore a tattered patch over one eye, though he didn't really need to. Despite his crooked back, the man's nearly bald head towered over those of nearly everyone they met (except Bull's, of course). Still, that wasn't why he went by the name High John. It was because his other shapes—the human guise he'd donned during his youth and middle age, when he went by the name John de Conquer, and his true form as a monstrous Rompo—were so much shorter.

They'd met on the ferry from Manhattan to Brooklyn. High John, then traveling with a group of sailors, claimed to have immediately recognized the gruff traveler in the threadbare coat as the famous Captain Stormalong. Another passenger then shocked Bull by revealing herself to be the mother of Peter Van Wagenen, the brave young man who had died, along with most of the crew of the *Courser*, in their doomed battle with the Kraken.

Loath to tell the sad woman what happened to her long-missing son, and the role played in his death by Bull's own reckless pride, the former sea captain hurried away as soon as the ferry reached Brooklyn. Stomping through town and into the woods, he eventually discovered that both High John and the Van Wagenen woman were following him—and that the two had been acquainted decades earlier, when she was a slave and the old sailor was an itinerant abolitionist. Indeed, John had helped her escape to freedom by distracting her tormenters with his Rompo form, an ungainly combination of the forelegs of a badger, the hind legs of a bear, a weasel-like body, a rat-like tail, and the head and ears of a rabbit.

Gez had once told Bull that shape-shifters were rare, but the Rompo was the fourth such monster Bull had met—after Diego, a Teumessian Fox; Shash, a Monster Bear; and Aki, a Water Monster. So, when High John had asked to travel with him for a time, Bull said yes. He'd learned much from Diego during their pursuit of the Elf ranger through the desert. He figured High John might have something to teach him as well, which proved to be true.

"Ain't no puzzle," the old Rompo said when asked about the many shape-shifters Bull had encountered. "Stands to reason. You's one of us."

"That's no explanation."

"Course it is. We's all part of Old Maker's plan. Bound to meet someday."

"Old Maker?"

"Maker of All Things. Author of the Universe, some call him. Or Providence. Can't see his hands, but they guides us sure 'nuff."

Bull had gnashed his teeth at that. "No one guides me. I make my own way." *And my own mistakes.*

"You ain't no puppet, that's so. But you ain't the writer of the play, neither."

"I don't understand."

"Ain't meant to, not fully. Just open your heart and see what's written. Open it and hear the drum beatin'. Folks with closed hearts, they done got so smart, they don't believe in nothin'."

When the two had traipsed all the way across Long Island to Sag Harbor, Bull expected John to join one of the whaling crews. The old man surprised him again. "I reckon to stay with you."

"Don't know where I'm goin.'"

"Then you best not go alone."

Later, when they got to the mainland and Bull decided to return to the town where he'd grown up, High John greeted the news with a belly laugh. "Ain't never been to Cape Cod!"

And when they found themselves penniless in Rhode Island, it was John who suggested they get jobs as firemen on the Boston and Providence Railroad to pay their way—even though it meant many hours of backbreaking work shoveling wood into the firebox. "Honest labor never hurt nobody," he'd said.

Bull had eyed his companion's stooped back and shook his head. "I'll go on alone."

"Don't be bullheaded," the Rompo replied. "I aim to see you home."

Now, as the slowing train sent puffs of steam and sparks into the midafternoon sky, Bull reflected once more on the old monster's words. *See me home? Provincetown is where the old captain and his wife took me in. I called it home once, but that doesn't mean there's anything left for me there.*

Still, as always, he couldn't think of anywhere else to go.

"Station ahead!" shouted the engineer. John reached into the little sack he always kept strapped across his back. Pulling out two bulbous roots, he tossed one to Bull and brought the other up to his grinning mouth.

~ ~ ~

The New Bedford station was a long, rectangular structure. Its ornately carved columns contrasted markedly with the plain Doric columns and scrolled Ionian columns of the other buildings on Pearl Street, just as its flat roof contrasted sharply with the gabled roofs of the nearby houses.

Bull had little interest in architecture, but the train station's vaguely Oriental look did serve to emphasize its novelty, and that of the mode of transportation it represented. When Bull was last in New Bedford, he'd watched many a workman load barrels of whale oil, crates of salt fish, and other harvests of the sea onto horse-drawn wagons to be hauled away for sale. He'd also watched them unload goods brought *by* wagon from inland farms and factories: grain, clothes, metal goods, and more.

This day, as he and High John walked out of the station, he again saw workmen loading and unload—only the incoming goods arrived by train and the outgoing goods would leave the same way. That was progress, he supposed, but that also meant fewer wainwrights and wheelwrights making wagons, fewer blacksmiths shooing horses, and fewer teamsters driving from town to town on plank roads and earthen trails. The coming of the railroad meant they'd all have to learn a new skill, a new identity, a new place in the world.

Will they find it as hard as I have?

"This way." John spat a wad of root pulp, turned left, and headed down Purchase Street at a brisk pace.

"Where we goin'?"

"To see a friend."

High John's legs were long. Bull's were longer. Soon they were walking side by side, Bull shooting him quizzical glances. John replied with cackles, smirks, and streams of reddish juice. They passed sweat-streaked laborers hurrying to and from the docks, finely tailored merchants hurrying to and from their shops, and elegant ladies in no hurry at all. New Bedford was no sprawling metropolis like New York or Philadelphia, but it was a thriving town.

When they reached Union Street, High John turned left toward the river. A disquieting notion came to Bull's mind. "Ain't interested in whalers."

"Me neither, Stormy!"

Sighing, Bull followed him three blocks down to Water Street, then along the riverfront for two more until they reached a wharf. John pointed to a large shop. "He's done added on, I think."

"Said you'd never been this way."

"Nah, ain't never been clear out to Cape Cod. I been—hey, Lewis!"

The blacksmith passing through the shop's door was of average height and wiry build. His nut-brown face was narrow, his dark eyes sharp and penetrating, his salt-and-pepper hair, mustache, and goatee neatly trimmed. His shirtsleeves were rolled up past his elbows, revealing well-muscled arms streaked with sweat and soot.

"Can I help ya?" said the smith.

John's face went blank. "Don't ya…know me?" he sputtered.

"Should I?" Lewis replied. "Are y'all from the *Corinthian*? Still workin' on those hooks and spikes."

The look of utter confusion on his companion's face made Bull queasy. How much did he really know about the wizened sailor? John's friendliness and evident familiarity with monsters and magic were disarming, but perhaps Bull should have been more cautious. He'd attributed John's odd sayings and mannerisms to eccentricity, when they could just as easily have been the ravages of old age.

"Simple mistake," Bull began. "My friend thought he'd—"

The corner of the blacksmith's mouth twitched.

John burst out laughing. "You rascal!"

"Learned from the best!" Lewis strode forward to shake the old man's hand.

John's uncovered eye twinkled. "We's ole friends, like I say. Lewis Temple, meet Alfred Bulltop Stormalong."

"Not ole Captain Stormy himself!" The blacksmith reached up to clap Bull on the back.

"No. Not anymore." Bull glared at John, who arched a mischievous eyebrow.

"Oh?" Lewis stroked his goatee. "Well, folks change. Once I was a slave down in Virginia. Then a funny little man with clever hands and dancing feet come along—and I'm a free man in Massachusetts. What name ya go by now?"

"Bull."

"And I go by High John," said the Rompo. "Back in Virginny, I s'pose I's *Low* John!" The two black men laughed.

Bull didn't. "So, you know that—"

"—that John's not what he seems," Lewis interjected. "I knew from the start. Got a knack for it, ya know, for *seeing* crooked things straight."

"You have the Sight."

"I figured him a monster before I ever saw 'im change. Just like I figured you at a glance. *Bulltop*. Hah!"

John nodded. "You should see them horns!"

Bull's eyes widened. *He knows I'm a monster! Even after many years on the* Courser, *Gez didn't know for sure what I was*. "I never heard of—"

Lewis cut him off. "That kind of tale's better told inside."

When they entered his shop, Bull felt momentarily disoriented. It was like walking into the blacksmith stall on his old ship. Harpoons, lances, boarding and rigging knives, hoops, pulleys—these and other whaling implements hung from wall hooks or lay in stacks on the floor.

"Whaling man?" Bull asked.

"Never been to sea, actually," Lewis replied. "Most of my customers are, though. Heard many a fish story in my time, though none so grand as the adventures of Captain Stormalong. Should've guessed Stormy was more than a man."

"Now you know." Bull glanced at John, but the old man had picked up a stirrup and was studying it. "*How* do you know?"

"Oh, that." Bemused, Lewis watched John run his finger along the stirrup's leather tread. "Saw the little people first, as a boy. Saw 'em in fields and woods and creeks. Some looked like me, except for strange clothes. Others like whites or Indians. Water Folk were the strangest, some with frog feet or no feet at all. They tried singing at me, so I just sang back at 'em. They didn't like that much."

"Folk like to be in charge," Bull said.

"Yep—and not just the magic kind." The blacksmith's eyes left John and seemed to stare at the wall, though Bull supposed they were looking through time, not space. "Anyway, spied my first monster when I was ten. A slinky, weaselly thing."

"John, you mean?"

"Nah, not yet. This one tried stealin' from the henhouse, but I ran it down good. Tried pretendin' to be the master's daughter, but I knew different."

"So you could see right through its human form?"

"In a way. Monsters don't sing on disguises like little Folk do. Y'all change your actual bodies, like tadpoles turnin' into frogs, only sudden-like and y'all can turn back again. I just got a knack for lookin' at frogs and seein' tails."

Or horns. "Didn't know the Sight worked like that."

"It don't, for most," said High John, who'd put down the stirrup and pointed at some irons on the worktable. "What's them things, Lewis?"

"Harpoons." The blacksmith's eyes had that far-off look again.

"That, I know," John scoffed, "only them's got odd heads."

"Just somethin' I been fiddlin' with."

The change of subject annoyed Bull. "John, you said his kind of Sight ain't normal."

"Shucks, Sight ain't *never* normal." The old man picked up a harpoon and waved it in the air. "But it ain't just one thing. It works diff'rent for diff'rent seers, like we ain't all the same just cuz we's monsters. Some humans got only a little bit o' Sight, like spyin' a shadow here and there but never the thing castin' it. Others got it more in the ears and the mouth than the eyes. They hear a spell and just blow it away before it can get 'em."

"And some men got a Sight for shape-shiftin' monsters, too," said Lewis Temple, deftly snatching the harpoon from John. "Or one does, anyhow."

"How many have you seen?" Bull asked.

"Countin' you?"

"Yeah, countin' me."

"Too many to count!" Both John and Lewis laughed.

Bull shook his head. "Can't be."

John chuckled. "Old Stormy ain't worked it out yet, Lewis."

"Worked what out?"

"Makes sense, if you think on it a spell. Magic Folk hunt all monsters, right? Kill us or put us in pens. Suck our magic dry. Only a shape-shifter's plenty hard to catch. We's safer from 'em. Safer still when we forget we ain't human, I reckon. Over the years, there come to be more of us slippery ones than other monsters. Maybe one day we's all that's left."

"I doubt it," Bull grunted.

He thought of the deadly Kraken, relentless and close to impregnable. He thought of fearless Mocha Dick, veteran of a hundred battles with doomed or defeated men, made vulnerable only by an exhausting fight with another great denizen of the deep. He thought of the lumbering Yeitso, colossus of the desert, vanquished only because it happened to encounter an improbable set of allies on the edge of a yawning chasm. He recalled the many other creatures Gez had told him about, terrible behemoths of sea and swamp, sand and sod, slope and sky.

"There are things more powerful than you imagine," Bull added.

"That so?" High John smirked.

"Too powerful for any little Folk to handle."

Lewis smiled, too. "Lots more humans than fairies."

"Don't matter!" Bull felt his face flush with anger. "When humans go after the *mighty* monsters, they die. Same as fairies."

"Not always."

"I've seen it!" the former sea captain snapped. "I know!"

Lewis shrugged. "So not *all* die."

"I ain't human!" Bull was in a rage now, stomping and bellowing as if he'd reverted to Minotaur form, though no horns sprouted to knock the cap off his head. "And I ain't no better! The great big monsters kill with fang and stalk and claw. I kill with foolish words and foolhardy deeds. Don't matter. Either way, my crew's just as dead."

"Never heard yer tale, I admit, but ya got that part wrong." Lewis still held the unfinished harpoon, tracing its length with the index finger of his other hand. "I once saw a man worked and lashed to death on the plantation, and another man shot tryin' to *escape* the plantation. Big difference."

"Both died."

"Yea, but one died like a mule, the other like a man."

John nodded. "Don't go talkin' like yer crew ain't men, like they ain't made a choice."

"Wasn't a real choice!" Bull insisted. "They didn't know the danger."

"And *you* did?" The old man pursed his lips, as if waiting for an answer and at the same time figuring he wouldn't get one.

He figured right. Presently, John's mouth resumed its twisted grin. "They *did* know their cap'n, though. They's willin' to fight for him."

Bull found his voice again. "Thought you were against fightin'."

"I ain't made for it," John allowed. "I like backdoors and briar patches and makin' a way out of no-way. Winnin' wars on the inside, not the outside. Still, Old Maker's not a wastin' sort. Some creatures *is* made for fightin'. Sometimes, a fight's all that's left."

"But what for?" Bull demanded. "The Kraken's a monster. *I'm* a monster.

What does it matter who wins? Your Old Maker ain't rootin' for one over the other!"

High John's crooked smile mocked him. And soothed him. "You sure?"

The fury left Bull. He felt hollow inside. *Why did the old monster bring me to this shop?* he wondered. Then his unspoken question broadened and deepened. It was *John* who'd enthusiastically endorsed Bull's notion of returning to his childhood home in Massachusetts. It was *John* who'd suggested they take jobs in Providence on a train bound for New Bedford.

Was this John's plan all along, to get me here? What for?

Lewis Temple flicked the harpoon, producing an odd click. John mimicked the sound with teeth and tongue. "Is it broke?"

The blacksmith shook his head. "Nah, the barbs are supposed to toggle out from the shank like that. Just haven't got the pivot quite right."

Bull's deeper questions cried out to be answered. He decided to ignore them, for the moment, and ask a shallower one. "Why make the barbs move?"

Lewis handed him the weapon. "A high-seas man can tell it better. Ever had a whale slip a harpoon?"

The honest answer was no. When Captain Stormalong harpooned a whale, it stayed harpooned. As Bull stared at the piece of iron, barbed at both ends, and watched it pivot on its joint at the head of the dart, he wasn't thinking about whale flesh. "If the beast can turn just right, the barb works itself out. The harpoon falls into the water."

"But what if the barbs could turn *sideways* under the skin?" Lewis demanded.

"Then"—it was as if Bull could *see* the result in his mind—"the harder the rope gets yanked, the harder the barbs dig in."

"Exactly!" The blacksmith turned to John, who was snickering with delight despite the obvious fact that he didn't understand what the others were talking about. Lewis grabbed his shoulder excitedly. "It's all in the pivot!"

~ ~ ~

Much later, when the two shape-shifters left the human's shop with goals, plans, and the latter's promise to keep working on his newfangled harpoon, Bull pointed an accusing finger at High John. "You knew what he'd been tinkerin' with all along. Fess up!"

"Shucks." As they walked down Water Street, sizing up the ships anchored nearby, John dug in his sack for a chewing root. "I's no whaler, Stormy, you know that. Still ain't got no notion what that pivot thing's for."

"Then why did you—"

"Lewis Temple's a mighty smart man. Sees more things, and more things clear, than anyone I knows. Figured he'd get ya seeing things clear, too."

Bull blew out an exasperated breath.

John let out a self-satisfied guffaw. "I figured right!" Then he handed his friend a root.

"You had me fooled," Bull admitted before taking a nibble.

"How's that?"

"All that connivin' talk about seeing me home. You never meant us to get to Provincetown."

"True." John cocked his head. The gesture made Bull think of a playful rabbit, which made perfect sense. "Never lied, though. Said I aimed to see ya home. Never said I thought yer home was on land."

Chapter 24 – The Agreement

April 1846

SAM HOUSTON TUGGED HIS CHEROKEE blanket so far up the back of his neck that its buff-colored folds, striped in black and orange, entirely covered his shoulders and hung down over his gray coat sleeves and the crimson armrests of his high-backed chair.

Across the room, John C. Calhoun sulked, his bushy eyebrows bristling.

Sam smiled. His smile was exaggerated, but hardly disingenuous. *You and I have a history, Senator Calhoun. I'll never let you forget it.*

They'd first met nearly thirty years ago, when Sam was an Indian agent and Calhoun was the secretary of war. Houston had led a delegation of Cherokee chiefs to meet President James Monroe. Calhoun took the young lieutenant aside to yell at him for entering the White House in native dress rather than standard uniform. Sam protested that wearing Cherokee clothing was a way to build rapport with the chiefs, but a furious Calhoun ordered him never to do it again. Later, based on false information from Sam's enemies, the South Carolinian repeatedly accused him of malfeasance. Sam had been vindicated every time, which only made Calhoun more resentful.

Three decades later, fate conspired to bring the two's interests into alignment. Using every tool at Sam's disposal—flowery speeches, misdirection, even assistance from the Elf ranger Thekla—he spent much of his second administration as president of Texas trying to persuade the United States to annex it. The alternatives, Sam made clear, did *not* include a perpetually independent republic. Either Mexico would reconquer it, or Texas would become a de facto protectorate of Britain or France. Surely neither outcome would be in the interest of the United States.

In early 1844, then-President John Tyler named Calhoun secretary of state. Ever suspicious of British meddling, the South Carolinian was a fit spectator for Sam's theatrics. And when Sam's old colleague from Tennessee, the pro-annexation James K. Polk, was elected president in November, the die was cast. On February 19, 1846, Sam Houston witnessed the flag of the Lone Star Republic lowered for the last time. Two days later, the legislature elected Sam and his former comrade in arms, Thomas Rusk, as the new senators from the new state of Texas.

Now here Sam was, two months later, staring across the chamber at a man who hated him but who also helped, however unwillingly, to send him back to Washington as a United States senator.

Sam stood up, the old blanket still draped over his shoulders.

Calhoun stiffened. Other members gasped. It was unheard of for senators to participate in floor debates during their first year in office. Sam was no political novice, though. He was a former congressman, governor, and president of an independent nation. Upon arrival in Washington, he'd immediately been named chairman of the Senate's Military Affairs Committee. He'd also made certain promises to President Polk—promises he meant to keep.

"For what purpose does the senator from Texas rise?" Vice President George Dallas sat on a raised platform on the east side of the chamber, slender hands resting on a table skirted in red.

"To speak on the resolution, Mr. President."

"The gentleman is recognized."

Sam scanned the chamber. Most seats were filled. Most of their occupants regarded him with surprise, irritation, or contempt. An exception was his oldest friend among the senators, Thomas Hart Benton of Missouri, under whom Sam had served during the War of 1812 and who'd first introduced the young lieutenant to their commanding general, Andrew Jackson. Benton nodded amiably.

Among the merely surprised were his fellow Texian Thomas Rusk and two men with whom Sam served in the House two decades earlier, Daniel Webster of Massachusetts and Willie Mangum of North Carolina. Among the irritated was Lewis Cass of Michigan, Jackson's former secretary of war and Sam's superior during his first mission to Texas. The most contemptuous was, of course, Calhoun.

"Mr. President," Sam began, "I am not insensible to the peculiarity of the position in which I find myself. To anyone—and more especially to one unaccustomed to participating in its debates—the occasion of addressing a body so influential and intelligent as the Senate of the United States must necessarily be attended with much embarrassment."

He paused, staring at Calhoun, and let the Cherokee blanket slip from his shoulders. The South Carolinian rolled his ice-blue eyes.

"I am, however, about to be called on to act as a member of this body on a subject of high importance," Sam continued, "and it therefore becomes my duty, as one of the representatives of a state which has recently become an integral part of the great confederacy of this Union, to present my reasons for the vote which I shall give on this occasion."

He paused one last time to look around the room before delivering his prepared remarks. Calhoun was clenching his jaw so furiously, it made his high cheekbones jut out like rocky crags. The other senators, friend or foe, looked at least curious about what Sam would say. The South Carolina one wasn't. He already knew.

He knew that in the Texian's first speech on the floor of the Senate, Sam Houston would *agree* with John C. Calhoun.

~ ~ ~

Three hours later, after Sam had completed his prepared remarks and met with fellow senators in executive session, he left the Capitol with much on his mind.

His first address was well received, winning support for President Polk's strategy of settling the Oregon question from a position of strength. During the 1844 election, backers of Polk's candidacy insisted on "Fifty-Four-Forty or Fight!"—an ultimatum to Britain that it cede all of the territory up to the border with Russian Alaska. For decades, Britain had asserted its own claim to Oregon as far south as the forty-second parallel, the border with Mexican California. In reality, Polk was willing to compromise by extending the current border with Canada due west, along the forty-ninth parallel to the Pacific. To drive Britain to the negotiating table, however, Polk wanted Senate approval to rattle a few American sabers. Thanks to Calhoun and Houston, he seemed poised to get it.

"Er, President Houston?"

Startled, Sam looked up and realized he'd walked down Pennsylvania Avenue to Third Street without so much as acknowledging a single passerby. This person would have been hard not to notice, however, even if he hadn't planted himself in Sam's path and called him by the wrong title. The first thing Sam noticed was the man's black silk hat, very tall with a flat brim. Beneath it, the lean-faced man was clean-shaven at the cheeks but white-whiskered along his neck and chin. A pair of spectacles rested precariously at the end of his nose. He wore a wrinkled coat, baggy pants, rumpled shirt, and ill-fitting cravat.

"I am a president no more, sir," Sam replied.

"Er, misspoke." The man removed his glasses. "Might I have a word, *Senator* Houston?"

"I have an appointment," Sam said, which was more or less the truth, though he couldn't know for sure when the emissaries would arrive.

"Won't keep you long. Just answer one question for my readers."

"Gentleman of the press, eh?" Sam inclined his head. "Have at it."

"Very well. Will there be war?"

Sam sighed. "A simple question, sir, but with no simple answer. The way to negotiation remains open, although we should not wait on the nods and becks of England to determine our own policy."

"Not with England," said the newsman. "I speak of Mexico."

"Ah." Instantly regretting his decision to accept the interview, Sam began plotting a graceful exit. After all, while Polk's saber-rattling might settle the Oregon question, it was unlikely to fix the country's southern and western borders. Mexico had never accepted the legality of the 1836 treaty Sam negotiated with Santa Anna to recognize the independence of Texas. And even some American leaders doubted the country's now inherited Texian claim that its jurisdiction extended all the way to the Rio Grande, including large swaths of New Mexico it had never governed.

President Polk was, however, committed to the Rio Grande border. Indeed, he sought to purchase the rest of New Mexico, and California to boot, from what he saw as a decrepit and unstable Mexican government that owed its American creditors vast sums in the form of defaulted debts and unjust seizures.

In his Mexican policy, Polk *didn't* enjoy overwhelming support. Senator Calhoun was among those against acquiring any more territory from Mexico, by purchase or force of arms. Nevertheless, Polk had instructed General Zachary Taylor and thirty-five hundred soldiers to cross the Nueces River into the disputed territory. During the executive session, Sam Houston and his colleagues had just learned of Mexican troops massing on the far bank of the Rio Grande. Had a senator already shared the news with the press?

"A more complicated question," Sam finally answered, "requiring more elaboration than time allows at present. Might I call upon you at some later date, sir?"

The man tugged nervously on his loose collar. "I *had* planned to leave for New York tomorrow."

So much the better. "Then may I, upon further reflection, send you my thoughts in a letter?"

"If you must." Reluctantly, he stepped aside to let Sam pass. "Address your correspondence to the *New York Tribune*, Horace Greeley, editor."

~ ~ ~

As he continued his walk, Sam rehearsed the answer he might have offered Greeley—but had been wise enough *not* to attempt off the cuff.

War with Mexico *did* appear imminent. Sam couldn't say he was against the prospect. It seemed the only way to resolve the border dispute once and for all, and extend stable governance from Texas to the Pacific. Still, the military forces of the United States were few and untested. Battles could be close-run things, he knew, and the outcome of a war often differed dramatically from the intentions of those who started it.

It was early evening when he reached the Indian Queen, his residence for the congressional session. Standing in front of its double doors, Sam traced his eyes up the hotel's white walls until he found the window to his fourth-floor room. It was dark.

"We tried there first."

Sam grinned. "It has been a long and eventful day, old friend."

Two familiar voices sang a familiar tune, a spell of concealment. Then Har the Tower appeared next to Sam, followed by Goran Lonefeather.

The Dwarf, he'd seen two days earlier. Although it had been many years since their last meeting, Sam perceived little change. Har still possessed the same sparkling eyes, unruly hair and beard, stocky build, and boisterous personality. The Sylph was another matter. Goran looked haggard, his oval face drawn, brown eyes dim, gold-tinged feathers dull and dry.

Sam knew why.

During his reunion with Har, the Dwarf had narrated the two rangers' adventures since departing Galveston Bay in 1840. So, Sam knew of Dela's rescue from the Nimerigar, as well as that cruel Folk's encouragement of Indian raids on Texas and New Mexico and their consumption of monster flesh. He knew Dela's former captors, the Elves, had robbed her of her memory, and that she chose to stay and heal in Tennessee even though it meant an indefinite separation from Goran.

In return, Sam had told Har about his own experiences: his second presidency of the Lone Star Republic, his ultimately successful machinations to bring Texas into the United States, and his dealings with Thekla the Elf. It had horrified Sam to learn Thekla was the Elf who'd dealt Dela a near-fatal wound and later nearly killed Goran and Diri by luring Water Panthers to attack them. Still, Har was gratified to learn what Sam had gleaned from Thekla about Cibola and the ongoing contest between her Folk and the Duendes over the legendary Seven Cities of Gold.

Har pointed. "Should we talk in your room?"

A gust of laughter blew from the open window to the dining room. "A less populated site might be better," Sam replied. He led them around the Indian Queen, then east on C Street. When they reached the First Presbyterian Church, Sam entered a small courtyard on its north side.

"Are you, at last, a church-going man, Sam?" asked a bemused Har.

"So my Margaret would have me, and she may get her wish in the end. She wants me baptized into her faith, though, not restored to my ancestral Presbyterianism. Still, I often find myself drawn to this place. President Jackson once worshipped here, as does President Polk."

"But not tonight, I take it."

"No, not on a Wednesday." Sam glanced up and spied two birds circling its tall steeple. "Did Har share my news, Goran?"

"About the Elves and Duendes? Yes. It clarified much that was murky. We knew both Folk pursued mysterious quests. Har witnessed Duendes exploring an abandoned Folk village beneath the Alamo. Later, we separately tracked Elf rangers to a canyon in New Mexico, but they escaped before we could divine their intentions."

"Thanks to a stone giant with a nasty disposition," Har added, "though we did learn from some new friends that the Elfish plot involved Carbuncle shells."

"Shells, you say?"

Goran nodded. "The Carbuncle is a small monster with a remarkable resistance to spellsong. Its shells provide similar protection for those who wear them."

"If my understanding is correct, spellsongs don't work on Folk." Sam frowned. "Why do Elves want the shells?"

"That riddle, we have yet to solve." Goran raised a finger. "And it isn't just the shells. We and our companions vanquished the giant Har mentioned by striking a vulnerable spot—a massive disk on its forehead. When I flew down to its carcass on the canyon floor to recover my arrows, the broken shards of the disk were missing. The Elves made off with them, too."

Sam scratched the cleft in his chin. "Thekla told me her Folk sought the Cibola sites to keep the Duendes from acquiring great wealth. Our legends describe them as Seven Cities of Gold, but maybe their true wealth isn't in precious metals but in—"

"—artifacts!" Har agreed. "Mages and craftsmen often use parts of monsters to make enchanted weapons and devices!"

Goran pursed his lips. "There is logic in what you both suggest, but it would be easier to harvest horns, claws, talons, and scales from their own monster pens or hunting grounds than to seek faraway Folk caches to loot. There must be something special about the magical items they hope to find in the abandoned villages."

"It is progress, my friend!" Beaming, Har slapped the Sylph's back. "We have narrowed the question."

Goran winced and shot Har a reproachful look. *That's not the question he cares most about,* Sam guessed. *He wants to restore Dela's memory.*

The Dwarf yanked back his hand and turned to gaze up at the church steeple. Sam's eyes widened. *Or there some other disagreement between the two?* He cleared his throat. "Har, have you thought more on what we discussed?"

"The Texas conflict, you mean." The Dwarf kept his eyes averted. "Goran learned much from his own interview."

The Sylph turned to Sam. "While you and Har met the other day, I sought out the only man in the Polk administration who, as far as we know, possesses the Sight: the secretary of your navy, George Bancroft. He has no objection to being introduced as such to other Sighted humans."

"I know him only by reputation," Sam said. "A scholar, as I recall. Ran for governor of Massachusetts a couple of years ago."

Goran nodded. "It was an emissary to Grünerberg from the Sprites of Boston who told us about Bancroft. He is not only acquainted with the Sprites—he met other Folk during lengthy studies in Europe. I found him a learned and perceptive man."

"Bancroft agrees with you, Sam." Har managed a wry smile. "He believes war may be the only way to settle your country's disputes with Mexico—and that the Folk of America should help the United States emerge victorious."

"Exactly!" Sam felt his pulse quicken. "I can give you the location—"

"King Alberich does *not* agree." Har's smiled faded. "He holds Elves responsible for provoking the war and refuses to act, however indirectly, as an ally of his bitter foe, Prince Veelund."

Sam was stunned. "The Elves didn't create our troubles with the Mexicans. Does your king really believe Texas would be better ruled by puppets from Mexico City, with Duendes pulling their strings?"

"Alberich is not concerned about the fate of Texas," Har admitted. "He believes Grünerberg's interests and Veelund's are always at odds. If Elfkind stands to gain, Dwarfkind must lose."

"Nonsense," Sam insisted. "That's the sort of fanaticism that threatens disunion in my own country. A sensible leader uses the tools at hand. I used Thekla as a source of information. That didn't make me beholden to her."

Goran put his hands on his hips. "You speak of fanaticism. If war comes, will not Southern fanatics be responsible, at least in part? Many Americans in the North say Polk merely schemes to add more slave states to your union."

"Is that what George Bancroft claims?"

"No, he supports the president's policy, though Bancroft is also a passionate opponent of slavery. He believes the westward expansion of American civilization and ideals will advance the cause of humanity."

"I believe that, too." Sam hadn't counted on having to argue with his own friends. "I will not defend the justice of an institution to which I am connected by fate, not by choice. Those in slave states may see the extension of American sovereignty to the Rio Grande, and perhaps beyond, as advancing their interests, just as free states see their interests advanced by our secure acquisition of Oregon. I consider both in *America's* interest, as does the administration."

"Even if blood be shed to accomplish it?"

"I have shed blood in the service of my country," Sam said. "I desire peace where there is a prospect of its proving more advantageous than war. But while I admit peace ought to be pursued and cultivated, another great principle of government is to resist oppression. If war becomes necessary to maintain this principle, I would endure it."

Goran arched an eyebrow. "Eloquent words, senator, but you are not on the campaign trail."

"I don't offer Alberich eloquence. I offer him truth."

"He will not budge," Har stated. "The king judges that if American troops march into battle with the full power of Veelund behind them, they will prove at least a match for Mexico and the Duendes."

Sam grunted in exasperation. "Sounds like he's not so opposed to Veelund after all."

"You are wrong." Har blew out a frustrated breath of his own. "I did not come to argue with you. I came to reach an agreement."

"What?" The image of John C. Calhoun's scowl sprang to Sam's mind. The South Carolinian wasn't just irritated by the ascension of a longtime foe. He resented Sam rising to speak in favor of Calhoun's own position, thus associating the tradition-minded veteran of the Senate with the brash, ill-dressed new member from America's newest state.

Calhoun preferred the clarity of disagreeing with Sam. Their agreement had mortified him. *Good.*

"The Dwarfs of Grünerberg will not actively enable a war against Mexico," Har repeated, "but we cannot allow Veelund to gain more power from one. If supplied intelligence on where hostilities may erupt, Alberich is prepared to send rangers to shadow any Elf rangers who take the field and discover their true intentions."

"Including Veelund's designs on the seven cities of Cibola," Goran explained. "I have already passed along Alberich's proposal to Secretary Bancroft."

"Now, the chairman of the Military Affairs Committee is offered the same." Sam looked first at the earnest face of Har the Tower, then at the weary face of Goran Lonefeather. He wondered if his own bewhiskered face reflected his frustration with Alberich's purported neutrality—as well as his relief that the rangers of Grünerberg, presumably including his own friends, would still play a role in whatever events unfolded in Texas and beyond.

The senator offered his rough hand to Har. "We are agreed."

Chapter 25 – The Blue

December 1846

"I NEVER DREAMED THE GOVERNOR would do that!"

Manuel struggled to hold his tongue. *Really? You never dreamed Armijo would run instead of fight? Are you a liar or a fool?*

He stared across the table at Diego Archuleta, studying the man's half-lidded eyes, hollow cheeks, and thin lips. No, Archuleta was no fool—that much, Manuel would grant him. Back in 1841, then-Captain Archuleta had supported Governor Armijo's dishonorable plan to execute Texians who'd been promised mercy. Since then, Archuleta had served in the National Congress and risen to the rank of colonel, second-in-command of the New Mexican militia.

After the United States declared war and invaded their country, Manuel Antonio Chaves and Diego Archuleta were among the thousands of New Mexicans who assembled at Apache Canyon, ten miles east of Santa Fe, to defend the capital. Before the Americans arrived, however, Governor Armijo ordered his men to disperse—and then fled New Mexico altogether.

Manuel frowned at the sly colonel. *Only I may see what is invisible, but Archuleta surely saw enough of the old scoundrel to know better.*

"Now is a time for new leadership!"

Seated on each side of Archuleta were two brothers. Juan Felipe Ortiz, rotund and passionate, was the vicar of Santa Fe. His brother Tomás Ortiz, lean and haughty, was a merchant and owner of the house in which they sat. It was Tomás who spoke of new leadership.

Manuel glared at him. *Only I may hear what is silent, but even the deaf could hear this man's unspoken words. Tomás Ortiz would be governor himself.*

"How can the militia be mustered without the Americans finding out?"

Two other brothers were next to Manuel. Nicolás Pino, who'd just asked the question, was tall and burly. He owned a large ranch south of Santa Fe. His brother, Miguel Pino, was the dashing young militia officer who, five years earlier, had sided with Manuel against Armijo's plan to massacre the Texians. The Pinos had become his close friends.

"My brother and the other men of the cloth hold the key," Tomás replied. "They can spread the word without arousing suspicions."

The vicar nodded. "Father Leyba and Father Martinez go east to San Miguel. Father Gallegos and I journey north to Rio Arriba and Taos. We will remind the loyal men of New Mexico that the Lord is a refuge for the oppressed, a stronghold in times of trouble. They will rise up to protect our towns, our women, our holy places from the evil Americans. They will do their duty bravely, I assure you."

Miguel Pino looked pensive. "It is not their loyalty or bravery I question. It is their ability to defeat a regular army in the field."

Diego Archuleta and Tomás Ortiz exchanged questioning glances. Then the latter shrugged. "If that were our only option, the risks might be too great. There is a better way, however."

"Our militia need not stand alone," Archuleta explained. "More will join our cause."

"General Santa Anna is sending us reinforcements?" Miguel's shocked face mirrored Manuel's own. Once again wielding power in Mexico after an exile in Cuba, Santa Anna was reportedly gathering forces to attack General Taylor's army in faraway Nuevo León. It made no sense for New Mexicans to expect help from Santa Anna.

Tomás glanced around the room. "Not help from the south. Help from the north."

Archuleta grinned. "The Indians of the Taos Pueblo will fight the Americans. Utes from north of the San Juan and Apaches from east of the Sangre de Cristo may join us as well."

Thus far, Manuel had observed the meeting in silence. He could do so no longer. "The Americans justify their occupation by saying they will protect us from marauders better than our own government has—and your solution is to invite *more* Indian attacks?"

"The Americans lie," Tomás snapped. "Everyone knows they *direct* the Indian raids that loot our caravans and destroy our towns. I say turn their own bloody hordes against them!"

Nicolás Pino shook his head. "Your claim makes no sense. American traders such as Charles Bent and Ceran St. Vrain have lived among us for years. The Indian raids cost them dearly, too. I want the American soldiers gone as much as anyone, but I do not believe they collude with Utes, Apaches, Navajos, and Comanches to steal our flocks and depopulate our towns."

"Believe what you like," Tomás sneered. "As for Bent, he already received his reward. The Americans named him governor, though he will not rule long."

Most crowded into the dining room cheered. Manuel agreed with their sentiment but had little confidence in Ortiz or Archuleta. Something about their plan didn't add up. How could a hastily assembled force of poorly armed militiamen and Indians hope to defeat American regulars?

It was Archuleta who supplied the answer. "All New Mexico shall become a nest of rattlesnakes, with Bent and his fellow spies the first to taste our venom. Deprived of friends and fodder, the Americans shall flee our country just as Armijo did."

"Spies?" Miguel Pino pointed an accusing finger. "You mean the American traders. You mean to murder them!"

"This is not murder. It is war."

Nicolás Pino pounded a meaty fist on the table. "Bent and the others are civilians, not soldiers! What of their wives, their children? What you propose is dishonorable."

"What we propose," Tomás Ortiz insisted, "is victory. If we do not now throw off the American yoke, New Mexicans will forever be sheep in a land once our own."

Again, the room erupted in cheers. There were four exceptions: Manuel, the Pino brothers, and a portly man on the other end of the room, a Navajo blanket draped over his rounded shoulders and ample midriff. He was yet another brother invited to the meeting, a man whose silence seemed unlikely to reflect moral scruples or tactical disputes with Archuleta and Ortiz. Manuel turned toward the big man seated in the corner, his bitterness mixed with pangs of regret.

Pedro Chaves added nothing to the conversation. He only had eyes for his little brother, and they were cold as ice.

~ ~ ~

The inn's colonnade was less crowded than usual for this time of year. In the waning days of December, leading citizens of Santa Fe typically congregated here to drink, smoke, exchange Christmas toasts, and talk business. Even before the occupation, the inn—across the street from the plaza of Santa Fe—was home to a large number of American traders, scouts, and diplomats freely mixing with their Mexican counterparts.

Since the arrival of the American army, the colonnade had been filled with as many foreign officers wearing light-blue uniforms as local merchants, farmers, and ranchers wearing dark coats. All the women socializing at the inn were, however, dressed in Mexican fashion. That the Americans had brought no wives of their own, and so frequently courted the company of the ladies of Santa Fe, created another grievance among a population already seething with resentment.

Manuel didn't share this particular grievance, for he was no longer "in the hunt," as his friend Aki jokingly put it. Two years before, Manuel had married the loveliest girl in New Mexico. María Vicenta Labadie de Chaves was more than a match for him—and for any boorish American she might encounter.

"Do you think they were discovered?"

Miguel Pino sat at the entrance to the inn, fingers laced on his lap. His tall brother, Nicolás, stood nearby, chatting with a business partner from Albuquerque.

Manuel pondered Miguel's suggestion. It made sense. Of all who had attended that first gathering in the home of Tomás Ortiz, only he and the Pino brothers were on the colonnade. Nor were there many blue uniforms visible. If the American commander in New Mexico, Colonel Sterling Price, *had* uncovered the plot against the occupiers, he'd doubtless have arrested the conspirators and placed his troops on alert. That would explain their absence from the normally crowded portico.

And what of Manuel's estranged brother? He hadn't seen Pedro since the meeting in the Ortiz home. Manuel looked across the plaza at the familiar outline of the Governor's Palace. He recalled the occasion, years ago, when he'd met with Governor Armijo in the palace after returning from exile in St.

Louis. He also remembered the night, years before that, when he'd waited in the plaza for Armijo to come out of the palace so he could put an arrow in the governor's spineless back.

Was his elder brother now a prisoner there? Manuel had a hard time believing Ortiz or Archuleta would entrust Pedro Chaves with a major role in any plot. He was no leader or fighter. Indeed, Manuel couldn't be sure Pedro had even attended the subsequent meetings to plan the attack on the Americans. Manuel and the Pinos were, of course, not invited, nor would they have accepted the invitation.

His eyes widened. An American officer appeared east of the palace and marched toward the plaza, followed by half a dozen soldiers. Their muskets bristled with bayonets. When they crossed the road, Manuel and Miguel rose from their chairs. Nicolás leaned against a column, eyeing the soldiers intently, his acquaintance from Albuquerque having scurried into the inn.

"They *are* making arrests," Miguel exclaimed. "Which conspirators do they come for now, I wonder?"

Manuel didn't wonder. He knew the answer even before the officer led his men briskly along the colonnade to where they stood. The American stroked his neatly trimmed beard and looked up at Nicolás. "Are you the Pino who owns a ranch down on Galisteo Creek?"

"He is." Manuel placed a hand on his friend's broad shoulder. "I am Manuel Antonio Chaves. Nicolás and his brother, Miguel, are my friends."

"Oh?" The officer's lips formed a faint smile. "Can your friends not speak for themselves?"

"Yes, but my English is better."

"I see." The American wiped his high forehead with a sleeve. "Well, Don Chaves, I am Captain William Zachary Angney, United States Army. Perhaps you can translate for me. I hereby place you, Nicolás Pino, and Miguel Pino under arrest."

"On what charge?"

Angney's smile disappeared. "Treason."

~ ~ ~

Despite all his conflicts with Governor Armijo, Manuel had somehow avoided being tossed into one of the cells on the west end of the Governor's Palace. He'd never dreamed it would finally happen under a different governor, one installed by a foreign power.

The cell was cold and sparsely furnished. He'd have endured it more easily in the company of friends, but to their surprise Miguel and Nicolás were quickly released upon a promise not to take up arms against the Americans. Manuel, on the other hand, had languished in jail for weeks. It wasn't exactly solitary confinement—he had frequent visitors, including his brother Román bringing meals—but it was still unjust.

Manuel pushed his empty bowl across the crude table and stared glumly at the dirt floor. The plot was, indeed, exposed long before its scheduled execution on Christmas Eve. While the wily Diego Archuleta had slipped away in the night, and Tomás Ortiz managed to escape by dressing in women's clothes, the other conspirators weren't so lucky. Some remained in custody or confined to their homes. Others were paroled when it became clear their involvement was, like the Pinos, limited only to the initial discussions.

So was mine! Manuel scanned the table, his fingers longing for the handle of his confiscated knife. He pictured Lionclaw carving a deep grove across its rough surface. The he imagined it cutting into something smoother, softer, and not yet dead.

It wasn't guilt that explained his imprisonment. It was revenge. He figured that out a few days after his arrest when, looking through the barred window of his cell, he spotted several friends of Governor Armijo leaving the palace. One was Pedro Chaves.

He knows I spoke against *murdering civilians,* Manuel fumed. *So do the others. Their lies are Armijo's parting shots at me.*

"Finished with supper, I see." The officer who'd arrested him stood outside the cell, holding a quill pen and stack of paper. "Might I ask you a few questions, Don Chaves?"

Manuel wanted to shout in reply. He wanted to reach through the bars and throttle the man. He did neither. *What would be the point? My real enemies are long gone.*

"I can spare a few moments," said the prisoner, hoping to sound amused, not annoyed.

William Angney pulled up a chair. "That you can."

"I have already told all."

"That was to your inquisitors." The American removed his cap, revealing wavy hair that matched the brown of his beard. "Now you speak to counsel."

"To *counsel*?"

"You face a court martial. Under our laws, the accused is entitled to representation. I practiced law in Missouri before my enlistment."

"You arrested me!"

"That was my duty. Now it is my duty to try to free you."

"Then you will fail." Manuel saw the officer flinch at that and smiled. "Words cannot deliver me from my enemies. It will take hot lead and cold steel."

Though enchanted bronze and bone would be better still. Shortly before the meeting at the Ortiz house, Aki left the Chaves ranch to spend the winter with Shash. Since Manuel's arrest, there'd been no way of getting word to the skinwalker. And he hadn't seen his Sylph friend Goran Lonefeather in years. Neither monster nor fairy was coming to his rescue.

"That's not true," Captain Angney said. "You'll get a fair trial—although if you speak about Americans that way in court, if you proclaim us your enemies, you'll doom your case."

Manuel sat back. "You occupy my country. That hardly makes us friends. Nevertheless, the enemies I speak of are not Americans."

"Then what do you—"

"I made these enemies long before you invaded New Mexico. I made them by telling the truth and acting on it."

The officer scribbled something with his quill. "I see. You refer to the witnesses against you."

"No, Captain Angney. What they *witnessed* was a citizen of Mexico desiring an end to the occupation of his country. To that, I freely admit. Everything else they say is false. That makes them liars, not witnesses."

The lawyer sighed. "I can understand your position, but you should know that my government considers most of this territory to have been surrendered by President Santa Anna in 1836, and thus part of the United States since the admission of Texas to our union."

"Conquerors often hide their blades within sheaves of worthless paper. I prefer the honesty of naked steel."

"Treaties are far from worthless paper," Angney replied. "My country has a long history of—"

"What of New Mexico *beyond* the Rio Grande? What of California? The bulk of your army marches west to conquer them. Which treaty justifies that?"

"There is no such treaty," the officer admitted, "but President Polk has enumerated our country's grievances. Abuses of American citizens and shipping in Mexican ports. Confiscations of American goods without compensation. Defaulted loans. Chronic instability and banditry along the border. Foreign intrigues that risk placing a new British or French protectorate at our doorstep."

"I have abused no Americans. My family, friends, and neighbors have abused no Americans. We owe them no debts. Yet the United States sent an army of conquest against *us*."

"No!" Angney was emphatic. "Our orders are to take possession of your land and extend over it the laws of the United States. We come amongst you as protectors, not conquerors. As friends, not enemies. Our purpose is your benefit, not your injury."

"I see. You would be stern but loving parents to wayward, ignorant children."

"That is not—"

"Mexico's independent government is young, true enough," Manuel interjected. "Younger even than yours, but ours is an ancient country. Centuries ago, our ancestors settled this land, farmed its valleys, and grazed our flocks on its grassy hills. Our churches dotted its countryside while most of your country was a wilderness. For generations, my forefathers have fought for their country—against fierce Indians, against grasping Spaniards, against unscrupulous Texians, against our own tyrants."

"Your country and mine have much in common," Angney said. "My government believes our destinies are intertwined. Under just laws, there is no limit to what we may accomplish together. One of those laws is that our government may not interfere with the religion of its people. Those churches of which you are rightly proud will be secure. Why, a third of our own army consists of Catholics."

"I am no village gossip," said Manuel. "I put no stock in fanciful rumors spread by the likes of Tomás Ortiz. I lived in Missouri for years and have done business with Americans for many more. It is not some mythical hostility to the Catholic faith that made your army my foe."

The officer's eyes widened. "*Made* it your foe? Or *makes* it?"

Manuel gave a weary nod. "I have no love for Santa Anna or the other rascals who rotate in and out of power in Mexico City. It was not at their command, or in defense of their ill-gotten gains, that I joined my fellow New Mexicans at Apache Canyon to repel your invasion. It was in defense of my country. It was as a soldier, willing to fight the soldiers of a foreign power."

"And now?"

"The army you serve is here. The army I served is no more."

"And yet you met with your former colonel, Diego Archuleta, and others to plot against the United States. To organize Indian raids and attacks on civilians, not a military campaign."

Manuel's neck flared as if touched by a hot poker. He wanted to pound his fist on the table. He wanted to pound it on the other man's neck. He wanted something else even more, however. He wanted to go home to his wife.

"Only another man present at the meeting could say I was there," he said, "and if he testifies I agreed to such a plot, he lies."

"Then *that* is what we must tell Colonel Price." Angney resumed scribbling. "Our orders are to treat your people with justice. All who remain peaceably at home, attending to their crops and herds, shall be protected in their persons, their property, and their religion. Only those who promise to be quiet and *then* take arms against us will be punished."

"You expect me to believe your colonel will accept my word and ignore the lies of my enemies?"

The attorney kept writing. "Oh, I'll sing you no spells, Don Chaves. Yours is a challenging case. Some have named you the most dangerous man in New Mexico. Still, I pledge to do my best on your behalf."

That Pedro and others might call Manuel dangerous was no shock. It might even have pleased Manuel a little, had he given it more than a fleeting thought, but he didn't. His mind was otherwise occupied.

I'll sing you no spells, Angney had said.

Hardly a common phrase, in English or Spanish. During Manuel's time with Goran, he'd learned much about monsters, magic, and Folk. *I could learn still more from another man with the Sight.*

If the American realized the import of those five words, he showed no sign of it. He put down his quill and stared at his notes, moving his lips as if rehearsing some legal argument.

Manuel decided to throw caution to the wind. "I understand. And you are too tall to be a spellsinger, anyway."

The American's lips formed a wry smile.

Manuel gasped. "You *knew*."

"I suspected. You have confirmed it."

"This was no wild guess. Why did you suspect I had the Sight?"

Holding a finger to his lips, Captain Angney glanced to his left. Apparently satisfied the guards were too far away to overhear, he replied. "It was a story I heard from an Elf ranger about a battle with a giant in a remote canyon. You fit her description of one of the combatants. When we took you into custody and confiscated this, that strengthened my suspicion."

He pulled an object from his pocket. Though the blade remained retracted, its bone handle gleamed in the lantern light.

"Lionclaw," said Manuel.

"A fitting name," said Angney. "The Elf said she saw a human strike the giant's head with such a weapon."

"You serve the Elves, then?"

The American returned the knife to his pocket. "No more than you serve the Duendes, if I am any judge of character."

I have already thrown caution to the wind. Might as well throw more. "I have heard of Duendes but never met any. I have dealt only with Elves, whom I distrust, and with friends I trust, who are not Elves."

"Who are these friends?"

Manuel paused, picturing the three fairies who'd fought at his side against the Yeitso. The narrow face of the Sylph. The broad face of the Dwarf. The comely face of the Water Maiden. "All I will say at present is that they are not enemies of yours."

Angney inclined his head. "Fair enough. Tell me what you know of Elves and Duendes, then."

"Elves, I know from personal experience. I fought them in Missouri and here in my own country. My friends say the Elves and Duendes foment conflict between your country and mine, though what they hope to gain is unclear."

"Power." The lawyer scratched his chin. "And game. May I assume you know the source of Folk magic?"

The prisoner nodded.

"The larger the territory controlled by humans under their sway," Angney pointed out, "the more monsters they harvest."

"True," Manuel allowed, "but there must be more to it."

The American sat back, eyes boring into those of his client. *Trying to decide how far to trust me*, Manuel thought. *Just as I am doing with him.*

"We understand Colonel Archuleta went north to Taos to raise the militia," Angney began, "and that the local Indians may join in rebellion."

Manuel sighed. "I know nothing of his whereabouts, but I can confirm the conspirators had hoped for Indian allies. Surely the Pinos and others have told you this."

"Yes, but my next question is meant only for you, Don Chaves. When the Elf visited me a few nights ago, she insisted the Duendes were behind the northern unrest—and that it was important *her* Folk, not their rivals, controlled the Taos Pueblo."

"Oh?" Manuel had visited the town of Taos many times but couldn't think of any reason the nearby Indian settlement was of special value. "Did the ranger—what is her name?"

"Thekla."

"Did this Thekla say anything more about her Folk's interest in Taos?"

"Yes, but it made no sense. She said it would be dangerous for the Duendes to possess 'the Blue Place.'"

Manuel recognized the reference. Being a stranger to New Mexico, Angney couldn't have known the Indians of Taos built their pueblo on a stream that flowed south to the Rio Grande—and that its source was a sparkling pond in the mountains above the town, a sacred place the Indians called *Ba Whyea.*

Blue Lake.

He was about to offer Angney an explanation when they heard the sound of approaching boots.

"That is all for now, Don Chaves," said the American, scooping up his papers.

Manuel rose quickly. "Captain, be kind enough to take my compliments to Colonel Price and say that he has nothing to fear from me now. When

Armijo disbanded the volunteers at Apache Canyon, I gave up all hope of being any service to my country at this time, and my record as a man will show that I am not at all likely to sympathize with any movement to murder people in cold blood."

"I understand, and I assure you that—"

"Tell him also," Manuel interjected, "that if the time ever comes when I can be of any service to my own country, Colonel Price will find me in the front ranks."

~ ~ ~

The last time Manuel sat in the governor's office, Armijo had asked him to help turn back the Texian invasion of 1841. Now, New Mexico was occupied by a foreign army and Armijo had long since fled south to safety. Six years ago, it was Manuel who'd stopped Armijo from murdering prisoners in cold blood. Now, it was *Manuel* accused of plotting to murder civilians in cold blood.

Sitting next to his legal counsel, Captain Angney, Manuel studied the faces of the nine officers who would decide his fate. They seemed open-minded. So far, witnesses had portrayed Manuel as a troublemaker, scoundrel, and hothead. When challenged by Angney to cite specific incidents, however, the witnesses equivocated or fell silent.

The most dangerous witness was yet to come, however. "Bring him in," muttered the presiding officer as he blotted his pale forehead. Colonel Price was still recovering from a bout with cholera.

The door opened. In strode a heavyset Mexican in a tan suit and white cravat. Stomping past Manuel, the witness gave the accused a sour look and sank into the chair next to Colonel Price. While other witnesses required a translator, this one did not.

The prosecutor, Captain John Burgwin, looked up from his notes. "You are Don Pedro Chaves of Santa Fe?"

"I was."

"What do you mean by—"

"I am Pedro Chaves, but no longer of Santa Fe. I have moved to my ancestral home of Cebolleta."

"No matter." Burgwin cleared his throat. "You are older brother to Manuel Antonio Chaves, the accused?"

"The one who remains, yes."

"That is no—"

"Our eldest brother, José, died long ago." Pedro's eyes met Manuel's. "Died on a fool's errand."

Colonel Price glowered. "It has been a long afternoon, sir. Simply answer the questions posed."

Pedro kept staring at Manuel. "Simple answers are my specialty."

"Don Chaves," Burgwin pressed on, "did you attend meetings in the home of Don Tomás Ortiz to plan a rebellion against the United States?"

"I attended one such meeting, yes."

"Was your brother Manuel present?"

"Certainly. If there is trouble to cause or glory to gain, he is sure to be nearby."

Why do you still hate me so? Manuel wanted to ask. The two had barely spoken in years. *Perhaps that is the reason, and as much my fault as yours.*

The prosecutor nodded. "Other men in attendance say the rebellion was to include not only military action against our troops but also the assassinations of Governor Bent and other American civilians. Is that so?"

"It is."

"The rebels sought to encourage Indian raids along the frontier, as well?"

"True enough."

Angney shot to his feet. "Colonel Price, the conspiracy is well attested. The defendant merely denies his involvement in it."

"I am getting to that, sir," Burgwin snapped. "Don Chaves, other witnesses spoke at length about your brother Manuel. His extensive business interests and friendships with Indians. His lengthy feud with your cousin, former Governor Armijo. His reputation as a marksman and warrior. Some even call him *El Leoncito*, the 'Little Lion.' Would such a man pass up the chance to help lead a military revolt against what he saw as foreign invaders?"

"No, he would not."

Manuel gnashed his teeth. *Even now, under oath, he names me a liar.*

Burgwin looked pleased. "Tell the court what he said when—"

"Little Lion, indeed," Pedro continued, seeming not to hear the prosecutor. "Manuel was never the giant of a man our brother José was. Never so strong, so graceful, so popular. In the shadow of such a giant, what else would a weak, headstrong little brother do but try desperately to prove himself a hero?"

Clenching his hands into fists, Manuel tried not to give into anger. Angney had warned him the prosecutor would try to get him to lose his temper, but he had never expected the provocation would come from his own brother's lips.

Pedro's jowly face contorted into a sneer. "Would such a man pass up the opportunity to bring glory and honor to the name Chaves?"

"This is not testimony!" Angney objected.

Burgwin actually nodded in agreement. "Don Chaves, let us talk only of the meeting that night at the home of Tomás—"

"The meeting Manuel tried to dominate, as usual." Pedro's voice was louder now, as if *he* were on the verge of losing his temper. "So dismissive. So high and mighty. Well, this was one time he did *not* get his way."

He paused. Though the room was crowded with Americans and Mexicans alike, no one else spoke. By their blank faces, it was clear to Manuel they were just as puzzled as he.

"You asked if my brother would pass up the chance to lead a military revolt," Pedro said, "but that was not the plan. The conspirators spoke of Indian raids and murders in the night. Tactics far beneath the famous Manuel Antonio Chaves. Nor were Archuleta and Ortiz ever going to permit him a role in leading their rebellion. There Manuel sat, his pretentious counsel spurned, his supposed prowess ignored. The exalted *El Leoncito*, reduced to the status of common peon. No wonder he and his pompous friends stormed out. No wonder they were excluded from all other meetings."

Angney glanced at his client. Manuel could only shrug. The prosecutor's face looked flushed. Colonel Price's face looked less pale than before. The other judges began whispering.

"That will…that will be all, Don Chaves," Burgwin croaked.

"Officers of the court," Angney said, "this testimony only serves to strengthen the defendant's denial that he was in any way involved in the conspiracy with which we are concerned."

"You go too far," said Burgwin. "Manuel Chaves chose to attend that meeting."

"As did his brother, and the Pinos, and many others." Angney said. "The defendant is charged with treason against the United States—but whatever the legal status of New Mexico may be, he does not consider himself a citizen of our country and has taken no oath to that effect. In his eyes he is a citizen of Mexico, to which he remains loyal. In seeking to discuss with his fellow militia officers the possibility of military resistance to an invading power, he acted as a patriot of his country, not a traitor to ours. And when he refused to participate in barbarities proposed by unscrupulous men, he acted as an officer and a gentleman."

The American pointed to his Mexican client. "Manuel Antonio Chaves deserves the admiration of all brave men. This court would forever bear the stain of disgrace if it undertook, under any pretext, to shoot a man for endeavoring to defend his country in time of need."

The defendant bowed his head. The prosecutor hadn't yet replied. Price and the other officers judging the case hadn't yet conferred. Still, Manuel knew in that moment he would soon be free. He'd owe his liberty in part to the eloquence and skill of an American officer, an enemy. Even more so, Manuel would get to go home to his wife thanks to another man he'd considered an enemy not just for months, but for years.

Had Pedro found it impossible not to express his contempt for Manuel even while defending him against an unjust accusation? Or had Pedro realized that expressing hostility toward an estranged brother would make his testimony *more* credible?

When Manuel looked up, he found Pedro heading toward the door—but he also found the answer he sought. One corner of his brother's wide mouth curved into a wry smile.

~ ~ ~

Freshly fallen snow covered the valley, the mountains ringing it, and the cluster of buildings between the ditch and the river. The blanket of white contrasted sharply with the blue uniforms of the infantrymen forming up in the largely deserted settlement.

Manuel looked down at the village of Taos and marveled at how radically his life had changed in two months. In December, he and his friends

Nicolás and Miguel had sat in the Santa Fe house of Tomás Ortiz, willing to entertain the notion of mounting a revolt against the Americans. In January, Manuel sat in jail, facing a capital charge of treason and blaming his estranged brother for it, while the Pinos were paroled to their homes but still under suspicion.

Now, just four days into the month of February, Manuel sat astride his palomino stallion on a ridge overlooking Taos. On his left was Nicolás Pino. On his right were William Angney, who'd defended Manuel in court, and John Burgwin, who'd prosecuted the case. All rode north to Taos under the overall command of Sterling Price, the same American colonel who'd ordered Manuel's arrest and presided over his trial.

All came to put down the Taos rebellion, though not necessarily for the same reasons. Captain Burgwin came to assert his country's sovereignty over New Mexico. Nicolás Pino came to protect his country from chaos and defend his family's honor, while Miguel stayed home to help protect Santa Fe. As for Manuel and Captain Angney, both shared their respective countrymen's goals while also pursuing a secret agenda of their own: to discover why Elves and Duendes were so eager to control the region.

Their expedition left Santa Fe so soon after Manuel's trial that he'd enjoyed only a few days' reunion with his wife, Vicenta, and managed only a brief conversation with Pedro. Although many issues still divided the Chaves brothers, Pedro admitted his past behavior toward Manuel was motivated more by envy than legitimate grievance. And Manuel admitted he'd done nothing to effect the reconciliation he knew his mother desired.

I will visit Pedro as soon as this is over. Manuel saw the first ranks of American soldiers marching out of the town. Whatever patriotic sentiment they brought to New Mexico had been replaced with a desire for revenge. Taos resident and merchant Charles Bent, named territorial governor by the Americans, lay dead—scalped and murdered by Indians from the pueblo at the same time Manuel was standing trial in Santa Fe.

"It is time to go," Burgwin told Angney. "Price will soon launch the assault. We best get into position."

Both captains had regiments of soldiers to lead. As for Nicolás and Manuel, they were among sixty-five new recruits, American and Mexican, who constituted Price's cavalry. Their task was to take up positions east of the pueblo and keep the rebels from escaping into the mountains. Colonel

Price had made similar use of the mounted volunteers during the army's northward advance from Santa Fe. In two brief battles, the Americans had outmaneuvered larger formations of rebels and Indian allies, forcing them to flee. Most had taken refuge in the heavily fortified Taos Pueblo.

Before following the other American officer down the slope, Angney gave Manuel a reassuring smile. Though acquainted for only a short time, the two had formed a strong bond not only during the trial, but over the course of their march from Santa Fe. Fighting side by side might do that for any men, even those from different lands, but Manuel also spent many nights talking with Angney about matters only Sighted humans could understand.

The American, it turned out, had glimpsed his first Elf ranger near the same Indian mound Manuel and Aki had discovered east of St. Louis. As for Manuel, he'd shared with the American not only his own experiences with Folk, but also his wife Vicenta's knowledge of Indian legends. During her childhood, one of the family servants had been an Indian from the Taos Pueblo. She'd told Vicenta fanciful tales about giant monsters, tiny demons, magic totems, glowing lights, and great battles between good and evil atop lonely mountains. Many of the legends centered on the sacred Blue Lake, from which the Taos Indians were said to be created.

Angney and Manuel agreed it must be the same Blue Lake the Elves and Duendes sought to control. So far, however, they'd witnessed no rangers of either Folk intervene in the skirmishes between the army and its foes. Perhaps today would be different.

~ ~ ~

The artillery felt silent. From their position east of the pueblo, Manuel and the other volunteers couldn't see what happened next, but a crackle of musket fire and chorus of shouts told the tale. As planned, Captain Burgwin's regiment attacked the pueblo from the west, Captain Angney's from the north. The melee was surely bloody, but its outcome seemed little in doubt.

The palomino snorted. Malcreado felt the same vibrations Manuel did. The latter exchanged glances with Nicolás, who sat astride his own horse, musket in hand, bearded jaw set in grim determination. After a couple of minutes, the vibrations became sounds. Footsteps up the slope. Hoofbeats along the ridge.

The volunteers scattered into small groups to cover more ground. Manuel turned left, nodding to Nicolás to follow. Soon, they reached a bluff overlooking the river that flowed from the mountains to the pueblo. If any of the rebels—or allied Duendes—chose to flee in the direction of Blue Lake, they'd go this way. Manuel cocked the rear trigger of his Hawken rifle and offered a silent prayer.

They didn't wait for long.

Something brown moved through some nearby pine trees, causing snow to tumble from low branches. Nicolás shouldered his musket and fired. Three fur-wrapped men, Indians from the pueblo, emerged from cover with bows drawn. The first never got a chance to shoot, thanks to Manuel's marksmanship. The second's aim was spoiled by the report of Manuel's rifle. His arrow passed well above the right shoulder of Nicolás Pino, who'd dismounted to reload his gun. Before the Indian could draw another arrow, Lionclaw found his throat. As for the third Indian, he was about to loose his arrow when another gun barked. The archer stiffened and sank to the icy ground.

Manuel glanced over his shoulder and saw the commander of the volunteers, Ceran St. Vrain, riding up, his own Hawken rifle tucked under his arm. "Figured I'd lend a hand," said the American, a longtime business partner of the murdered Charles Bent.

"It is well you did," Manuel replied. Both men reached for their ammunition pouches. Nicolás was already aiming his reloaded musket into the trees.

The next wave of rebels announced their presence with arrows and bullets. Three guns blazed in response before a hulking figure emerged from a thicket of mahogany and bitterbrush. It was an Apache wielding a long hunting knife. With a fierce cry, he leapt at St. Vrain and grabbed his coat, yanking the American from his saddle.

There was no time for Manuel to reload or recover his thrown knife. As the American struggled in the grip of his foe, trying to keep the Apache's blade from puncturing his chest, Manuel leapt from his horse and brought his rifle barrel down on the head of the Indian. There was a loud crack. The Apache fell limp.

"Manuel!" Nicolás pointed to the far side of the ridge. A sure-footed mare was scrambling up the hill, a broad-shouldered Indian on her brown back. That was, at least, what Nicolás saw. Manuel saw another figure sitting behind the Indian, a slender fairy clad in a strange garment fashioned of stems, leaves, and moss. And in the air above them, he spotted a green-clad fairy soaring on gossamer wings.

Elves? Duendes? Or one of each? Manuel had to find out. Hurrying to the bodies of their fallen foes, he recovered Lionclaw. "Others may be coming!" he called to his companions as he remounted. "I will follow this one."

~ ~ ~

Deep into the rugged mountains they rode, Manuel and his quarry, following the river as it wound east, then north. Though it seemed impossible he could escape notice, neither the Indian nor the fairies paid him any attention. Manuel couldn't even tell if the fairy on the horse was aware of the winged fairy following overhead.

It was when they reached the source of the stream, Blue Lake, that the situation drastically changed. More to the point, when Manuel saw what was occurring above the tree-lined lake, he realized he'd stumbled into a situation he didn't understand.

The sky was filled with fairies, some hovering and shooting, others grappling with or hurtling at their foes. Their clothes and weapons varied widely, though Manuel soon found he could distinguish the two sides by the nature of their flying implements. Some wore the now familiar packs and artificial wings of Elves. Others, whom he took to be Duendes, kept themselves aloft with natural wings similar to those of Goran Lonefeather.

Three sounds drew his attention from the sky battle. First, bursts of gunfire from the ground signaled the aerial combatants weren't alone. Manuel spotted several Elves standing on the other side of the lake, each working a ramrod down the bronze barrel of a gun.

Second, the Duende he'd tailed hopped from the horse and landed with a splash in the edge of the lake. Crouching among low reeds, she yanked a flute from her belt and began to play.

Third, Manuel heard hoofbeats. Another horse was approaching.

A moment later, the Indian wheeled his mare and headed back the way he'd come—that is, toward Manuel. Was the Duende using spellsong to send her minion after him? No, he decided. The Indian was in no hurry and drew no weapon. Manuel decided to act the part, wheeling his own horse as if succumbing to the same spellsong. Still, he drew the knife from his belt. He couldn't be sure the Indian wouldn't attack.

The third horseman on the trail proved no more charmed by the Duende spell than Manuel was. *Play along*, he mouthed to Captain Angney, whose blue uniform was streaked with sweat, soot, and blood.

The American's eyes narrowed. *Understood*, he replied silently, turning to retrace his path.

When the three humans passed out of sight of the Duende spellsinger, Manuel halted. Angney did, too, while the Indian continued to ride back toward Taos.

"You followed the winged Elf?" Manuel asked.

"I did."

"How goes the battle at the pueblo?"

"It is won, Don Chaves. Once we got the guns close enough to fire grapeshot and breached the walls of the church, the rebels began to withdraw. Most surrendered, though a few seek refuge in the mountains."

"Some have already found it—in death." Manuel tucked Lionclaw back into his belt.

"I fear Captain Burgwin will soon join them," Angney said. "He was grievously wounded in the assault."

Manuel had little reason to mourn the man. Burgwin had prosecuted the spurious treason case against him. Still, he bowed his head in respect. *The man but did his duty, as I must do mine—once I am confident what my duty requires.*

Angney appeared just as uncertain. "Elves and Duendes contest control of the lake, I take it. What do they seek?"

Manuel shrugged. "The Elves have their foes outnumbered. I do not know whether to be pleased or troubled by that."

The two found their way back to the lake and rode around its thickly forested shore, using the foliage to shield their movements. As they watched, three Duendes and one Elf fell from the sky, dead or about to be. With great sweeps of feathered wings, the remaining Duende fliers turned and fled eastward.

"The Elves have won the day," Angney observed.

Manuel made no reply. His eyes were trained not on the Elf fliers descending toward their fellows on the west bank of the lake but on the east bank, where the Duende spellsinger had stopped playing her flute and stood in the shallow water, watching her enemies celebrate their victory.

Even at a great distance, Manuel saw a sly smile crease the round face of the Duende. Then she whirled and dashed into the woods. *Was that the look of a defeated foe?*

"We will not find our answer here," Manuel told the astonished American. "Our adventure is not yet complete."

~ ~ ~

The riders followed the spoor of the Duende for many hours. At first they could see the ranger in the distance, scurrying along ridges and down gullies with impressive speed. Then she passed out of sight, though tumbling rocks and swinging limbs marked her passage sufficiently to keep them headed in the right direction. Even so, the coming of night would have proved their undoing had they not soon spotted two Duende fliers headed southeast, their figures illuminated by the light of the crescent moon.

Just before dawn, Manuel and Angney finally found their answer. It wasn't the winged fairies who led them to it. They'd vanished an hour earlier, leaving the two humans nonplussed. Nor was it the dwindling moonlight that ultimately revealed the destination they sought. It was another source of illumination, one shining up instead of down—an eerie, otherworldly radiance from the top of a far-off mesa.

A glow of brilliant blue.

"It was never about the lake, Don Chaves!" Angney exclaimed, spurring his horse to a gallop.

Manuel nodded and followed. *The Duendes never meant to win the lake battle with the Elves*, he realized. *They meant to lose it.*

When the riders reached the base of the mesa, they saw two shapes soar from the trees to the summit. Although perhaps the same flying fairies they'd followed the night before, the figures brought a memory to Manuel's mind. He'd passed this rugged butte before, during trading missions. He'd heard it called Urraca Mesa, named in Spanish for a bird native to the region, the magpie.

Perhaps the local Indians had some other reason to associate the place with winged creatures.

Angney pointed upward. "Should we confront the Duendes? Try to make them tell us about the blue glow?"

There was no need for Manuel to respond. The wind did it for him. It was no natural breeze that brushed their cheeks and tousled the manes of their horses, for they could not just feel it but *see* it—a ripple of light, a trail of sparks. An instant later, they heard what traveled along the glistening funnel that formed over their heads. They heard voices speaking Folktongue.

And when the two humans returned their gaze to the summit, they saw no blue glow.

Manuel frowned. "A transport spell. We are too late, Captain Angney."

"I would not say that."

The voice didn't belong to the American. It was female.

"Drop your rifle, Manuel Antonio Chaves," said the voice. "My arrow is aimed at your back—and as your companion can attest, I do not miss."

Manuel dropped his gun, then glanced over at Angney. The American was shaking his head vigorously. "There is no need to—"

"*And* the knife, Don Chaves," the fairy interrupted. "I have seen what you can do with it."

Reluctantly, Manuel complied. Lionclaw struck the stony ground with a clink. At least now he knew her identity—for she knew his. *The Elf ranger Angney spoke of. Thekla.*

Reckoning it was safe to do so, Manuel wheeled his palomino to face the archer. Thekla stood on a rocky ledge, bowstring drawn back to her square chin.

Angney raised a hand in protest. "You've found what you sought. Now stand down."

The Elf glared at him. "You have done my Folk and your own a great service, Captain, but do not presume to give me orders. You are not in command."

Manuel glared at the American. "You were in league with her all along."

"No," Angney insisted. "I didn't know Thekla followed me from Taos, though I admit I'm not surprised by it."

"Why should I believe you?"

"Because I've never—"

"Enough!" The Elf rolled her green eyes. "Your petty quarrel does not interest me. You are right, Captain Angney. Thanks to you, I have found the true location of the treasure. The Duendes may have transported away many stones, but I am confident more can be found."

Despite the threat she posed, Manuel found his curiosity surging. "Stones, you say? Stones that give off a blue glow?"

"They do far more than that," said the Elf. "Of all the treasures hidden in the abandoned villages of Cibola, these may be the most important, or so Grandmaster Runa has concluded. Only a special kind of ore may store the elemental magic required."

"Required for what?"

"To fuel the spellsong."

Manuel cocked his head. "Are you not a ranger? Why would you need glowing stones to sing spells? And don't your kind wield temperamental magic, not elemental magic?"

"You may possess the Sight, human, but that hardly makes you an expert on spellsong." Thekla said. "Or forever safe from it."

"What does that—"

"Silence!" Thekla hissed. "I will waste no more words on you. Captain Angney, I suggest you return to Taos and your army."

The American started. "What about Don Chaves?"

"He is no longer any of your concern." She sneered at Manuel. "Perhaps he was never the Duendes' catspaw, as I once suspected. That does not mean I trust him."

"But I do," Angney said.

Thekla shook her head. "It is the will of my grandmaster and my prince that your government extend its authority over the states of Mexico. So, I offered my assistance. That does not make me your servant. There are forces at work you do not and need not understand. There are decisions I alone must make, for the good of Elfkind and the humans we herd. There are secrets I must protect."

She lowered her head to peer down the shaft of the arrow. Her intentions were clear.

"Captain Angney," Manuel began, "she means to—"

He never finished the sentence. The shot made it unnecessary.

"Let's have no more of that."

The bow dropped from the Elf ranger's suddenly stiff fingers. She tumbled from the ledge and lay, forever motionless, on the ground.

"No more of that 'Captain Angney' and 'Don Chaves' business, I mean," said the grinning American, smoke trailing from the muzzle of his gun. "From now on, I call you Manuel."

"And I?"

"You may call me Bill."

Chapter 26 – The Castle

September 1847

BUM PA-DA BUM.

Though Folk varied in appearance, dress, culture, and other respects, they shared the same language. That's why one spellsinger could identify the *type* of magic another is attempting—even if the melody, meter, and lyrics are unfamiliar.

Bum pa-da bum.

It's why Goran knew someone was casting a mood spell, accompanied by a drum. And it's why he couldn't tell for sure whether the unseen spellsinger was Duende, Elfish, or Dwarfish.

Bum pa-da bum.

"One of yours?" he asked. His companion shook his head.

No ranger of Grünerberg, then.

The Sylph shot up from the fencepost, his eyes scanning the tents, wagons, and corrals illuminated by flickering campfires and twinkling starlight. As Goran hovered over the fence, Har the Tower climbed it and turned right, skirting the edges of the American camp. They'd only just found General Scott's army and had no idea which Folk—if any—had accompanied it from Veracruz to the outskirts of Mexico City.

Bum pa-da bum.

So far, the rangers' experience of the war with Mexico was unfamiliar. During prior conflicts, Goran and Har had frequently witnessed and even took a hand in major battles. This time, they'd reached the southern border of Texas in late 1846, long after General Taylor's forces won their initial battles and marched hundreds of miles into northern Mexico. After a lengthy search along the Rio Grande yielded no sign of Elves or Duendes, the rangers had decided to find their way to General Taylor's command. By the time they caught up with Taylor in Mexico, however, he'd already won his largest and bloodiest engagement yet—with General Santa Anna himself, near a little village called Buena Vista—and was under orders not to advance any further into the country.

Bum pa-da bum.

Taylor's orders came from his superior Winfield Scott, who'd also commandeered most of Taylor's troops for his plan to take Mexico City and force a negotiated end to the war. Again, Goran and Har headed into the Mexican countryside, this time eastward to the port city of Tampico, where the American soldiers were to meet up with General Scott and his transports. Again, the fairy rangers arrived too late. By using spellsong on naval officers occupying Tampico, they'd learned Scott's army had already landed on the Gulf coast, won two key victories, and was closing in on Mexico City.

Perhaps, if their instructions had been to assist the Americans, Goran and Har would have traveled more quickly and seen more action. That wasn't the mission King Alberich had given them, however. Their orders were to investigate Elf and Duende activity. If there were powerful magical artifacts to be found, Alberich wanted to claim them for Grünerberg—or, at least, to keep them out of the hands of his hated enemy, Prince Veelund.

Bum pa-da bum.

Now, for the first time in months, Goran and Har had a trail to follow. Somewhere nearby, a fairy ranger was casting a mood spell. Also nearby were encamped the opposing armies of Winfield Scott and Antonio Lopez de Santa Anna.

That is no coincidence, Goran thought. He got Har's attention and pointed to a crossroads east of the camp. The Dwarf acknowledged Goran's gesture but was already trotting in the same direction.

Bum pa-da bum.

The Sylph smiled. Though their experience of the current war had been uncharacteristically uneventful, the two rangers fell into a comfortable rhythm: Goran surveilling from above, Har exploring from below, using their different perspectives to see things more clearly. Employing their complementary strengths—Goran's speed to Har's brawn, his bow to Har's axe, his strategic insight to Har's tactical skill. It was almost as if the two had repaired a friendship damaged by Dela's loss of memory and her feelings, however fleeting and confused, for the Dwarf.

Almost.

As he banked his wings into a slight turn, Goran tried to keep the image of Dela kissing Har from springing back to mind. He failed.

Bum pa-da bum.

The settlement comprised several houses along the east-west road and a larger building at its juncture with the causeway stretching northward to Mexico City. Goran soon spotted a steeple framed against the moonlight sky. *A church. Of course.* In every Mexican town they'd visited so far, religious institutions—chapels, missions, cathedrals—were by far the most prominent landmarks.

When he reached the church, the Sylph tilted his wings to circle the roof, ears straining, eyes searching. Loud voices came from the church but they were speaking English, not Folktongue. There were also officers and soldiers milling around outside, many conversing in low tones.

None sang.

Bum pa-da bum.

Just one ranger sang the mood spell, which Goran could still hear over the human voices from the church. Together, he and Har could easily overcome the spell with a counterspell. That would, however, reveal their presence to the other spellsinger and any other Folk in the vicinity. The Sylph circled the steeple once more, then landed on the pitched roof. It required but a hand wave to the approaching Dwarf to set a different plan in motion.

That much of their bond remained intact.

Bum pa-da bum.

"We are not getting anywhere, gentlemen, and the hour is late!"

Goran peered through an open window. A dozen American officers in dark-blue uniforms formed a rough oval in the sanctuary. Nearly all were arguing with the officers beside them. The two exceptions were notable not just for their silence, but for their extreme difference in size. The biggest man in the room stood in the center, staring reproachfully at the other officers. The smallest man sat some distance away from the rest, his half-lidded eyes staring distractedly at the floor as he stroked his neatly trimmed goatee.

"One at a time, I insist!" the big man thundered. By his tone and the design of his immaculate uniform, Goran concluded he was the commander, Winfield Scott.

Bum pa-da bum.

A dour-faced officer glared back at him. "Did you not invite our counsel, sir?" he demanded.

"I did, General Pierce, but this is not counsel. It is bedlam."

Another general, his thick hair swept back rakishly from a high forehead, pointed a shaking finger. "You may call it bedlam, sir. I call it a spirited consensus against your proposed course of action."

Scott worked his square jaw, obviously trying to quell a roiling temper. "The risks are considerable, General Pillow, but so are the rewards."

"We heard Major Lee's report," Pillow drawled. "Sickness has reduced our strength by a third. The southern approach to Mexico City is more direct than the western, and does not first require the capture of a castle."

Bum pa-da bum.

"Chapultepec is no true castle," Scott snapped. "It is a half-built palace defended by unsteady soldiers and untested cadets."

General Pierce shook his head. "It remains a formidable position." He gestured toward a dark-eyed officer seated behind him. "Robert Lee just explained that our artillery may be insufficient to breach its walls."

"No one has more respect than I for Major Lee's talents," Scott allowed, "but he is not the only engineer on my staff. Major Beauregard believes—"

"The little Creole!" Pillow spat. "Why, I would no more trust a—"

"That is quite enough!" With one great stride, General Scott closed the distance with Pillow and looked down with undisguised fury.

Goran looked around. *These are the leaders of a victorious army?* With the obvious exception of the man in the corner, whom he guessed was the previously mentioned Major Beauregard, the Americans were unnaturally anxious and quarrelsome.

Bum pa-da bum.

The Sylph rolled his eyes. *I have been out of action too long.* Their behavior was precisely that: unnatural. As the other officers fell silent, watching Scott and Pillow glower at each other, Goran could again hear the mood spell from the unseen ranger, just as he could see its effects on the humans.

Then, in the middle of a phrase, the song stopped.

Well done, Har.

The relief wasn't instantaneous—that's not how mood spells worked. Winfield Scott and his subordinate continued their wordless war of wills for several moments. As the now silenced ranger's temperamental magic began to fade, however, whatever preexisting enmity there was between the two no longer dominated their thoughts. Other considerations reasserted themselves. Tact. Prudence. Duty.

General Scott stepped back. "I think it would greatly aid the discussion, gentlemen, to hear the report of our other engineering officer." Then he lowered his immense bulk into a chair, making sure to jerk the bottom edge of his uniform to smooth out any wrinkles.

General Pillow sat down as well, glancing at the man in the corner. The others turned their heads, too, but the young officer, eyes closed, seemed not to notice. After a moment of awkward silence, Scott cleared his throat. "We are waiting, Major Beauregard."

The engineer's dark eyes shot open. "My apologies, sir."

He leapt to his feet and hurried forward. "You have heard much about the challenges of taking Chapultepec Castle, and of the advantages afforded us by assaulting Mexico City from the south rather than the west. It cost many casualties to get within striking distance of Chapultepec. With so many men laid up with the yellow fever or the other afflictions of this swampy land, risking further losses by attacking the castle seems reckless."

Goran felt as confused as the Americans officers looked. "Have you altered your opinion, major?" Pierce demanded.

"No, sir. Don't you see? These facts are no more a secret to Santa Anna than to us. He *expects* us to assault his capital along the southern causeways. He's placed obstacles in our path, and trained most of his guns southward. He doesn't expect us to risk a costly attack on Chapultepec, as a prelude to attacking his capital from the west. That's *precisely* why we should."

"Bah," grunted General Pillow. "Santa Anna won't be so easily fooled."

"Not *easily* fooled, no." Beauregard spoke as if he were answering Pillow but kept looking at Pierce. "So we'll make a great show of it. Fire at his southern gates. Assemble our men south of the city in daylight, then march them west under cover of night."

"The risk is great."

"*Not* attacking the castle presents its own risk, sir. If we leave Chapultepec in enemy hands and attack from the south, the Mexicans may threaten our left flank."

Pierce sighed. "Your position is well argued, major. May Providence smile on us all." He turned to Winfield Scott and offered a slight nod.

The commander returned it and got to his feet. "Franklin Pierce sees wisdom in the plan. What say the rest of you?"

The other officers began murmuring. Sensing the discussion might continue for some time, Goran stepped back from the window to look for Har. He was about to take wing when the sound of footfalls on gravel drew his attention to the north side of the church, where the Dwarf was crossing the road. Har waved a brawny hand. It wasn't empty. It held something long and thin.

A weapon? Goran mouthed.

No, Har mouthed in reply. Then he struck the top of the object with his other hand, producing a low note.

The drum! Although Goran was no expert on Duendes, he couldn't remember any record of rangers from old Spain using such an odd-looking instrument, nor did it resemble any Elfish drum he'd seen.

"Then it is settled." The booming voice of Winfield Scott drew Goran back to the window. "Gentlemen, we will attack by the western gates. This meeting is dissolved."

~ ~ ~

The shed where the Dwarf had found the mysterious spellsinger was as good a place as any to interrogate him. Standing a head shorter than Goran—so, scarcely half as tall as Har—the captive had dark eyes, skin a shade darker than copper, and hair that might once have been dark. Much of it was swept up into a topknot, the remaining wisps of white cut long in back and in short bangs across his forehead. The old ranger's garments consisted of a skimpy loincloth and a long cape, each woven of white linen and festooned with feathers, beads, and precious stones.

Wrists and ankles bound with ropes tethered to the wall, the captive regarded his captors with undisguised contempt.

"What is your name?" Goran asked.

"I have nothing more to say," the captive muttered in a gravelly voice.

"Nothing...*more*?"

"Well, *one* thing more." The spellsinger inclined his head slightly. "You two are not as gullible as your companions."

"Who do you think we—"

It took only a raised eyebrow for Goran to cut Har off in midsentence. And it took only a moment of wordless communication for the Sylph to help the Dwarf reword his question. "Why do you think we alone saw through your ruse?"

"Because I saw the rest depart for Puebla days ago. Perhaps they still search in vain for the Eyes. Perhaps the others killed them. I do not know. Still, of your entire host, only two now stand before me."

The Sylph allowed himself to look surprised. "You recognize us?"

"No," the captive admitted. "Your faces look much the same to me, but I have come to know your kind. The winged ones, Ventolin. Your hulking friend there, Enanos. Different bodies, different names, yet sharing the same mad dreams and foolish pride."

He thinks us Duendes, Goran realized. *Let him.* "You do us a disservice. I do not assume others of your Folk I meet must think and act as you do. Why not treat us the same?"

The spellsinger snickered. "You seek now to trick *me*?"

"It is no trick."

"True. You lack the wit to deceive me. Speaking nonsense will never do it."

"What nonsense?"

All signs of levity left the captive's wrinkled face. "You know as well as I that you will *never* meet another Chaneque. That I, Laca the Leaper, am the last man at my post. And, as far as I know, the last of my kind in this land—thanks to *your* kind."

Both Har and Goran tried to suppress their surprise. Only the Sylph succeeded. The Chaneque caught the Dwarf's fleeting expression. He stared at Har, lips pursed, then reopened them. "Who has captured me?"

Goran shrugged. "I am Goran Lonefeather. My companion is called Har the Tower. We are *not* Duende."

"I see." The ranger Laca looked down. "You are of the others, then."

"What others?"

"The Elves."

"Certainly not," Har said. "They are our enemies."

Laca sighed. "So, yet another Folk covets the Eyes."

Careful, Goran told himself. *Keep him talking.* "We are here to thwart the plans of the Elves and Duendes if we can. That much is true, but the Eyes you speak of are unknown to us."

The Chaneque met his gaze. "If you know of their plans, you must know of the Eyes of Ahuizotl."

"I assure you," said Har, "we have never heard that name."

Laca made no response. Frustration was written on the Dwarf's ruddy face. Goran shared it. For all he knew, Winfield Scott was already preparing his assault on Chapultepec—and, after that, Mexico City. While it wasn't their mission to aid the Americans, Goran couldn't see any way a bloody defeat of Scott's army would aid their cause. They needed information only this captive could supply.

From some reason, a bit of Christian scripture sprang to mind, something he'd once heard George Washington quote: "*Give, and it shall be given unto you.*"

"Laca," the Sylph began, "might these Eyes of Ahuizotl have something to do with the Seven Cities of Gold?"

"That you know to pose the question is its own answer."

"And you are the Eyes' guardian?"

"In a way, as was my friend Yoli. Now he is dead. Only I remain."

Goran raised a finger. "Earlier, when you thought us Duendes, you claimed we were responsible for that. They killed your friend?"

The captive's brow furrowed. "Yes, though not quickly enough. First they tortured Yoli, insisting he reveal the location of the Eyes. I watched from my hiding place, powerless to act against a dozen foes."

"And when he refused, the Duendes killed him?"

Laca blew out a ragged breath. "No, it was only after he talked that they put him out of his misery."

"You mean," Har fumed, "the Duendes already know the location of the treasure?"

"No." The Chaneque glared at the Dwarf. "I said he talked. I did not say he told all. Yoli feigned ignorance of the actual location, revealing only that the Eyes of Ahuizotl lay buried beneath a place of learning. When he refused to say more—indeed, after Yoli passed out from the pain—the Duende female with the golden hair drove a spear through his heart."

Har turned to Goran. "That could be Aya, the Xana ranger. She led the

Duendes I met in Nacogdoches."

Then the Sylph recalled what Laca had said when they entered the shed. *I saw the rest depart for Puebla days ago. Perhaps they still search in vain for the Eyes. Perhaps the others killed them.*

"Your friend was not the only Chaneque who talked," Goran said. "What did you say to convince the Duendes to depart?"

Laca grinned at that. "You are clever, winged one. Yes, after I witnessed Yoli's death, I allowed myself to be taken by his killers. I pretended to be less courageous than he, more willing to talk without being tortured. I told them the place of learning where the Eyes are hidden. Then, before they could finish me off, I made my escape."

Goran returned his smile. "You must *not* think me clever enough, Laca the Leaper. First you say you were too outnumbered to save your friend. Now you claim to have overcome a dozen Duendes, yet you evidently could not defeat a single Dwarf."

The Chaneque glanced up at Har the Tower. "He counts as two, at least."

"Nevertheless, you expect us to—"

"I never claimed to have *fought* the Duendes," Laca pointed out, "only that I *escaped* them. Clever, you may be, but a careful listener you are not."

The Sylph kept smiling. "You said the Duendes departed for the city of Puebla. That is where you told them the Eyes could be found?"

"In a tunnel beneath the city," Laca agreed. "The human priests, the Jesuits, built a school there hundreds of Blur years ago. They called it the College of the Holy Spirit."

"And you later told the same story to the Elves when *they* questioned you."

Laca nodded.

"That is," the Sylph said, "you told both the same lie."

This time, the captive's only reply was to blink.

"You see, I *have* been listening carefully," said Goran. "When I first entered, I heard you say the Duendes were searching in vain, and it was possible the 'others'—meaning the Elves—had killed them. You sent them all to the same place, the *wrong* place, hoping to guard your secret while getting your foes to battle and weaken each other."

The Chaneque blew out an exasperated breath. "The longer you hold me, the greater the danger."

"Danger from any Elves and Duendes who make it back from Puebla?"

The captive gave a curt nod.

Goran took another step closer. "Then offer us more than riddles."

Laca's defiance seemed to leave him. "Very well. Ask."

"Tell us of the Seven Cities and the treasures they hold."

"Not gold—or at least not *only* gold." Laca wrinkled his nose, then struggled against his bonds. "Might you free my hands? I need to scratch."

Har laughed. "We are not easily fooled."

"I was obliged to try." The captive's lips quivered. "The tale begins not with the seven, but with the one. Cibola, the great city of the Chaneque. The city of my birth."

Goran swept his hand to the side. "Hidden nearby, I take it."

"Hardly." Laca tried to sound bored, but the tremor in his voice betrayed him. "Our once mighty Folk lived far north of here, beyond the burning deserts, in what is now called New Mexico. The humans we herded from our village on the Mountain of Storms were plentiful and industrious, building their homes in verdant valleys and shaded cliffs."

"We know this land," said Har. "Do you speak of the Zuni? The Hopi?"

"The humans had many names for themselves, most now forgotten—especially by me. Much later, after the Catastrophe, their descendants remembered them only as *Hisatsinom*, the 'Ancient Ones.' Their rivals, the Navajo, called them *Anasazi*, the 'Ancestral Enemies.'"

Goran stepped closer. "This Catastrophe you speak of. Was it a war between the humans?"

"No, not at first. We Chaneque sowed its seeds ourselves. With our lust for power. Our arrogance. And its subject, our great talent for magic."

Har and Goran exchanged skeptical looks.

Laca noticed. "You think I boast, but that is not so. Our gift for magecraft and spellsong was truly unparalleled. It served us well as we contended with the Paakniwat to our west and other Folk to our north and east. Though they outnumbered us, our enchanted weapons and charmed human warriors gave us victory more often than not."

"So the Catastrophe—"

"Arose from within, not without. You see, we Chaneque desired more than victory. Instead of merely winning battles, we would prevent them. Instead of merely guarding our hunting grounds, we would expand them.

Instead of merely keeping our enemies at bay, we would add them to our herds."

"Add other *Folk* to your herds?" Goran found Laca's turn of phrase confusing. One fairy nation conquering another was nothing new, but he'd never heard it described that way.

The captive ranger smiled. "Again, you misunderstand. You think I use a poetic metaphor. No, I *mean* what I say. Our chiefs devoted their vast knowledge and unrivaled skill to the task. It took many tries over many years. It even took lives—some lost while obtaining the powerful artifacts our magecrafters demanded, others while testing their handiwork. In the end, however, we achieved our aim. We accomplished the greatest feat in all Folklore. We solved its greatest riddle."

No!

Like a dam burst in his mind, Goran was overwhelmed by a flood of images, emotions, and visions of doom. *It cannot be. It is impossible. And yet it explains so much. Maker of All Things, forgive them!*

Staggered by the weight of it all, he turned to Har, whose ashen face revealed his own stark realization.

Unnecessarily, Laca continued. "The Chaneque finally learned how to wield spellsong against Folk. And it destroyed us."

~ ~ ~

Boom! belched the mortar placed fifty feet in front of them.

Boom! Boom! roared the cannons placed several hundred feet to their right.

Goran and Har watched the bombardment from behind a fallen cypress. It had been two hours since dawn. Two hours since the artillery resumed their fire at Chapultepec Hill. The Americans had spent much of the previous day blasting away at it as well. Apparently, General Scott didn't think he'd weakened the position enough for his soldiers and marines to assault without heavy casualties.

Boom! Boom! Boom! Boom! bellowed the two other American batteries.

The Sylph studied their target, clearly visible in the early morning light. Chapultepec Hill looked to be about two hundred feet high and six hundred feet across. A brick wall encircled much of it, while the old palace on the top, the "castle," consisted of stone walls and circular towers. Although the constant barrage had silenced the Mexican guns and damaged the Mexican walls, it remained a formidable position.

Goran grunted in frustration. As soon as Laca had revealed what the Elves and Duendes were really after—magical items that, used in concert, made fairies vulnerable to spellsong—Goran was intent on finding the Eyes of Ahuizotl before the others did.

The mysterious artifacts weren't beneath a college in Puebla. Still, Goran figured the other Chaneque *had* uttered the truth under torture. The Eyes *were* hidden under a "place of learning," presumably a college in Mexico City, though Laca refused to confirm that.

The Sylph suggested they immediately dash into the capital to look. It was the normally impetuous Har who urged caution. Despite Laca's switch from taciturn to talkative, they couldn't be sure he was being honest. Perhaps he *wasn't* the last surviving Chaneque after all. Perhaps the old man, still trussed and gagged in the shed, had allies lurking nearby, ready to strike. Nor could they know how long the Elves and Duende would chase Laca's false trail in Puebla, eighty miles away. They might come back soon or already be in the city.

Goran and Har were on their own, in an unfamiliar land, facing foes of unknown number and identity. Their best move, the Dwarf insisted, was to wait for the American assault on the capital. If other Folk *were* present, they'd reveal themselves during the battle—Elves assisting the attackers, Duendes and maybe even Chaneque assisting the defenders. On the other hand, if no Folk intervened, Goran and Har might safely search for the Eyes. Loath as the Sylph was to admit it, Har was right.

Their hours-long vigil had, at least, given them a closer look at humans Goran had first glimpsed in the church. Major Beauregard helped place the artillery to their east. Major Robert Lee, assisted by a young lieutenant named George McClellan, constructed the other batteries. All three seemed both highly capable and dog-tired, as did the other Americans passing close enough to examine. *These men may be tough fighters*, Goran thought, *but General Scott is not wrong to be cautious about ordering them up a steep slope against stone walls.*

The Sylph sighed. The long wait had also given him time to mull over what Laca had called the Catastrophe.

According to his account, after the Chaneque had devised a means of using spellsong against enemy fairies, they unsurprisingly won a series of smashing victories against the Paakniwat, a Water Folk of the Pacific coast. Soon, however, the Chaneque rangers who knew how to wield the new "domination magic," as Laca termed it, quarreled over the spoils of conquest. Each also began to fear the rest would use the awesome power not just to expand the Chaneque domain, but to seize personal control of it. So, they turned on each other: clan against clan, chief against chief, friend against friend. With domination spells, spellsingers assembled huge hordes of Folk, humans, and monsters and hurled them against each other. The few mages and craftsmen who initially escaped domination devised powerfully enchanted weapons of their own to fight back, adding to the chaos and destruction.

One Chaneque did, indeed, emerge supreme in the end—but his victory was accompanied by devastation and death on a massive scale. Horrified and chastened, the victor swore off domination magic. Nevertheless, nearly all the surviving Chaneque fled Cibola. Bereft of the monsters and mages needed to maintain Shimmer protection, most perished in the Blur. A few managed to establish new villages in far-flung lands or found refuge among other Folk.

Among the refugees, Laca admitted after some prodding, were seven rangers with a secret mission: to guard the seven elements necessary to cast domination spells. Each knew only of the element with which he had been entrusted. Whether the victorious spellsinger of the Catastrophe was among the seven or remained behind in Cibola, Laca claimed not to know.

Goran understood why the victor hadn't tried to eradicate all traces of domination magic and its constituent elements. After all, the Chaneque spellsinger couldn't be completely certain his rivals were dead. If one came back, intent on making himself the invincible emperor of all Folk on the continent, the repentant victor would have preserved the means to resist him.

Whatever his intention, the Chaneque had laid the foundation for a highly compelling legend. Even as separate elements, the treasures of the so-called Seven Cities were surely powerful in their own right. They'd be noticed and coveted—and not just by Folk. It had taken only the chance discovery of the cave painting beneath Cahokia for the Elves to guess what the fabled cities really contained.

If Prince Veelund acquires domination magic, Goran mused, *neither Folk nor human will be safe from him. The same goes for the ruler of the Duendes. And King Alberich.*

Goran glanced at Har, who was watching the Americans reload their cannons. The Sylph wanted to believe his longtime friend shared his conclusion, that *no* Folk could be trusted with domination magic, but for some reason he hadn't broached the subject.

Is it because I do not trust him? Goran wanted *not* to believe that.

He knew only that he *had* to find the Eyes and destroy them, along with as many other elements as he could acquire. Based on the tales told by Bull, Zorro, Har, and Dela, he counted four known treasures: the Carbuncle shells hoarded by the Paakniwat at Santa Cruz Island, the forehead disc of the Yeitso at Canyon de Chelly, the spellsong lyrics carved onto columns beneath the Alamo, and the painting at Cahokia that showed how to bring the artifacts together as a mask, presumably worn by the spellsinger when casting a domination spell.

The Eyes of Ahuizotl, whatever they were, constituted the fifth element—and the first he would deny to both Elf and Duende.

Boom! Boom!

This time, the roar of the cannons seemed to reverberate for several moments. Then Goran realized he wasn't hearing echoes. It was the sound of boots pounding the earth. He looked to his left, spotting a detachment of Americans forming up. He estimated their number at two hundred, maybe more. Behind them were distant figures in motion in far greater numbers.

Har touched the Sylph's shoulder, then pointed in the direction of the artillery to their east. Another two hundred troops, soldiers and marines, were lining up on a road. Once again, behind the forward formation was a much bigger column.

"Do they attack or pretend?" Har whispered. The previous day, they'd watched the Americans stage feints south of Mexico City and west of Chapultepec. Winfield Scott clearly wanted to keep Santa Anna guessing.

Then the bombardment ceased. "They attack," said the Sylph.

With savage cries, the two storming parties—the Americans called them "forlorn hopes," Goran recalled—broke into a run. The soldiers west of Chapultepec crossed the field and reached a cypress grove. Some wove their way through the trees while others ran around them to reach the Mexican ramparts. Meanwhile, the other storming party hurried up the road, intent on striking Chapultepec from the south.

Scaling ladders thudded against brick walls. Bayonets flashed. Muskets blared. Men shouted in defiance or shrieked in agony. Many attackers in light-blue uniforms fell short of the ramparts, some wounded and crawling, others forever motionless. Many Mexican defenders fell, too, or turned to flee up to the palace. They soon covered the hillside with running, wriggling, or writhing figures in varied uniforms of blue, red, gray, and white.

Though the battle produced an ear-splitting bedlam, they'd have heard spellsong by now if enemy Folk were present. "Come on!" Goran shouted, scrambling to the top of the fallen tree and taking to the air. The Dwarf clambered over the log and followed him. They headed for the cypress grove and the melee unfolding just beyond it.

Boom!

Goran spotted an American lieutenant and several soldiers north of Chapultepec Hill, manning a cannon placed on a causeway to provide a clear shot at the Mexican breastworks. Another crew was struggling to push a second gun through marshy ground to the same position.

Blam! Blam!

At least one Mexican battery remained serviceable. Its answering fire felled two American gunners and scattered most of the rest. Their officer wasn't among them. Having lost his forage cap, the lieutenant ran his fingers through the sweat-soaked hair covering his eyes, sweeping it back to reveal a high, soot-streaked forehead. "Come back, men!" he exhorted. "We can take 'em!"

Only a single sergeant stumbled toward his lieutenant. The rest cowered in the mud.

Blam!

Another Mexican gun fired. To Goran's amazement, he saw a cannonball hit the ground a few feet from the American officer, throw up rocks and dust as it bounced, then roll between the young lieutenant's firmly planted legs.

The stony-faced American didn't flinch. "There is no danger!" he yelled to his fleeing men. "See? I am not hit!"

They saw. They saw their steadfast lieutenant and his loyal sergeant hurrying to load their cannon. Two gunners ran back to help, and several more resumed wheeling the second gun onto the causeway.

To Goran, their display of courage was further evidence that no Duendes were present to aid the defenders. Executing a turn, he soared over the west slope of Chapultepec Hill. Below him, American soldiers were swarming over trenches and breastworks. A few surviving Mexicans fought back with bayonets and gun butts, but most were in rapid retreat.

He spotted Har working his way around a crumbled section of wall. "No other Folk!" Goran shouted down. "Head into the city!"

The Dwarf shook his head furiously and pointed. It was then that Goran Lonefeather glimpsed the first of three sights that changed everything. It was the tiny figure of Laca the Leaper, his white cape swirling behind him as he scrambled up the hill. How he'd slipped his bonds and escaped the shed was a mystery.

A chorus of shouts and a flash of movement in the distance drew Goran's attention to a second even more surprising development: Some attackers had already made their way into the castle itself. Dead bodies from both armies covered the inner courtyard. The sight that really caught his eye, however, was a small figure atop the southern-facing wall of the complex. It didn't look human. There were two curved shapes jutting from its back.

Wings?

Was this a Ventolin, one of the Spanish fairies from the Duende host? Goran beat his own wings with as much force as he could muster. At the same time, the other winged figure walked to the edge of the rampart as if preparing to spring into the air. Opting not to break his momentum by slipping his bow over his head, Goran reached for the hunting knife at his belt.

He never drew it—for when the figure leapt from Chapultepec Castle, it did not soar. It plummeted. What fluttered behind it weren't wings. They were the flapping corners of a large cloth that enveloped the falling body. Vertical stripes of green, white, and red rippled in the wind like waves on a stormy sea. And when the doomed jumper struck the hard ground, the tattered flag of the Mexican Republic covered his corpse like a shroud.

Even before Goran witnessed a third unexpected event—Laca vanishing into the side of the hill—the Sylph had begun to suspect the truth. He saw three Americans lift the flag off the body. He saw the broken, slender form of the defender, his light coat and garrison cap bearing the red stains of his final sacrifice. Goran saw the unlined face of youth that would never grow old.

And he remembered Winfield Scott's words during the debate in the church. The castle, the general said, was nothing but "a half-built palace defended by unsteady soldiers and untested cadets." *Untested cadets.* The Mexicans had been using Chapultepec as a military academy.

A place of learning.

The treasure was *here*.

~ ~ ~

If the tunnel was ever magically shielded, its enchantments had long since faded away. No Shimmer wall divided the Blur without from the realm within. No secret spell was required to traverse its length, though at several points the stocky Dwarf had to turn sideways to wriggle through the tunnel's narrow confines.

The Chaneque had a significant head start as well, as he possessed, they assumed, an intimate knowledge of the route. Loath to stumble into a trap, Goran led the way with small, deliberate steps. Niches cut at regular intervals suggested the tunnel had once been lit by torches, now missing. Balancing their need for sight and stealth, Goran opted for a small bundle of glowing sticks held close to the floor.

It was sound, not sight, that prompted the Sylph to halt in midstride. After a few moments, he heard it again. *Water lapping stone*.

After two more sharp turns, the tunnel widened into a cavern so vast, they couldn't see its full expanse with the feeble light from their puny torch. A moment's reflection revealed to Goran that its ceiling must be far above ground level, perhaps extending into Chapultepec Hill itself. The cave floor was moist, its air dank and foul.

Although the top and sides were shrouded in darkness, the far wall of the cavern was readily distinguishable—but not by torchlight. Two glowing shapes cast a faint ochre hue along its uneven surface, like dying coals embedded in cold stone.

A shiver crawled up Goran's spine and along his wing bones, causing his feathers to twitch. He looked back at Har, who'd armed himself with throwing axes and looked as uneasy as Goran felt. Holding his torch aloft, the Sylph edged into the cavern, followed closely by the Dwarf. He returned his gaze to the two inward-sloping ovals shining in the darkness.

To the two *eyes* shining in the darkness!

"The Eyes of Ahuizotl," Goran hissed.

Har grunted behind him. "Should we—"

Whoosh!

A wall of water struck both fairies. Knocked sideways, Goran tottered for an instant on the outer edge of his right foot. Then a hand grabbed his other foot and yanked him leftward.

The hand was *not* Har's.

Although the Sylph dropped his torch, its fizzling embers yielded enough light for him to see what was dragging him along the cave floor. The hand was attached not to an arm but to a *tail*, long and sinewy, which in turn was attached to one of the oddest-looking creatures Goran had ever seen. Although in form and proportions it resembled the sheepdog of his native Cornwall, it was far larger in size—and its dark fur stuck out in all directions like spikes. Like most monsters, its eyes had no whites. They gleamed a shade of orange similar to the shapes embedded in the wall. Strangest of all, the beast walked not on paws, but on claw-tipped hands similar to the one gripping his leg.

Goran's hands, however, were free. He whipped his knife from its sheath and brought its sharp bronze blade down on the tail with all the force he could muster. That didn't sever it, but the wound was sufficiently painful, or at least startling, to prompt the canine monster to let go.

His freedom was brief. Two more hands seized him, one by each leg, followed an instant later by a third just below the elbow of his knife arm.

"It is a pack!" Har exclaimed. "Killed one, but four more have me!"

The Sylph resisted fruitlessly for a moment, then had a better idea. "Confuse them!"

The two fairies began a confusion spell, Goran's tenor voice harmonizing resonantly with Har's bass. Though the monsters continued to drag the struggling fairies, Goran figured it would only be a matter of time before the creatures succumbed to the magic and relaxed their hold.

He figured wrong.

After the entire first stanza of the spell, the canines showed no signs of distraction or weakening. For some reason Goran could see them more clearly, as well as the underground pond from which they'd sprung and to which they were now pulling their prey. With a splash, one of his attackers leapt into the murky water, still yanking Goran's ankle with its tail.

"Try another spell?" Har suggested.

"Go ahead—perhaps you will succeed," said a gravelly voice.

Laca the Leaper leaned against the far wall of the cavern, arms folded. The triumph on his squat face was easily seen, for the ovals above him no longer glowed a faint ochre. They blazed a brilliant yellow.

Goran heard splashing and growling. The fiercest growls were Har's. The Sylph fought back, too, wrenching his body and beating his wings to keep from going under.

"Help us!" he called to Laca.

The Chaneque laughed. "Are you such poor spellsingers?"

Goran tried a discouragement spell, but it availed him nothing. His legs were now half submerged. "Do you control these creatures?" he demanded.

"The Ahuizotl do as nature commands," Laca croaked. "I merely harvest the result."

Harvest the result? Goran paled. *Does he mean he eats the flesh of the monsters' victims?* Turning his head back toward Laca, he found he had to squint. The light from the fiery ovals was blinding.

Harvest the result. He recalled a detail from Laca's story. He understood.

"Our spellsong!" The Sylph was fighting to keep his upper body above the surface. "The monsters divert it!"

"No, not the Ahuizotl." The Chaneque pointed upward. "The *Eyes*. Crystals of clear obsidian, engraved with runes. An Ahuizotl merely feeds his constant hunger, but when Folk are its prey, their spellsong feeds the Eyes."

"And *they* power domination spells?"

"No. The Eyes steal temperamental magic, but only the Horn can store it."

"Stop this!" Har bellowed. "We are not your foes!"

"Perhaps," said Laca, "but duty requires I have no friends."

The water was lapping Goran's chin. "You can trust us!"

The Chaneque shook his head. "May your death be—aheeeee!"

The butt of a spear struck Laca so hard that he doubled over in agony. Just before the canine monsters pulled Goran under, he glimpsed the fairy holding the spear. So much like Dela: a lithe figure wearing a shimmering shift cinched at the waist, long hair cascading over shapely shoulders.

The hair was sparkling gold, not lustrous blue.

Water closed over Goran's head. His fate seemed sealed, but he wouldn't let his last moment be one of resignation. Rather than continuing to struggle, the Sylph went limp. He sank. The grip on his arm loosened. Twisting free, Goran reached down to slash his blade across the clawed hand holding his right ankle.

It let go. Hope surging, lungs bursting, the Sylph tried to strike the tail of his remaining foe. His knife parted only water. Again a hand seized his free leg, but the once-dark water was now brightly lit. Goran saw it was a paw from the same Ahuizotl that held his other leg with its tail.

One enemy is better than three. Goran swept his wings against the water to push his torso into a tight bend at the waist. Feeling his strength ebbing, he managed a last, desperate thrust. The tip of his knife pierced the shaggy fur of the beast between its two front paws, then drove deep. The Sylph felt something warm and sticky flow over his clammy hand.

His legs were free. Two feeble kicks were enough for Goran's head to break the surface of the pond. He gulped the dank, foul-smelling air. Nothing had ever tasted sweeter.

A terrifying image sprang to mind. *Har!*

The Sylph spun around, trying to find his friend. What he found were several Ahuizotl floating in the water, most with arrows protruding from their backs or sides. *I did not prevail on my own.*

Then he spotted Har at the water's edge, swatting his axe not at a fiery-eyed Ahuizotl but at a swordsman hovering over his head. The fairy's wings weren't flapping—they were rigid. *An Elf!*

A battle raged around him—in the pond, on the cavern floor, in the air above. Nearly a dozen Elves were fighting a smaller number of what Goran guessed were Duendes. At the far wall, Laca lay crumpled on the floor while two rangers battled furiously beneath the blazing obsidian Eyes. One was rail-thin and mousy-haired. Her two dagger blades flashed bright yellow as she wove a curtain of cuts and thrusts around her foe. The other, shapely and golden-haired, dodged some attacks and parried others with her barbed spear. *Aya.*

The Sylph didn't know whether Har had actively chosen sides or simply responded to an attack. What he did know was that Prince Veelund and his minions had long fomented violence and injustice, that neither Folk could be trusted with the powerful treasures of Cibola, and that joining the outnumbered side, Aya and her Duendes, might prolong the battle, giving the Sylph and Dwarf a slight chance of achieving their own ends.

Alas, the choice was made for him. The arrow passed within inches of his right arm and hit the pond with a splash. Goran looked up. An archer hovered a dozen feet above, nocking another arrow to the string of his beechwood bow. Reflexively, the Sylph sprang into the air. Then he noticed the bowman's wings were beating. *A Ventolin!*

Goran beat his own soggy wings to gain altitude, choosing a zigzag pattern to make himself harder to target. "Do not shoot!" he called. "We are not—"

The Ventolin's second bronze-tipped arrow grazed his shoulder, stinging but not greatly wounding him. Seeing no alternative but to defend himself, Goran's hands reached for his bow to draw it over his head.

They found only the strap of his quiver. His bow was gone. It had either broken or fallen off during his fray with the Ahuizotl. There was no time for surprise or frustration. Goran abruptly withdrew his limbs and twisted, allowing his body to drop an instant before the Ventolin's third arrow clattered harmlessly against the cave wall. Then he spread his wings at an angle, banking left until he reached a spot several feet below two other fliers, an Elf and Ventolin locked in swordplay. Darting back and forth to keep the distracted combatants between himself and the approaching archer, Goran drew his knife and waited.

When he saw green wingtips poke above the head of the dueling Elf, Goran struck. Diving below the swordsmen, then hurtling upward, the Sylph so startled the Ventolin that his final shot went wide. Goran was on him before the archer could reach for a blade. Again, he bloodied his knife. The Ventolin screamed, shuddered, and fell.

The Sylph dropped into a glide, eyes searching frantically for a towering figure in a red cap. The search failed at first, though not because of darkness. Although the oval insets in the cave wall had dimmed a bit, they still glowed. No, it was because the figure was no longer towering over his foes, and his cap had fallen off. Har lay sprawled on the ground, howling in pain and rage, a wound in his thigh, one burly arm struggling to keep an Elfish spearpoint from reaching his chest and the other wrapped around a second Elf's bearded throat.

All grievance and doubt fled Goran's mind. With a fierce cry of his own, the Sylph dove blade-first at the back of the spearman. The Elf never knew what hit him, nor anything else after that. Har pushed up with his now free hand, yanked the one wrapped around the other Elf's neck, and grunted triumphantly when his efforts produced the desired cracking sound. Spotting a discarded bow—he couldn't tell its make—Goran snatched it up and nocked an arrow.

"Back off or she dies!"

Aya's voice was both melodious and menacing. Whether from anxiety, exhaustion, or curiosity, all the combatants paused to see what was transpiring beneath the Eyes of Ahuizotl. Three Elves had bows trained on Aya. The Xana ranger, in turn, had the point of her spear against the throat of a prostrate Elf—the mousy-haired one she'd fought earlier. Laca still lay motionless.

"Do not listen," snarled Aya's defeated foe. "Strike now."

"How can we, Runa?" an Elf demanded. "What use are the treasures without you?"

Aya beamed. "What use, indeed? Lower your weapons, Elves, or your efforts will be for naught!"

Goran scanned the cavern. Eight Elves still lived, two fliers and six on foot, including Runa. Other than Aya, only three Duendes remained standing: another yellow-haired Xana hefting a barbed spear, a dark-featured woman dressed in odd-looking clothes of vines and leaves, and the Ventolin swordsman.

Reluctantly, the Elves complied. Spotting Goran next to Har, Aya's gray eyes flashed. "You as well, winged one."

The Sylph smirked. "I am no Elf. If you wish to slay this Runa, I have no objection."

At that, the three Elfish archers turned their backs on Aya, exchanged astonished looks, and trained their weapons on him. "We do," one warned.

Goran's smile vanished. Seeing no alternative, he lowered his bow. The Elves did, too, though all kept arrows nocked.

"I suspected as much." Aya looked down at Runa. Though the Elf stared defiantly back at her, the Xana's expression was softer. "You and I have much in common, Grandmaster. Both of us have studied the legend of Cibola. Both know the tantalizing truths it contains and seek to control the

Seven Cities for the good of our Folk. And both have kept knowledge of our quest from all but a chosen few—and full knowledge of its purpose, even closer than that."

Runa said nothing, which Aya clearly took as confirmation.

"Yet here we are, at each other's throats," she continued. "Precious lives lost. Others hang in the balance—not just here in this desolate burrow of death, but across the sprawling realms of Duende and Elf."

"My life is a small price to purchase victory for Elfkind," Runa snapped.

"Noble words." Aya twisted her spearpoint. "As for me, I find the prospect of martyrdom less enticing. Perhaps that is because while you lead a guild, I lead a nation. You are but a grandmaster. I am a queen."

Several of the Elves reacted with gasps and whispers. Goran happen to notice one other ranger react to Aya's words as well. The Ventolin, standing only a few paces away, balled his fists and looked down, a sour expression on his thin face.

Aya noticed too. "Come here, Lum," she said, "your queen has need of your blade."

Sighing, the Ventolin flapped his wings, rose several feet into the air, then soared over the Elfish archers.

"Afraid to do the deed yourself?" Runa cackled.

"Hardly." Aya pointed to the grandmaster's throat. Landing beside her, Lum placed the tip of his blade next to the Xana's spearpoint. Then Aya drew back her weapon. "You may consider your life a price worth paying, Runa, but I do not deem it a price worth *taking*. And we both know it will *not* purchase victory for your Folk—just as sacrificing my life will not win victory for mine."

The Elf grandmaster's lips formed a sullen line.

"That scowl you wear does not become you, Runa, though perhaps in your case, a smile would do little good." Aya turned away with a dramatic flick of golden hair. Goran found himself loathing her.

"Nevertheless," the queen went on, "I am determined to find out. I have a proposal for you, one I believe will put a smile on that bony face of yours. A way for both of us to complete our quests without further bloodshed. A way for each to leave here alive, parting not as allies but also not as enemies."

Runa's eyelids fluttered. "I have already guessed what you would say. It is unthinkable."

"Oh?" Aya glanced coquettishly over her shoulder. "Can *you* think of any better solution to our common problem?"

The Elf rolled her eyes. "We have you outnumbered. If you take my life, my rangers will take yours—and one more treasure of Cibola."

"Which no one else in your guild knows how to use." Aya rolled her own eyes mockingly. "A trade that leaves you poorer than before is no trade worth making. Mine is."

Goran gave Har a questioning glance. The Dwarf nodded slightly. Both already guessed what Aya's next words confirmed.

"I tell you now, Grandmaster Runa, that my rangers of the Duende, Guardians of the Unity, Servants of the Throne, are currently in possession of three treasures of Cibola. We have the Blue Stones of Taos, the Lyric Columns of Yanaguana, and a drawing of the Mask Painting of Cahokia."

Runa gasped the last revelation.

"Do not be so shocked," Aya beamed. "Of all your host and mine, few rangers are as clever and stealthy as the Trenti of Northern Iberia. Why, Oina here managed to slip in and out of your best-guarded stronghold without detection." The queen pointed to the Duende in the moss-covered clothes. The dark-featured woman took a playful bow.

"Now, here I stand beneath a fourth treasure of Cibola," Aya continued. "I see two Eyes of Ahuizotl. Why not take one with you, and I the other?"

"That, we could," Runa replied, "but in return, you would have us reveal the treasures of Cibola we possess?"

"Naturally—assuming you can offer an equal trade."

"We can," Runa confirmed, "but to what end? Neither would have all seven. Confirmation of that fact will bring only full-scale war between our Folk. By now you know that the humans we herd, these Americans of the United States, are more than a match for yours. You cannot be so foolish as to think you and your Mexican minions can prevail in such a conflict. So, if I reveal our secrets, your swordsman here will slay me. Then our rangers will resume this battle, which you apparently *are* foolish enough to believe you can win. As I said, your proposal is unthinkable."

"That," Aya insisted, "is because you are not thinking clearly. First, we Duende have no interest in preserving or expanding this misbegotten Mexican republic. Have you not been listening? The Duende of America serve the *Throne*."

Runa gaped. "You mean—"

"Yes, of course. We seek to return all of Mexico, indeed all of Spanish-speaking America, to the orderly rule of she who sits in the Royal Palace of Madrid, whom the humans call Queen Isabella II. Of course, the true authority rests with we who control Isabella and her court."

"The Unity?"

"That is what we call the confederation of all Duendes of Iberia," Aya said. "All serve the Unity as their gifts allow. Enanos are our mightiest warriors, Ventolins our most skillful hunters, Trenti our cleverest rangers, and Trasgu our best mages, craftsmen, and greenweavers. As our humans ventured off to conquer other lands, we have welcomed still more Folk into our great Unity."

Runa gave her a sly look. "And what of your kind, the Xanas?"

"We Folk of the lakes and streams of fabled Asturias shoulder the greatest burden of all," said the queen. "The Xanas rule the Unity."

There was more murmuring. "Well," said the grandmaster after a time, "the Elves of America have no desire to join this Unity of yours."

"Nor do we ask it of you." Aya put her hands on her hips. "I propose a fair trade, as I said. Let us leave this place under truce, each with four of the seven treasures of Cibola, and knowledge that the other holds the remaining three. Next, we exchange emissaries to end this war between the Americans and Mexicans and negotiate a final accommodation."

"Under what conditions?"

"Your humans will keep the northern provinces they already occupy. In return, you will ensure the Americans leave the capital and the rest of Mexico to us. In truth, we are more interested in reasserting our authority in Central and South America than in retaining those faraway northern lands."

Runa shook her head. "Such matters are of comparatively little importance."

"You care only for the treasures of Cibola?" Aya looked amused. "I thought the solution to that dilemma was obvious. Each of us will supply the other the missing elements. Each will gain complete domination over the Folk within our respective realms, but not over each other. All the northern lands will be yours forever. And all the southern, ours."

The grandmaster closed her yes. *Is Runa really considering Aya's proposal?* Goran couldn't imagine anyone believing such an accommodation between two dangerous neighbors could last. On the other hand, both Runa and Aya clearly believed something just as absurd: that their Folk could survive what the Chaneque of Cibola had not—the acquisition of domination magic.

"We do, indeed, possess three treasures of our own," Runa admitted. "The Carbuncles of Limuw. The Crest of the Yeitso. And the Horn of Uktena, the river dragon. Before agreeing to your proposal, however, I have one more condition."

"And that is?"

"There are two rangers here who serve neither Elf nor Duende."

All eyes turned to Goran and Har.

The grandmaster raised a bony finger. "They must be left in our custody."

Aya snorted. "Why bother with custody? Just slay them and be done with it."

"No," said Runa. "I have other…uses for them." Then she grinned at Goran.

The Xana queen had been right about one thing, the Sylph realized. Smiling didn't make Runa look any less homely—or less menacing.

Chapter 27 — The Vortex

October 1849

BULL RESISTED THE IMPULSE TO crumple the newspaper and toss it into the corner of his cabin. Instead, he grabbed each end, pulled it taut, and tried again.

The nameplate wasn't the problem. "THE FLAG OF OUR UNION," it screamed. It was the text underneath that was the problem: eight columns of dense type interrupted only sporadically by chapter breaks. Bull had attempted twice to work his way through the florid romance filling most it. He'd failed.

Having spent two pennies on the newspaper back in Boston, he was determined to get his money's worth. Then the text in the right-hand column, darker and closer set, drew his attention. The item was entitled "Extent of the Gold Region."

With difficulty, Bull deciphered the first few lines. It was an account of recent gold mining in California and a speculation about similar riches in the Rocky Mountains. He frowned. He'd visited both places. He'd found his own treasures there. By comparison, gold nuggets were just yellow rocks.

On a different ship, with a different crew, he'd spent countless hours in his cabin listening to Gez. The Kabouter had read him stories, articles, poems. Here on his new ship, Bull had many fine companions, but none like Gez. None with the learning and patience required to read to his captain.

And none who could sing spells.

With a frustrated sweep of his hand, Bull brushed the newspaper off the table. It fluttered for a moment, then plopped onto the floor. The front page blew back, revealing a two-page spread. Glancing down, Bull noticed an item about two-thirds of the way down. It was brief and surrounded by white space. Perhaps that's why he felt compelled to scoop it up, or perhaps the byline caught his eye.

Bull put the paper back on the table and scrutinized the item. "Written for the *Flag of our Union,*" stated the header. He read the rest with growing excitement:

Eldorado
By Edgar A. Poe

Gaily bedight,
A gallant knight,
In sunshine and in shadow,
Had journeyed long,
Singing a song,
In search of Eldorado.

But he grew old—
This knight so bold—
And o'er his heart a shadow—
Fell as he found
No spot of ground
That looked like Eldorado.

And, as his strength
Failed him at length,
He met a pilgrim shadow—
'Shadow,' said he,
'Where can it be—
This land of Eldorado?'

'Over the Mountains
Of the Moon,
Down the Valley of the Shadow,
Ride, boldly ride,'
The shade replied,—
'If you seek for Eldorado!'

Bull sat for a long while, eyes fixed on the poem. Though its meaning eluded him, his mind reeled at the images it conjured. A "gallant knight" who'd "journeyed long, singing a song." Bull couldn't think of a better description of Gez.

The thought brought him no joy. *The Kabouter's journey ended because of me. Because I was reckless. Because I failed him.*

Bull also recalled a folk tale his friend Diego Vega had told him about a fabled city of gold called El Dorado. And he recalled the long-ago day the *Courser* first encountered the Kraken. Just before the battle, Gez had read him a story, "Manuscript Found in a Bottle," about a ghost ship, a luckless sailor, and a deadly whirlpool. Its author was this very same Edgar A. Poe, whom the Kabouter had insisted must be at least partially Sighted.

From beyond his door came a gale of laughter. It didn't interrupt his thoughts. They remained on his friend. *Laughing came naturally to Gez. Never did to me.*

It was only when he heard other voices from midship, cackling in response to the first, that Bull's mind snapped back to the present. He looked up, no longer ruminating on what he'd lost—his ship, his crew, his old friend—and instead considering what he'd gained.

The *Courser* had been swift and sleek. This new ship, the *Tuscarora*, was strong and stout. A massive four-masted vessel carrying eight whaleboats, three rows of side-mounted guns, two special guns at bow and stern, and a crew of sixty, the *Tuscarora* was like no other whaler on the seven seas.

The ship's complement was like no other, too. Bull had recruited each sailor personally, as before, but this time he screened not only for experience, but also for men who neither scoffed nor blanched at talk of fairies and monsters. No crewman had yet exhibited the Sight, like Manuel Chaves or Lewis Temple possessed, but many claimed to have glimpsed Kelpies, Hippocampi, Makaras, Merfolk, Mugwumps, or other unnatural creatures while serving on other ships.

Bull figured open minds would come in handy on the new ship. *Already did.*

As for old friends, Captain Stormalong brought two with him. One was Gunnar, the only other survivor of the *Courser*. Ashamed of his cowardice during the battle with the Kraken, the Norwegian begged for the chance to prove himself as first mate of the *Tuscarora*.

Speaking of which, there would be no *Tuscarora* if Bull hadn't met John de Conquer six years earlier, on the ferry to Brooklyn. It wasn't just that during their subsequent travels, John had helped him come to terms with Gez's death and his identity as a monster. The shape-shifting Rompo had helped him find new purpose, and a way back to the sea. And because the loss of the *Courser* also represented the loss of all of Bull's worldly possessions, he'd built and equipped the *Tuscarora* with money provided entirely by John, from some hidden trove his friend refused to identify or explain.

"Old Maker's plan," is all he said on the matter. "You and me, we's part of it."

God. Heavenly Father. The Almighty. Maker of All Things. Over the years, Bull had ferried, served, skippered, or fought alongside a wide range of folk. Even *Folk*. Many discussed or prayed to a higher power, High John more than most. Though they practiced different customs and spoke different words, Bull got the sense they were all talking about the same idea, the same person.

Which don't mean I understand it. Or Him.

Bull glanced back at the newspaper. It was like the poem. He could stare at it for hours, perhaps even be moved by it, but never really get what its creator was trying to say.

His sepia eyes shot wide open. *Maybe that ain't the point.*

For he, Alfred Bulltop Stormalong, was on a quest of his own. It wasn't for a city of gold or personal gain of any sort. Nor was his quest—this time—just vengeance. He sought a chance to serve, to protect, to make things right. To *do* right.

To fly his "true colors," as Gez put it, whether on tranquil ocean or stormy sea.

In sunshine and in shadow.

What hands had placed him here, on this ship, at this moment, to stumble across these very words, written by the very author most likely to remind him of what his long-lost friend had tried to teach him?

Bull's own hands, surely, though not on their own. They'd had help from people he'd met during his trek across the continent. The humans Manuel Chaves, Lewis Temple, even Isabella Van Wegener. The fairies Goran, Har, and Dela. His fellow shape-shifters Aki, Shash, Diego Vega, and especially John de Conquer. Many hands, each playing a role in placing him here.

And, maybe, there was one more set of hands. Never seen but always present. Never touching but always felt.

~ ~ ~

The captain wasn't surprised to find High John responsible for the revelry heard throughout the cavernous lower decks. He found his grinning friend in the forecastle, tapping out a rhythm on the pinewood floor with his bare feet and surrounded by clapping, whooping, laughing crewmen.

"Mornin', Cap'n Stormy!" John hollered. "Come to show us a step or two?"

Bull tried to keep a straight face. "Nay. Come for breakfast, if cook be found to fix it."

"Sure 'nough." The old man smiled even broader. "How 'bout serpent steak?"

"Eggs and coffee'll do."

Offering a good-natured shrug, John trotted away. Although the old shape-shifter claimed to have spent "many a year" crewing barges and riverboats—and his encouragement and financial investment had made the *Tuscarora* possible in the first place—he'd refused to accept officer rank. "She's a huntin' and fightin' ship," John insisted, "and neither's my way." Instead, he signed on as ship's cook. In practice, he tended to the men's morale at least as skillfully as he tended to their appetites.

Though averse to violence, John did indirectly contribute to one of the *Tuscarora*'s two innovations in weaponry. The toggle design acquired from his friend Lewis Temple was found on every harpoon they carried. It had already proven its worth many times on the ship's maiden voyage from New Bedford to the South Atlantic, around Cape Horn, and into the rich hunting grounds of the Pacific. Under the fabled Captain Stormalong, the giant whaler amassed a truly legendary haul of oil, spermaceti, baleen, and ambergris—though she never encountered the prey for which she was specifically designed.

It was during their second voyage, heading not south but north, that Bull and his men got to test their ship's other innovation, an innovation for which not John de Conquer but Gunnar the Norwegian was responsible. After the loss of the *Courser*, while a deeply disenchanted Bull was making his way from California to New England, a deeply discouraged Gunnar had sought refuge with a newly founded colony of fellow Norwegians in Texas. One of the settlers, Elise Wærenskjold, was once the wife of a whaling captain who'd spent years tinkering with new devices for launching harpoons. Both shoulder-fired harpoon guns and swivel guns on whaleboats had been known for decades, but possessed limited range and often misfired. Based on what Elise could recall of her former husband's work, Gunnar designed a swivel cannon capable of hurling harpoons a hundred yards. Far too powerful to be fired from light whaleboats, two such guns were mounted on the *Tuscarora* itself, at bow and stern.

As Bull climbed to the deck, he spied the head of the swivel guns' first kill lashed to the end of the bowsprit. Its once-glowing eyes and scaly skin were gone, leaving only a weathered skull and gaping jaws. Though gruesome, the sight made his heart swell with pride for ship and crew.

They'd encountered the enormous Sea Serpent near Gloucester, Massachusetts. Knowing instantly the hump in the distance wasn't a whale, Captain Stormalong had issued the call to battle, not to hunt. Well-trained, his crew executed his tactics to the letter. After weakening the monster with broadsides, they shot it with the bow swivel gun. The harpoon struck the beast just behind its shiny head. When it jerked back, the motion deployed the toggled barbs beneath its slimy skin, securing the monster to the *Tuscarora*. Big as it was, the Sea Serpent lacked sufficient might either to snap the rope or to drag the far-heavier ship under the sea. Once the aquatic tug-of-war exhausted the beast, the men lowered the whaleboats and moved in for the kill.

John really *had* offered to reward them with grilled filet of Sea Serpent. No one took him up on it, for the monster's horrid stench proved stomach-turning. Moreover, being only a day out of port, the *Tuscarora* remained stocked with far more appetizing provisions.

"All clear, cap'n."

As first mate, Gunnar had the early watch. Weaving his way through sailors swabbing the deck, he joined Bull by the port rail.

The captain pointed up at the gray clouds blocking the rising sun. "Storm brewin'."

"Aye, sir, but sea's clear."

The Norwegian's meaning was plain enough. He'd objected when Bull charted a northeasterly course for the ship's second voyage, taking them past Newfoundland into the Labrador Sea. It was a common-enough hunting ground, but the *Tuscarora* was built for more than common whaling. And despite hearing tales of the Kraken as a boy in Norway, Gunnar was convinced the prey they sought must be where they'd fought it before, in the Pacific. What the Norwegian didn't know—and Bull had good reason not to tell him—was that Gez the Kabouter had first encountered the Kraken in the North Atlantic.

"Clear *now*," said Bull, glancing again at the grisly trophy on the bowsprit. "Maybe not for long."

Gunnar followed his gaze and harrumphed. "Leettle worm."

Only by comparison. The Sea Serpent off Gloucester was no Kraken, true, but it was still a fearsome beast. Bull studied the first mate's craggy face. He saw more than frustration in the clenched jaw and knitted brow. *Was it fear?* Gunnar's every word and deed signaled an earnest desire to meet the Kraken. *Still might be worried he'll lose his nerve again.*

Bull wasn't just worried about it. He was *certain* Gunnar would lose his nerve in the end, as would the others. During previous battles, Gez had been on hand to sing courage spells—and even *then* terror magic overcame his crew.

Good thing I ain't counting on courage this time. Just loyalty.

~ ~ ~

The sky continued to darken. By midday, light drizzle fell onto a crowded deck and choppy sea.

After gobbling his breakfast, Bull spent the morning inspecting the guns and early afternoon drilling the crew with polearms. Two men, new recruits for the second voyage, struggled to keep their footing on the increasingly slippery deck. One, a harpooneer from the Ashanti country of West Africa, was nearly as tall as Bull but much leaner. The second, even-slighter man had been a schoolteacher in New York before becoming a sailor. Though both were solid hands in their respective professions, neither had experience with a two-handed halberd—and how the heavy axeblade could throw its wielder off-balance, especially at sea.

The wind suddenly picked up. The drizzle became a driving rain. "Sorry, skipper," stammered the smaller man, grabbing the harpooneer's arm to steady himself. "We'll get the hang of it, eh, Daggoo?"

The lanky African wasn't looking at his friend or his captain. He'd craned his long neck to see around the foremast. "There!" he cried, pointing a long finger. "Right ahead!"

The other men scrambled to look. Bull didn't need to. Another sense, a sixth sense no one else possessed, told him all he needed to know.

"Stations!" The captain's deep voice cut through the now-wailing wind. The sailors on deck snapped to while Gunnar and the other mates relayed the order to the lower decks. Among the first heads to emerge from below, one bore an uncharacteristically serious expression on his dark face.

"Come time?" asked High John.

Bull nodded. Remembering the halberd in his hands, he offered it to the old man.

John waved a dismissive hand. "Who ya think ya foolin'?"

He already knows, then. Should've guessed. Bull motioned for John to follow and headed for the bow, knowing Gunnar would head aft to take the wheel. "Want another job?" he yelled over his shoulder.

"Nah, but I gotta do it anyhow," John called back. "Only one who can, right?"

He knows that too.

Bull's first glimpse of the creature ahead was reassuring. Only two arms were visible in the distance, two bright arches above darkening water. Although Bull was sure the Kraken was aware of their presence, it hadn't yet rushed upon its prey. There was time to execute the first stage of his battle plan.

"Hard-a-starboard!" he cried. Relayed to Gunnar, the command soon presented a battery of long guns at the beast. Lightning flashed over flailing tentacles, as if to illuminate their target. Thunder rolled back to the *Tuscarora*, as if to awe and deter her crew.

The ship's captain glanced leftward at the cook. High John had never looked less jolly. Still, the old man inclined his bald head, one eyebrow arched. "Time's a-wastin'."

Bull nodded. "Fire!"

Cannons blared in reply, spewing shot and smoke over angry waves.

"Hard-a-port!" Bull ordered, adding his own crack of thunder to the rumbling cacophony.

The second battery erupted in a furious fusillade.

It had all happened before. Bull took in the familiar sounds, sights, and smells of battle. The crash of water and creak of wood. Small figures hurling balls of iron at a massive beast before moving in to hack and stab it with iron blades. Thick, salty air and thin, acrid fumes. Relentless men battling a remorseless foe on a restless sea.

His dark eyes stayed fixed on distant scarlet curves. Small became large. Two became four. The captain rapped the *Tuscarora*'s bow rail with his fist. *Time to test your mettle, lass.*

When the approaching monster reached optimal range, Bull turned to the crewman on his right. Daggoo stood at his station, weapon ready. The rangy harpooneer was second only to Gunnar in mastery of the swivel gun. It required but a jerk of Bull's head to signal the African. With a powerful blast, the gun cast its missile unerringly through the pounding rain. Darting through two waving stalks, the harpoon hit the ocean with a splash and pierced red flesh just below the surface.

Although the Kraken was already hurling itself at the *Tuscarora* by spurting wastewater out of its rearward-facing funnel, no wild thing likes a leash. The monster twisted the steering fin behind its carapace to execute a sudden turn, trying to dislodge the buried iron before resuming its attack unencumbered.

Bull had seen the maneuver work before. This time, as he hoped, the Kraken's change of direction served only to activate the toggled head of the iron. Its barbs dug deep. Despite the immense bulk of the *Tuscarora*, the captain and his crew felt the ship lurch as the monster tried a second time to free itself.

"To starboard!" shouted the captain, though Gunnar had already discerned the significance of the lurch and begun implementing the next phase of their prearranged plan. When the Kraken yanked a third time, it merely hastened the rotation of the *Tuscarora*. As soon as most of her guns were parallel with the monster, Bull gave the order to fire again.

Whether their first two artillery barrages, conducted at long range, did any damage to the Kraken was impossible to tell. This time, the effects were visible from nearly half a furlong away. One ball hit the carapace, sending a torrent of shell fragments upward against the driving rain. At least two others struck softer targets, for one tentacle was cut in half and another fell limp against the churning water.

Witnessing such results, any captain might feel pride in his ship and confidence in his crew. Instead, Bull was irritated. Most of his gunners missed. *Don't they get the stakes?*

He felt a tug on his sleeve. "Take it," said the voice of John de Conquer.

Bull wrenched his arm away. He was in no mood for the Rompo's silly distractions. *Do I have to go below and shoot the blasted beast myself?*

Then, out of the corner of one half-lidded eye, he saw Daggoo shiver. "Red ghost!" the African breathed. "Kee-hee. Kee-hee!"

The captain had never seen his harpooneer less than fierce—and that's what broke the spell. *Terror magic*. It was making Daggoo anxious and Bull angry.

There was another tug on his left arm. He turned.

"Take it now!" John insisted. In his hand was a length of leather cord threaded through several small shells and a larger one, oblong-shaped and red as the Kraken. Snatching it up, Bull removed his hat and slipped the necklace over his head—grateful to Diego Vega for the gift of a Carbuncle and to John for keeping it close at hand.

Bull had decided not to wear the protective shell too soon. He thought it would keep him from detecting the Kraken from afar. He had, however, underestimated how quickly the gigantic cephalopod's magic would fill him with rage. He couldn't afford to let irrational fury cloud his judgment.

It took just moments for the Carbuncle to take effect. The anger subsided. He blew out a breath, then turned and cupped his mouth. "Hard-a-port!"

As the ship began its turn, Bull dropped his halberd, whipped out his rigging knife, and cut the line tethering it to the Kraken. Lewis Temple's toggling harpoon had done its work, helping them weaken the beast. Perhaps they'd need it again. At the moment, though, there were other tools to use. Bull pointed aft. "Clear away starboard and larboard boats."

A dozen sailors looked back at him, some fearful, some just confused. The *Tuscarora* appeared to be turning to flee. To them, it made no sense to ready whaleboats. After all, they had no way of knowing what the Kraken would do next.

Bull did. He stomped a foot. "I said clear away them boats!"

A big wave crashed against the port bow, sending several men careening. Others scrambled aft. Bull followed, not only to ensure his nervous crewmen properly outfitted the boats but also to see if he'd correctly foreseen the Kraken's next move.

Confirmation came long before he reached the stern. Although storm winds filled her sails, the *Tuscarora* didn't accelerate. She slowed to a crawl. Bull could feel her creaking and shuddering, as if struggling against the pull of a massive anchor.

When he reached the mizzenmast, he found his third mate, Flask, seemingly frozen, eyes wide. "Wha-wha-what is it, sir?" stammered the stout New Englander.

Bull followed the man's gaze astern, soon spotting a reddish blur over the oddly contorted sea. "A Demon from the heart of Hell," he replied. "Time to send it back."

Even wounded and lacking two arms, the Kraken retained enough strength to spin. The *Tuscarora* hadn't retreated fast enough to escape the resulting vortex. *Figured as much.*

Leaving the astonished mate behind, he hurried to the port quarter, finding Gunnar bent over the larboard boat. "Clear?" Bull asked.

"Aye, cap'n. Both."

"Then lower away!"

When the larboard boat touched water, anxious oarsmen began to climb down after it. "Nei," grunted an alarmed-looking Gunnar. "Avast dat."

"Whacha mean?" asked one of them.

"'Avast boardin','" Bull insisted. "Leave it be!"

Puzzled but clearly relieved, the oarsmen backed away. Once untethered, the boats darted backward. After bouncing along the unnaturally flat surface of the water behind the ship, each made an abrupt turn to starboard. Caught on the outer edge of the whirlpool, the boats spun into a fog bank and disappeared from sight.

The captain looked at Gunnar, who'd reassumed his post. "How long?"

"Hard da say," said the first mate, eyes fixed on the wheel in an apparent attempt to resist the Kraken's terror magic. "Must make guess."

Lightning cracked the turbid sky. By its light, the two whaleboats were visible in the distance, about to come around after circling the still-spinning Kraken.

Another enormous wave crashed into the *Tuscarora,* tossing two sailors hard against the steeply angled deck. When Bull turned to help, he found High John lifting one to his feet. "Quite a squall," said the old man. "Squid's doin'?"

"Don't know." Bull jerked his thumb at the swirling sea. "But that is."

"Figured so," John said, "but how—"

There was another flash of light, though far dimmer than the first and coming from the surface, not the sky. A tongue of fire jutted briefly above the lip of the whirlpool, then snuffed out. Bull cast a questioning glance at the first mate.

"Bad guess," Gunnar wailed.

The next waves were notably weaker than their predecessors. Bull took no solace from that, for the ship also ceased her forward motion. The same powerful current flattening the waves was pulling incessantly on the *Tuscarora* from behind. Bull could hear her masts, planks, and joints straining, groaning, putting up a fight.

He grimaced. *Gunnar's other guess best be right.*

It was.

There was no flash, no glimpse of flame. If smoke rose from the center of the whirlpool, Bull couldn't see it. Still, he knew their plan had worked. He knew the first mate had cut the proper length of fuse for the second boat, that its powder kegs had exploded on or near the Kraken.

He knew because the creaking from his ship's wooden skeleton grew softer, then stopped. She shot forward, her billowing sails no longer competing with the pull of the vortex. Bull also knew because Gunnar looked up, his weathered face no longer pale, his jaws no longer clenched. The other human faces around him visibly relaxed. Even John de Conquer, who'd never appeared particularly fearful, now cracked a playful smile. "Clever trick y'all pulled," he said. "Magic's gone."

Bull's only response was a slight nod. "Hard-a-starboard," he told Gunnar.

The first mate complied with evident relish. Her crew hurried to their stations with evident pride and relief.

John's smile faded. "Hope you ain't huntin' a trophy."

"No." Bull pulled an iron from the case next to the swivel gun and looked for a pole. "Just huntin'."

"I see." The Rompo reached into the pouch at his hip and pulled out the nub of a chewing root. Biting off half, he offered the other to Bull. "Makin' sure, I s'pose."

The captain found a pole and jammed the harpoon home, then accepted

John's gift. "Might still need that job done."

The old man chewed in a regular rhythm, savoring the pungent taste. He seemed completely oblivious to the wailing wind, rough sea, and unsettling implications of his friend's words.

Bull chewed along with him for a few moments until the pulp was soft enough to push between his cheek and gum. "Come on," he said.

When the two reached the other end of the ship, he seized the bow rail and shot John a sideways glance. *Gotta be certain.* "Terror magic," he began. "You don't feel it?"

"Never said that." John spit over the bouncing rail. "Truth is, makes me right scared."

"Then how come you don't—"

"Cuz I got my own witchin' way, same as you. When most critters suck in whatever meanness another spews out, it sorta takes 'em over. Can't break their minds free, least not easy. Then they's other critters, like us. Some kinds of magic, we ain't gotta swallow. We can chew it, swish it around, switch it to somethin' else."

"Like fear spells just make me angrier."

"Yep. You switch it before you swallow." John turned away, a strange expression on his scarred face. The two stood there for some time, looking for something bright and solid in the dark, roiling water. Then the old man puckered his lips and shot a stream of juice over the rail.

"Some critters don't just swallow. They spit it out again."

Bull's eyes widened. "*You* make terror magic?"

"Me?" John shook his head. "Naw, ain't my knack. Can't spit fear."

"Then what?"

"Mine's the drummin' way. The singin' way. Beatin' away a whole mess of sorrow and finishin' off with a laugh."

Spying the puzzled look on Bull's face, John cackled and tapped his captain's thick forearm. "Can't ya guess? It's not fear I spit. It's hope."

~ ~ ~

Their first two circuits yielded no sign of the Kraken. Keeping his Carbuncle necklace on as a precaution, Bull relied on his crew to detect any resumption of terror magic. It was on the *Tuscarora*'s third and last pass that Gunnar allowed himself a broad smile. "Is done fer!"

"Maybe," said the captain.

The Norwegian's smile disappeared.

John de Conquer slapped the first mate's back. "Ain't no harm in checkin.' Got a meetin' in Iceland to get to?" Then his smile faded, too.

Mood magic. Bull glanced around the deck. The truth stared back at him. Proud, confident, jovial faces became timid, anxious, morose. *It's still alive*. "Lower my boat!"

No one moved. Faster than he thought possible, fear overwhelmed his crew. Bull scanned the sea. He saw nothing but choppy waves.

It's alive—and below us. "Lower the boat!" repeated the captain, gripping the pole with white knuckles.

Then High John began to hum. The tune, high-pitched and jaunty, seemed out of place among a terrified crew on a bobbing ship under a stormy sky. That was the point. John slapped a foot on the puddly deck, splashing water on Gunnar's pantaloons. He clapped, stamped, then repeated the sequence over and over in cadence with his song.

Bull unclenched his hands. *John's spitting hope*.

Though the old man's manner was playful, Bull could see the exertion in his furrowed brow and twitching mouth. The Rompo admitted he wasn't fully immune to terror magic. He was converting some of it and, with effort, resisting what was left.

Gunnar was the first to regain some control of himself, thanks to John. He took a couple of faltering steps forward. "Your…your boat, cap'n?"

"Gotta finish this." Two nearby sailors shook their heads as if waking up from a nap. Bull pointed aft. "Take 'em. Lower away."

Trusting them to obey, the captain returned his attention to John, who tried to reassure him with a smile. The completion of Bull's plan required a sufficient number of able seamen to manage the *Tuscarora*. John's mood magic, his "spittin' hope," was helping—but at this rate, it might take too long.

If only Gez were here. Two spellsingers are better than one.

It was at that moment, with many more lives than his own at stake, that Bull remembered the words of his friend Diego Vega on the day they first met. *I possess many talents*, the shape-changing Teumessian Fox had said. *Hidden talents*.

Diego had hidden talents. So did Shash, Aki, and John de Conquer. *Maybe I do, too.*

Then Bull did something that made John's eyes widen in surprise and concern. The captain lifted the Carbuncle necklace over his head and wrapped it around his harpoon. Suddenly the air around him felt thick and heavy, as if he'd been cast into a vat of taffy. It pressed against his flesh, assaulted his ears, invaded his nose and mouth. It wasn't air heavy-laden with moisture or bunched into a heavy wind. Indeed, it wasn't air at all.

It was fear.

Countless times, he'd felt it press against him. Countless times, without any conscious thought, Bull had let it in. It had never scared him—it just made him angry. The effect wasn't to weaken him. If anything, the angrier he got, the stronger he felt. Still, the emotion impaired his judgment. That's why he'd started wearing the Carbuncle, to keep his mind clear.

Now, though, it was time to try something else. Rather than letting the fear flow through him, Bull tried conscious direction. He imagined himself gulping it in, "swishin' it around," as John put it, and spitting out hope to his stricken crew.

The outcome wasn't what he expected. Bull gulped in fear, all right, more than he ever had in the past. As before, he felt a surge of anger inside him, not terror. Even more so, however, he felt a surge of strength, of stamina, of possibility filling his lungs and coursing through his veins. His legs felt like skeins of rope, his arms like bars of iron, his hands like cudgels of the stoutest oak.

He gulped, he swished, but found he couldn't spit. He could only swallow.

Can't let the fury take me. Bull sucked in more fear, as if through a hundred rye-grass straws, and tried thinking only hopeful thoughts. He recalled youthful exploits on fishing vessels and riverboats. He recalled sailing a schooner up the Hudson River. He recalled his first ocean-going ship. He recalled the whaling voyages he'd made, the kills he'd made, the friends he'd made. He recalled Mike Fink, and Ichabod Crane, and Zorro, and Gez, and John de Conquer. He let go of his disappointment, his regret, his anger. He swished, and swished, and swished.

And only swallowed.

Not a drop of magic escaped him, no matter how hard he tried to expel it, but Bull's efforts weren't ineffectual. He had never felt hardier, sturdier, mightier. His body seemed broader and deeper somehow, like an unfathomable well containing inexhaustible power. His mood changed as well, but not to anger. He felt confident. Purposeful. Indomitable.

"Cap'n?"

Gunnar's voice no longer sounded tremulous. It sounded inquisitive. The question jerked Bull out of his introspection. He realized most of his men were now doing their jobs, not quivering in fear. His first mate was at his side. A quick glance aft confirmed that his whaleboat was ready, its oarsmen about to board. And, for the first time, he noticed High John was no longer humming and dancing. The old man was leaning against the rail, his face contorted into an expression Bull had never seen on him before.

Pity.

Then, finally, he understood. He knew what Gez never had the heart to tell him. He knew what John had let Bull discover for himself. He knew what the Kraken really was, for he knew what Alfred Bulltop Stormalong really was.

And he knew why he had to get the *Tuscarora* away from here, as far as possible, as fast as possible.

Bull spun and bounded toward the starboard quarter. "Nay!" he shouted to the oarsmen, waving them away from the boat. "Back to stations!"

He heard lighter feet pounding the deck behind him. *Gunnar. And John.* When he reached the whaleboat, Bull leapt aboard and began securing a line to his harpoon.

"Not alone!" cried the horrified Norwegian.

"Gotta be." Bull removed the Carbuncle necklace from the iron and pointed at the boarding knife thrust into Gunnar's belt. "Swap."

The first mate did so. The captain thrust the long thin blade through his own belt. "Put it on," he commanded. Befuddled but compliant, Gunnar donned the necklace.

John gravely bowed his head. "We'll get her away," he vowed.

Bull met his eyes. "See that you do." Then he picked up two oars and used one to push away. Amidst the protestations of her crew, Bull heard a high-pitched hum and rhythmic tapping. John de Conquer had gone back to spitting.

Three sweeps of oars by the legendary Captain Stormalong would have propelled even the heaviest of boats a great distance. Most of the rapidly yawning gap between his boat and the *Tuscarora* was, however, due to the latter's four masts of full sails and the velocity with which they propelled her in the opposite direction.

The next three pulls shot the boat a much greater distance, because Captain Stormalong was no longer at the oars. It was a Minotaur, his hulking frame barely contained within what had been the captain's already oversized clothing. Now safely away from his ship, Bull assumed his true shape. Sipping from his inner reservoir of power, the Minotaur felt his muscles grow stronger and his senses keener.

Whether he would *feel* the Kraken's presence before he spotted it, Bull neither knew nor cared. He was no longer concerned about terror magic, for he knew it wouldn't cloud his judgment. It never had. His anger had come from *inside*, not outside. It was an instinctual reaction to a misunderstood threat. Now that he understood the true nature of the Kraken, he'd keep his fury in check.

As it happened, it was Bull's huge eyes—sepia marbled with cracks of glowing orange—that detected its presence. They glimpsed a blur of motion to his left. He let go of the oars and picked up the harpoon. Although obviously weaker than before, the cephalopod would be no mean antagonist. Best to tire and bleed it more, if he could, before the final confrontation.

The next signal was invisible but no less definitive. The Minotaur *felt* the Kraken reach out with magic, trying to find and terrify its prey. "Not this time," he whispered. "Not from me." For he now knew what the monster really wanted, what it *needed.* Immobilizing its prey was but a welcome side-effect—the true purpose of the spell was to *produce the fear itself.* The Kraken fed on human fear, healed with it, grew stronger from it.

Just as the Minotaur did.

That was why the *Courser* had lost her previous battles with the creature. Though badly wounded at first, the aquatic beast had gotten close enough to Bull's crew to harvest their fear, like a gargantuan leech drawing sustenance from its host. Wounds healed, vitality restored, the Kraken had been too powerful to defeat.

When planning his new hunt, Bull had intended to keep the *Tuscarora* at a distance during his killing stroke so he wouldn't worry about her terrified crew. It was only after Bull felt *himself* absorbing the fear of his own sailors, growing ever more powerful as he fed, that he understood what lent the Kraken its power—and why, in the end, he had to face his nemesis alone.

Because he'd felt its psychic tendril touch his mind, Bull wasn't surprised when its physical one darted out of the sea at him. Knocking it aside with one furry arm, he tossed his harpoon with the other. It struck the tentacle below the water line. When the Kraken jerked its limb back, Lewis Temple's toggled head proved its worth again. The barbs anchored the iron in flesh and muscle.

Bull glimpsed a dark cylindrical shape in the ocean off the portside bow and guessed it was a stream of wastewater expelled from the Kraken's steering funnel. The whir of rope against the loggerhead confirmed the monster's flight. Bull drew more stored magic into his arms and legs, braced himself, and waited.

When the coiled line ran out, the whaleboat leapt from the water like a sturgeon, hurtling through the air for several moments before hitting the surface with an enormous splash. The force might have sent a human oarsman or harpooneer tumbling into the water, but Bull held fast, more concerned about his boat capsizing or breaking than his grip weakening.

On the Kraken rocketed, abruptly changing direction several times in an attempt to dislodge the iron. It failed. Glancing over his shoulder, Bull saw no sign of the *Tuscarora* on the misty horizon. He guessed the beast had dragged him in a northeasterly direction, though he couldn't be sure without instruments or a cloudless sky. If he survived the battle, his chances of finding his way back to his ship, or to succor of any kind, seemed remote.

Always knew this might be it. Fittin' end to Captain Stormalong.

The towline went slack.

Was it doubling back to attack? Diving? Bull saw no red shape approaching. He decided to assume the latter. Unlike a whale, the Kraken could breathe underwater. It wouldn't have to surface. Even tired and bloodied, its sheer bulk might be enough to yank his boat under or tear it asunder.

Bull was ready for that, too. The Kraken was cunning, but it wasn't a thinking monster. He was. Holding his eyelids shut, he tapped his inner reservoir again. He concentrated not on strength, but on size. He heard his already ragged coat and shirt rip to shreds. He felt his feet and calves become bare and his previously loose pantaloons become tight. Opening his giant eyes, the Minotaur—now so large that his feet barely fit within the bottom of the boat—grabbed the tow rope and wrenched it free. Filling his now-enormous lungs, Bull jumped overboard.

Within seconds, the rope went taut again. Down into the murky depths dove the Kraken, pulling the Minotaur with it. Knowing time wasn't on his side, Bull started working his way down the rope, shaggy hand over shaggy hand, using some stored magic to keep a tight grip on the tether and feeding the rest into his already gigantic frame. The heavier he got, the slower the Kraken's dive became.

The glowing cracks in his obsidian eyes were enough to illuminate the water ahead. So, when the scarlet tip of a tentacle came into view, Bull had an instant to draw his rigging knife. Unfortunately, his hand was now so big that he could only hold the weapon between thumb and forefinger. Flicking it aside, he seized the Kraken's stalk and wrapped it around his own enormous forearm.

The tug-of-war would have been longer if the *Tuscarora* hadn't taken its toll on the Kraken—and if he were still just Captain Stormalong instead of a horned colossus determined to prevail. He pulled. His foe pulled back. It lost.

Bull extricated his arm and grabbed the rope with both hands. Lungs bursting for air, he considered trying to swim to the surface while keeping a hold on the creature. He couldn't tell how deep he'd been pulled under, however, or how long his reservoir of magic would last.

Come here. He pulled the rope again and again, drawing the struggling Kraken ever closer. He could see it below him now, a wriggling mass of power and evil. His hands reached the end of the rope and the iron embedded in the tentacle. Bull grabbed the shank and yanked with all his might. The iron gave, ripping off a large chunk of bloody flesh.

Another arm snaked around Bull's torso.

Grapple with me, will you? The Minotaur smiled and reached for the weapon he could still wield. His huge hand covered the handle of the boarding knife and more. Nevertheless, there was enough of its long blade showing to plunge into the unwounded tentacle.

It didn't stay unwounded.

Now we finish this. Although his lungs burned in protest, Bull kicked his massive legs and shot downward. Approaching the body of the beast, he noted with satisfaction multiple holes and deep cracks in its carapace.

Another tentacle tried to block his path. Brushing it aside, Bull spotted a huge eye glowing faintly. Holding the boarding knife before him like the head of a spear, he kicked his legs once more. The blade struck home, forever extinguishing the golden glow. Bull withdrew the knife and targeted the pink hide between dead eye and damaged carapace. At last, allowing hate and rage to take over, he stabbed again and again and again, willingly spending his last breath to save the living and avenge the dead.

~ ~ ~

The sea and its Master have its own plans, however. They weren't yet done with the seafaring Minotaur whom humans named Alfred Bulltop Stormalong.

He found himself on the now-placid surface of a frigid ocean, grasping a plank that may have once been part of his whaleboat, though it could just as easily have been a rafter from Triton's palace. How he made it to the surface alive, Bull had no idea. Nor did he know how far from his ship he was, or from land, or how long he might cling to his wooden float before exhaustion or exposure brought his tale to a quiet end.

One thing he knew for certain, though, and it was enough. The Kraken was dead.

Then a most unexpected sound came to his wide-spaced ears: a tinkling bell. Voices followed, distant and muffled. Bull turned his head. Only a few dozen feet away was the side of a large vessel. It was one of the new ocean-going liners by the looks of it, equipped with both sails and a steam engine.

He tried to swim toward the passing ship, but his limbs wouldn't cooperate. The titanic struggle had consumed nearly all his strength. Only a tiny ember of magic smoldered inside him.

"Not again!"

Bull was stunned. He *recognized* the voice. He'd heard it before, years ago, on a different sea.

"I'll throw no more lines to the likes of you. Learned my lesson."

He sees me! Bull attempted to clear his parched throat to cry out. All that produced was a feeble croak. Then he remembered his appearance. If the man on the passing ship got close enough to see a horned monster bobbing in the water, he'd become even less inclined to help.

Bull had been willing to die in the service of others. He'd "shown his true colors." Now, for reasons perhaps known only to John's beloved Old Maker, he was being given a chance at rescue, to live and serve again.

Thinking of John de Conquer gave him an idea. He'd seen the Rompo assume more than one human shape. Could he do the same? Summoning the last bit of magic he'd absorbed, Bull fixed his mind on the unremarkable face and form of one of the sailors on the *Tuscarora*, the former schoolteacher from New York.

"You there!" said the voice again. Through unfamiliar eyes, Bull looked up at the familiar face of the passenger peering down from the ship's deck. "Do you truly wish rescue, or are you determined to perish like the other?

"Re-rescue," Bull sputtered.

"All right, then." A rope struck the water. "But let us strike a bargain, you and me. If I reel you in, you have to tell me how you ended up here."

"De-deal."

Later, Bull lay wrapped in a blanket on the deck, marveling at the improbable twist of fate. He *knew* this man. He'd met him in the South Pacific, aboard the whaler *Acushnet*. He was the rather sardonic sailor who'd brought Bull word that Gez was dead. He couldn't tell this man the truth, of course. He tried to imagine how his fairy friend or John de Conquer might construct an entertaining but expurgated version of the truth, one a human might believe.

The passenger wagged a finger impishly. "I played my part. Now play yours! My name is Herman Melville. And you?"

Bull managed a wan smile. "Call me Ishmael."

Chapter 28 – The Asylum

June 1852

HENRY CLAY WASN'T COMING.

That much, Sam Houston knew before he left the Indian Queen and crossed 6th Street to the National Hotel, where Clay resided. The last time Sam had seen him, the elderly senator from Kentucky was frail, emaciated, and incapable of uttering more than a few words without gagging. Although the two men differed by party and generation and much else, Sam found it painful to see one of America's foremost orators rendered virtually speechless by consumption and other infirmities. Clay hadn't stood on the Senate floor in months. Only a miracle could make him fit for the day's outing.

When Willie Mangum shuffled out of the National Hotel, the venerable senator's glum face said it all. *Of course* Henry Clay wasn't coming. Indeed, the North Carolinian's anguished expression suggested Clay might not survive the week.

"Shall we go, gentlemen?"

Unlike Sam Houston and Willie Mangum, the white-bearded man waiting by the carriage was no senator. John Pendleton Kennedy was a former Whig congressman, speaker of the Maryland House, and, rumor had it, about to be appointed secretary of the navy by President Millard Fillmore.

The visibly shaken Mangum leaned against the portico. "Give me a moment, sir."

"Of course." Kennedy offered the North Carolinian a sympathetic smile, then turned to Sam and pointed across the street. "Isn't that where you and I first met?"

Sam smiled. "In the dining room of the Indian Queen, yes."

"Must have been fifteen years ago."

"Eighteen." Sam remembered the occasion well. It was the same day

Goran and Har had arrived in Washington to inform him of Dela's capture at Spirit Forest. That dinner was also the first time he'd heard David Crockett vow to leave for Texas if his fellow Tennesseans chose not to reelect him.

If the voters had made a different choice, Crockett might still be alive. The thought made him wince.

"Age is no foe to the likes of you and me," said Kennedy, misinterpreting Sam's reaction to the memory. "We but grow stronger and sweeter, like a fine wine."

"It's not the passing years that sadden me," Sam replied. "It's the thought of friends absent from them."

Now it was the Marylander who looked distracted. "I recall now. Congressman Crockett joined us for dinner that evening, as did another no longer with us."

"Indeed." Back in 1834, the nervous-looking guest accompanying Kennedy to the Indian Queen had made little impression. Only much later had Sam realized the extent of the man's talents. His poem "The Raven" was a particular favorite, for obvious reasons. "Edgar Allan Poe died in Baltimore, didn't he?"

"Yes, nearly three years ago."

"A tragedy not just for his friends, but for readers everywhere."

"Kind words, sir. Speaking of wine, after we get back to the city, might you join me to toast our lost companions, Crockett and Poe?"

Noticing Mangum had recovered his composure, Sam opened the carriage door. "You know I never drink anymore, John."

As Kennedy stepped aside and indicated the North Carolinian should enter first, he forced another smile to his lips. "Then come and watch me perform the act for us both."

~ ~ ~

Their destination lay just north of the city, but the ride was still long enough for an argument.

"It will surely be Mister Clay's last service to our country," Mangum insisted, "a work of prudence and bravery."

"Its prudence, I doubt," Kennedy replied, "and its bravery, I reject. You know what would take courage? To settle for all time the question of slavery—not to postpone it for future generations to contest."

The North Carolinian glared at the Marylander. "The question is not for Congress to settle. The Constitution no more gives us the power to regulate local institutions than it gives us the power to tax local commerce."

Kennedy raised a finger. "And yet, within the framework Henry Clay suggested and Stephen Douglas brought to fruition, Congress admitted California as a free state and outlawed the slave trade here in Washington. Were *these* the acts of tyrants?"

"You confuse the issue," said Mangum, annoyance adding a faint flush to his pallid cheeks. "The people of California *requested* admission as a free state. The people in the new territories of New Mexico and Utah will decide the question for themselves. As for Washington, it lies within no state. Congress lawfully governs the capital, as you well know."

"I know this supposed 'compromise' Congress enacted in 1850 will not hold. It cannot. It should not."

Sam shook his head. "You best hope you are wrong, John. The rights and interests of all Americans depend upon the inviolability of our Union. Whatever impairs it will earn my disapproval, whether it be fanaticism born in the North or in the South, for a nation divided against itself cannot stand."

Kennedy grimaced. "It is our national division that troubles me, Sam, and your part in bringing it about."

"*My* part?"

"There was no louder advocate for annexing Texas than her former president, and few more supportive of the late Mister Polk's aggressive diplomacy over Oregon and war against Mexico. Adding so many new and different lands to the Union is what brought on the crisis."

"You give me too large a role in the drama, sir." Sam glanced at Mangum, but his Senate colleague was gazing out the carriage window, lost in thought. "The machinations of England and the outrages of Mexico required decisive action. By victory and treaty, we made acquisitions of territory necessary for the United States to carry out her destiny and secure the peace of the continent."

"The peace of conquest. The peace of the sword."

"War may sometimes be productive of good," Sam allowed, "but I speak of more than force of arms. I speak of America's enterprise, and the character of her population and institutions, uniting in the extension of human happiness."

"Happiness for some. Bondage and misery for others."

Frustrated, Sam turned to look out the other window. During his many years in the Senate, he'd argued countless times for the Oregon Treaty, the Mexican War, and conciliation between North and South. He didn't feel like repeating the arguments again. As for slavery, he had no love for the institution but considered immediate abolition unrealistic. If the newly freed slaves stayed on the same farms and plantations, working for the same overseers, what would be gained? And if they didn't, who would take care of them? Would they not be cast into the streets, objects of want and wretchedness?

"If there is a simple solution to our dilemma," Sam eventually said, "I cannot find it. So, I prefer to find a way for jarring interests to be reconciled, and for millions yet unborn to enjoy happiness under a Union which it is our duty to transmit to them unimpaired. If it be dissolved, I wish that its ruins may be the monument of my grave, and the graves of my family. I wish no epitaph to be written to tell that I survived the ruin of this glorious Union."

The corners of Kennedy's mouth twitched. "I, too, desire fondly to preserve our Union. We merely differ on how best to accomplish it. As for your exalted language, it is impressive but misplaced. I cannot vote for you. Your party already selected another candidate for president."

If he meant to insult Sam by mentioning the just concluded Democratic Convention, it wouldn't work. Although he'd once hoped to be the party's nominee for the 1852 election, Sam realized months ago it was not to be. That he received as many as a dozen votes at the Baltimore convention and stayed in the running until the forty-ninth ballot—the one that nominated former general and senator Franklin Pierce—was a source of pride, not shame.

On the other hand, if his Whig friend was merely being playful, Sam welcomed the chance to end their argument. "You sell me too short, John. Your party's delegates will journey soon to Baltimore, as well, for its convention. Might I not aspire to at least earn your nomination for vice president?"

Sam had judged correctly. Kennedy threw back his head and laughed. "A Democrat from Texas on the Whig ticket? Why, if we fashioned such a chimera with you and, say, General Scott, which would be the lion's head and which the goat?"

"You consider my former commander the frontrunner, then?" Sam had his political disagreements with Winfield Scott but respected the general's prowess and patriotism.

Kennedy shrugged. "I'm a Fillmore man, but Scott enjoys the support of such venerable Whigs as our own companion here, Senator Mangum."

"What's that?" the North Carolinian sputtered.

"We speak of the Whig convention, sir," said Kennedy. "You declared for Scott, did you not?"

"I did."

"I was joking to Sam that the vice presidential slot would—"

"I cannot accept," Mangum insisted. "It will not serve the Whig cause. My fellow Southerners no longer revere me. They resent me. They see Scott as William Seward's tool."

"Why, that is rank nonsense," Kennedy said. "I share Senator Seward's anti-slavery views, but Winfield Scott is his own man, for good or ill."

Mangum coughed, then wipe his mouth with a handkerchief. "I am an old man. I feel I have misspent much of my life."

Exchanging concerned looks with Kennedy, Sam patted the North Carolinian's arm. "Hardly, sir. Your visit with Senator Clay has upset you."

Blotting his forehead, Mangum closed his eyes as if in concentration. "What was it my teacher said long ago? He asked what course of life I intend to pursue. Why I kept shifting about, turning my coat for one cause and then another. I should have listened. I should have heeded John Chavis."

Sam started. "Chavis, you say? Could you possibly mean John Chavis, the colored minister from North Carolina?"

Mangum opened his eyes. "You know of my old teacher?"

"Why, yes! We met long ago. It was my own father who brought John Chavis to study at Washington College. John, you'll appreciate this: this same Chavis was present when I first met David Crockett as a boy."

"You don't say." Kennedy cocked an eyebrow. "A black man tutored a future North Carolina senator. If I put that in one of my stories, my readers would reject it as incredible."

"I should have listened to John," Mangum repeated in a whisper.

"We will speak no more of it," said Sam. "Besides, we have reached our destination."

As their carriage trundled to a stop, Sam peered out the window at the stone cottage built atop a gentle rise. Two stories across much of its length, the former summer home of banker George Washington Riggs and his family was now home to a family of a different sort—thanks in large measure to the very man seeking the Whig nomination, Winfield Scott.

Rather than pocketing the enormous sum paid to him as tribute by the people of Mexico City after his 1847 conquest, General Scott had donated it to the cause of housing America's wounded and disabled soldiers. Years later, another veteran of the Mexican War, then-Senator Jefferson Davis of Mississippi, fought off attempts by the War Department to repurpose the funds and shepherded through a bill to purchase the Riggs Estate for the new United States Military Asylum.

"The estate's ample cornfields and pastures should keep the men well-supplied," said Kennedy. "Take my arm if you please, Senator Mangum."

When Sam followed them out of the coach, he was surprised to find another carriage nearby, its driver chatting with a paunchy soldier in a faded uniform. "We aren't the only visitors, I see."

"Nor will we be the last," Kennedy said. "Some will come here to honor the soldiers' sacrifice, others to claim credit for their new home."

Long before he reached the porch, Sam learned the identity of the asylum's other visitors. He recognized each of the three voices blaring from the house, for each belonged to a current or former colleague.

"I could not consent to introduce slavery into any part of this continent already exempt from what seems to me so great an evil," said the first. "That was my reason for declining the compromise."

William Seward.

"Nor could I abide an unholy crusade against the domestic institution of the South," intoned a deeper voice, "perverting religion from its mission of peace and brotherly love to sanctify such unprovoked hostile aggression."

Jefferson Davis.

"Gentlemen," a third voice intervened. "Neither North nor South can afford to act under so fatal a delusion as total victory. Our compromise was predicated on the fundamental principle that every people ought to possess the right of forming and regulating their own internal institutions in their own way."

Stephen Douglas.

When Sam opened the door, he found the unkempt senator from New

York towering over his diminutive colleague from Illinois. "The Fugitive Slave Act has rendered it more than just an internal institution," Seward complained.

"The duty to return fugitives to their owners is no new obligation," Douglas replied. "It was clearly stated in that most sacred of instruments, the Constitution of the United States."

Seward sniffed. "There is a higher law than the Constitution."

"You see?" Though standing next to the New Yorker, Jefferson Davis directed his words at Douglas. "All obligations, social and political, these self-canonized saints proclaim to be annulled by the higher law are revealed only to them, and theirs alone to execute."

Sam cleared his throat. "I am far from a saint, but may my fellow travelers and I be allowed to cross your battlefield unscathed?"

"Senator Houston!" Douglas beamed, although Sam couldn't tell whether the Illinois senator was pleased to see him or just welcomed the interruption. "And Senator Mangum, too. Why, we are nearly a full committee convened."

"Nearly," Sam agreed, "but our task isn't to debate legislation, past or present."

Neither Seward nor Davis seemed inclined to agree. Still, when they spied Mangum crossing the threshold with an unsteady gait, both men dropped their eyes in deference to the longest-serving senator.

"I quite agree."

The new voice was one Sam *didn't* recognize. An officer in a rumpled blue uniform stood behind them on the porch. He was rather tall and might have once been lean and vigorous. Many years of service had taken their toll, however. His back was stooped, his face jowly, his midriff portly. The officer's overlarge ears stuck out at odd angles and were partially covered by unruly strands of gray hair. Only his green eyes, keen and perceptive, belied his decrepit appearance.

"I welcome you on behalf of the garrison of this post," said the officer. "We will be pleased to conduct you on a brief tour, so long as you refrain from any further disputation that might disturb our residents."

Stephen Douglas tittered. "I do not believe you understand, general. We are—"

"Colonel." The tall officer nodded politely.

"Sir?"

"My superiors never saw fit to recommend me for a generalship."

Jefferson Davis looked offended. "Are you questioning the justice of your rank, colonel?"

"Not at all. I sought no such promotion and lodged no such complaint. My service has been its own reward. Now I have the privilege of serving the asylum as its governor."

"Nevertheless," Douglas said, "I think you should know that you address current and former members of Congress."

The colonel smiled. "I do. That explains my confidence in your ability to exhibit proper decorum while within this institution, this home of heroes."

Sam found the man's unbridled honesty refreshing. "Are the residents all veterans of the late war with Mexico?"

"Most are, though some suffered wounds in earlier service—including the conflict in which you and I were first bloodied, the War of 1812."

Taken aback, Sam gave the man's weathered face a closer look. "Did you and I serve together, Colonel? I confess I do not remember you."

"No, Senator Houston, I know you only by reputation."

John Kennedy tugged Sam's sleeve. "I suggest we proceed. Not everyone in our company is fit for lengthy conversation."

Glancing over his shoulder at Senator Mangum, who was breathing heavily, Sam nodded. "Perhaps you and I may speak another time, sir."

"I would welcome that, senator." The colonel strode across the room. "Gentlemen, I didn't mean to be disrespectful. I know weighty matters command your attention and that much depends on your efforts to address them. Perhaps what you see today will clarify the stakes. The warriors who live here do so because the leaders of our republic saw fit to send them to war. These soldiers obeyed. They performed their duty as best they could, and came home forever changed by it. Some wounds are visible. Others, just as deep, are not."

His words had the intended effect. The visitors fell silent as they followed him down the hallway.

"It pleases all soldiers to review their careers with pride," the officer continued, "to consider their years of service part of a larger design. Those who give the greatest sacrifice feel the greatest need to invest it with meaning."

He stopped at another doorway, gesturing for the others to enter. Last in line, Sam was about to walk past when the officer locked eyes with him.

"It comforts them," the colonel added, "to imagine more than human hands at work in the world—even if they lack the Sight to witness them."

The two men stared at each other. Much passed between them, much that required no words to impart and yet promised a hundred dinner conversations to explore in full.

Presently, Sam broke the silence. "What is your name, sir?"

The colonel grinned. "One you have heard before, though we never met before today."

"How can you be sure?"

"Because I know you to be well-read. I am Ichabod Crane."

Chapter 29 — The Lost City

THE NET STRUCK HOME, WRAPPING itself around the flyer's neck, arm, and artificial wings. Twisting, shrieking, he slammed into the mound, then tumbled down its grassy slope.

That settled it. She was just as adept at casting a net as she was at wielding a trident.

Though I have no memory of mastering either skill.

Dela scanned the area. Nothing moved. Having chosen a cloudy, moonless night, she wasn't surprised her attack went undetected. She dashed along the mound's middle terrace until she reached the unconscious ranger. Drawing a fishbone-handled knife, she held its bronze point to the Elf's throat while unwrapping the net and removing the flying apparatus from his motionless body.

Now was the moment of decision. Yes, she'd journeyed more than five hundred miles to the outskirts of St. Louis. Yes, she'd lurked among the Cahokia mounds for days, watching rangers come and go. And yes, she'd just brought one of them down and threatened his life.

She could, however, still turn back. Dela could leave before he regained consciousness, or after ensuring he never would. She didn't have to press ahead. She could return home. Or, rather, the Water Maiden who *used* to be Dela could go back to Long Island and *pretend* it was home. The person she was now had no real past, no real relationships, no real home to go back to.

I have tried everything else. If I am to be Dela once more, I have no choice.

Keeping the knife at the ready, she turned the Elf onto his back. Blood oozed from a cut on his bruised forehead. After a few moments, his eyelids fluttered.

"Do not move," Dela hissed.

The Elf's emerald eyes widened.

"Give me the security song."

His eyes narrowed again. "No."

"I have you in my power."

"You may have my life, nothing more."

He was clearly made of braver stuff than the first Elf she remembered capturing, the one who'd swiftly offered up the song she needed to escape the mound years before. The Elves had, of course, long since changed the spellsong for passing through the Shimmer. That's why she needed him to surrender it.

Dela pressed the knifepoint against his skin. "Is your life worth so little?"

Impressively, the Elf smiled. "It is dear to me, but the safety of my Folk is dearer."

She sighed. *I must play the savage.* "If you refuse, I will kill you and capture another."

"Who will also refuse you."

"I will keep killing Elves until I get the spell. Someone will, in the end, give it up—so all the lives I take, including yours, will be wasted."

Her captive gulped, his eyes darting from side to side. *Is he wavering?*

"You will fail," the Elf insisted, sounding more fanatical than fearful. "Your raiding party cannot stay hidden for long."

"Are you willing to risk—"

Dela stopped herself in midsentence. She'd thought it best to intimidate the man, but his assertion prompted her to rethink. *Perhaps a fool can obtain what a savage cannot.* "What makes you think I come with a raiding party?"

"Your army, then. Whatever your numbers, the defenders of Cahokia are more than a match for you."

"There is no army, no raiding party."

For the first time, the Elf looked her straight in the eye. "You lie."

"No. I come alone."

"Nonsense," he scoffed. "What could you hope to accomplish?"

Dela tried to look crazed. "I was once held prisoner here. I return to collect a debt."

"Revenge?" The Elf's face softened, though the sight of her blade kept him from laughing. "You must be mad!"

"No, but I *am* angry." It was close enough to the truth for her to mean it.

"If I offer the spell, you spare my life?"

"You were not among my jailers, so yes."

He sang. Dela listened. Then she withdrew the knife, lifted her trident, and gave his forehead another nasty bruise.

~ ~ ~

This is *madness, of a sort.*

Her body pressed against the wall, the Water Maiden poked her head out to check the corridor. She'd encountered no Elves when she passed through the Shimmer. Once she descended into the heart of the mound, however, her likelihood of avoiding detection would decline rapidly.

She *had* tried other ways.

She'd let the mages of her village attempt countless remedies. None succeeded. She'd read countless books and scrolls in her guildhall. None triggered a recollection. She'd spent countless hours interviewing her mother, friends from her youth, and Grandmaster Gwyla. She'd even talked at length with Gwyla's sister Diri, leader of a Gwragedd Annwn colony in Texas, when Diri visited Long Island during an ultimately doomed effort at reconciling the two communities. None of the conversations brought her any closer to restoring her memory, nor made her feel any less a stranger among her own Folk. They all insisted that it didn't matter, that Dela would always have a home with them, a life with them.

They were wrong. *I can reside in their village but never truly find a home there. Deprived of identity and purpose, I can* exist *but never truly* live *again.*

Perhaps if Dela possessed *no* memories of her former life, she might find a way forward. Alas, that wasn't the case. When she first awoke in Cahokia, her mind retained a confusing muddle of fleeting images and encroaching shadows. Over time, the latter overwhelmed the former until just two memories remained from her before-time.

One was distinct and horrifying, the image of a haughty face leering down at Dela with menace. Whenever it sprung to mind, she felt a sharp pain in her chest.

The other was indistinct and tantalizing, the image of a kindly face gazing down at her with affection. Whenever it sprung to mind, she also felt a pain in her chest, more a dull ache than a sharp sting.

She recognized the first face. *Grandmaster Runa.*

The identity of the second eluded her. Was it Goran Lonefeather, who by all accounts loved her? Har the Tower, whose feelings for her were less clear? Some other man? And did her heart ache in response because she returned the man's love—or because she did not?

How else could she know but to regain her memory? As far as she knew, the only person who could bring that about was Runa.

The clank of metal on metal prompted Dela yank her head back. An Elf was trudging up the tunnel. She held her breath.

"Then she pulled me from the roster entirely!" snapped a gruff voice.

"Tough luck," answered a nasally voice.

So, there are two.

"I would rather be bored on guard duty than gored by some river monster."

No, three.

"How long ago did Enti send the message?"

"Nearly a Blur day ago. Should be here."

So, the ranger brought down by Dela's net was named Enti, and his absence had already been noticed. The Water Maiden sighed. No longer able to retreat without being spotted, she readied herself.

When the first Elf entered the chamber, sturdy strands crushed his arm against his armored chest. Yanking hard and then releasing her left hand, Dela hurled the netted warrior against the wall and used the momentum to spin on one heel. The tip of the trident in her right hand slashed the throat of the next Elf in line, an archer wearing a wing pack.

"Intruder!" shouted the third Elf. Another flyer, he bore javelins. Quick as a flash, one of the short, bronze-tipped missiles shot from his practiced hand.

Quicker than a flash, Dela ducked. The javelin missed. She sprang forward, knocking the body of the gurgling archer into that of his companion. The two rangers tumbled to the floor. Determined not to waste her advantage, the Water Maiden hopped over the twitching legs of the mortally wounded man and stabbed the chest of the javelineer.

He was the first to die.

Wheeling, Dela found herself face-to-face with the armored warrior, who'd cut her net away with one of his two drawn shortswords. His eyes took in the two prone rangers, then narrowed. "You have much to answer for!"

"Undoubtedly," she agreed.

Growling, the thickset Elf swung a blade at Dela's head. Rather than ducking—and thus giving him a stationary target—she swept the trident across her body to parry the blow, then lashed out at his forearm with the butt. The Elf knocked it aside and stabbed with the other sword. The edge grazed Dela's hip, producing a gasp of pain and a trickle of blue blood.

"Surrender and I will show mercy!" he snarled.

In response, the Water Maiden knocked his next thrust aside with her weapon, then kicked out with her unwounded leg. It hit his belly, but the Elf was armored and stout. The force pushed him back only a couple of steps.

Dela was outmatched in both strength and equipment. Both combatants knew it. "Say the words," he spat, "and I will make it quick."

She spoke no words. Instead, she began to sing. Annoyed by her defiance, the Elf aimed another hack at her head. This time Dela *did* duck, gripping her trident with both hands and using it to block his second attack. Continuing her song, the Water Maiden pushed her weapon at the warrior, causing him to take two more backward steps.

The Elf sneered. "However many you call, they will arrive too late to save you."

When she blocked his next attack, her trident made his bronze sword ring. When his other blade struck, it made only a thud as it chopped a deep wedge in the wooden haft. Another blow and her weapon might well break in two.

"Had enough?" he demanded.

Dela stopped singing and smirked. "Yes."

The Elf's eyelids flickered in confusion. The Water Maiden thrust the butt of her trident against his torso and shoved with all her might.

Which didn't amount to much, actually. It forced the warrior back but one more step. However, that was all it took. With a yelp of surprise that soon became a scream, he fell through the unshielded entrance to the mound.

No longer concerned, Dela turned away. If the fall didn't eliminate him as a threat, exposure to the Blur would. She hurried to the two rangers on the floor. Both were done for. Glancing down at her hip, she was relieved to see it no longer bleeding. The wound stung, but not enough to hinder her movements. She dragged each body across the floor and sang the first few bars of the security song again. Pushing the rangers through the entrance after their erstwhile companion, she paused to make sure the Shimmer reconstituted itself. Then she recovered her net and headed down the tunnel.

Perilous though it was, her plan had one stroke in its favor. Cahokia's rangers had built their guildhall on the extreme edge of the underground complex, close to the flyers' entrance. She soon reached the guildhall's double doors. Offering a silent prayer to the Maker of All Things, Dela pushed lightly on the right-hand door. It gave way. Hearing no shuffling feet or other response, the Water Maiden slipped inside.

Except for its lack of sentries, the sparse anteroom looked the same as it did the day she'd escaped Runa's clutches. Crossing to the other side, she crept cautiously through the passage into the adjoining library. It was empty as well. As Dela entered, however, she discovered the guildhall wasn't unoccupied. From the hallway beyond came a voice. It was too faint to decipher, but the chill running up her spine was confirmation enough. It belonged to Runa.

Unable to resist the impulse, the Water Maiden dashed into the hallway. The voice was louder but muffled. She couldn't make out any words, nor did she have much time to try. Two flashes illuminated the dark passage. Two blasts temporarily drowned out Runa's voice. Two musket balls flew at Dela.

One missed.

The other drew a line of fire from her right temple to the back of her head. Stifling a scream, the Water Maiden dropped into a crouch and jabbed her trident into the dark. A smoking muzzle swatted it aside. The Elfish musketeer, a head taller and far brawnier than Dela, stepped from the shadows. Behind him skulked another Elf, nimble and dark-featured, her bronze musket discarded and a wicked-looking knife in each lithe hand.

"How dare you interrupt the grandmaster!" the male Elf barked.

Trying to ignore her burning scalp, Dela willed her shoulders to shrug. "Runa and I are old friends."

"We will relay your regards," said the other Elf, slipping past her companion and circling to the left.

Blue fluid trickled into Dela's eye, making it sting. Winded, wounded, and now bleeding profusely, she also couldn't rule out Elfish reinforcements. *A long duel might seal my doom.* Gritting her teeth, the Water Maiden thrust at the musketeer's scowling face. He parried, as expected, but Dela's real attack was with her heel. The surprised knife-wielder beside her took it on the chin, reeling and slashing the air ineffectually. Determined to maintain the initiative, Dela shoved the butt of the trident into the female Elf's midsection.

"You will pay—" the male Elf began.

"I *have*!" growled the Water Maiden as she sprang, aiming her weapon at his left leg. Its blades pierced his thigh. Though he jerked back, howling in pain, he managed to swing his gun at Dela's head.

It was just the opening she sought. Dela dodged rightward. The barrel just missed her shoulder, then clanged as it hit the floor. Thrown off-balance, the musketeer pitched forward—directly into the trident. It opened his throat.

Wincing and wheezing, the Water Maiden turned to face her smaller foe. The Elf had resumed a fighting stance, one knife low and the other at eye level. She easily parried Dela's first two attacks, then responded to the third by deflecting the trident and jabbing the other knife at the Water Maiden's right arm. Dela drew back just in time, feeling its tip touch her forearm but not break the skin.

The Elf wove a shroud of bronze around Dela, parrying, stabbing, and slashing with effortless grace. Every moment they sparred, the Water Maiden's prospects diminished. She could still hear Runa's voice coming from the hallway. It was still too muffled for Dela to make out the words, but the grandmaster was apparently delivering a lengthy speech to someone in the great hall.

I am running out of time. The Water Maiden took a deep breath, then a chance.

The Elf jabbed at her chest. Dela parried, then gasped as she let go of the trident. The Elf grunted with satisfaction as it clattered onto the stone floor. That was all the distraction Dela required. She yanked the damaged net from her shoulder and hurled it at the Elf's head, then dropped low and lashed out with one pale-blue leg, sweeping the yellow-stockinged legs of the other.

Down went the Elf, dropping one knife so she could break her fall while hacking at the net with the other. Dela kicked again, sending the remaining blade spinning across the floor. Her third kick produced a cracking sound that announced the end of the fight.

Lungs heaving, blood running down her face, the Water Maiden recovered her trident and trotted down the hallway. She soon discovered why Runa's voice sounded muffled. Two heavy blankets, one cloth and the other hide, hung over the door to the great hall.

Dela had journeyed hundreds of miles. She'd fought her way into the mound, suffering wounds and dispatching six foes. The Elf who took her memories was just beyond that door. Even curtains of steel couldn't stop her now. A single swipe of the trident parted the rings holding the drapes in place. They swirled to the floor. Dela tried the latch, expecting the door to be locked.

It wasn't. She threw open the door—and collapsed in a heap.

Bash the walls, batter, bust,
No fortress stand against the horde,
Stone to sand, wood to dust,
No holdfast left to be restored.

The grandmaster wasn't speaking. She was singing. It was thunderous, deafening. More than sheer force crushed Dela to the floor. The song exuded malevolence, contempt, malice:

Douse the spark, drown the flame
That dares to blaze against the night.
Heat to cold, pride to shame,
From steamy haze to clearest sight.

Dela tried to focus. She didn't recognize it, though that meant little. Perhaps Runa was casting a spell she'd forgotten, or that the Gwragedd Annwn didn't use.

Close a link, forge a chain,
Each stumbling soul to others bind,

Page to book, thread to skein,
And liberate each lonely mind.

Then Dela drew in a ragged breath. *This cannot be a spellsong. Folk are immune!* With difficulty, she raised her head. The great hall was large and square. The shelves on its walls were filled with books, scrolls, and flasks. *I have been here before. This is where Runa questioned me about my lost memories.*

"Why is it not working?"

The grandmaster was no longer singing. Freer to move her head, Dela soon spotted Runa standing before a cluttered table. The Elf wore a mask of hammered copper, much like the one she'd once shown Dela. Crystals were set in its eyes, a colorful agate in its forehead, and a red-orange horn in place of a nose. The mask's sides was lined with blue stones, from which dangled red shells shaped like miniature masks. All of them—the crystals, the agate, the horn, the stones, the shells—were flickering and sparkling, as if lit by internal flames.

"Tell me now—or forfeit your lives!"

Dela's eyes followed Runa's pointed finger. What she saw made the Water Maiden cry out. Goran Lonefeather and Har the Tower lay against the far wall. Each was securely trussed, their bodies covered in cuts and bruises. The cords binding the Sylph's limbs looked strong. The ropes wrapped around the Dwarf's arms, legs, and midsection looked enormous.

Her yelp hadn't gone unnoticed. "So, my first specimen has returned," Runa jeered. "How convenient."

Fury renewed Dela's strength. She rose to her feet, trident in her hands, determination in her head, anguish in her heart. "Release my friends."

"You think to command me in my own hall?" The grandmaster took a step toward her. "Fool that you are, I admire your audacity."

The Water Maiden moved forward, too. She trembled, but not from fear. She felt like a coiled spring, a drawn bowstring, a snake about to strike. "Release my friends."

"They have information I require," Runa said. "The Duendes tricked us, trading worthless baubles for our treasures. I suspect your 'friends' conspired with them."

"You are wr-wrong." Goran's voice was raspy. "H-have all the se-secrets of Cibola. You j-just do n-not know h-how to use them."

"Then show me how!"

"Do not know," Har muttered. The Dwarf's mouth was battered and bruised, making it hard to move his lips. "Would not show, anyway."

Goran cleared his throat and tried to spit. The reddish liquid made it as far as his chin. "Give up your m-mad scheme."

The Elf shook her head. "I was meant to find the painting. I was meant to wield the power of the mask, for the good of all."

The Water Maiden halted in midstride. When Runa mentioned the painting, an image sprang to mind of the first conversation she could recall with the grandmaster. *It was not my intention to wipe your mind's slate clean,* Runa had told her in this very room. *We did not realize at first the importance of the colored lines in the painting, but now we know their meaning.*

Then Dela recalled another memory, murky and incomplete. Another memory from her before-time. A painting on the wall of a tunnel. A person in a loincloth and cloak wearing a multicolored mask. Her pulse quickened. Before Dela was robbed of her identity, she'd seen the painting Runa mentioned! *Perhaps I was there when she found it.*

"You cannot," Goran said, his voice strengthening. "Domination magic brought the Catastrophe. Destroyed Cibola. Drove the refugees to the Seven Cities."

"We are not foolish Chaneque," Runa replied. "We are Elves. It is our destiny to rule, to bring order from chaos. It is *my* destiny to supply the means."

"No," insisted the Sylph. "True order is learned, chosen, practiced. Not forced. You will bring more chaos, more suffering."

The grandmaster sighed. "That you are in league with the Duende is obvious. Whether that makes you a villain or a dupe, I cannot—come no closer!"

Dela had resumed her advance. Now she froze, still a dozen paces from Runa. Whatever the Elf intended with her spellsong, it *had* served to immobilize the Water Maiden when she entered. Runa could do it again. *I must keep her talking until another option presents itself.* "This mask you wear, Elf. I have seen it before. You used its power on me."

"The first model, yes," the grandmaster replied. "Before I truly understood its design. Before we acquired all the elements."

"I remember the red horn."

"The one treasure we already possessed, along with the painting. Elf rangers found the engraved Uktena horn near the river the humans call Black Warrior. It stores temperamental magic. It powered the spell I tested on you."

"Your test failed."

"Yes, but from such failures come knowledge. I learned the mask could not focus the spell without the Crest of the Yeitso. It could not draw more temperamental magic *into* itself without the Eyes of Ahuizotl, or store elemental magic to boost its range without the Blue Stones of Urraca, or shield me from its effects without the Carbuncles of Limuw. And I could not truly wield domination magic without the lyrics to its activation spell, lyrics preserved on columns in the underground village of Yanaguana."

The Elf took a couple of steps back and snatched a parchment from the table, showing it to Dela. Written on it were seven blocks of text.

Lyrics of Yanaguana? Stones of Urraca? Little of what Runa said made any sense to the Water Maiden, though she did remember the multicolored crest in the Yeitso's forehead—and Goran's report that Elf rangers had made off with its broken shards. She glanced at the Sylph and Dwarf. Both were straining against their bonds. Given their pale complexions and wan expressions, both seemed destined to fail.

"Now your knowledge is complete," said Dela.

"Or so I was led to believe." Runa pointed a finger. "Why have you come? Perhaps *you* have what I seek. Perhaps I interrogate the wrong specimens."

Dela glared. "I came for answers, not questions."

"Who sent you?"

"Vengeance."

"How dramatic." The mask covered most of Runa's face, but Dela guessed her words brought a derisive smile to the Elf's lips. "For taking your memories?"

"For taking my identity."

"I suppose your question is whether I can restore it. And I suppose you now have your answer."

Dela did, although it wasn't until that moment that she really accepted the truth. There *was* no way to restore all her lost memories. Runa didn't know how. The Elf had yet to master the magic of the mask. And even if she did, that would only allow the grandmaster to sing spells against Folk, not to mend what was previously broken.

Accepting her fate didn't enrage the Water Maiden. It didn't push her to the brink of despair. It left her hollow. And it left her craving the one thing that might fill the cavity, at least a little: the blood of an enemy. "Then I will—"

The magic blast struck Dela like a punch to the face. She glimpsed the elements of the mask glimmer with power, then sank to her knees. She cupped her ears, trying in vain not to hear Runa's song:

Lustrous gem, shining horn,
Bewitching eyes that do not see.

She felt as though the obsidian eyes were bearing down on her, boring into her, yanking at her.

Conjured dreams, flesh reborn
And dancing to their melody.

Then the pressure returned, the crushing burden of Runa's distorted spell. If the grandmaster sought to break her will, however, she had failed. Something about the power of the mask, what Goran called "domination magic," still eluded Runa.

Bash the walls, batter, bust,
No fortress stand against the horde.

Dela managed another sidelong look. Goran and Har were both twisting on the floor.

Stone to sand, wood to dust,
No holdfast left to be restored.

Despite her best efforts, she couldn't block out Runa's words. Then she stopped trying, for something about the last two lines grabbed her attention. It wasn't the words. It was the rhythm.

Douse the spark, drown the flame
That dares to blaze against the night.

The next lines bore the same meter. It was *so* familiar. Dela realized she'd heard it many times before. Did it resemble a spellsong of the Gwragedd Annwn?

Heat to cold, pride to shame,
From steamy haze to clearest sight.

No. She'd picked it up somewhere else. The pattern of the song, not the lyrics. Dela could swear she'd sung different words to the same rhythm.

Close a link, forge a chain,
Each stumbling soul to others bind.

She reviewed what she'd learned in the few past minutes. The Chaneque had invented domination magic, and as a result suffered a catastrophe.

Page to book, thread to skein,
And liberate each lonely mind.

Goran has spoken of *refugees*, Runa of *wanderers* and *hidden treasures*. The crystals, shells, stones, crest, and horn. The lyrics and the painting of the mask. Seven treasures. Seven cities.

Lose to gain, to belong,
A wind to calm unruly seas.

Dela's eyes widened. *Catastrophe. Refugees. Wanderers*. What if the Elves, the Duende, even Goran—what if they had it wrong? What if they misidentified one of the treasures, a necessary element to cast a domination spell?

Quiet words, silent song,
In stillness hear the harmonies.

If the Water Maiden was right, she was the only ranger in the room—perhaps the only ranger in the *world*—who was at that moment capable of wielding domination magic. Twisting her head, Dela found Goran staring back at her. He fluttered the tip of his wings, then jerked his chin at the masked grandmaster, who'd restarted the domination song:

Listen now, fellow Folk,
In savage Blur or Shimmer shell.

Goran couldn't have guessed what Dela now knew, but his meaning was clear. The more they waited to try an escape, the less likely they were to succeed. She nodded.

Rhythm wrought, rhyme awoke,
And not for human ears—

"Now!" Goran exclaimed.

With a great sweep of feathered wings—which, unlike his arms and legs, had finally slipped their fetters—the Sylph shot from the floor. Startled, Runa stopped singing and drew back, reaching for her sheathed knife. Now free of the magical force directed mostly at her, Dela rose and lifted the trident over her head.

Goran fell short of his target. The distance was too great for his weakened muscles to close. Recovering her composure, Runa restarted the song, aiming its force at the Sylph:

Rhythm wrought, rhyme—

This time, it wasn't a sudden movement by the Sylph that interrupted her—it was a hurled trident finding its mark. The blades took Runa in the shoulder, spinning her around. The mask flew from her head, bounced off the table, and collided with the far wall. Minutes before, smashing the mask would have delighted Dela. Now, as she hurried across the room, her fondest wish was to find it intact.

"Dela!" Goran shouted.

She scooped up the mask, then wheeled to discover Runa coming at her, trident in hand. The Elf had pulled it from her shoulder, leaving a ghastly wound. Dela circled to her left, her foe matching her gait, until the Water Maiden stood next to the grandmaster's cluttered table.

Runa slammed the butt of the trident against the far wall. It must have touched a hidden button, for a series of bells gonged loudly. "My rangers come," the Elf sputtered. "There is no escape for you. Not this time."

Dela confounded her by smiling. "Escape is not my plan."

Then she snatched the parchment off the table, lifted the mask to her face, and sang the opening lines to the domination song:

Listen now, fellow Folk,
In savage Blur or Shimmer shell.

Relief washed over her when she saw Runa's face slacken. It went from angry to surly to merely dour. Then it lost all expression. On Dela sang, reading the lyrics and turning around to survey the rest of the room. Goran lay on the floor, motionless, his face just as blank as Runa's. Har was in the same condition, as were three Elves who'd rushed into the great hall in response to Runa's summons.

Dela sang the same words. She wore the same strange mask, its magical components ablaze with surging power. In one crucial respect, however, her performance was different.

While the Water Maiden had much to relearn about being a spellsinger, she knew rangers could employ a variety of lyrics, melodies, and accompaniment to cast their chosen spells. One ranger's courage spell could sound unlike another's and yet be equally effective. It stood to reason, however, that any spell capable of affecting Folk must be more challenging. It wouldn't be enough to use precisely enchanted objects to power the spell, and precisely chosen words to activate it. The spell would also require a precisely delivered melody.

If refugees fleeing the destruction of Cibola carried away the seven elements needed to wield domination magic, one of them *had* to be the melody. Runa thought the seventh treasure was the painting of the masked spellsinger, found in the lost city of Cahokia. She was mistaken. The painting was just a painting. Cahokia was just an abandoned Folk village.

The seventh lost city was Quivira, cofounded on the plains by a winged Folk from the east, the Mialuka, and a band of refugees from the south who called themselves the Teihiihan, the "Strong Ones." The latter had fled north from some great catastrophe. The Teihiihan—who Dela now knew were once Chaneque, and whose fiercest descendants became the Nimerigar—had shared a traditional song with the Mialuka. The winged Folk added new lyrics. During her time in Quivira, Dela had learned to sing their joint creation, "The Great Lament."

Which was why she knew the melody required to use domination magic.

~ ~ ~

Much later, after she removed all memory of Cibola, the mask, and its components from the minds of Runa and the other surviving rangers of Cahokia, Dela stood before what remained of the painting of the masked spellsinger. The rest was covered with brown paint foraged from the grandmaster's supply shelf. Goran and Har stood beside her. Exhausted and drained though they were, the two could wield paintbrushes.

"When we are done, I must hurry south to the Yucatan," said the Water Maiden. "The sooner I find Aya and the other Duende you spoke of, the better."

"You said *I*," the Dwarf observed, "not *we*."

Goran hung his head. "You and I are in no condition, Har. We will only slow her down."

Dela stopped painting but kept staring at the wall. "What you say is true, but it is not the whole truth. There is another reason I must make the journey alone."

Her peripheral vision was enough to reveal a puzzled Har turning to face her—and a melancholy Goran turning away. "I was about to suggest you go by way of Cedar Point," the Dwarf said, "so Diri or some other ranger of the

Gwragedd Annwn can accompany you into Mexico. Even with you wielding that infernal mask, the task is too dangerous to attempt by yourself."

"I appreciate your concern, but the Duendes do not pose the only danger."

Har grunted. "That, we know well. The monsters of Mex—"

"She does not speak of enemies," said the Sylph. "She speaks of… friends."

Goran said nothing more. Nor did Har. As silent moments turned to minutes, Dela struggled to come up with the right words to explain her decision without hurting two men for whom she cared deeply, two men who'd suffered so much for her sake and for the cause they shared.

Explanation was, in the end, unnecessary. Har lay a hand on her shoulder. "My apologies. I have just figured it out. You and Goran were always better at such things. My talents run more to knocking down doors, not thinking up plans."

Dela covered his beefy hand with her own slender one. "You sell yourself too short, my friend."

"Too short, eh?" Har grinned. "An unfamiliar accusation of me, I admit."

She returned his smile. "And you, Goran?"

The Sylph's wings, discolored from poor diet and worse treatment, were drawn up so high on his back that she couldn't see his head. He stood there for a moment, motionless, wordless. Then he broke the silence with a single word.

"No."

It was not what Dela had expected to hear. "Well," she began hesitantly, "the Chaneque invention of domination magic led to catastrophe. I cannot in good conscience—"

"I know," he said, keeping his face averted. "The Elves and Duendes are not your only targets. You mean to remove all memory of domination magic and the secrets of Cibola from those who know about them. Including us."

"It is the best way to prevent all this from happening again," she said. "Only I will remember—and even I will lack the ability to use it, for I will destroy the mask and destroy or hide the treasures that would allow another to be constructed."

Har stroked his beard thoughtfully. "To keep so terrible a secret is a great burden to shoulder alone."

"I see no alternative."

"Then look again!" Goran spun around. His gaunt face was no longer pale. It was flushed with emotion. Sorrow? Anger? Fear? Perhaps none of them. Perhaps all, and more. "I will not let you take my memories!"

The vehemence of his protest shocked her. "It is for the good of all, including yourself. I will remove only your recollection of domination magic and—"

"Temperamental magic is never so exact, even for rangers expert at memory spells," he insisted. "You may have taken more from the minds of Runa and her minions than you intended."

Dela knitted her brows. "I *am* expert at memory spells. You told me so yourself."

"No." He shook his head. "You *were* an expert. Now, you are a novice."

"Goran!" Har glared down at his friend. "She is doing the best she can."

The Sylph blinked. "That is not…I do not question your efforts, Dela, or your intentions. I question your precision."

Astonished, dismayed, confused, hurt—Dela's emotions were just as jumbled and deeply felt as Goran's appeared to be. By all accounts, this man loved her with a passion Dela could neither comprehend nor return. With so much at stake, how could he not trust her?

She gazed into his eyes. There was distrust there, yes, but not only that. There was something else, something that threatened to engulf his light-brown eyes in bright-orange flame. It spoke to her, as clearly as words, *more* clearly than words. It shook her jumble of emotions until they fell in place. Until she clearly, painfully understood.

It was *because* he loved her that he could not trust her. *He cannot bear the thought of losing any memories of me.*

Slowly, deliberately, the Water Maiden drew close to the Sylph. Slowly, hesitantly, she reached for his hand. Slowly, reverently, she placed the paint-brush in his palm and closed his fingers around it with her own.

"I trust you," she whispered.

"I love you," he breathed.

"I know."

Releasing his hand, Dela turned and eyed the taciturn Dwarf. "Finish without me?"

"Aye. And then we leave this accursed place."

Nodding, the Water Maiden reached for her trident and the pack in which she'd stowed supplies and the mask. Her first step was the hardest. In truth, however, each step out of the tunnel was a struggle—and an eternity.

"We will keep the secret, Goran and I," Har called after her. "You can rely on us."

Of that, she had no doubt.

Epilogue — The Pecos

September 1864

THEY WERE WAITING AT THE main house. Some had been there an hour. Knowing him as well as they did, however, none of his guests would begrudge Manuel Antonio Chaves a few more minutes by the river.

The light of the corn moon dappled the surface of the Pecos with orange ripples. Sitting astride his black stallion on the west bank, Manuel gazed across the river at the orb looming large on the horizon, framed between two faraway hills, and thought of a campfire tale popular in the nearby settlement of Puerto de Luna.

It seemed that more than three centuries ago, a Spanish adventurer named Francisco Vásquez de Coronado left the Mexican state of Nueva Galicia and traveled north in search of the fabled Seven Cities of Gold. When his expedition reached the Pecos River, the explorer stopped to rest. Watching the moon rise between those same eastern hills, Coronado proclaimed the place *Puerto de Luna*, the "gateway of the moon"—or so the story went. Manuel figured the Luna family, whose verdant pastures abutted those of his own ranch, were more responsible for naming the new village than some long-dead adventurer.

From his left came a long, lugubrious howl.

Manuel sucked in a breath. The stallion snorted. Both whipped their heads around to peer upriver, where one of the flocks had not yet been brought in for the evening. Manuel picked out three tiny shapes in the distance.

The second howl was short and shrill, more warning than wail. Manuel judged it too low-pitched to be a fox and too monotone to be a coyote. A gray wolf, perhaps?

"Steady," he whispered to his mount. "My men can handle it."

The stallion didn't agree. He snorted again and yanked at his reins.

"Very well, Níyoltsoh," said the rider, kicking his steed into a trot. "Who am I to defy a storm?"

As the trot became a gallop, Manuel smiled. When he bought the stallion fifteen years ago, Manuel had named him *Níyoltsoh*, the Navajo word for tornado. He'd done so to honor the trusted steed of his friend Diego Vega, the shape-shifting caballero of California. Since then, Níyoltsoh had repeatedly lived up to the name, exhibiting both a blinding speed and a stormy temper.

As they dashed up the riverbank, the far-off shapes grew more distinct. One was a fat white ewe. Another was one of the black goats interspersed with the sheep to make it easier to count and herd them. The third, originally a brown blur of motion, soon resolved into the familiar outline of Manuel's longest-serving ranch hand on a brown mare.

"Took off!" the vaquero shouted.

"How many?"

There was a puzzled expression on the man's weathered face. "Just the one. Funny-looking critter, pale and scrawny."

Manuel shook his head. "No, I mean, how many did we lose?"

"Not a head. Went after one of the bell goats but stumbled. Got spooked and ran. Fast little thing, whatever it is."

"Well, we should chase it down. Could be a cub from a larger pack."

The ranch hand grinned. "I can handle it. You have other duties."

The sound of hoofbeats interrupted Manuel's reply. He sighed when he saw the approaching rider. "That, I do."

"Mamá sent me," said thirteen-year-old Amado, his eldest son. "Your guests are restless."

"Perhaps they should come join the hunt," Manuel mused.

"Mamá thought you might say something like that. She says a cold meal is no fit way to send the colonel off against the Comanches."

"Your wife speaks the truth," said the vaquero. "Besides, if I let you ruin dinner, my wife will have my head. She has been cooking all day."

Manuel sighed. Angering Vicenta was bad enough. If Shash got mad, too, he wouldn't hear the end of it. "Very well. Tell me later what it was."

"Sure—if I catch it." Aki wheeled the mare and rode back toward the herd.

If I catch it. Manuel marveled at how strange those words sounded, even though many years had passed since Aki, Shash, and their children came to live permanently on Manuel's Pecos River ranch.

Once, the notion that the fleet-footed Aki couldn't run down some scraggly wolf would have struck them all as ridiculous. Now it was the speed of his *mount* that mattered, not that of Aki's all-too-human legs. He could no longer turn into the Water Monster, nor could Shash assume the form of a Monster Bear. Neither could remember how. Neither could remember *knowing* how.

~ ~ ~

"Why is their rotten corn our problem? The savages were brought to the Pecos to stop them from raiding our homes and thieving our herds."

"You didn't give 'em much of a choice. Thinnin' out the game. Crowdin' out the pastures. They act from absolute necessity, from starvation, and you call 'em savages."

This was something else the "Little Lion" wasn't accustomed to, despite years of practice: looking *down* at a superior officer and looking *up* at his brother. Yet here he was, standing between the two with hands raised, trying to end their spirited argument.

Standing to his left in the dining room was the thin, bow-legged, long-haired, soft-voiced man Manuel had called friend for the better part of two decades. Dressed in a rumpled blue uniform denoting his rank, the colonel's scarred, freckled face bore a shocked expression, though the twinkle in his gray eyes belied it.

"Think your brother needs rescuing, eh?" drawled Kit Carson. "Why, he's as wide as I am tall!"

That wasn't saying much, since even in his prime the famous adventurer was all of five feet, four inches tall—and the stoop-shouldered Carson had long outlived his prime years.

"My size does not trouble you," said the man on Manuel's right. "My words do."

Small and ungainly during most of his childhood, Román Baca had experienced a growth spurt in his teens. Tall and powerfully built as a young man, Manuel's half-brother became more portly than burly by the age of thirty, but still remained one of New Mexico's fiercest warriors.

"My words—and your own actions, Kit," Román went on. "When the generals needed the Navajos cleared out and marched to their new reservation on the Pecos, who did they put in charge? The same man who had already done the same to the Mescalero Apaches. The great Kit Carson!"

Colonel Carson's eyes twitched. Manuel could tell his friend was trying to restrain his temper. "I did my duty, distasteful as it was, but that was only the beginning. The Navajos aren't like the Apaches. They're a growin' people, a herdin' people. They deserve a fair shot. So far, they aren't gettin' it here."

Román pointed at Manuel. "Look at my brother. While he was away fighting the Confederates, the Navajos raided his ranch on the Rio Grande. Stole thirty thousand sheep and all his horses and cattle! So, Manuel moved his whole business east to the Pecos. He is prospering here. The Indians can, too."

Carson sighed. "The valley can support a few ranches, yes, but the Navajos and Apaches number many thousands. Every promise made to them should be observed to the letter. It is in the interest of all New Mexicans that they become a source of wealth to the territory, not a source of dread and poverty."

Román didn't reply. Manuel took the opportunity to think through his own conflicting views about the crowded Indian reservation at Bosque Redondo, just down the Pecos from his ranch.

Thirty years ago, he'd emerged from the desert as the lone survivor of his brother José's expedition into Navajo country. It was thanks to the devotion of Pahe that he'd survived. Manuel had repaid the debt by protecting innocent Navajos from vengeance-minded Cebolletans, including his own brother Pedro.

Ever since, Manuel had sought to deal fairly with the Indians of the territory. Sometimes he befriended and traded with them. When they raided his lands or those of his countrymen, however, Manuel fought back. He tried to conduct himself honorably and spare innocent lives. When he thought of his brother's lean body riddled with arrows, Manuel tried to act as José would have acted, with justice and mercy. And when in the winter of 1850 he found Pedro Chaves lifeless in a canyon near Cebolleta, his fat body also riddled with arrows, Manuel tried to remember that while his brothers' killers had been Navajos, not all Navajos were killers.

He tried not to let vengeance consume him. Most of the time, he succeeded.

As the balding Román Baca and the stringy-haired Kit Carson continued their staring match—it was a good-faith disagreement, Manuel knew, not personal animus—it was one of the other guests who defused the situation.

"My friends," said Miguel Pino, "we did not come here to settle the Navajo question. We gather to wish Colonel Carson the best in a cause we all support: his expedition against the Comanches."

Román shrugged. "That, we do. They are a menace to everyone."

"Including those on the reservation," Carson added. "In their last raid on Bosque Redondo, the Comanches didn't just make off with Navajo horses and cattle—they stole women and children, too. The Navajos and Apaches were disarmed by order of our own government. They don't stand a chance without help."

Every man in the room nodded, some more vigorously than others. Besides Manuel, Román, Miguel, and Kit Carson, the dinner party included Miguel's brother Nicolás and the American trader Ceran St. Vrain. All had at one time or another seen combat alongside Manuel. They knew the dangers of war. They knew the challenge Carson faced.

St. Vrain stepped forward and clapped the colonel on the back. "How many men you takin'?"

"Three hundred regulars and militia," Carson replied, "plus seventy-five Utes. They have their own score to settle with the Comanches."

Nicolás Pino was next to shake Carson's hand. "The Comancheria is vast and perilous. Perhaps you should wait for reinforcements."

Carson shook his head. "No more's comin'. Gotta make do with the men at hand, just like we did against the Texans."

Two years earlier, every man in the room had joined the ranks of the Union army to resist a Confederate invasion of the territory. St. Vrain had helped organize the First New Mexico Infantry Regiment. Its battlefield commander was Colonel Kit Carson. The Second New Mexico Infantry Regiment was led by Colonel Miguel Pino, with Lieutenant Colonel Manuel Chaves as second-in-command. At the pivotal Battle of Glorieta Pass, it was Manuel who had guided Union troops through the forested mountains to destroy the enemy's supply train, ultimately forcing the Confederates—most of them Texans—to call off their attempted conquest of New Mexico.

As for Nicolás, he had served as a colonel in the New Mexico militia where, for a time, his commanding officer was Diego Archuleta, of all people—the same Archuleta who'd supported Governor Armijo's attempted execution of Texian prisoners in 1841 and later helped organize the murderous Taos Revolt of 1847. Not surprisingly, Archuleta had initially flirted with the Confederacy before switching sides. What *did* surprise Manuel was that Archuleta had ended up outranking them all as a brigadier general in the American army.

"Well," said Miguel Pino, "if anyone can enter the Comancheria and come back victorious, it is Kit Carson. No man ever made more enemies run—excerpt, perhaps, for our host, Manuel Antonio Chaves."

Everyone laughed, Manuel most of all, but it was Carson who got the last word. "Yep, I made 'em run. Sometimes I run after them, but most times they were runnin' after me!"

~ ~ ~

Much later, after his friends left the hacienda well-fed and much-cheered, Manuel saddled his stallion and rode out into the night. Thrust into the saddle holster was his Hawken rifle. Thrust into his belt was the weapon he trusted even more, Lionclaw.

Aki had, indeed, come back from his hunt empty-handed. Whatever had menaced the flock earlier that night remained on the loose. Manuel wasn't truly worried about a lone predator getting past his ranch hands and causing trouble. It was solitude he craved, and some time to think things over.

How *had* Diego Archuleta managed to become a general? For most of his life, Manuel had prided himself on his perceptual ability, his honed senses. *I hear what is silent. I see what is invisible. I know what is hidden. Yet there are still many mysteries I cannot solve.*

That wasn't really what bothered him, though. The talk at dinner of Kit Carson taking on the Comanches with so small a force made Manuel feel queasy. *Should I have volunteered to recruit more men? To go myself?*

He'd already spent so much time away from Vicenta and the children, first warring against the Confederates and then seeking the return of lost property. His last exploit had nearly cost him his life. Leading fourteen ranchers and vaqueros against a hundred Navajo raiders, Manuel was the only one to ride away unscathed—and with just three bullets left for his gun.

If Carson had asked for his help, Manuel would have said yes. Still, the expedition into the Comancheria was a mission for the United States Army, not Manuel and his friends. *Is it really guilt I feel, or is it envy?* He recalled the dying words of his brother José:

"Papá never believed. Weak...headstrong...I knew better...proved him wrong. I challenged...pushed myself...a step ahead. How else...can a cub grow...to be a lion?"

Originally, Manuel had believed his brother spent his last breaths boasting about his own prowess. Only years later did he come to understand José was talking about *Manuel*, about the love of an elder brother for an unruly and ungrateful cub, and about his efforts to prove Manuel worthy in the eyes of a demanding father.

Ever since, Manuel sought to become that lion. He had nurtured and challenged young Román Baca as José had nurtured and challenged him. He'd done the same for the children he and Vicenta brought into the world, and for the men and women who worked for him. Although he refused to go on slave raids with other New Mexicans, his punitive expeditions against Indian raiders sometimes produced widows or orphans he brought home to work in his businesses or household—including Lupe, a Comanche girl who now worked happily alongside Shash in the kitchen.

Thinking of Shash made him feel queasy again. *Guilt? Envy?* No, neither was what unsettled him. During dinner, his friends had discussed many matters—the rebellion of the Confederacy, Mexican politics, Indian affairs, even reports of eerie beasts prowling the valleys and deserts of New Mexico—without fully understanding them. After all, none possessed the Sight.

Among Manuel's closest companions, only Bill Angney shared that particular gift. But he no longer lived in New Mexico, having recently endured the death of his beloved wife and decided to relocate to California. With Aki and Shash now living fully as humans, retaining no memory of their origins, Manuel was left with questions he could not answer and secrets he dared not share.

Níyoltsoh heard the creature before he did.

One moment, the horse was trotting along the Pecos, carrying his distracted rider further and further north of the Chaves ranch. The next moment, Níyoltsoh took off at a gallop, with an instantly alert Manuel reaching for his rifle.

It wasn't a shrill canine howl they'd heard. It was the deep, rumbling roar of a mountain lion.

On they sped away from the river, the master and his mount, the edge of the former's poncho fluttering behind them like a lady's fan. There was another roar, then a shriek. Had the lion found a stray sheep the vaqueros left behind? Or some wild animal to stalk?

When Manuel passed a clump of cottonwoods, a primordial scene came into view a hundred yards away. The long, lithe, tawny body of a lion dashing across the plain. Its puny prey, swift but terrified, trying desperately to escape.

It wouldn't succeed. Manuel knew it at a glance. With every second the lion grew closer, its huge jaws thrust open to seize its doomed quarry.

Every second also brought Manuel closer to the action. He was ready. He felt no angst, no uncertainty, no guilt. Raising the rifle to his shoulder, he peered down its bouncing barrel at a target bathed in moonlight. With skill practiced over decades and confidence bred over a lifetime, he squeezed the trigger.

The bullet struck a heavily muscled shoulder. The lion grunted, hissed, and stumbled to a stop. Whipping its head around, the wounded beast bared its fangs and roared at the approaching rider. Shoving his smoking gun into its saddle holster and drawing his knife, Manuel stared into the lion's eyes, a fiery yellow ringed by charcoal black. They stared back with a boundless fury, the eyes of a remorseless killer.

What the *lion* saw, however, were the steely gray eyes of another killer. Not a remorseless killer, exactly, but one just as deadly with his Lionclaw as the beast was with its own. The massive feline glanced at its shivering prey, snarled in frustration, and turned to limp away as fast as its injured foreleg would allow.

Manuel considered reloading and finishing it off. Then he spied the lion's quarry—and the shock of it chased all other thoughts from his previously troubled mind.

Small and skinny, its ribs outlined in stark relief along its pale hide, the creature was roughly the shape of a coyote but lacked the lush coat, bushy tail, and upraised ears. Its skin was mottled and scaly, more reptilian than canine. Its spindly legs ended in clawed feet, not furry paws. Strangest of all were the stubby spines running from the top of its oblong head to the base of its whiplike tail—and its bulbous eyes, widely set and glowing blood red.

A monster! Manuel's pulse raced.

Then the creature's unnaturally glowing eyes met his. It whimpered and shuddered. The pale skin lost its scales. The clawed hands and feet lost their claws. The spines and tail retracted into nubs, then disappeared, except for the ones on the beast's head that split and spread into a tuft of blond hair. The bulbous eyes sank into its flattening head, lost their glow, and faded from red to hazel.

The towheaded boy, for that's what he now was, lay naked and shivering on the hard ground. Manuel judged him no more than nine years old, and probably much younger—although when it came to unnatural beings such as changelings, who could say for sure?

Dismounting, he removed his poncho and wrapped it around the scrawny child. Then he hefted his new bundle and got back up on Níyoltsoh. "Sorry, my friend," he whispered. "Your burden must be heavier than usual tonight."

By this time, the lion was long gone. Just to be sure, however, Manuel reloaded his Hawken rifle before nudging the stallion into a steady trot. He made straight for the bank of the river, then turned right to follow its course back home. The boy whined and coughed a few times before falling into a fitful sleep.

As Manuel tried to devise a plausible explanation for Vicenta about the newest addition to their household, his mind kept returning to the one close friend who'd been missing from the dinner party—the one friend for whom the truth about the shape-shifter would have sufficed. Bill Angney would have understood Manuel's decision, and approved.

Níyoltsoh nickered and shook his head, as if eavesdropping on his rider's thoughts and registering a complaint. Manuel patted the horse's neck. "Yes, perhaps you too understand, Níyoltsoh, at least a little."

Speaking the horse's name aloud gave Manuel an idea. He gazed down at the sleeping boy in his arms. "I have just the name for you, little one. A name to ground you, to challenge you as my brother once challenged me. And a name that honors an old friend."

Manuel smiled. "I will call you Pecos Bill."